THE LONG RUN

THE LONG RUN

A NOVEL

Leo Furey

Trumpeter · *Boston* · 2007

Trumpeter Books
An imprint of
Shambhala Publications, Inc.
Horticultural Hall
300 Massachusetts Avenue
Boston, Massachusetts 02115
www.shambhala.com

9 8 7 6 5 4 3 2 1

First Paperback Edition
Printed in the United States of America

♾ This edition is printed on acid-free paper that meets
the American National Standards Institute Z39.48 Standard.

Distributed in the United States by Random House, Inc.,
and in Canada by Random House of Canada Ltd

Designed by James D. Skatges

The Library of Congress catalogues the previous edition
of this book as follows:
Furey, Leo.
The long run: a novel/Leo Furey.—1st. Trumpeter ed.
p. cm.
ISBN 978-1-59030-411-2 (hardcover)
ISBN 978-1-59030-528-7 (paperback)
1. Boys—Fiction. 2. Orphanages—Fiction. 3. Male friendship—
Fiction. 4. St. John's (N.L.)—Fiction. I. Title.
PR9199.4.F865L66 2006
813'.6—dc22
2006014924

To
REVEREND RJ MACSWEEN
(1915–1990)

priest of the invisible

Two things cannot alter
Since time was, nor today
The flowing of water
And Love's strange, sweet way.

Japanese lyric

Contents

Autumn 1960

1

THE FIRST PERIOD in the afternoon is religion. Brother McCann takes attendance, gets up from behind his desk, shakes chalk dust from his soutane and struts to the middle of the classroom. As he walks, his right shoulder sags. His huge head tilts permanently to the right as if he's listening to his shoulder, and his left ear juts straight out so it looks like it came off and he glued it back on wrong. As usual, specks of greenish white saliva cling to the corners of his mouth. A few wisps of reddish hair dance on his bald head and look like they'd waltz away on a windy day. He's an odd duck with the worst temper of all the brothers at the Mount. When he speaks, he sprays spit. The boys in the front row shield their faces with their hands. Oberstein calls McCann's classroom "the shower."

When Brother McCann moves to the middle of the room, we know what's up. He's about to launch into one of his sessions. Monologues and Dialogues he calls them. Ten to fifteen minutes of ranting and raving. We painfully participate "for the sole purpose of the salvation of souls." His raving makes no sense. "Monologues and Dialogues is like a game of fish," he says. "You all have playing cards. I see all the Mount Kildare boys playing fish in the halls. You play fish in the halls, don't you, Spencers?"

His hazel eyes stare hungrily from beneath bushy brows. He has the odd habit of always adding an *s* to a boy's name: Murphys, Ryans, Kavanaghs, Obersteins. And if a boy's name ends in *s*, he drops it: Hyne, Roger, Jone, Brooke.

"Murphys, you play fish?"

"Yes, Brother."

"Littlejohns?"

"Yes, Brother."

"And you, Ryans?"

"Yes, Brother."

"And are you good at it, Murphys?"

"Yes, pretty good, Brother."

"Well, Monologues and Dialogues is like the card game fish. During the monologue, you, the class, are dealt the cards, information, and during a dialogue you are to match the cards, *information*, with the information, *cards*, given out during the monologue. Is that clear, Kavanaghs?"

"Yes, Brother."

"Carmichaels?"

"Yes, Brother McCann." I watch him remove the large ivory crucifix from above the blackboard.

"Quite clear, Mr. Burn?"

"Oh yes, Brother, quite clear."

"Clear, Nevilles?"

"Yes, Brother McCann."

None of us has a clue what the hell he's talking about. But you don't dare disagree with Brother McCann unless you want a knuckle sandwich. His game is very simple. There is no dialogue, just monologues where Brother McCann tries to stump you with a question and you answer as best you can, hoping to avoid the strap. Each monologue has a theme, and he announces the theme by reading from a book or a magazine. There are always props, as he calls them, to help get the point across. Today's props are the huge ivory crucifix, a copy of the *Nazareth Foreign Missions Magazine* and a *National Geographic* photograph of a monkey. He raises each prop slowly and places each item on his desk.

The classes are always crazy, and most days somebody gets a bad strapping. Usually drowsy Rowsell or bucktoothed O'Grady. They're the slowpokes in the class. Blackie thinks Brother McCann is crazy. He says that Monologues and Dialogues is all the proof you need to put Brother McCann in a rubber room at the Mental and throw away the key.

"Today's theme is Christ, the Evangelist. Are you paying attention, boys?" A thread of spittle hangs between his lips.

"Yes, Brother," we chant. The air in the classroom is very hot, and I can feel the sweat soaking the back of my shirt.

"And do you know what an evangelist is, Kellys?"

"No, Brother."

"Well then, pay very close attention and you shall find out, Mr. Kellys."

"Yes, Brother."

"Bradburys, are you paying attention?"

"Yes, Brrr."

"Pardon me, Bradburys?" McCann's eyes narrow as he speaks.

"Yes, Brother McCann."

"That's better, Bradburys. Now, I know many of you boys abbreviate the word 'Brother.' In fact, you use this abbreviated form in other classes. But not in my class, boys. There will be no lapses in my class. You will not say Brrr or Burr or Bruh or Bro in my class. Is that clear, boys?"

"Yes, Brother McCann."

"Bradburys?"

"Yes, Brother McCann."

"Some of the other brothers may permit you to say Burr and Bruh and Bro. But not this brother. This brother does not permit such speech. With this brother, it will always be Brother and nothing else. Never forget that, class. Brother and nothing else. Repeat that now."

"Brother and nothing else, Brother."

He looks at us dully before reading from the *Nazareth Foreign Missions Magazine*, the corners of his mouth wet with saliva. After reading for a few minutes, he stops short, rolls the magazine into his fist and begins his raving.

"We are being accused of buying souls. Buying souls, boys. Trading in salvation. Us, boys. You. And me. And not just Mount Kildare Orphanage. All Romans around the world."

Romans is his word for Roman Catholics.

"We are the majority, boys. The largest single denomination on God's earth is being accused of buying the souls of the poor. How? How, boys? Why, with money and jobs. That's how. That's the accusation. That's the allegation. Money and jobs, boys. As if Romans need to stoop so low."

A fly lands on Tracey's desk. Brother McCann eyes it cautiously. "Don't move Traceys," he whispers, and whacks at it with the rolled magazine. It buzzes away. "I told you not to move, Traceys."

"I didn't, Brother."

He whacks Tracey on the side of the head with the magazine.

"Don't talk back, boy. Money and jobs," he continues. "Can you imagine? They are accusing us of buying souls?" He pauses, snickers and strolls to the other side of the room. "Of what is our Church being accused, boys?"

"Buying souls, Brother."

"Very good, class. And what do we say to this accusation? Is it true, class?"

"No, Brother," we chant.

"Well done, class. Well done." He breathes a deep sigh, raises his eyebrows and unrolls the magazine. "Pay close attention,

boys, as I read the pack of lies being propagated against Holy
Mother Church. Against all Romans worldwide. Listen carefully now to what I read. And remember our theme. Christ the
Evangelist. Ready now. This is the monologue. Pay close attention. The dialogue will follow." He sighs deeply and reads:

> Little Pundhu Ghanga, seven years old, shudders as he
> recalls the Hindu radicals who came to his dirt poor vil-
> lage and dragged him to a river to be scrubbed clean of
> Christ.

"You heard right, class. That's what the text says: 'to be
scrubbed clean of Christ, scrubbed with the bark of trees and
with jagged rocks.' Now listen to this, boys. Listen: 'When the
cleansing was complete, little Pundhu was forced...' That's
what it says, boys—*forced*—'to worship a picture of Hanuman.'
That's right, class. You all heard correctly. Your ears did not
deceive you. Little Pundhu was forced to worship a picture of
Hanuman. And do you know who Hanuman is, class?"
"No, Brother."
"Hanuman is a monkey, class. That's right, boys. A monkey.
But Hanuman is no ordinary monkey, boys. Oh nooooo."
Bug Bradbury puckers his lips and points toward Brookes,
who has a monkey face. Bug can be as bold as brass.
"No ordinary monkey, this...this Hanuman. And do you
know why, boys? Do you know, Murphys?
"No, Brother."
"No. Of course not. How would you? Then I shall tell you,
class. Make good note of it. Your souls depend on such knowl-
edge. Hanuman is none other than the Hindu Monkey God."
Brother McCann shakes his head and looks up at the ceiling.
His mouth is wide open, and the boys in the front rows can see
his crooked yellow teeth. "The Hindu Monkey God. And little

Pundhu, baptized in the blood of our Lord and Savior is *forced* to worship Hanuman, to bow down to a monkey. Little Pundhu is *forced* to ignore this—*this* ..."

He swirls around and grabs the ivory crucifix from his desk, raises it high above his head. "*This,*" he screams, spraying spit everywhere. "Jesus, his Savior. Can you imagine it? He must ignore the blood of Christ and worship *this.*" He swirls again and grabs the *National Geographic* picture of the monkey, and with his free hand raises it above his head. "This? Or *this?*" he shouts, the veins in his neck standing out. "This is little Pundhu's choice. Can you imagine it, boys? Can you? Hanuman or Jesus?" He shakes his head, opens his mouth wide and gapes again at the ceiling, gasping for breath. "A monkey, for God's sakes. Or ... or Jesus our Savior? A monkey? Or God? Some choice, class. Some choice, boys. But little Pundhu's choice. Little Pundhu Ghanga. That little Roman's choice. Much younger than most of you, boys. Half your age in fact. And that little Roman made the right choice. A little martyr in the making. Little Pundhu chose the Son of Man, who died on the cross for our vile sins."

Silence. Rapid breathing. He does not look at us but seems to gaze on some faraway scene. A line of blue spruce trees outside the classroom window splinters the sunlight.

"And who would you choose, boys?"

"Jesus our Savior, Brother."

"Mr. Spencers, Jesus or Hanuman?"

"Jesus, Brother."

"Kellys?"

"Jesus, Brother."

"Wait for the complete dialogue, Kellys."

"Yes, Brother."

"Hanuman or Jesus?"

"Jesus, Brother."

"Ryans, choose ye this day whom ye shall serve. Jesus or Hanuman?"

"Jesus, Brother."

He goes around the room questioning everyone, and we all answer Jesus. Except for Smokin' Joe. That's Rowsell's nickname. But most of the time we just call him Rowsell. He smokes like a Labrador tilt, every finger is yellow. He always carries a Zippo lighter. Every time someone takes out a cigarette, Rowsell's there clicking open his Zippo. He's large-eyed, with a big moon face that turns beet.red whenever he has a cigarette. Rowsell's not the sharpest knife in the drawer, and when his turn comes to answer, Brother McCann slightly changes the question.

"Rowsells? Jesus, human and divine, named by God. Or a monkey, named by . . . God knows who. A monkey! Who, Mr. Rowsells?"

Rowsell thinks he is being asked to name the Hindu monkey god.

"Hanuman," Rowsell says.

What happens next takes place at lightning speed. Brother McCann bolts toward Rowsell's desk.

"Jesus, I mean Jesus, not Hanuman. *God*, not the monkey god. Jesus."

Too late. Brother McCann's strap is out.

"Up, Mr. Rowsells. Get them up. Higher. *Higher.* Hanuman over Jesus, is it, Rowsells?" Specks of spit splash on desks and school clothes. "A monkey? An animal over our Savior, is it? Well, let's see if you can endure some of the pain for your monkey god that little Pundhu endured for Jesus, our Lord and Savior."

"Jesus, I meant *Jesus*, Brother." Rowsell is crying. "Not Hanuman. Please. *Jesus.* I don't know what got into me."

"Oh, I know very well what got into you, Rowsells. Very well. The devil got into you, sir. The very devil I'm about to exorcise." McCann's spit is flying everywhere. "The **very devil** the Little

Missionary Brothers must fight each day in the battle for souls that rages in the jungles of Africa and India." The strap strikes at bullet speed, and with each blow Brother McCann shouts a letter. His voice is high and hysterical: "H-A-N-U-M-A-N." He returns to the front of the classroom. "Now, is there anyone else who would like to worship Hanuman, the monkey god?" He's spitting like crazy and breathing so hard it sounds like he's having a heart attack. "Any more worshippers of Hanuman?"

"No, Brother."

"Very good, class. Very wise."

Silence. The radiator hisses. It seems like a good deal of time passes, but it is really only a few seconds.

Bug Bradbury, who'll say anything to get some attention, asks if Pundhu's cleansing would be an example of Baptism by Desire, which was the subject of Brother McCann's last Monologues and Dialogues. Bug cocks his head to one side and grins proudly at us. He's more interested in outdoing everyone than sucking up.

Brother McCann's eyes bulge. "Yes, oh yes." He sounds like he's just won top prize at a raffle. "It certainly would be. Or blood. Yes, of course, blood. Probably more an example of Baptism by Blood. That is, if he hadn't already been baptized," he stammers, and stares excitedly at the ceiling. "If little Pundhu bled profusely during the cleansing, he would most certainly have experienced the Christian soldier's Baptism by Blood. A very good question, Mr. Bradburys, very good."

Catching McCann's excitement, Bug propels his hand and asks if a boy, like Oberstein, has a monkey teddy which he sleeps with at night, would that be a sin or an occasion of sin, a sort of monkey worship? Bug's always trying to stump other boys, especially Oberstein, who's the smartest in the class. Brother McCann rolls his eyes so that only the whites are visible. He stares up at the ceiling as if receiving divine intervention.

"Yes. It could be so. It could be an occasion of sin ... if the requirements were met." He reaches for Tracey's catechism and raises it high. "And what are those requirements, class?"

"Knowledge and awareness, freedom to choose," we chant the memorized response.

"If a boy ignores his rosary, his night prayers, and asks protection of his monkey, treating his teddy as a sort of Hanuman, that would definitely be a sin, a mortal sin, wouldn't it, Brother? And that little teddy monkey would be an occasion of sin?" Bug cocks his head at Oberstein.

"Well, let's ask Mr. Obersteins. Do you worship your little monkey teddy, Mr. Obersteins?"

"No, Brother McCann, I do not," Oberstein is much quicker than McCann. "I worship Jesus, Brother." The words race back to him from a previous lesson. "Jesus, the Son of the living God." Oberstein is Jewish. Brother McCann wants to make him a soldier in the army of Jesus Christ, but Oberstein wants to stay Jewish, like his father and grandfather. Oberstein memorizes a lot more than the rest of us. He has to, in order to keep McCann off his back. Oberstein is always a step or two ahead of everyone, including McCann.

"The Son of the living God," Brother McCann parrots the words. He repeats them again, slowly. Then he stares at the ceiling as if entering a trance. "Peter's response to Jesus when he inquired, 'Who do you say that I am?' Yes. Yes." He cocks his head but does not look at us. He stares instead at some distant thing he seems to have spied outside the window.

"Besides, Brother, I gave up my teddy last year. I'm too big for a teddy now." Oberstein's cheeks flush as if he's been slapped.

"Too big for teddy, Mr. Obersteins, but not too small for the Son of the living God." He stares off into space for a long time. Then he looks at his watch. "You would all do well to respond as Mr. Obersteins, class. A very fine response. Very eloquent. A divinely inspired response. Worthy of a true disciple. Which I'm sure you will one day become." He turns, walks to the blackboard and begins writing out our homework assignment.

Oberstein looks over at Bug, who cocks his head and winks. Oberstein grins, returns the wink and gives Bug the finger. Bug turns away sheepishly. Oberstein has won another round. Lucky for all of us. Oberstein's really got McCann's number. He knows how to settle him down, prevent him from flipping out.

McCann flips out a lot. Almost every day. I watch him spin from the blackboard, as Sullivan is drifting off a bit, grab the metal mission box and rifle it at him. Sullivan ducks, and it hits McCarthy in the forehead. He has a purple lump there now and maybe a dent for the rest of his life. McCann pulls his strap out of his soutane. He has the longest and thickest strap in the Mount. He waves it above his head and charges Sullivan, who jumps from his seat and runs around the classroom. McCann chases after him, striking him—his neck, his shoulders, his back, his face, his arms—wherever the strap strikes, until poor Sullivan falls to the floor, exhausted.

McCann crouches over him and straps his face. "And do you know why you are being punished, Mr. Sullivans?"

"Yes, Brother," Sullivan whimpers. "Because I ducked."

"Nooooo, Mr. Sullivans, nooooo! Not because you *ducked*. Because you were daydreaming, Mr. Sullivans. Daydreaming in *my* class."

"I wasn't, Brother. Honest," Sullivan sulks.

Whack. "But I saw you, Mr. Sullivans. Do not lie. I saw you daydreaming. I saw you with my own eyes."

Sullivan moans and weeps loudly. "I was paying attention, Brother. Honest, I was."

Whack. "More lying. More deceit, you young devil."

"I *was* listening to you." More tears.

"Well, one thing is certain, Mr. Sullivans. One thing is

certain. You won't be daydreaming in this class ever again. Nor will anyone else. Isn't that right, class?"

"Yes, Brother McCann."

"Good. Very good. That's what I want to hear, class." He spins around, slime hanging from the stubble on his chin. His breath comes in quick sharp wheezes. He scans the class. "And does anyone else? Is there another young devil thinks he can get away with daydreaming?" His eyes freeze on Kelly. Instead of shying away, Kelly freezes and lowers his head. But it's too late. He's a goner. McCann grabs a fistful of his shirt. He buckles him over the desk top and slaps him hard, bouncing his head off the wood.

"Look at me when I speak to you, Mr. Kellys," he screams, spit spraying into Kelly's face. "Do you think you can get away with it, Mr. Kellys? Do you?"

Kelly cringes.

"Well, doooo you? Stand up, sir." Silence. "Doooo you?"

Kelly stands up.

"Do I what, Brother?" Tears drip from Kelly's cheeks.

Whack. McCann knocks him back into his desk. "Do you think you can get away with daydreaming?" He screams so loud Kavanagh puts a hand over one of his ears.

"No, Brother. I don't, Brother."

"Good. Good. Because you will not." He scans the class. "Nobody will get away with it. Not Mr. Kellys. Not Mr. Sullivans. Not Murphys. Not Brooke. Not Kavanaghs . . . Not anyone. Not anyone. Is that clear, class?"

"Yes, Brother McCann."

"Is that crystal clear, class?"

"Yes, Brother McCann, crystal clear."

"Am I ever going to see another boy daydreaming ever again in this class, boys?"

"No, Brother McCann. Never again."

"And if I do, if I so much as see a boy staring out the window, the strap will come out. What will come out, boys?"

"The strap will come out, Brother McCann." Fear of the strap hangs over every class.

"That's right. And the boy who feels its sting will feel it until his body is black and blue. Is that clear? Until his body is what color, class?"

"Black and blue, Brother McCann."

Silence.

"Now, take out your catechisms and answer the assigned questions. And don't let me hear so much as a peep out of one of you."

Silence.

"You got no right to hit anybody," Blackie's voice is low but clear. The words hang in the air long after the sound stops. It's as if we've all stopped breathing.

McCann turns. He has the face of a mad dog. "Who said that? Who is the young daredevil who said that?" There is froth on his lips.

Blackie Neville raises his hand. He's a stocky boy with a curly black afro and tiny black eyes set way back in their sockets. McCann crosses the room, jumps an empty table, his soutane flying. He charges, scattering a row of empty desks, and smacks Blackie on the side of the head with his fist. Blackie's desk is opposite mine. I can see the greenish white saliva in the corners of McCann's mouth.

"*What*, Mr. Nevilles? What did you say?"

"Said you got no right to hit somebody."

Whack. "What? No what? No right? No right, did you say?" *Whack.* "You think you're in charge here, Mr. Nevilles? You think you're the Brother here?" *Whack.*

"No, don't think I'm—"

"Good." *Whack.* "That's good, Mr. Nevilles. Because you are not, sir." *Whack.* "You are not in charge, sir."

Blackie's pink plastic glasses fall to the floor. *Whack*. Left hand. Right hand. Left. Right. "You are not in charge." *Smash*. "You will never be in charge. And if I want..." *Whack*. "...to strike someone..." *Whack*. "...I'll bloody well do so, Mr. Nevilles." *Whack*.

Blackie is bleeding. From the nose. From the mouth. He crouches in his seat, defeated and crying. I want to go to him and give him a tissue. I want to wash the blood away from his face, his clothes, his books. I want to put my arm around his shoulder and tell him what a brave soldier he is, that what he said was right and true. And I want to whisper to him not to worry, that everything will be fine, that we will all look after him. We will take him to the dorm after class and clean him up and care for him. But I don't dare move. None of us dares to move. And the silence lasts an eternity.

2

SOMEONE IS MAKING a soft scratching noise. There are always sounds in the dorm throughout the night, especially creaking bed springs. All the mattresses are old and sag. And the gray blankets that cover them are stale and smell like licorice. But this sound is different. Quietly, so as not to wake anyone, I climb out of my bunk and listen again for the scratching. In the far corner, O'Connor rocks lightly, a squeaky bedspring rhythm. But that isn't it. From the far side of the dorm, Spencer snores gently, but it isn't a snoring sound. I scan the dorm for a brother or for Spook, the night watchman, and skulk in the direction of the scratching. The hardwood floor is cold. And there's always a slight breeze in the dorm, as if the windows are left open. Except for the flickering nightlight at the far end, it is dark. The long shape dividing the room is a row of wooden lockers. I rub my hands and blow on them.

"It's a rat. Maybe two," Blackie whispers from two bunks away. "Could be three." He speaks only when it's necessary and says only what's needed. His curly black head pops in and out of the big window as it always does when he smokes late at night. As I get close, he strikes a match. His face is still swollen from the beating. He grins, flashing a gold tooth, and blows out the match.

His name is William Jefferson Neville but everyone calls him Blackie because that's what Brother McCann nicknamed him the first day of class when everyone still thought he was deaf. "You're black. So we'll have to call you Blackie," Brother McCann said to a chorus of laughter. He might easily have been nicknamed Blackie because of his curly hair and his beady black eyes that seem never to close, never to blink. They're darting eyes, behind pink plastic glasses that rest on a broad nose, and they take in everything. He's short and sturdy and lives here with us in St. Martin's, the dorm for junior boys, because when he entered the Mount last year, nobody knew his age.

He was left at the monastery doorstep and didn't speak for weeks. For a while everyone thought he was deaf. The rumor is that he's from the States, New York. Or *New Yawk*, as Oberstein would say. Oberstein and Blackie are really close. They are the closest in our dorm. We think it's because they're both Americans. Oberstein overheard Brother Mc-Murtry, the Superior, telling Brother McCann that Blackie's mother is a prostitute. McMurtry said a bigwig from Fort Pepperrell, the American military base between Quidi Vidi Lake and the White Hills, came to see him and told him that Blackie's mother was with a sergeant from Harlem who used to beat Blackie. She came to Newfoundland with Blackie looking for the soldier when he went missing. She found him and left Blackie.

Blackie's sure he'll find his mother if he can just get back to the States. Oberstein wants to write his own mother and ask her to take out an ad in the newspaper, but Blackie says that won't do any good because his mother can't read. He says he has to get to New York and find her himself. He knows he will find her if he can only get there. McMurtry put Blackie with our group because our dorm had the most empty beds. Even brainy Oberstein thinks he should've been put in St. Luke's with the senior boys. We all think he's a lot older. And smarter. Blackie's a different kind of smart. He's smarter than everyone except Oberstein, who's smarter than some of the brothers.

"Been at it for days. Three, maybe four rats. Could be a nest. Comin' before the snow. Eatin' the wallpaper by now, I reckon." He flicks his cigarette butt out the window and leaps from his upper bunk to the cold hardwood, landing softly on all fours, like a cat. "Comin' from the closet in the corner. By Ryan's bunk."

I stare at his swollen nose and wonder if it's broken. In the dark, his skin looks lit from within. It's the color of Brother McCann's big mahogany desk.

"Don't worry. They can't get out. It's locked," I say, trying to convince myself.

"Me 'n' Murphy are headin' to the bakery for a fresh loaf. C'mon, I'm hungry as a hound."

You can say and do a lot of things at the Mount, but one thing you never, ever do is say no to Blackie. So I follow at his heels.

He slaps Murphy awake and orders him to scout ahead. Murphy wipes the sleep from his eyes and scratches his jug-ears. Brother McCann always leaves the bakery locked so that the boys can't get inside until he's there to supervise them in the morning after seven o'clock Mass. The bakery door is divided into two parts, an upper and a lower that both swing in and out. Both have padlocks. Blackie can pick any lock in the place, and the bakery is his specialty. Murphy and I watch in amazement as he slides a thin piece of wire inside the lock and within seconds pops it. "Thank you, Jesus," he says. He squints and grinds his teeth, again exposing that beautiful gold tooth.

"Jesus, Blackie, how do you do it?" Murphy says, as we push through the lower door and inhale the most beautiful smell in the world, Mount Kildare bread, fresh out of the oven.

"*Believe*," Blackie whispers.

The loaves are all laid out in perfect rows on a long stainless steel table near the cleaned dough mixer. Each loaf consists of three buns. Blackie greedily rips one of the loaves into three parts and passes Murphy and me a hunk. We sink our teeth into the soft dough.

"How is it, Blackie?

"Real good. You?"

"Good. Be perfect if we had a swig of altar wine."

"Wine smugglin's always midweek," Blackie says. "That's the rule."

Murphy stares at Blackie's bruised face. "I wish I had the balls to kill McCann," he says, flashing a side-slanting grin.

Blackie says nothing. We eat in silence. We are the best of brothers at such moments. We eat slowly, in complete communion. More complete than the sleepy communion we will share at seven o'clock Mass. When Blackie finishes, he lights a cigarette, inhales, and passes it to Murphy.

"Let's take a loaf to Bug and Oberstein," Murphy laughs quickly, showing small white teeth.

"No," Blackie snaps. Blackie has a quick temper.

"It's too risky," I say. "Blackie's right."

Occasionally, there is a row of toutons left out. These are lumps of leftover dough deep-fried in chip fat. Dipped in molasses, a touton is an unbelievable treat. Noses are bloodied and sometimes broken over a treasured touton.

"Our lucky day," Murphy says, scooping up a handful of toutons in his big hands. Murphy is large-framed and almost six feet tall. Everything about him is big. Big hands, big feet, big freckles, big red head. Big heart. He's forever running a hand through his straight red hair, a thick shock of which keeps falling in front of his glasses, which are pink plastic like Blackie's, like every pair at the Mount. An arm of his crooked glasses is held on by hockey tape. His lips are always cracked, so much so that they sometimes bleed.

"One each," Blackie says. "Arrange the tray so it looks full. Nobody been at it."

Murphy knows better than to question Blackie's authority. He passes us each a touton and rearranges the tray.

"A bit of molasses would be nice," I say.

Blackie nods a firm no. "Gotta go," he says, glancing at his watch. "Been ten minutes out. We're enterin' the danger zone." There is a creaking noise overhead. We freeze.

"*Spook*," Murphy whispers, meaning the night watchman is on the move. He squints, crinkling the freckles around his eyes.

We bolt the bakery, a touton in one hand, a hunk of fresh loaf in the other. As always, we take the same route back to the dorm, Murphy scouting ahead, dropping bits of paper along the way to let us know the coast is clear—through the huge dining hall, up the two flights of stairs, past the chapel, down the long dark hall to St. Martin's dormitory. We head straight for our beds, and I lie there frozen for a long time before eating my touton and the rest of my delicious hunk of fresh loaf. As I eat, I listen for the scratching sound I heard earlier. I want to be able to report to Blackie in the morning whether there are two or three rats or a whole nest in the closet, the place that is soon to be known by everyone at the Mount as the Rat Locker—a small room at the far end of the dorm that the brothers use for storing the big boxes of winter clothes. But there are no scratching sounds to be heard. Only stillness. The long, lonely stillness that will be broken in a few hours by the sound of the ugly buzzer waking all the boys for seven o'clock Mass.

I'm jittery and can't sleep, so I get up and go to the fire escape for a smoke. As I open the door to the long tunnel, a musty smell rushes past me. It reminds me of the smell in Dad's old blue bus. It's so strong the memories flood back, and I start to cry. I slam the door shut. That smell will always remind me of death. The door makes a sharp click, which rouses Blackie.

"Whatcha doin'?" he whispers, hopping from his bunk.

"Nuthin'," I say.

"Time is it?"

"Five o'clock."

"Why you up?" He offers me a piece of touton.

"Can't sleep." We go to the big window at the back of the dorm. Blackie slides the window up and coos gently to the pigeons. He drops a few pieces of bread on the window ledge. But the pigeons are asleep and don't answer.

"Poor little birds," I say. "Always hungry."

"Trouble sleepin'?"

"I'm really worried, Blackie. About getting caught."

He wrinkles his brow and taps his gold tooth. "Cut the sleep-talk." That's what Blackie says when he thinks someone is speaking without thinking. "Nobody's gettin' caught. Believe it."

"I want to, Blackie, but . . ."

"No buts. *Believe.*"

Soft footsteps startle us. They come from the other side of the dorm. Oberstein's still shadow looks like a Buddha statue. That's what Brother McMurtry calls him, the little Buddha. He's really chubby.

"We're over here," I whisper. "Feeding the pigeons."

Blackie stretches as we listen to Oberstein's footsteps padding across the dorm. It's still dark, but by the flickering night-light in the big window we can see the reflection of the long row of wooden lockers down the middle of the dorm. On top of the lockers Rags, our favorite brother, has left a stack of comic books.

"What time is it?" Oberstein asks, squinting through thick round eyeglasses that magnify his eyes.

"Five."

"It's cold." Oberstein pulls his flannelette pajamas tighter. Like every pair of drawstring PJs, his are washed out.

"I can't sleep," he says. "I'm worried. What if they find out the wine's missing? What if ... What if they find it?"

"Buried in the woods up in Major's Path?" Blackie smirks.

"We should stick with the bakery. I don't think we should steal old Flynn's altar wine anymore."

"That's a lotta shit you're gettin' on with. Nobody's gettin' caught. You want outta the Dare Klub, maybe? You want out?"

"No. But what if we get caught? What if someone squeals? What if..."

"What if ... What if ..." Blackie growls, his beady eyes darting from me to Oberstein as he speaks. "Nobody's gettin' caught. If we do, I'll take the rap. I'm in charge. So, cut the sleep-talk. Nobody's gettin' in trouble 'cept *me*."

The night watchman's clock chain jingles in the washroom, so we race to our bunks. When Spook finishes his walkabout, I lie there peacefully, thinking about my older sister, Clare, until the tears come. I think about her every night. She's at St. Martha's, the girl's orphanage, which is run by the nuns. The boys' orphanage, where I am, was built in 1888, seventy-two years ago. It's run by the Irish Christian Brothers. There are hundreds of boys here, from age four to seventeen. That's when you have to leave, when you're seventeen. Most of the boys are orphans, but some are half-orphans. No boys come here for school or anything. There's just the orphans and half-orphans.

St. Martha's was opened around the same time. It's run by the Sisters of Mary. They're nuns from Ireland and Newfoundland. Clare visits me every now and then, when the nuns let her. Once I had the spells so bad the brothers had to go get her to come and talk to me. I felt like I was wandering through an old abandoned house that was half falling down. It was a terrible feeling, and I couldn't shake it. I had the spells *really* bad when I first came here. Clare was a big help. She told me I was feeling like I was because of Mom and Dad's death and that if I prayed really hard for them—even to them—the spells would go away. Not much changed when I prayed for them. But things got a bit better when I prayed to them.

Clare told me the last time I saw her that she and some of the senior girls at St. Martha's might come to work at the Mount Kildare Bakery on weekends. Mount Kildare is famous for its bread and hardtack, which are little rough oval-shaped cakes baked without salt. The brothers sell the bread and biscuits around the city to make money for clothes and food for the boys. Bread and biscuits and the famous Mount Kildare Raffle are how the brothers raise money to run the place. I sure hope it's true that Clare is coming to work at the bakery. That way I'll get to see her more. I really miss her a lot. She's the nicest person in the world. Lying alone in my bed thinking of her makes me feel as lonesome as a gull on a rock.

I finish my feast and stretch awhile and enjoy my nightly entertainment, the scratching in the Rat Locker, Bradbury's distant snoring, Fitzpatrick talking in his sleep, usually about girls, and O'Connor's periodic rocking. Then I listen to the stillness again, and drink it in for awhile before slipping into a deep sleep.

·   ·   ·   ·   ·

The youngest boy in our dorm is Oberstein and he's always the first to wake. Most mornings he's up before the buzzer. Sometimes he'll wake one of us and chat about one of his discoveries. He's always reading and always making discoveries. But this morning he's not first up. He's in the infirmary. He has the spells. Like Blackie, who's the oldest boy in our group, Oberstein is proud he's from the United States. He's from Washington. Home of our president, Oberstein beams each time he's asked what part of the States he's from. Everyone loves to hear him speak. He has the most beautiful accent. And he has a beautiful singing voice. His father was an American soldier stationed at Fort Pepperrell, half a mile down the road.

There are five American bases throughout Newfoundland. Rags says we can thank FDR, his favorite president, for Fort Pepperrell and all the jobs it created. He made a deal with Prime Minister Churchill, destroyers for land for ninety-nine years.

Oberstein's mother is from St. John's. When his father went back to the States with her they had two boys before he was killed in an accident.

"It was a terrible accident," Oberstein once told me. But he won't say anything else about it. "My mother asked the brothers to keep me until she has enough money to come and get me and take care of me." But it's been two years and she hasn't come. "I want to be just like my dad who was *one hundred percent* Jewish," he says. "If my Dad was alive, there's no doubt about it, that's how I'd be raised," he says. He doesn't let the brothers know that he's learning everything he can about being Jewish. He's afraid they'll stop him. He says he might be a rabbi when he grows up. His mother's not Jewish. She's Catholic. Oberstein carries a photograph of her and his little brother, Jack, everywhere he goes. He looks a lot like her. She's round as a barrel and has the same silky blond hair. Oberstein says he's got her genes.

He's an amazing guy, Oberstein is. He's smart as a bee. And he knows lots of wonderful songs, like "Joshua Fought the Battle of Jericho," which we get him to sing for us when we're sitting around bored. Or he'll wake us up singing it before the brother on duty gets us up for morning chapel. He says his father taught him tons of Jewish songs before he died. He's only a little guy, but he has this deep, booming voice. You'd never think a little guy like that could have such a deep voice. It's really funny. We all howl with laughter whenever he sings "And the walls came tumbling down." His voice echoes like the walls are really tumbling. And he sings other songs too, like "Amazing Grace," which the brothers get him to sing in chapel. And "The Streets of Laredo." Cross lends him his black cowboy hat, and Oberstein puts it on and goes down on one knee and booms, "As I walked out in the streets of Laredo. As I walked out in Laredo one day." And immediately a crowd gathers. They come from every-where, because his beautiful voice can be heard all over the Mount. Even some of the brothers come to hear him. We could be out in the yard playing or way down in the soccer field, and when he starts singing we drop everything and come running the second we hear "As I walked out in the streets of Laredo." We all freeze and stare at him, bug-eyed every time, until the song is over. He has a huge throat and neck, like a tree trunk. Blackie says that's because he needs a big house for his big voice.

And he's a great storyteller too. He tells us all kinds of stories, mostly from the Bible: Abraham trying to kill his son, Isaac, Samson and Delilah, Moses and the burning bush, Jonah and the whale, David using his slingshot to kill the giant, Goliath, Ezekiel and the fiery chariot. Sometimes at night, after the brother on duty is gone, we crowd around Oberstein's bunk and listen to a story. He can keep you interested for a long time, from beginning to end. Halloween is just around the corner. That's when he's at his best. He can tell some pretty spooky stories. He really scares the little ones. He's really tiny and chubby, and has a moon face, and his hair falls over his round glasses like silk. His hair is shiny like my sister, Clare's, but hers isn't silky, it's as thick as rope, hangs almost to her shoulders, and has a perfect part down the middle.

In class, Rags always calls Oberstein the chubby cherub. "Well, I guess we'll have to check with the chubby cherub for that answer," he says whenever the class is stuck on something. Rags is so kind. Instead of strapping us for cursing, like the other brothers, he tells us to try and say words like "pistil" or "shuttlecock." That really cracks everyone up.

Rags is a string bean with a ghostly face dotted with pimples. Clare says he has what's called a lazy eye. He has the most amazing eyes, tiny liquid brown eyes that are extremely close together. And you can always see more of the white of his right eye than his left. He wears square rimless glasses, which are always perched low on his nose. "Rags is the only guy I know can look himself in the eye," Oberstein once joked. And he has the pointiest Adam's apple you've ever seen. Your eyes go straight to it every time you see him. He told the little ones it's called your Adam's apple because Adam ate the forbidden apple in the Garden of Eden and it got stuck in his throat. He's always sliding his hand through his salt-and-pepper brush cut and rhyming a nickname for one of the little ones: "How's little Randy the candy today?"

Oberstein always has a good answer to every question. He's only twelve and really shouldn't be in our group, the grade eights and nines, but Oberstein's so smart he skipped two grades. He's the best reader in the Mount, and he's an amazing speller. He wins every spelling bee. He can spell words that aren't even in the dictionary. And he beats some of the brothers at chess. He's quite amazing at everything; everything, that is, except sports. He hates sports, and he hates the cold weather. Sometimes in winter, when it's so cold your cheeks sting and we're all told to go outside and play in the yard until supper, Oberstein finds a comfortable spot in the shadows of the massive stone buildings and sandwiches himself there and stands out of the wind stamping his feet and clapping his mitts together. We pass him by, playing caught in the bumper or frozen tag and he just smiles and waves and stays put like a Newfoundland pony—solemn and beautiful and dumb. When we all go inside, Oberstein has the rosiest cheeks. You wouldn't believe it if you saw them. It's as if someone took a paintbrush and painted him up to play Santa Claus. Such rosy cheeks, he almost looks like a girl.

He's been at the Mount for two years, and he's still homesick. Not a month goes by without Oberstein getting the spells. But it always seems to be the worst at the beginning of the school year. That's when he first came here. Every boy at the Mount gets the spells one time or another. But it's usually only once in a while for most of us. With Oberstein, it's once a month. Twelve months in a year, twelve spells for poor Oberstein. Anyone else with the spells usually wanders off by himself and cries for a few hours and then he's okay. But not Oberstein. It really hits him harder than anyone else. Bug Bradbury says it's because Oberstein's like a girl, he's extra sensitive.

One Saturday, taking a shortcut through the chapel, I heard his voice in the choir loft. I stopped dead in my tracks, thinking it was Brother Walsh and some of the senior boys come to wax the floors. The wax machines hum everywhere Saturday mornings, even in the corridors after we wash the floors on hands and knees with scrubbing brushes and Spic 'n' Span. I ducked into one of the pews and slunk to the kicked-up kneelers. The pews always smell of Sunlight soap, and the air is always thick with a mixture of floor wax and candle wax. The chapel is the brightest room in the Mount, light shining through the stained glass windows by day and streaming from a thousand candles by night. During Christmas and Easter, the chapel is on fire with light.

When I was sure it wasn't Brother Walsh, I thought it was the old geezer brother, JD Wright. He usually prays in a high voice, half wheezing, half crying. Brother JD is the oldest brother in the Mount. He looks like he's about a hundred years old. Oberstein says he found out from Rags that JD was once in a bad car accident. He's got a lot wrong with him. He forgets a lot. He never remembers names. If JD asks Bug his name, Bug says Boris Karloff or Jesse James or Errol Flynn. A different name every time. Murphy's not as brave. He always says Audie Murphy because of the movie *To Hell and Back*, which we saw a while ago. Anyway, old JD pats them on the head and says run along now Audie or Jesse or Boris.

When he's out of bed, which is rare, he limps around like a spider on two aluminum canes. He has bad eyes and wears heavy, thick glasses. Once in a while he works in the canteen, and when you hand him your canteen card he holds it up so close to his eyes you'd think he was looking through it or trying to find a watermark. His eyes are really weak. And he has a mop of thin gray hair that bounces with each step he takes. And there are always rings under his eyes. He looks really odd when he's spidering around the place. Like something out of a cartoon.

He's bedridden most of the time, and we're always praying for him. Once, Brother McMurtry asked us to say a special novena for him. Rags said he was at death's door. Monsignor Flynn had to give him extreme unction. Extreme unction is pretty serious. It's given only to the dying. Oberstein calls him the terminal man. But he's been okay lately. In the chapel during rosary or Benediction or Mass you can hear this high wheezing sighing, followed by a few words of the Hail Mary. Or, out of the blue, old JD starts shouting at the devil: "You get the hell outta here . . . Get . . . Now . . . Go . . . Go on . . . Get the hell outta here . . . Get."

I thought it might've been old JD, and I froze in my tracks. You weren't allowed to cut through the chapel. Anyone caught was a goner. But it wasn't Brother JD. It was Oberstein. He was crying and talking at the same time. I thought he was praying to the Virgin Mary at first, but then I realized that it was *his* mother. I stood beside the big statue of St. Raphael and looked up at him, his head buried in his crossed arms on the choir loft railing. He was talking to his mother, who lives in

Washington. He looked up and the tears dripped down his cheeks. I thought of a wounded sparrow I'd seen once, trying to get a few crumbs from its angry brothers.

"You told me you'd come in two months, and I believed you. And you haven't. You haven't come. And it's been two years." And he'd sob, his chubby little body bouncing up and down, like a dory on the ocean.

"And who's lookin' after your hands? You know how bad they get. They never break into a rash when I do the dishes. When my hands are in the soapy water. My hands aren't allergic. But who's there now to do it? Little Jack can't. He's too small, and he doesn't understand. I hope you wear gloves when you put your hands into that soapy water, but I know you don't." More sobbing.

I knew exactly what was going on. What he was talking to her about. One weekend when he had a bad case of the spells, I found him alone in the yard by the handball court. He cried and cried that he was worried about his mother. "Her hands always break out in a rash," he said. After his father died, he said he was the only one to look after her hands, to put special cream on them when they got red and sore. "She's supposed to wear rubber gloves," he said, "but she never does. She hates rubber gloves. She says it makes her hands worse when she wears them." He was crying, he said, because he wasn't there to wash the dishes every time for her so her hands wouldn't get sore. And he was crying for little Jack, who couldn't look after her and who didn't have a father or a big brother to look after him.

He's so homesick, and Thanksgiving always makes the spells worse because he always gets a letter from home. That's why he's in the infirmary. For the past week Oberstein has been really excited. His mother has written to him from Washington telling him she has saved up enough money to pay for the fare to come to Newfoundland to see him. Every few months Oberstein gets a letter from his mother, and every time it's the same. She's already packing her suitcase, and she should arrive any day now. Oberstein doesn't sleep. He doesn't eat. He loses so much weight he doesn't even look chubby. He gives away his baloney and mustard potatoes, which he loves. Even his Jell-O, his favorite, he gives to Murphy or Bug. He carries the two sheets of creased and wrinkled stationery with him everywhere around the Mount. Each night he sleeps with the letter. Everyone has read it. Every boy and every brother. He's cornered me more than once, asking me to read the part where it says she'll be bringing little Jack. The envelope is dirty from the many finger marks. And the stamp of the White House with the red USA beneath it is marked with spots of grease and food. Eventually, what's happened in the past, happens again. Oberstein gets sick, develops a temperature and is sent to the infirmary.

He's received lots of letters, and he has not seen his mother once since she left him at the Mount two years ago. Oberstein gets more upset each time she doesn't come. And his stay in the infirmary gets longer with each letter. This time he was sure that she would come with little Jack and they would fly back to Washington where she lives in an apartment with a kitchen, a living room, a bathroom, and two bedrooms.

Oberstein has cornered every boy in our dorm and discussed all his plans with each one time and again. How he and little Jack will share the big bedroom and his mother will have the small one. Where he will go to school. How he will take little Jack to see the Yankees when they come to play the Senators. How he will teach him to score the games. How they will all arrive home just in time for the World Series. We all listen and nod and agree with everything he says.

"Will you get to see Mickey Mantle, Oberstein?" Blackie says. "Will you see Yogi Berra?"

"And if you catch a ball at the game, will you keep it or give it to little Jack?" Murphy asks. "Will you wait around after the game for an autograph?"

"*Yes*," Oberstein says, "yes, yes, yes."

But what's the use? It's like a bad dream that won't go away. Oberstein lies in the infirmary with a high temperature, worrying worse than ever about his mother's hands and little Jack. We all visit him and play cards or jacks with him and tell him how much we miss him and promise to help him get over it. We hope that his mother won't send another letter a few months from now. And we hope that Oberstein will soon get back to class because he always knows the answers to everything and helps everyone with homework. And there always seems to be much less strapping going on when Oberstein's around.

Kavanagh crouches down by his bed to talk to him. As though he can stop Oberstein's tears. "Don't worry Oberstein, you'll be visiting the White House soon enough. Maybe seeing the president. Maybe shaking his hand. Soon you'll be in your own bedroom with little Jack. You'll come and go and never have to ask permission once to watch TV or go to the fridge or anything. It'll be worth waiting for, Oberstein, you'll see. Just think, study when you feel like it, not even study at all, sometimes. Just loaf around and do nothing."

I lean down over his infirmary bed. And stare into his blue eyes. They look like water. His face is as pale as his pillow. His cheeks are rosy from his high temperature. As rosy as they are when he stands outside in the cold. He doesn't say anything. Not a sound, except a feeble sigh now and then. The tears sting his eyes and run down his face as he pulls the white sheet up to his chin. I turn and close my eyes and try to blank out the tears glistening on his rosy cheeks. He does not speak of his mother or little Jack or the apartment in Washington. He is silent. He is thinking of the lie that is fading away.

•   •   •   •   •

Next morning at breakfast, we pick up our tin trays with the US Army indentation in the middle where the hard boiled egg and fried baloney are placed. I look at Oberstein's reflection in his tray, his thick eyeglasses catching the light. He really does look like an angel. We slide the tin trays silently along the steel counter. Sunshine floods through the windows, making huge squares of light on the floor.

It's in the air. That dreadful feeling. It only comes once in a long while, the way it must come to animals when they sense the weather changing. It's not like the spells. It's sudden. Like lightning. It'll be here and gone before you know it. And everyone feels it at once. Animals must feel it when they sense a forest fire is on the way. Everyone's edgy. Everyone will be fidgeting in class. The same as they were in chapel. Boys are toying with their food, picking at their green woollen sweaters, fiddling with their silverware. Blackie keeps wiping his glasses on his sweater. Oberstein, who always has a Classics comic or a paperback, isn't reading. Some are only half-eating, even though they're hungry. It's always a strange time when something big's brewing. I can feel it in my gut. A big fight's about to take place. It might happen after school, unannounced. But everyone will know. Everyone will know at the same time. And everyone will be there. Behind the outdoor swimming pool. Or in Brother JD's garden. One of the usual places. The word will go out, like fire through dry grass. After school, behind the outdoor swimming pool or down near the bog: Hynes against Jones or Jones against Littlejohn. There will be animal fear. And blood.

Or maybe it's not a fight at all. Maybe a storm's coming. A big one. A hurricane. Like the one four years ago. All the heating will be shut down for days. And the American soldiers from Fort Pepperrell will bring us food in big stainless steel vats branded USA. We'll all go around wearing extra clothes for protection against the cold winds that blow through the big buildings late at night. We'll even wear our clothes to bed.

Or maybe somebody has stolen something—money or food—or something from the monastery. And somebody's gonna be made an example of. Or they've found out about the stolen altar wine. I search for Blackie. He's at the front of the line, whispering something to Oberstein. Or there's gonna be a big announcement. There will be no choices for Christmas this year. A month or so before Christmas, every boy receives a white index card with Christmas Choices typed at the top and three numbered lines neatly listed below. Each boy fills out his three choices, the last choice being the gift he least wants. You never get your first choice, rarely your second and sometimes not even your third choice. Maybe that's the reason for the feeling that's in the air. That would be awful. It happened once before. No choices for Christmas. That year everyone received a pair of shoes, brown penny loafers.

But there's no doubt about it. Everyone's thinking the same way. Everyone's expecting something awful to happen. But nobody's saying anything. You can see it in the twitching of Murphy's eyebrows. The lazy way Kavanagh scratches his carroty head. In the dangerous one-handed way Kelly carries his food tray. In the tapping of feet. In the confusion of seating arrangements. Kavanagh and Brookes changing seats without a fuss. Ryan, who usually sits between Murphy and me, is missing. I can feel Blackie nervous and angry beside me. The tension is thick; you can touch it.

Then, *bang*—it happens. "Mayday! Mayday!" Oberstein whispers. Brother McMurtry's snow-white hair appears at the front of the cafeteria. He's small and pale and wears round steel-rimmed spectacles beneath a swollen forehead. He has a tiny nose, no chin, and icy eyes. Eyes that glow and always stare sternly. As usual, when he has something serious to say, he removes his spectacles, bites the tip of one of the arms and stares at us through X-ray eyes. Wolf eyes, Blackie calls them. Eyes that see through you and beyond, Oberstein says. I watch his gaze pass slowly around the room, over green sweaters and gray flannel pants, over frightened faces, to the holy pictures and statues at the back, till they find their resting place, the podium, which is only brought out when a boy is to be severely disciplined. Murphy looks at me. I look at Blackie, who looks at Murphy. We are all thinking of last night's raid on the bakery. The silence of air rushing to fill a vacuum descends upon the hall. McMurtry waits, lets us drink in the silence. Then he clenches his fists, clears his throat and speaks.

"Gentlemen, your attention, please! After three years of living at Mount Kildare, of being cared for at Mount Kildare, of being educated at Mount Kildare, one of our boys, one of our family, one of your *brothers*, has done a terrible thing. One Eddie Ryan, formerly of Parson's Pond, has done a foolish, foolish thing. Mr. Eddie Ryan has run away."

Suddenly, it's as if we are all naked on an ice floe. Blackie's glance is a laser beam. Kavanagh has turned ghostly. Murphy's eyes are blinking madly. We all know what will happen to Skinny Ryan. You'd have to be mad to even think about running away.

"Mr. Ryan disappeared yesterday after supper." Brother McMurtry snaps his fingers for effect and wrinkles his lips into a half-smile. "Simply vanished into thin air. A disappearing act. Mr. Eddie Ryan performed an amazing trick. An escape artist! A little Houdini! He became invisible. That's correct. Invisible. But Mr. Eddie Ryan did not perform the impossible trick. Mr. Ryan did not disappear permanently. That trick has never been performed by a boy at Mount Kildare. Not since its doors were opened in 1888. And I can assure you, gentlemen, such a trick will never be performed ... never while I am the Brother

Superior." He nods and smiles. Murphy lowers his head and glances toward Blackie, who is tapping his gold tooth.

"But Mr. Eddie Ryan did vanish. He did disappear for a few hours. His absence was discovered last night by Brother Walsh when Mr. Ryan failed to sign what you boys affectionately call The Doomsday Book. The police were called. Mr. Ryan was found not far away, less than a mile from Mount Kildare, hiding in the woods at Virginia Waters. He was discovered sleeping under fir and pine branches. Like an animal. Instead of sleeping comfortably in the warmth of his bed, like a human being, Mr. Ryan chose to sleep in the cold autumn woods. He was tracked down not by the police, but by the grace of God, the night watchman and Brother McCann, who dragged him home crying and kicking and cursing. Yes, boys, *cursing*. Now, isn't that something for a young Catholic boy. *Cursing!* In a moment, Brother McCann will lock him away in what some of you call the Rat Locker, located in St. Martin's dormitory. He will remain there until we see fit to remove him." Brother McMurtry's fists are rigid.

There's a long silence, as if everything has suddenly become dark, and Brother McCann appears with Eddie Ryan, who looks skinnier than usual, like he needs a new nickname. Skinny arms, skinny legs, skinny wrists. As he walks by us, we notice that his hands are tied behind his back. Brother McCann leads him through the cafeteria by thick ropes knotted around his waist. Eddie Ryan's jet-black hair is ruffled, and his baby face is mud-splattered. His black-and-white canvas sneakers are still wet, and they leave prints on the linoleum. There are pine needles and twigs and wads of clay on his red-checkered shirt and in his greasy hair. He's dirty as a duck's puddle. The silence is so strong you can hear it. I close my eyes and think of the movie we saw last week about a soldier facing a firing squad. All Ryan is missing is the blindfold.

"Untie him." Brother McMurtry's voice is a controlled whisper, but louder than a shout. Every boy strains to see and hear. Brother McCann unties his hands and drops the lead rope. "Step forward, Mr. Ryan," Brother McMurtry says. He snorts and releases White Lightning from his black soutane. It's the only leather strap at the Mount that isn't black or brown. It's a dull yellow color that looks like a flash of white when Brother McMurtry wields it, working himself into a rage with each blow. "Up. Up. Higher." Brother McMurtry's voice is shrill and loud and angry. We've never seen or heard him like this. Eddie Ryan raises his hands high. From behind, Brother McCann holds Eddie Ryan's skinny wrists. The sounds remind me of a shoot-out in *Gunsmoke*. The shots echo. Skinny Ryan sounds like a wounded animal. It seems the firing will never cease. But it does. It stops. When Eddie Ryan has received the prescribed number of strokes for runaways: twenty on each hand. And when he has fallen to the floor, sulking and broken. It ends as it starts. With silence. The silence of air slowly slipping away, recreating the vacuum.

We steal shy glances at each other while staring at the floor and the scraps of food on our plates. "Sonofabitch," Blackie whispers between his teeth. Tearfully, Oberstein looks at Murphy, who winces and bites his lip. Some of us cry silently. Some close their eyes and see pictures they would never want anyone else to see. And some think terrible thoughts, which they will carry with them through the rest of the day and late into the night. Into their dreams. But nobody speaks. And nobody, nobody dares to look in the direction of Skinny Ryan.

3

First Friday of the month. First Friday of the month.
First Friday ... First Friday ...

ONE OF THE MOUNT CRIERS, as Oberstein calls them, is
shouting in the hallways. There's always a crier or two racing
around, half-singing, half-screaming something or other that
may or may not be true. Usually, there's more than one. They
get a big kick out of running around shouting out something
at the top of their lungs. The brothers never mind. Rags says it's
a good way to remind us of things. For the boys, it's like a competition to see who can be first to break some news or remind
everyone of some scheduled event.

There's always a million things happening at the Mount. So
it's easy to forget Skinny Ryan's strapping or Oberstein's spells
or Blackie's beating. Every minute there's something new.
"Every day is mayday at the Mount," Oberstein always cheer-
fully reminds us.

Today, the crier is right. It is the first Friday of the month.
We always have confession after breakfast. Monsignor Flynn,
who has gray wisps of hair and thick eyebrows that stick out
like antennae, says that if you go to Mass and confession and
make a novena seven First Fridays in a row you will not die

without being in a state of grace. "Ergo," he says, "you will go straight to heaven." He always uses that word. "No stops," he says. "No transfers. You're on the Express Line to heaven. And pray to Jesus, boys. Remember, you can do all things through Jesus." Monsignor Flynn lives in a small apartment attached to the Mount. He says Mass every day for the brothers and boys and hears confessions every Saturday and on special occasions like First Fridays. He walks with a stoop in his shoulders, and whenever he speaks there's always a rattle in his throat.

Bug Bradbury sighs and waves his hand. Oberstein thinks that Bug's not really a believer. He says Bug has what Brother McMurtry calls the *doubts*. It's hard to tell with Bug because he loves to annoy everyone, especially old Flynn. Once, during confession, I was on the other side of the box, and he started telling his sins without saying, "Bless me, Father, for I have sinned." Old Flynn blasted him for not saying "Bless me, Father." Then I heard Bug say, "Excuse me. Scripture says, thou shalt have but one Father, thy Father in heaven, *sir*." Next thing I heard was the screen sliding across and Bug screaming. Old Flynn must've given him quite a poke.

"But, Monsignor, how can you be so sure? Maybe there's a stain or two on your soul, and you need to spend a day or two in purgatory on the way."

Monsignor Flynn's antennae twitch furiously. He stares at Bug with sad eyes. "If a boy makes the seven First Fridays, there are no exceptions. Ergo, no stops, not a single stop. Making the seven First Fridays guarantees the penitent the last rites of Holy Mother Church. Ergo, the Express Line to heaven, Mr. Bradbury. Is that clear, sir?" Bug hunches his shoulders and turtles his head. He knows when to shut his mouth. Another word and old Flynn would poke a finger in Bug's eye. That's how he punishes a boy. If he stops you in the chapel hall or on the stairway and asks you a question from the catechism, like what is a sacrament, and you don't say right away, "A sacrament is an outward sign of God's grace," he pokes a finger in your eye. It hurts. You see stars for a few minutes, but it's better than the strap.

The entire dorm is on the way to the chapel for confession. Monsignor Flynn will lead us in the general act of contrition, followed by his usual lecture on how God is listening. "God is always listening, boys. God knows all. Omni*potent* and omni*present*! Be sure to tell everything. You will be forgiven, and your souls will be washed clean. Remember, boys, no sin is too great. Our God is a loving God. And He's an all-knowing God. All-knowing but all-loving."

Bug Bradbury's hand becomes a propeller again. "What if I got a gun and killed everyone in Mount Kildare? Like that guy in *Gunsmoke*. Every last soul? God wouldn't forgive me then, would he?"

Monsignor Flynn smiles a knowing smile. "God would forgive you, yes."

"But wouldn't you get excommunicated?" Bug asks, with windmill arm motions.

"No, you would not, Mr. Bradbury. You would be forgiven. Our God is a loving God. You are only excommunicated for opposing Church doctrine."

Bug slumps in his seat, mute as a mouse, defeated again.

Before chapel, we're permitted twenty minutes to wander about the building during the examination of conscience. We all wander off, even Oberstein. Although he's Jewish, he has to participate in all the Catholic stuff, even confession. The brothers take the examination of conscience very seriously. My sister, Clare, says it's the most important thing about being a Catholic, because when you examine your conscience you have to follow what you find even if it means going against your own church. "Conscience decides everything," Clare once said to me. "That's all that matters in the long run, not the rules, not the catechism book, not the sacraments, only conscience . . . conscience decides." She kinda scared me when she said it. She was so deadly serious. Oberstein says she's right, and that conscience is just a fancy name for common sense. And if you lose that, you lose everything.

Bug Bradbury and Oberstein and I wander toward the gymnasium, which is always empty at such times. Most boys wander off with Blackie for a smoke behind the outdoor pool. It's a safe spot with high wooden walls. Fast runners stand guard at either end to warn the swarm of smokers in the middle if a brother appears. We have great fun there in the summertime. A few boys head to their lockers to munch on a hidden treat. Bradbury and Oberstein are arguing about telling the truth in confession. Bug would argue with the devil.

He's a little guy with a squeaky voice and a bad heart. He's just over three feet tall, and he walks around with his deformed chest puffed out like he owns the place. He's really cocky for a little deformed guy. Saucy as a mutt. Out of the blue, he once said to Oberstein, who is really proud of his silky hair, "Oberstein, you got too much soft, silky hair. Why dontcha do yourself a big favor and get it all cut off?" He whistles when he breathes, and he has a saucy, high-pitched voice, which wouldn't sound so bad if he didn't act like he knew everything about everything. Because of his poor health, he has to go for extra meals in the morning and afternoon, and he has mug-ups—hot cocoa and toast—at night before bed. When we tell him he's spoiled rotten, he snaps, "You guys want extra meals, go get a hole in your heart." He got the nickname Bug because Blackie said one day that he looked like a ladybug.

"If someone gotta big brush and painted you red with black dots you'd look just like a ladybug, a ladybug with a human head," Blackie said.

"Ladybug, ladybug, fly away home," Murphy and Ryan always tease him. "Your house is on fire and your children are gone."

I never tell the truth in confession. Old Monsignor Flynn can get pretty cranked up if you say you stole a loaf from the bakery or robbed someone's canteen card. Instead of saying I stole a loaf, I say I cursed six times. You have to say something like that. Even if you haven't sinned, you have to make something up. You can't just kneel down and say, "Bless me, Father, for I have sinned, it's been two weeks since my last confession, I've been good." Old Monsignor Flynn depends on lots of sins to make him feel good about his job.

As we enter the empty gymnasium, Bug squeaks, "Ain't you guys afraid?" His voice is becoming more nasal.

"Afraid of what?" I ask.

"Hell!" Bug whistles. "You stupid sonofabritch."

"Bitch," Oberstein says. "It's sonofa*bitch*."

I tell Bug I'm not afraid, that I don't believe in hell, so it doesn't scare me one bit.

Oberstein agrees that there's no such place. "You can't have an all-loving God and innocent children in hell," he says. "It's contradictory."

Bug sighs a few whistle breaths and says he's not sure about heaven but he believes in hell. "It's like a bad horror movie," he complains, "like the ones that give you nightmares. Like *Night of the Zombies* or *The Fly*. And maybe Monsignor Flynn is right. God *is* everywhere. Ergo, He knows everything. And maybe He punishes you when you're bad. That's why I'm going to confess to Monsignor Flynn that I snapped the lizard six times since my last confession."

"Don't!" I shout. "You can't crank up old Flynn. He'll have a canary if you tell him that. Tell him you took the Lord's name in vain twenty times or you had five hundred impure thoughts."

"My God is a loving God," Bug squeaks, mimicking old Flynn, "and He's always listening. He knows all. I gotta confess. I gotta get the big solution."

"*Absolution*," Oberstein corrects.

"Besides, Monsignor Flynn won't believe me if I lie. He'll know." His eyes flutter and close as he speaks.

"Oberstein, tell him it doesn't matter if he jacked off or stole a loaf. Tell him it's all the same. It's all sin. Tell him, Oberstein," I plead. "Tell him it's a worse sin to crank up old Flynn. Tell him, Oberstein, he'll listen to you."

"You can say you had a few hundred impure thoughts about girls, Bradbury, you don't have to say you actually snapped your lizard," Oberstein says.

"I believe in hell. And I'm not going there. I'm getting the Express Line to heaven. And I believe God knows all. He's listening to us right now." Bug puffs out his chest. "I can't lie. I just can't." He makes a fluttering gesture and clamps his hands over his ears.

"I can't tell the truth," Oberstein says. "If I steal a loaf from the bakery, I say I took the Lord's name in vain seven times. If I haven't sinned, I say I swore or I had a thousand impure thoughts. I never confess the truth. And I rarely do penance. If I do, two Hail Marys and an Our Father becomes half a Hail Mary and a Glory Be. I just mumble through the act of contrition. I never do any of it right. And God hasn't struck me dead yet. Tell Monsignor Flynn you took the Lord's name in vain a hundred times since your last confession, and that you're really, really sorry. Spell it out, Bradbury. Tell him you said two hundred God-damns, one hundred Christ Almightys, and three hundred Jesus Christs. Believe me, he'll believe you."

"Ask him for extra penance, Bradbury," I say. "That always throws old Flynn off. He'll tell you not to be so hard on yourself."

"You're a dope, Carmichael. God is listening. Ergo, He

knows everything," Bug whistle-breathes and squeaks like crazy. "He will know. Monsignor Flynn will know. And besides, your sins won't be forgiven. My sins *will* be forgiven if I confess. Every sin will get the big solution. My soul will be washed clean. *Your* souls will remain stained, *stained*, throughout all eternity." He jumps around like a cat on hot rocks.

"But you can't tell old Flynn you were tugging the toad," I say. "He'll have a friggin' heart attack. For God's sake, Bradbury, make something up."

"I don't have any choice," Bug squeaks. "I'm confessing to everything ever, masturbating, swearing, dropping a roll of toilet paper in the toilet."

"Jesus, you don't confess to that, do you?" Oberstein says. We both howl. Oberstein's stomach shakes as he laughs.

"Certainly," Bug squeaks. "And once, I peed on the bathroom wall, and another time, I soiled my underwear during class."

We laugh so hard we almost fall down. Murphy wanders into the gym, asks what's so funny and joins in laughing. Bug is so serious he has us in stitches.

"You don't have to confess everything, Bradbury. Nobody confesses everything. Not even Father Cross," Murphy tells him. Father Cross is Chris Cross's nickname. He wants to be a priest.

"Well, I'm not Father Cross," Bradbury squeaks and puffs his chest at Murphy. "I reckon it's better to confess than not. It's better to have a clean plate."

"*Slate*," Oberstein corrects him.

"The brothers don't even confess all their sins," Murphy says, his mouth a side-slanting grin.

"You can't prove that. You got no proof of that." Bug is angry now, and his voice is squeakier and saucier than ever.

"Well, they put saltpeter in our food, and none of them confesses to that," Murphy says.

"What's saltpeter?" Bug whistles.

"Chemical stuff they put in the food to stop you from getting a hard-on," Oberstein says. "They get it from the Americans at the base, at Fort Pepperrell."

"Well, it doesn't stop me," Bug squeaks. "I get a hard-on all the time, a hundred times a day, at least."

"I don't think that's normal," Oberstein says.

"Do you confess to wetting the bed?" Murphy asks, his freckles brightening as he speaks.

"Yes," Bug wheezes, backing away. "I confess to everything. I don't wanna get excommunicated."

"You can't get excommunicated for that," Murphy says, poking me in the ribs and laughing. "Besides, you've got a waterproof rubber sheet, so even if you piss yourself it's okay. So why confess?"

"It's not a sin to wet the bed anyway," Oberstein says. "It's natural, same as snapping the lizard. God might see it, but He's not gonna send you to hell for doing something that's natural. And they're both natural, like eating and sleeping."

"I'm also gonna tell Monsignor Flynn that Blackie stole money from the collection box. I saw him. And *God* saw him. Last Sunday during public Mass. He threw a dollar bill behind the statue of the Virgin and got it after Mass when he was cleaning up. I'm gonna confess it. I gotta. And I'm gonna tell him about the wine stealing and the fresh loafs from the bakery too. I gotta." He turns and puffs his chest and pushes past us, stomping toward the door. Bug is mad now.

I grab him. "Where are you going, Bradbury?"

"To confession. To tell all," he whistles, and tries to pull away.

Murphy towers over tiny Bug Bradbury.

"Just a minute. You can't squeal on Blackie. That will ruin all our plans."

"What plans?" Bug squeaks.

"None of your business what plans. Just don't squeal on Blackie, or you're a dead duck. You say one word, and I'll crown you." Murphy makes two big fists. "One word, and I'll get the whole Dare Klub to dog-pile you. I mean it, Bradbury."

Bug listens, and all we can hear is his whistle breathing. Then he puffs his chest again and shoves me aside.

"Just a minute." Murphy grabs him by the neck with his big hands and shakes him. Oberstein jumps in, and we hold him as he squeaks and raves.

"Leave me go. Lemme outta here. I wanna go to the chapel. For the big solution. Leave me go. I wanna go to confession." His arms are windmills.

"The only place you're going is the Rat Locker," Murphy shouts.

"Leave me go."

He won't listen to us and kicks and strikes out, his squeaky mouth wet with spit as Murphy grabs him by the throat, choking meaningless gibberish out of him. He lets out a shrill little scream and reddens, his voice coming from nowhere and everywhere at once. He wants to get away from us, to get to chapel to squeal on Blackie to Monsignor Flynn, who will tell Brother McMurtry, who will punish Blackie. And that cannot happen. And though Bradbury raves and squeaks and kicks, we give him a hiding to let him know what's in store for him if he squeals on Blackie. We do it quickly and efficiently, and he falls to the gymnasium floor, whimpering for a few minutes. And then he sits there, whistling, trying to catch his breath. We are pale and a little shocked at our actions, and we are breathing as quickly as Bug Bradbury.

"That's just a taste, Bradbury," Murphy says, holding up his big fist. "And that's nothing to what you'll get if you squeal on Blackie. Do you understand?"

Bug does not answer.

"Do you understand, Bradbury?" Murphy shouts, and the words echo through the gymnasium.

"Yes," Bug sobs. "Please don't dog-pile me. Please don't put me in the Rat Locker."

Murphy picks him up off the floor and wipes his eyes with the cuff of his shirt.

"If I don't confess to snapping the lizard and seeing Blackie steal the money," Bug whimpers, "I won't have anything to say."

"Just tell him you had impure thoughts," Oberstein says.

"Yes," Murphy says, "and confess to being in a fight once since your last confession. No, twice. Say you fought twice since your last confession."

Bug sulks and nods his head slowly, and we know Blackie is safe. And we all head off to chapel as I lose myself in thought, wondering if I should confess to a hundred impure thoughts or cursing a hundred times instead of beating up Bug Bradbury.

4

OBERSTEIN ALWAYS SAYS that Blackie has the wisdom of Solomon. I wasn't convinced until Blackie came up with the idea for the marathon. That convinced me. It came to him one Saturday afternoon when Abe Richardson's little brother, Aaron, whose nickname is Shorty, insisted on running a suicide mission for Abe. Shorty's small-boned, but he's light and thin and long like a bird.

Saturday and Sunday afternoons, boys in grade seven and up are allowed to go to town. We can leave the Mount Kildare grounds between the hours of two and six o'clock. You can go anywhere in the city you want—visit anyone, walk anywhere. There are only two rules: Don't get into any trouble, and be back by six o'clock. Most of us go fishing at Virginia Waters, where we have a boil-up and roast wieners and potatoes on sticks over an open fire. Or we walk to Major's Path near the Bat Cave and pick gallons of blueberries and raspberries. Or we hike to Signal Hill and play in the barracks and storehouses where the French and the English fought in 1700. That's why it's called Signal Hill, because the British sailors used it as a look-out. It's a great place to play. Murphy always climbs the noonday gun, which is a big black cannon they've been firing off every twelve o'clock since 1842. Or we just hang around

Bannerman Park, looking for girls, or walk to the west end to Victoria Park or Bowering Park and watch the swans or skip stones in the pond or play war games, climbing the statue of the Fighting Newfoundlander. If we go to the west end, we always have two timekeepers because it takes us about an hour to get back. If we aren't in the dining hall by six, we're in big trouble. "Back by six or we're in a fix," Blackie warns us, as we sign the big black register chained to the lectern outside the dining hall. The Doomsday Book, Oberstein called it one day after history class. We sign out at two, and we sign in before six. It is better not to show up at all than to show up after six o'clock on a Saturday or Sunday.

Every boy who leaves the grounds visits some place or just wanders around St. John's. Some visit an aunt or uncle or cousin or friend of the family. One or two of the older boys arrange to meet with their girlfriends—to get a piece of skin, as the saying goes. Murphy and I have a long chat about that. "It must be the greatest feeling in the world," he says after he's admitted that he's never gotten his skin. "Can you imagine lying down naked up in Major's Path in the swampy woods with your girl, the smell of raspberries all around and the warm wind blowing over your naked bodies? Imagine eating raspberries and kissing her sweet red lips and the taste of her sweetness burning your mouth. And smelling her hair. And the touch of her soft, smooth breasts, just lying there, feeling her nipples get hard. Getting hard as a rock yourself and slipping it inside her like a tadpole sliding through the grass. It must be *soooo* good to be inside your girl, lying on the cool mossy earth. Getting a good rocking rhythm going until—*whamo*—you explode like one of those supernovas Rags talks about in science class, shock waves rippling through every layer of your skin. You'd shine brighter than the entire galaxy for a second, I betcha. Dontcha think it'd be the greatest feeling in the world?" he says.

"I do. But you don't need to convince me, Murphy," I say. "I can't wait to get my skin."

The punishment for returning one minute after six o'clock is an instant strapping. Twenty whacks. Ten on each hand. Your hands sting till they're numb. And you lose all privileges for three months, including smoking, TV, and your canteen card. In addition, you are given extra chores like cleaning stairways every morning for three months. Nobody ever takes a chance on getting back after six. Although Shorty Richardson did one time.

That's what put the marathon idea in Blackie's head. Shorty's race against the clock one Saturday. Abe and Aaron Richardson used to live on Garrison Hill in the row housing just below the Basilica. It's a little over two miles from the Mount. Abe and Shorty spent the afternoon with their aunt, returning around five o'clock. Ten minutes after they got back, Abe realized he'd forgotten his green V-neck sweater, part of his school uniform. When you go to town, you wear your school uniform—white shirt, green V-neck sweater, green necktie, gray flannels. Most of our scratchy woollen sweaters and gray flannels are hand-me-downs. Nobody has clothes that fit. Oberstein's pants are always too tight. Mine are always too baggy. Murphy's pants never reach his ankles. Bug's shirt is always miles too big. And there isn't a woollen sweater in the Mount that doesn't have at least one hole in it. Our shoes and sneakers are never the right size. Almost everyone's clothes have patches. Patches that are never the same color. Where there's a hole, the tailor, Brother Young, cuts a piece of cloth from his pile of old clothes and sews a patch over the hole. There's a piece of gray pajamas sewn on one of the elbows of my sweater. You get new clothing when you can't fit inside your old clothes. As long as you can wear it, you get patches. We don't mind wearing patchy clothes most of the time, but it's embarrassing when you're trying to impress a girl.

"Over forty minutes. I can make it. Twenty there and twenty back. I can do it. I know I can. Let's not waste time fighting about it," Shorty says.

"No, it's too risky," Abe says. "You'll be killed if you don't make it back by six. I'm not going to chance it." As he speaks, his brother begins to cry.

"You'll get a worse shit-kickin' than me if you shows up Monday to class without your sweater. You'll be killed if you shows up to Walsh's class with no sweater."

"That's my problem," Abe says, squinting in the blinding sunshine.

"It's my problem too," Shorty says. His eyes are glassy.

"I don't want you to chance it, Aaron. It's too risky." Abe puts his long arm around his scrawny brother, who pulls back as if he's been stung and bolts toward the big Celtic cross posts lining the entrance to the Mount. I look at my Mickey Mouse watch. It is five-fifteen. I love my Mickey. Clare gave it to me when she came to visit the time I had a really bad bout of the spells. It glows in the dark.

"Jesus, come back. Come back!" Abe screams, and starts to cry.

"Come back to the five and dime, Jimmy Dean, Jimmy Dean," Bug mocks.

Murphy races to find Blackie, who instantly takes charge.

"Murphy, see who got supper duty. Maybe we'll be lucky." Blackie's eyes are on fire. "Rags, we can con for ten, maybe fifteen minutes." Rags lets us get away with a lot. "Maybe keep him from the Doomsday Book. Brother Walsh, we'll get five. Six, tops. McCann or Madman Malone, we're shagged. We'll forge Shorty's signature. Hope he ain't missed. Get Rumsey on red alert. Rifle through Shorty's desk for a signed book. Gotta start practicin' his signature right away."

"Done, Blackie," Murphy says.

"How far to Garrison Hill?" Blackie asks.

"About two miles," Abe says.

"One way?" Blackie removes his plastic glasses and wipes them on his shirt. There's an ugly yellow streak across his nose.

"Each way. Four miles altogether."

"Jesus, more than a ten-minute mile. He can't run a ten-minute mile, can he?"

"He's a good runner. Best runner in the Mount," I say. "He wins every race every Sports Day. He even beats the grade elevens."

"He runs like the wind, Blackie," Oberstein says.

"He'll never do it in a million years," Bug says.

"He looks like a bird, and he flies like one," Murphy says, flicking the shock of hair from his eyes.

Blackie looks at his watch. "Fuck of a run. He think about the quickest route?"

"No, he just took off. He'll probably go the way we always go. When we walk to town. Over Elizabeth, down Bonaventure to the Basilica."

"Probably the quickest route. Can he do a ten-minute mile?"

"Dunno," Abe says. "I just watch him run. I never time him or nothin'. He's like the wind. If it can be done, he'll do it."

"Better," Blackie says, "or he'll pay a helluva price."

We all head to the dining hall to check the roster. A stroke of luck. Rags is on duty.

"Thank you, Jesus," Blackie says, and tells Murphy to pretend he's been knocked out playing frozen tag in the gym if Shorty isn't back by six. That will divert Rags for at least five or ten minutes. Murphy is to pretend that he's knocked out for as long as he can. Rags will call for a stretcher to take him to the infirmary. Someone will go for medicine. That'll take time.

Blackie and I are the only ones with watches. We are in the middle of the group, staring at the seconds ticking away, standing in front of the big Celtic crosses leading to Elizabeth

Avenue. Blackie has that same sad stare in his eyes every time he looks across Elizabeth Avenue. He's always thinking the same thing. At the end of that road is Harlem, where his mother is. The huge stone walls of the Mount are always visible from Elizabeth Avenue and Torbay Road. As we wait, a passing car slows down. A passenger rolls down a window and gawks. "They have come to take home a norphan," Oberstein's voice is a falsetto. "I'm a *norphan*. I'm a norphan. We're all norphs in here. Come and visit the little *norphs*." Then he looks sad and says in his normal voice, "That's what I love about Rags. He never makes you feel like a norph."

Rags is so easygoing. After washup each night, we line up in our pajamas, and the brother on duty inspects us. If your nails are still dirty or you missed a spot behind your ears or something, most brothers thump you on the head or give you a whack and send you back to the sink. Or worse, they grab a facecloth and scrub you till it hurts. Not Rags. "Oops," Rags says, looking over the top of his rimless glasses. "I think I see a potato in Oberstein's ear. Or is that a carrot the chubby cherub's growing in there?" Which makes us all giggle like crazy. And after night prayers, Rags always tells us a story. Usually he makes one up about Chop-Chops, a cat with a missing leg, who has nine lives and who's full of mischief. The stories make us laugh and they make us cry. Chop-Chops prowls around the Bronx, getting in and out of trouble. Once, he had a really rich owner who used to beat him. Another time, he had a really poor owner who used to give him his supper. Both times, Chop-Chops ran away. We hate it when Chop-Chops gets to his last life. We beg Rags to bring him back with another nine lives. And he always does. That's the difference between Rags and most of the other brothers. Rags does what a *real* brother would do. We trust him an awful lot. Although we got suspicious when he asked if we knew anything about the wine missing from the sacristy. "Tell the truth and shame the devil," he said. That's an expression he uses all the time. Tell the truth and shame the devil.

"If I find out anything about that, I'm going straight to Brother McMurtry right away," Oberstein said, and we all nodded.

"That's good. I'm glad to hear that," Rags sighed. It was like the thought of us getting caught stealing was painful for him. Anyhow, we knew Oberstein had thrown him off our trail.

Oberstein stares at the car and says dolefully, "The monkeys have come to visit the zoo." And I know he's thinking of his mother and little Jack. Today, the few cars that pass come almost to a full stop to examine our little group, shivering and staring intently across Elizabeth Avenue, waiting for the figure of Shorty Richardson to appear.

Bug is driving everyone nuts, whining that Shorty will never make it.

"Looks like rain. It's clouding over. That'll slow him down," Bug whines.

Even Blackie's getting pissed off with Bug. Blackie hates anyone being negative. At precisely quarter to six, Blackie directs Murphy to prepare to head to the gymnasium and get ready to con Rags. It is ten to six exactly when Ryan yells, "There he is! There he is!" We climb the chain-link fence but can see no one. Ryan yells that he's at the lower gate, that he's coming up Kenna's Hill. We all look, and there he is, the green-and-white sweater draped over his scrawny body, sleeves flapping. He looks like a scarecrow in a wind storm.

Loud cheers! Everyone races to him, slapping and hugging him. Abe kisses him and says he loves him over and over. Shorty takes off the sweater and gives it to his brother. "I told you I could do it," he whispers.

Abe starts to cry and laugh at the same time, hugs Shorty and says, "Jesus, I couldn't ask for a better brother."

Blackie looks at his watch. "Kenna's Hill's a longer route. *Better* than a ten-minute mile," he says. "*Fantastic* run! Helluva run." His beady eyes are dancing.

As everyone gathers around Shorty, whooping it up, I notice Blackie pulling Oberstein aside. He speaks as his eyes shift to catch what's happening with the crowd. I can hardly hear them for all the cheering and hooting. Another loud shout goes up as I edge closer, and all I can make out as they split apart are the words "New York City."

Shorty Richardson beams as we raise him high on our shoulders and head to the cafeteria. It is not until Shorty is signing the Doomsday Book that we notice he's wearing penny loafers.

● ● ● ● ●

Diefenbaker meat for supper. Diefenbaker meat for supper.
Diefenbaker meat again.

We're all getting pretty sick of Diefenbaker meat. A month ago two big transport trucks pulled into the Mount and dumped about a million tins of Spam. Rags told us it was donated by the government. Some guy had a loan from the government to open a food business and couldn't pay back the loan so the government took all his merchandise. We got a warehouse full of Spam. St. Martha's got a ton of canned tomatoes. Oberstein calls the Spam Diefenbaker meat, after the prime minister. Brother Walsh and a few senior boys built a huge shed out in the yard to store it. We'll never eat it all in a million years. And they've sectioned off a square at the back of the cafeteria and made a storage room. Tins and tins of Diefenbaker meat, stacked to the ceiling.

During supper Murphy kicks me under the table with his dandy long legs and gives me the double nose twitch, a secret sign we use that means he has a checker for me. A checker means that Blackie has called a meeting of the Dare Klub. A black checker means we'll find out the meeting time and place later in the day. There's an important meeting, but it's not an emergency. A red checker means it's an emergency and the meeting will take place during Saturday free time at the Bat Cave. The Bat Cave is an old American army bunker hidden deep in the woods. It's dome-shaped and has a sodded roof, which Oberstein says was once used for military camouflage. We love going to the Bat Cave. It's great fun. We play cowboys and Indians or light a small fire in the doorway and boil tea, roast potatoes, and tell spooky stories. There are rusty double doors, wide as the devil's boots, at the opening of the cave, with old, rusty iron bars across them that take two boys to remove. Inside, Chris Cross has painted a huge black bat on the gray cement wall.

Whenever Blackie calls an emergency meeting, the special members, which Blackie calls The Brotherhood, must attend. The Brotherhood consists of Blackie and Oberstein, and sometimes me and Bug. If you're given a red checker, you don't dare miss the meeting. If you don't get one, you don't dare attend. If you're given a crown, two red checkers, it means the meeting can't proceed without you. If someone tells you about the meeting, you don't really have to attend. It means Blackie's planning a boil-up or a fishing trip and is looking for a few buddies to go along.

Murphy points to his bog juice. I stare at the milky sweet tea we have at every meal and shrug. He triple nose twitches, jabs a finger into his cup and points to mine. I gulp down the luke-warm tea. Sure enough, two red checkers sit at the bottom of the cup. A crown! The meeting can't go ahead without me. I learn after lunch that it's the biggest meeting of the Klub ever. There are even rumors of new members.

Ryan, who can steal anything if you give him a few hours

notice, receives a crown as well. That means there'll be research, and I'll be asked to act as scribe. I like doing that. Writing things down and putting them in order. Sorting out what people say and do. It's like putting together a puzzle. Blackie and Oberstein tell me I'm really good at it. Blackie says I should become a writer. Keeping good records means there'll be a small salary for me. Blackie always seems to have tons of money. He'll pay you a nickel for this, a dime for that, whenever he thinks the job's an important one. "He's always got a few shekels," Oberstein says. He gets his money from everywhere. He steals from the collection at Sunday public Mass. He gambles for things like comics and cigarettes and trades them for cash. New guys are always a source of quick money. Most new guys have a few bucks, and they're usually sitting ducks.

Everyone is really excited about the meeting. There's something big brewing, and we're all very tense. The last big meeting like this was months ago. It dealt with Ryan's revenge. Greg Smith, a bigger boy from St. Luke's, the senior dorm, picked on Ryan, and Ryan asked Blackie for a meeting to get revenge on Smith. It took hours to decide on Smith's punishment and how it would be secretly administered. Blackie calls these meetings his trials. And he's always the judge. Sometimes he picks a jury to help, but not very often. Rumors about the Saturday meeting are rampant. A really ripe one is that Blackie is planning a breakout. But we doubt that's true. Not after what happened to Skinny Ryan. Bug thinks it's about next Wednesday's wine raid. King Kelly is convinced that the meeting has something to do with Shorty Richardson's run.

"Oberstein's been yakking about nothing since," King Kelly says.

"I was hoping for a boil-up," Kavanagh says. "Shuttlecocks."

"*Cock*," Oberstein says, "shuttle*cock*."

After supper, during free time before study hall, Blackie, Oberstein, and Bug ask me to join them for a smoke out behind the pool.

"My last cigarette." Blackie taps a pack of Chesterfields against his wrist until one juts out. "And yours too."

"Why, Blackie?" I laugh.

"Got plans for you. For all of us."

"We're going in the regatta marathon this summer," Oberstein says, taking the cigarette.

I laugh harder. "The brothers will never allow that. You know the rules. We only compete with visiting teams. On Mount Kildare grounds."

Brother McMurtry brought in that rule two years ago after the senior boys' soccer team got into a free-for-all at Prince of Wales Collegiate. Some of the PWC students wound up in the hospital.

"Brothers ain't gonna know," Blackie says, rubbing his fingers. "Puttin' some big money on Shorty Richardson. Gotta chance to make some real money. Shorty can beat anyone if we train him right."

"*If* we train him right. That's a big if, *brother*," Bug says, opening his silver case.

"Besides the money, it'll be a great adventure. Lotsa fun," Oberstein says.

"And lotsa work," Blackie says.

"Want you to keep a record of everything," he says to me. "Meetings. Training schedule. You know. You're good at that sorta stuff. Writin' everythin' down."

He passes me his cigarette. "You in?"

"Sure," I say.

"Have a long haul," he says, nodding at the cigarette, "it's your last."

Time really drags, as it always does when you're looking

forward to something. Ryan gives me the red checkers on Wednesday. It seems like forever to Saturday.

Thursday isn't so bad. In the morning we go outside to clean up the grounds. In the afternoon Rags has us practicing parts from a play called *Julius Caesar*. He says we may perform it for the Christmas concert. During study hall Brother McMurtry asks me to supervise the little ones. I really like that because you get to sit around and read. This time I read a book Blackie stole from the library about Floyd Patterson, the famous American boxer who knocked out Gene Tunney to win the heavyweight championship of the world. I love Floyd Patterson. Blackie and I watched him being interviewed on TV one day, and I started to cry. What made me cry was what he was saying during the interview, or rather, what he *wasn't* saying. He couldn't remember things. Like the names of people. He seemed dazed. Like he'd just been knocked down. The interviewer asked him what year he beat Archie Moore, and he just shrugged and smiled that shy smile of his. He couldn't recall. He'd just lost the title to Ingemar Johansson and couldn't remember the number of rounds. He kept saying he was really tired. And he kept asking for his wife. "I gotta go," he said to the interviewer. "Where's my wife? Sometimes I can't even remember her name." I looked at Blackie and knew we were thinking the same thing. "All them head punches finally catchin' up with him," Blackie said. I thought of McCann and how he could never hit us as hard or as much as Floyd Patterson had been hit.

I love Floyd Patterson because he's small and shy and looks like he could be knocked down with one punch. And yet he's the king of boxing. And Blackie is powerfully drawn to him too. He says when he gets out of the Mount he's gonna change his name to Floyd something, in honor of Floyd Patterson. When McCann asked us once in religion class to write an essay on the man you admire most, everyone wrote about one of the saints.

Oberstein wrote on Moses dividing the Red Sea. Father Cross wrote about St. Francis Xavier. His essay was called "The Saint with the Strong Right Arm." He baptized so many people, one of the other Jesuits had to hold up his arm for days as he poured the water. I wrote about Floyd Patterson, how he grew up poor and spent a lot of time alone and got the spells a lot. The book about him said that he would go off to a dark hiding place for hours on end. I knew that was how he dealt with the spells. It was a pretty good essay. It was called "The Saint with the Mean Left." I showed it to Blackie and Oberstein. They liked it a lot. But I didn't pass it in. I knew McCann wouldn't understand.

Friday crawls along. I squirm through classes and can't concentrate one bit in study hall. But Saturday finally comes, and when we meet at the cave, it's the largest group ever. I collect the checkers, and Blackie swears in Shorty Richardson, and everyone knows the meeting's got something to do with running.

Every new member of the Klub has to be branded. Blackie is the only one who can brand a member. He plucks a homemade branding iron—two tiny metal K's representing the Kildare Klub—from the fire and brands the new member on the heel of his left foot. The letters are so tiny you can hardly see them. Shorty screams, but only for a second. We are all branded on the heel so that our logo is always out of sight. If anyone's is seen by one of the brothers you're supposed to say that you walked barefooted on a dare over bits of metal out by the incinerator.

Everyone goes through a special ritual on branding day. Once you're branded, everyone sits down in the cave and Blackie swears you in. He puts on his poncho, a gray blanket stolen from the infirmary, and we place a white sheet around the boy getting sworn in. Blackie never looks so serious as when he sits with his hands stretched out on the arms of his log throne. Like the statue of Abraham Lincoln, Oberstein says. He points to the drawing Chris Cross made behind the throne, a huge drinking glass, half-full, with our motto—*Poculum Semi Plenum*, the glass half-full—written in large golden letters beneath it. Blackie calls out, "How full the glass?" And we all chant, "The glass half-full."

Blackie then reads from a scroll, asking you to be faithful to the Klub's Magna Carta, which is what Blackie named it. It's a list of ten rules he reads out. Oberstein calls them the ten commandments. They're written on the wall of the cave, five on each side of the half-full glass. Then Blackie asks you to promise to protect all members of the Klub, even if it means placing your life in danger. He asks you to repeat Jesus' words from the Bible: "No greater love hath any man than to lay down his life for a friend."

Once the swearing-in is over, everyone takes a sip from a bottle of wine stolen from the sacristy. Everyone except the new member, who is given a half-glass of wine to drink. Shorty swallows the wine in one gulp as we chant his name over and over. "Shorty, Shorty, Shorty ..." When he's finished, he puts his shoe on his branded foot, and as we chant his name again he stamps on the glass until it is broken into tiny pieces. A Jewish custom Oberstein read about.

Shorty then signs the register, which is kept in the vault, and we all line up in front of Blackie's throne and shake hands with Shorty, Roman-style, the same way they do it in the movies. Blackie is always the last to shake hands, and he always finishes by placing his right hand on the new member's head and extending his left hand toward the painting of the half-full glass, saying, "All welcome the new brother. What half the glass?" We all chant in unison, "Welcome, Brother. The glass half-full." Then Blackie looks at our new brother and asks, "Shorty, what half the glass?" And Shorty answers, "*Poculum semi plenum.*" Then Blackie slaps him on the cheek, the way the Archbishop does at confirmation, only it's a much harder slap.

Then the business of the meeting is conducted. The bosun whistle sounds, and Blackie waves the speaking stick, a knotty Newfoundland birch, and passes it to Kavanagh, whose turn it is to be the treasurer. After the treasurer's report, I take the stick and read from the minutes book.

1. "New shirt for Ryan! Action: Father Cross, by today's meeting."

Blackie waves and the stick is passed along to him. "Ryan, you okay?" Ryan nods yes. Blackie returns the stick to me.

2. "Fines! Murphy—twenty-five cents. Brookes—thirty cents. All fines received in full."

3. "Slugs! Receipts from pop machines—eleven dollars and thirty cents, including sales of soda pop."

Slugs are small metal discs the size of quarters that we obtain from construction sites. They come from electrical panels and, when filed down by Father Cross, work perfectly in pop machines. A slug gets you a free pop and fifteen cents change.

Kavanagh waves for the stick and passes it to Oberstein.

"Brookes was caught last week putting a slug in the pop machine at the Golden Eagle Gas Station. He told the attendant it was a mistake and paid him a quarter. Recommendation: No slugs ever be used again at the Golden Eagle Station."

Blackie waves for the stick. "Motion?" Every hand goes up. "Golden Eagle off the list." He stares at Oberstein. "Any other incidents?" Oberstein shakes his head. Blackie returns the stick.

4. "Lost! Bradbury's cigarette case—found and returned by Kelly."

After the reading of the minutes, Blackie waves the speaking stick and asks if there is any news to report. He means about the wine stealing. Oberstein says that one of the little ones, Ian Smith, told Rags that he stole wine. "Happened after Mass," Oberstein says, "when little Smith was collecting the hymn books. He said he took it from the cruets 'cause he already drank silver and wanted to know what it would be like to drink gold."

"Rags say anything?" Blackie asks.

Oberstein says, "Nuthin'. Just laughed."

Blackie waves the speaking stick again and announces the reason for the gathering. He tells the Klub members he's got a big job for us, one the brothers must not find out about. He tells us he has a plan to make a lot of money.

"Shorty Richardson's enterin' the Royal Regatta Marathon," Blackie says, "and he's gonna win." He smiles, and I can see the glint of his gold tooth as he lectures us on what's at stake for the Klub.

"In order to win," Blackie says, "we gotta do this thing right. Professionally. Ain't no other way. Everyone gotta pitch in. There's a price on the tag and we all gotta chip in to pay that price. We'll be a real team together. Believe it. *Believe. Believe.*" When Blackie is really excited about something, he always says that. *Believe. Believe.* And he taps his gold tooth like crazy.

There's a long silence, and everyone senses something very important is happening. Then Blackie takes charge. "Oberstein, see what you can find in the library on runnin'. Check the public library next Saturday." He gives orders as though he's been thinking and planning the marathon all his life.

"Oberstein, I wanna professional program for Shorty, starting next week. Exercise, diet, sleep, clothin', everything that must be considered. The ABC of marathon runnin'. Go to the university, speak with someone who coaches runnin' teams. Find out everythin' you can. Take notes. Ask for advice. Borrow books. Whatever you can get your hands on. Find out who's in charge. Don't tell him you're a *norph*. Tell 'em you're trainin' for the regatta marathon and you wanna win. Ask whatcha gotta do. And Shorty'll need sneakers, the best. Not the black-and-white crap we get from Rags. Real runners. We'll steal them. Ryan, case the Sport Store on Water Street next Saturday. We need a good plan on how to steal clean. Nobody gets caught. Practice hard at it. We'll need two, maybe three pairs of the best runners. Oberstein, find out everythin' you can 'bout weather conditions, runnin' in hot weather, runnin' in cold, rain, sleet, snow, hail. When's the marathon?"

"Summer. August. Same time's the Royal Regatta," Oberstein says. "Always the first Wednesday in August. It's the 143rd running. Oldest sporting event in North America. Older than the Boston Marathon."

"Summer. Could be blistering hot."

"Might not," Oberstein complains. "It's Newfoundland. Could be freezing cold."

"We'll prepare for all types of weather," Blackie says. "Gonna be ready, no matter what." There is a buzz in the cave now. Everyone wants something to do. Blackie raises the knotty birch branch. "Shuddup!" he yells. "We'll need money. Lotsa money. To buy the things we can't steal. Murphy, you and Kavanagh make a list of all our needs. Cards, marbles, yo-yos, jacks, comic books, the popular ones. *Superman* and *Batman*. What's most popular now?"

"*Betty and Veronica*, a few of the Classics, *Gulliver's Travels*," Murphy says. His lips are dry cracks that are bleeding.

"'Specially *Betty and Veronica*," Blackie says. "Sunday collection durin' public Mass will be our main source. But don't get too greedy. Remember the rule. Never go over two dollars a collection. We'll make the rounds. See what boys have money. Kavanagh, start stealin' canteen cards. Sell them at a discount. We'll need to get up a few gamblin' games. A stack of canteen cards. That's everyone's job. Work with each other. And we need food. Everyone's job too. Start squirrelin' from the kitchen, the storeroom, the canteen. Steal from the Dominion Stores Saturdays. We'll need lots of liquid, especially juice. Murphy, get cola from the canteen. Gettin' the keys from ole JD will be a breeze. And we'll need flashlights. Father Cross, make four of those homemade flashlights. We may need more."

"Why do we need flashlights, Blackie?" Bug asks.

Blackie stops. He waves the stick. "This is top secret," he says. "Night runnin'. That's when we'll do our best trainin'. Nobody—*nobody's* gonna know about it. You break the secret, I break your bones. We'll train an hour or so each night, very late, almost early mornin' before the brothers rise. Oh, and no smokin' while in trainin'. Not a single cigarette from now on."

"I'd like to train at night," Bug says, eager to be a part of it all.

"Gonna need a stopwatch." Blackie ignores Bug. "A real good stopwatch."

I wave my hand. "There's one at the stadium. In the penalty box."

"Okay, Carmichael, that's your job." Blackie stands and raises the speaking stick, the signal that it's time to adjourn the meeting. "We'll meet here at our regular times until the marathon plan's in place. For emergencies, we'll use the checker system or meet in the chapel, using the prayer system." The prayer system means that we meet in the chapel and sit according to an arranged order. We bring our rosary beads and the lead boy prays a Hail Mary out loud. When the Hail Mary is finished, Blackie uses the volume of the chorus response to give orders or to whisper a message to one of us. The chorus is used as a cover in case a brother discovers us. It's a tricky system, but it always works. If a brother comes to the chapel and questions our presence there, the lead cantor says he got a letter saying his aunt is very sick and we're praying to the Blessed Virgin for her good health. It always works like a charm. "Next meetin', one week from today. Here at the cave," Blackie says. "Everyone's gonna be busy as a nailer. Everyone's gotta do his job. You don't do your job, don't bother comin' back. You're outta the Dare Klub. No longer a member. For good."

"Pistil, I've got to serve a funeral Mass for Monsignor Flynn next Saturday," Kavanagh says.

"Come late, then," Blackie says. "If your job's done. Do the bird whistle. Ryan's gonna let you in."

•   •   •   •   •

When Bug goes crying to Blackie about the beating we gave him, Blackie's really pissed off. He calls me and Oberstein and Murphy into the TV room, like he's one of the brothers. The fear in my gut is the same as when McCann shouts the death roll, as Oberstein calls it. After wash-up and night inspection, you stand by your bed in your PJs and pray your name isn't called to go to the TV room to be strapped for some mistake you made during the day.

"Bug, handicap," he keeps saying, over and over, pounding the wall with his fist. "You never hit a handicap, never." His eyes jump madly.

We think we're in deep trouble until Oberstein says that Bug was gonna squeal to Monsignor Flynn about the wine smuggling and stealing from the bakery. That settles Blackie down a bit. But he warns us never to hit Bug again. "Never ever hit a handicap," he says.

From that minute on, Blackie takes Bug under his wing. He even makes him a permanent part of the Brotherhood. Bug becomes Blackie's pet. The way some of the boys are pets of some of the brothers. Bug loves it because nobody dares stand up to Blackie. Blackie's the best scrapper in our dorm. He's hard as nails. Nobody messes with Blackie. If you get in trouble with Blackie, it's not the same as with the brothers. If a brother punishes you, you expect it, and it doesn't bother you so much. They do what they have to do. But if Blackie gets mad at you, it really hurts because Blackie really cares about you. He's the king of our Klub. Nobody crosses Blackie. And he looks after everyone, no matter what the problem. He's probably the best person in the world to talk to about the spells.

Bug figures out pretty soon that he can be as saucy as he wants to be and nothing will happen to him. Nobody dares to hit Bug ever again. And most of the time we don't even back-sauce him for fear of Blackie's wrath. Nobody ever back-sauces or double-crosses Blackie. If Blackie tells you to keep something secret, you don't think twice about it.

We all think Blackie's a great leader. Better than any of the brothers. He's amazing, really, when you consider he's just a kid. But he isn't perfect. For one thing, he always likes to get his own way. And he usually does. There's one thing I really hate about him. It's a game. Called palms.

Here's how it works. The challenger stretches out his hands, palms up. The opponent places his hands on top, palms down. The action begins immediately. The object of the game is for the aggressor, the challenger, to turn one of his hands over, or both, and slap his opponent as hard as he can. The sting is worse than getting the strap. If his opponent pulls away quickly enough and the challenger misses, they switch positions and it's the opponent's turn to strike. The aggressor holds his position as long as he slaps his opponent. Nippers or nips, making the slightest of contact, are counted. But if the contestants do not agree on whether contact was made, they flip a coin and the game continues. A variation on the game of palms is the game of knuckles. The exact same rules apply, with opponents squaring off, only this time it's fist to fist instead of palm on palm. It's a much more brutal game, and one that is rarely played because the loser winds up in a lot of pain.

The main strategy of the challenger in palms is to twitch his fingers so that his opponent pulls away unnecessarily, thus creating a guessing game on the part of the opponent, giving the challenger a decided advantage.

My introduction to palms came one day when one of the criers was running around the halls screaming, "Kelly wants a game of palms. The King of Pain wants a game of palms." It was a Sunday before study hall. Some of the runners were standing around the smoking room, sneaking a puff of Oberstein's fag. I was soon to learn that palms is a deadly game. It wasn't very often that someone took up the challenge for a game of palms, especially with King Kelly, so called for the crown of hair on the back of his head as well as his mastery of palms. He's the undisputed king of palms. The King of Pain, Oberstein calls him. Kelly would never have thrown down the gauntlet if he had known Blackie was nearby. Palms is not a game you wanna be on the losing end of.

About five minutes into the game, King Kelly gave Blackie several stunners, as we call a really fierce slap. Five uninterrupted stunners, and the game is over. It's like a technical knockout in boxing. And it's a terribly embarrassing way to lose, as the word goes out that you've been skunked at palms.

"That's five stunners in a row," Kelly's horsy mouth cheered, after he delivered a crossover strike that most of us felt. "I win. I'm the king of palms."

Blackie got that faraway look in his eyes. He shook the pain out of his fingers, flexed them several times and without warning, punched Kelly in the mouth, knocking out one of his front teeth.

"Yeah. You're still the king of palms," Blackie said, "but you ain't the king of punching in the mouth."

And Blackie walked away as we stood there in shock, staring at Kelly's bloodied mouth.

Palm Sunday, Oberstein forever referred to it. The Mount was abuzz the whole day about what happened. By the time we sat down to supper, the rumor mill had it that Blackie had beaten King Kelly at palms. We knew Blackie wouldn't speak for days. That's the way he gets when things aren't going right for him. He freezes up for a while, doesn't talk to anyone. That's what I mean about Blackie. He's a great leader, but he can be scary sometimes. He's a good guy to have on your side. But you don't ever want to cross him.

5

I'M OUT BACK, which is what everyone calls the yard, even the brothers. The yard is a huge open gravel area where boys play marbles or king of the castle or stretch or become the batter or a hundred other games. I am feeding the pigeons. There are always pigeons around the Mount. They hang out in the eaves of the three old stone buildings. You can always hear them cooing from their nests and flapping their wings a lot this time of year. Perhaps it's because of the cold. Soon we will get our winter jackets. I can't wait. It's cold in the yard with just your school shirt and sweater. All the wing flapping reminds me of one of the poems we memorized in Brother Mansfield's class. Only this one's about a robin.

> *When winter frost makes earth as steel,*
> *I search and search but find no meal*
> *And most unhappy*
> *Then I feel.*

Words like that really make you feel for the little fellas with winter coming on. I really like poetry. Most of the boys hate it, but Oberstein and I talk up a storm about it. Oberstein says I should be a teacher. He says I really have the knack for poems and stories. Clare told me my mother used to read me nursery rhymes and fairy tales all the time. And my dad used to quiz me about what my mother read. Clare said that he'd kid around with me all the time, asking crazy things like why Jack in "Jack and the Beanstalk" had an ugly duckling that laid golden eggs. She said I would laugh and laugh until the tears came to my eyes and say to my dad, "That's not Jack 'n' the Bean Talk."

Blackie wants to turn one of the pigeons into a homing pigeon. He got the idea from a movie, where most of our ideas come from. He thinks it will be a great way to send messages back and forth to girls. I think it's a cockamamie idea but you never know. Some of Blackie's crazy ideas have turned out pretty good.

I have a few hunks of fresh loaf, and I'm tearing off bits for a scrawny little pigeon with a nick in its beak. It's amazing how he eats. He struts about with his head bobbing back and forth really fast and snaps his broken beak at the bit of bread, flicking it a few inches before pecking at it. The only reason I figure he does that is to prove the bit of bread is dead and not an animal that can peck back. His head is black with specks of gray, and he has a thick neck that flashes green and violet when he turns quickly. He coos a lot and fans out his tail and sweeps with it. He seems very affectionate.

After I've given him a second bit of bread, two fat pigeons appear out of nowhere, then three more. One of the new ones is almost completely white. He's beautiful but he's a bully. Pretty soon there are a dozen or so fighting fiercely over the few morsels of bread, attacking the poor scrawny one. Since I'm trying to train the scrawny one, I refuse to throw out any more bread. I shoo away the other birds and manage to give the scrawny one, who I decide to call Nick, a few more morsels. It's incredible how he responds. Training him isn't gonna be a problem, I can see that.

A small wind comes up and blows the dead leaves and scattered candy wrappers toward the big maples, almost as high as their lowest branches. Some of the trees are so bare and bent back now they look like something from a vampire movie. On the roof of the cement porch near the handball court is a crow with a mouse in its beak. Blackie and Oberstein and Ryan arrive on the scene, blowing on their hands. I ask them if they've been strapped or if it's just the cold.

"Fun-nee," Oberstein says.

Quickly, they make a sort of fence out of old cardboard boxes to protect Nick so he can eat in peace.

"Gonna be as chubby as Oberstein by next week," Blackie laughs.

"How are you gonna train him to be a homing pigeon, Blackie?" I ask.

Blackie removes his pink plastic glasses, puts an arm in his mouth like Brother McMurtry does, squints and flashes his gold tooth. The ugly yellow bruise is almost gone. "Dunno," he says. "Gonna figure that out soon. By the time you fatten him up, we gonna have a message for the Doyle sisters."

I throw Nick a big hunk. "Geez, Blackie, wouldn't that be something? Sending messages back and forth to the Doyle sisters." They're a bunch of girls we knock around with at Bannerman Park during weekends. I think immediately of Ruthie Peckford, the first girl I ever kissed, and I can see my note tied to Nick's foot.

"Just like in the movies," Oberstein says. "Homing pigeons saved a lot of lives during the war."

"Yeah, like the movies," Blackie repeats.

"Eat up, Nicky," I say. "Eat up little fella. We gotta get you as chubby as Oberstein as soon as we can."

Blackie laughs. Bug and Murphy and Shorty Richardson happen by and ask why we're feeding only the ugly pigeon.

"Name's *Nicky*," Blackie says.

"Because of the nick in his beak," I say.

"We're gonna train him to be a homin' pigeon. Send messages."

"You mean like in the movies?" Murphy asks.

"Never work," Bug says. "Movies are one thing, birds are another. Didja tag him yet?"

"Nope," I say. "Why do we need to tag him, Bug?"

"They do it in the movies," Bug says. "There must be a good reason. Nicky's a stupid name. I would of called him Chicken. He's skinny as a rake."

Blackie and Oberstein howl.

"How we gonna get him to be a homin' pigeon, Ladybug?" Blackie asks, nudging Oberstein, his eyes twitching.

"You gotta train the shit outta him. Get him to eat outta your hand and sit on your shoulder."

"Shit on your shoulder?" Blackie teases.

"*Sit*. Not shit. *Sit*. Like the parrots in the pirate movies. And that ain't gonna be easy, brother. That's gonna take a while. By then we'll read up on how they deliver messages. And we'll have a few to tie to his feet."

"By then you might have a girlfriend in town to send a message to, Bug," Oberstein says.

"Won't be needing no pigeon to bring my messages," Bug snaps. "What I gotta say won't fit around a bird's foot. Anyway, I'll be delivering what I gotta say in person."

"Yeah, you got those long steamy love letters, right, Bug?" Oberstein says.

"You got that right, brother." With one hand, Bug clicks open his little silver cigarette case, lights one and takes a long drag.

"Maybe we'll fit what you say on a roll of toilet paper. That way, she cries, she won't be stuck for tissues, Bug."

We all howl.

"Yeah," Murphy says, "or if she finds it so ridiculous she shits herself, she'll have lotsa toilet paper."

Even Bug laughs this time.

Father Cross gallops up in his Lone Ranger costume. "Hi Ho, Silver!" he sings, tugging at invisible reins and whinnying like a horse. Cross is really artistic. He paints and draws everything. He can do a realistic sketch of everyone at the Mount, including the brothers. He once drew Rags, and Rags said it was as good as any professional could do. And he makes costumes. The Lone Ranger, Batman and Robin, Superman, Captain Marvel. You name it, he can make it. Which is amazing, considering what he has to work with. He scavenges the tools of his sewing trade from Brother Young's tailor shop, the laundry room and the store room, and from his aunt, who lives on Patrick Street in the west end of St. John's.

He has a ton of stuff: sewing needles of all shapes and sizes, spools of colored thread, bits of wool, boxes of dye, a pen knife, tweezers, two pairs of scissors, a thimble, elastic bands, a pin cushion, razor blades, a bottle of buttons, packets of glue, patches, a roll of colored ribbon—all stored in a small wooden box he keeps in his dorm locker. Sometimes I watch him puttering away at an old curtain or a bed sheet, and it's amazing what materializes—a tie-dyed T-shirt or a beautiful pair of pants or a button shirt with a collar. Nobody knows how he does it, but he creates magic with almost no materials. Brother Young, who patches our worn-out clothes and was trained in Toronto, can't hold a candle to Cross. Neither can Brother Taylor, who cuts our hair. Cross uses an old pair of stolen scissors to touch up everyone's haircut. He's a much better barber than Brother Taylor. When we praise him for his creations, he just shrugs and says, "It's nothing, just a bit of fun." He's a really humble guy.

When he's in his Lone Ranger costume, he races around the

Mount, wild as a goat, yelling, "Hi Ho, Silver . . . Away!" He's older than most of us and taller than Murphy, over six feet, and we're afraid of him, which is strange because he's head altar boy and as timid as a mouse and very kind. He'd give you anything, the shirt off his back. You just have to ask, and he'll give it to you. And we have loads of fun with him. He doesn't mind being teased, like most of the boys. He's more like Rags, he gets a kick outta things. "Don't be so cross, Father Cross," Oberstein loves saying. Or he'll say, "Have you picked up your cross today, Father?" Oberstein has a lot of fun with him. Cross is Brother Walsh's pet and the half-pet, as we call it, of every other brother except McCann, who has no pets. But even McCann likes Cross because he wants to become a priest. Oberstein calls Cross the chosen one.

Chris Cross's face is covered with acne, and it is so raw-looking we nicknamed him Soup after the rich red tomato soup we receive at every noon meal during the winter months. When he smiles, he blushes, and his face becomes a red smile. But the nickname never stuck. Blackie still calls him Soup once in a while, but nobody else does. He isn't a really popular boy, but he isn't disliked. He's a crazy mix, really.

He loves girls, which is strange for someone who wants to become a priest. I'll never forget the Sunday Murphy and Ryan and I arrived at the Bat Cave later than usual. It was freezing cold, and not many Klub members came to the cave when it was that cold. The few who did usually opened the heavy doors and made a fire in the doorway and roasted a few stolen potatoes. This day, as we approached the cave, we heard what sounded like a cry for help. It was a weak singsong cry that came from inside the cave. We were about to race to the sound when Murphy grabbed both of us and, putting a finger to his lips, cautioned us to approach quietly. As we did so, we heard the cries get louder, but they no longer seemed like cries for help. They seemed more like giggles. We opened the door a crack and peeked inside. As our eyes became accustomed to the darkness, we noticed two naked bodies rolling around on the earth. They appeared to be wrestling. One was Cross and the other was a young girl. She was skinny, with a flat chest and long brown hair that fell below her shoulders

"Jesus! *Father Cross!*" Murphy whispered.

"Well, I'll be. Father Cross is getting his skin," Ryan said.

"Father Cross," Murphy laughed. "Father fucken Cross."

I tell him why we're feeding Nicky, and he tips his cowboy hat, tears off a few pieces of bread and flips them on the ground. "I love birds," he says. "If I get enough seagull feathers, I'm gonna make a big headdress like Geronimo wears."

Blackie decides to have a game of become the batter. "C'mon, season's almost over," he says. "Batter up." It's another game he made up. Blackie usually wins because he's a great catcher. He catches like Willie Mays. Blackie tells me to keep score while I'm fattening up Nicky. Become the batter is a great game. The batter hits grounders and fly balls while the rest try to be first to get a hundred points and become the batter. You get ten points for snagging a grounder, twenty for a one-hopper, and twenty-five for a fly ball. If you miss, you wind up that many points in the minus column. It's really hard to get points, so you gotta be careful what you try for. There are no rules. Anything is allowed. Tripping a guy so he misses the ball. Kicking stones at grounders. Even tackling a guy is allowed. But it's good fun.

Blackie wins the second game by diving for a line drive that caroms off the building. As we cheer his catch, he gets up with that faraway look in his eyes, whispers something to Oberstein and wanders off for a while. When he returns, he whistles for us to huddle around him. He reminds us it's Wednesday, hump day. He slaps his rump like he's on a horse and races to the cement porch by the handball court. We all mount up and ride after him. Inside, we huddle again, and he tells us this will be our last wine raid for a while.

"Things are gettin' a bit spooky," he says. "Better lay low after this one. Skinny's joinin' us tonight. Ryan, you still in?"

Ryan is nervous. "Yeah, yeah," he shakes his head.

"Nobody forcin' you," Blackie says.

"I'm in, I'm in," Ryan says.

Blackie reviews the drill for the midnight raid. When he's sure we all know what to do, he slaps his rump and races back into the yard. "I'm the king of the castle and you're the dirty rascals," he hollers. "Three out of five wins."

"Last norph to the hill's the rotten egg," Murphy shouts, squinting in the sun.

Blackie charges toward the high bank on the far side of the handball court. We love playing king of castle. It's such fun getting knocked down the bank. Sometimes you laugh till your sides are sore.

After the last game, we have an hour before supper, so Blackie asks Rags if it's okay to have a race around the block. By that he means over Elizabeth Avenue, down Portugal Cove Road and up Kenna's Hill. Rags says okay, and we grab our sneakers. Bug says he wants to be the timer and takes my Mickey. Oberstein gets his scribbler to record the times. Since Shorty Richardson's magical run, Blackie takes every opportunity to have a race. Even during recess, we go outside and have hundred-yard dashes. And Blackie says soon we'll start sprinting races to the Bat Cave.

Ryan is first out of the blocks. He always starts and finishes with a kamikaze kick that's good for ten to twenty yards. The funniest thing about running is watching everyone. You get to see everyone in a different way. Murphy almost kicks himself in the bum his feet go so high behind him when he runs. Cross is a huffy runner. Kavanagh runs like one leg wants to go east and the other wants to go west. But Shorty Richardson and Ryan don't even look like they're running. They look so graceful they seem to be gliding. No up-and-down head motion. No movement of their shoulders. They look like they have motors in their sneakers. They don't seem like they're doing any work. And unlike the rest of us, they don't seem to work up a sweat. At times, they don't even look like they're breathing.

In no time we race through the leafy streets to Kenna's Hill, which is really steep. Blackie loves taking that route because Ryan always makes great time on the hill. And Blackie's always rooting for Ryan so he'll push Shorty Richardson harder. Ryan's only hope for beating Richardson is to open a wide lead on Kenna's Hill. Nobody can catch Ryan on hills. And nobody catches Shorty on the flats. As we approach the uphill slope, where Ryan overtook Shorty once when Shorty's knee was sore, we all know that if Ryan can get to the top well ahead of Shorty, this might be the day he'll beat him to the soccer field. Sometimes when you're running, if you're having a great day and the other runners aren't doing so good, they feel worse when you pass them, especially on a hill. Lotsa races are won and lost on a steep hill coming into the home stretch.

Richardson is well ahead of the pack when we pass Memorial Stadium. At the bottom of Kenna's Hill, Ryan's kamikaze kick rockets him past Shorty Richardson. In no time, he opens up a big lead. With about thirty yards between them he approaches Mount Carmel Cemetery. We are all chugging uphill, well behind them, slick-faced with sweat, our eyes glued to Ryan, who does the most amazing thing. He stops by the cemetery gate, pulls out his lizard and takes a leak. We are all flabbergasted. Blackie laughs so hard he stops running for a minute. Richardson closes the gap on the hill and they race neck and neck halfway up Torbay Road. A few hundred yards from the soccer field, with Oberstein, Bug, and a huddle of Klub members hollering their excitement, Shorty Richardson blows by Ryan.

When we finish up, Blackie tells Ryan he would've won if he hadn't pissed by the graveyard.

"I know," Ryan gasps. "But I had to spring a leak. Hadda leaky faucet."

Blackie laughs hard. "I know," he repeats. "Ain't nuthin' you can do when Mother Nature calls."

Oberstein passes me a tiny square of paper with my time on it. "Make a note of it. Blackie wants you to drop a few seconds off next time you do that route. Forget about cheating. I'm recording every run in my scribbler." Then he leans against the side of the cement handball court and gazes at the building. A huge shadow cast by the Mount falls over the yard and stretches slowly toward the row of shuddering pine trees lining JD's garden. The last of the runners enters the building. Oberstein stands perfectly still, staring at the Mount a long time, his round glasses catching the light. He looks as if he's trying to remember something. He has that faraway look Blackie gets sometimes.

"What is it, Oberstein?" I ask.

"Nothing," he says. "It just struck me. How much I love this place sometimes. Like now. It will always be a part of me."

For a few minutes we both stand there, staring at the huge shadow. Neither of us speaking. Then Oberstein walks away as though I'm not there. A soft breeze moves through JD's pine trees, carrying the last of autumn's leaves from the yard. When we reach the big aluminum door, Oberstein says, "It's funny, isn't it? How it happens."

"What?" I ask.

"The way this place grows on you."

I really don't know what he means. I don't feel that way. So I don't say anything.

. . . . .

There's no color in Ryan's face. He looks white as a ghost. He's sweating and biting his nails. It's his first time on a wine raid. The last thing he wants is another strapping or a trip to the Rat Locker. Skinny Ryan is the untidiest boy at the Mount, shirt always hanging out, holes in his pants, socks, shirt, even his PJs. His sneakers always look like they've been through the war. His buttons are always half undone. Rags calls him his little orphan. He's so skinny and puny. But the wide gap between his front teeth somehow makes him look strong. He's a very popular boy. Everyone likes him because he never sucks up. And he's really brave. He'll try anything, even run away. Nobody has ever tried that before. But tonight he's a nervous Nellie. He looks panicky, as if the floor is about to give way beneath his feet.

"You'll get used to it," I tell him, patting his shoulder.

He jerks away. "Don't touch me," he says. There isn't much worse you can do to Ryan than touch him.

His baby face turns whiter. He always has headaches because he worries too much and studies too hard. There are beads of sweat on his jet-black eyebrows. His eyes dart left and right, as if one of the brothers is about to catch us red-handed. Blackie spots the stool by the radiator. He motions with a flick of his hand. I understand at once, grab the stool and put it in front of Monsignor Flynn's locker. Blackie stands on the stool, climbs the vestment table and picks the sacristy wine lock. Ryan passes me the empty Crown Cola bottle. Spots darken his pajamas. He blushes and puts his hand in front of his crotch. He's so frightened he has wet his PJs.

"Don't worry about it. You can dry them on the radiator," I whisper. "They'll be dry as a bone in no time." Ryan turns red with embarrassment.

I hold the Crown Cola bottle while Blackie pops the cork

on a used wine bottle. Every second is precious. Blackie is working fast, thinking fast, his eyes are moving fast. As we pour, Ryan opens the next wine bottle. Now the sweat breaks out on Blackie as he pours slowly, steadily into the Crown Cola bottle. "Perfect!" he whispers. "Thank you, Jesus." He replaces the wine with water. An inch or two from each of the bottles is all we take. Any more and we risk discovery. The punishment for such a crime is unthinkable. It's a slow process and usually takes about ten minutes of nerve-wracking time. I keep an eye on my Mickey.

"I wish I was back in my bed," Ryan whispers.

"It won't be much longer," I say.

Ryan is a nervous wreck. I've never seen him so bad. He must be overtired. His constant flinching and nail-biting is getting under Blackie's skin.

"What if we get caught? Jesus!" Ryan says. "They'll kill us."

"Shuddup," Blackie says, and corks the last wine bottle.

We finish up and return the wine bottles to their exact spots, and Blackie gives us the nod to head out. I check my Mickey. It's three o'clock in the morning.

Back in the dorm, I fling myself onto the bed and try to sleep. Not a moment too soon. A hand grabs my pajama sleeve. I open my eyes. It's Spook, the night watchman, rousing everyone to take a leak. He leans his long gray face toward me and flicks on his flashlight. I cover my eyes and get out of bed. I trudge to the bathroom and join the lineup behind a urinal. Sleepy heads wander in and out of the bathroom under Spook's watchful eye. I return to bed, frightened that he may know something about the raid. It's not until gray light filters through the windows that I finally fall asleep.

I wake just before the alarm. It's a cloudy morning. On the way to chapel it begins to rain. Ryan sits between me and Blackie at Mass. During the Confiteor he whispers that Spook woke him during the night and asked why he was away from his bed.

"What did you say?" I ask.

"Told him I was using the toilet and fell asleep."

"Did he buy it?"

"Think so. He said I was lucky I was only missing for about five minutes."

"No matter what happens, stick to your guns," I tell him. He nods and turns white. "Remember what happened to the guy on *Perry Mason* who never stuck to his guns?"

"Yeah, I remember," Ryan says.

At breakfast, Blackie says there's a rumor going around that the brothers know someone is stealing wine from the sacristy. Someone has reported that Brother McCann heard two of the boys talking about getting drunk. We don't know if it's true. There's a new rumor every minute at the Mount. Blackie warns everyone to lie low. Code Red. An expression he got from a spy comic. It means we're not to talk to anyone, not even members of the Kildare Klub, about the wine raids, the bakery, or the marathon.

Blackie's worried. One look at his face and you can see what he's thinking. Ryan has become a nervous Nellie again. I hate it when he's such a worrywart. Kavanagh has stopped eating. Even Oberstein, usually pretty cool under fire, is worried. Everyone is worried. There'll be hell to pay if the brothers find out we've been stealing wine.

During cleanup, as we carry the full trays of cups to the washing machine, Oberstein tells Blackie he's having trouble sleeping. He mentions the Book of Psalms and says, "The sorrow of death compassed me, and the pains of hell got hold of me. I found trouble and sorrow."

"We're caught with all that wine," Blackie says, "you got no idea the trouble and sorrow."

•   •   •   •   •

Sunday is always the longest day. Mass followed by a breakfast of cream of wheat and one very hardboiled egg. Followed by study hall. Followed by lunch—raw Diefenbaker sandwiches and bog juice. Followed by free time. Followed by supper, which is always the same every Sunday: a scoop of mustard potatoes, a slice of fried Diefenbaker meat, a canned tomato and a date crumble. Followed by study hall, then TV time before bed. It's the loneliest day of the week. If you're gonna get a bout of the spells, Sunday's usually the time they'll start. If it wasn't for the running, a lot of us would have a lot more spells.

Before we head out Brookes crouches and rubs his bruised shin, which he hurt playing frozen tag. We run on and on in silence, staring at the scattered fir trees along Logy Bay Road, which give us a bit of shade off and on until the sun gleams at us for a long stretch. Our feet grow hot as we pound the pavement, sweat running through our hair under our baseball caps. Far ahead, Murphy doesn't look as big and gangly. Nearby, Brookes, running with pain, is first to pick up the pace. Before the run he told me he would rather die than lag behind, even though his shin was sore as a boil. I watch him struggle with every stride, the strain fixed on his face like it has been painted there. He seems to sweat more than any of us. And yet his breathing is lighter than Cross's or mine. Compared to him, Cross and I pant like dogs. I watch his chest heave as he makes an effort to speak. He kicks hard and moves slightly ahead of me, turns and backpedals as he speaks, his cap throwing a dark shadow over his light blue eyes, his mouth hanging slightly open, like Rowsell's in class when McCann asks him a question.

"Water at Sugar Loaf will be sweet today."

I smile and work my dry throat. "Sure will," I say, hoping he stays a pace ahead so I don't have to waste energy speaking. I'm getting used to having a parched throat when I run. For that reason alone, I know Brookes is right. The water will be sweet. The day of the marathon, Blackie says, there will be bottles of water stashed along the route for Shorty Richardson and Ryan.

There's the sound of rustling breath behind me. I think of swirling autumn leaves as Father Cross, who always lags behind, pulls up. His face looks more pimply today. He jogs along without speaking. Like me, he hates to talk while running. His face is flushed and he's panting.

"Check out the crow," Brookes says, pointing to a tree top.

As if hearing us, the crow caws.

"I hate crows," Brookes says. "They're ugly."

"I love them," Cross says. "Look how black their feathers are. And they're smart."

"Let's see," Brookes says, picking up a stone and firing it. The crow doesn't move.

"Dumb bird."

"He knew you'd miss," I say.

We run without speaking until the turnoff to Sugar Loaf. Pulling ahead, Brookes says, "See you at the water hole." But he advances only a few strides. This run is a hard one. We are all lazy. It's one of those days when you run like you're half asleep. Today, our pack will not catch the others, coming or going. We are tired and sluggish, like we're having a bad sleep.

At Sugar Loaf Pond, the others cluster around, waiting for us to drink. A creamy mist hovers high above the water. Brookes and Cross take off their baseball caps, and the steam rises from their wet hair. Cross dunks his head in the water twice, while Brookes slurps greedily. I lay down, exhausted, with a severe pain in my head. I close my eyes and put my face in the water, hoping the pain will go away.

"Pick it up," Blackie hollers, as the sun comes out from behind a cloud bank. "We're losin' time. And the Logy Bay fog's rollin' in."

Halfway home, as it starts to drizzle, my throat is parched again. A hot flash races through my body, and I can hear my heart beating heavily. I consider asking Cross to jump my temperature when we get back so I can spend a day in the infirmary. But I know that thought too, like so many others, will pass. As we near Logy Bay Store, the sun pales, barely burning through the gray sky. A crow shakes its black feathers. I think how right Cross is. Crows are beautiful. And I think of Nicky and the other pigeons and wish they were as strong as crows. Then I think of that poor little mouse in the crow's beak, and I'm glad Nicky's just the way he is.

Surprisingly, we close the gap on Blackie's pack. I peek over my shoulder. Murphy has stopped to wipe his foggy glasses. The drizzle turns to cold rain and falls through the black boughs onto the swirling leaves as we pass Bally Haley Golf Course, where any day now we'll come during free time to slide for hours on the snowy hills. As we pass Fort Pepperrell and head up through the bog, we watch Shorty Richardson race toward a tiny piece of the sun peeking over the edge of the soccer field.

6

WHENEVER BROTHER WALSH has something very impor-
tant to say, he stands in front of the class and stares at the floor
for several minutes, tapping his foot. He's a short, stocky man,
with a face that looks like it's been chipped out of stone. He has
two nicknames—Jawbreaker because of his huge square jaw
and Killer because of the way he straps.

"Some of the boys, not all, mind you, some . . . quite a few,
too many boys . . . are using too many squares."

Silence. I look over at Ryan, who shrugs and looks at
Kavanagh, who looks oddly at Murphy, who also shrugs and
stretches his big, sneakered feet.

"Too many. Too many squares. And it must stop. It is an
unnecessary, an ungodly expense. Too many, too many squares.
Four per sitting is plenty. Six at most."

It is Jawbreaker's manner to lecture a group of boys in a sort
of code. He lectures away, warning and threatening dire consequences for those boys who don't pull up their socks. Those
are two of his favorite expressions: dire consequences and pull
up your socks.

"Too many squares, far too many. We have to pull up our
socks. It has to stop." He walks through the speckles of light
lying across the floor. "There is just too, too much waste. You

are living, boys, in an orphanage. This is not Buckingham Palace, boys. Money does not grow on trees. There is no money tree at Mount Kildare. If we had a money tree, boys, there would be no need of the bakery, no need of the raffle. Each and every boy will have to pull up his socks. If every boy does his little bit, the problem will be licked. Dire consequences will be avoided."

Connelly raises his hand. "What squares, Bruh? What do you mean by squares?"

Jawbreaker frowns. "Why the squares of toilet paper, Mr. Connolly. What other squares are there? Some of you boys are using twenty, fifty, over a hundred squares of toilet paper per sitting. It's outrageous. I once found a whole roll of unused paper in a toilet bowl. An entire roll! Shameful. *Four squares*, boys, four squares is sufficient. Five at most per sitting is plenty. The brothers use only four squares per sitting, and we are adults. Some boys are going through almost half a roll of toilet paper per sitting. Do you think we are rich? Do you think toilet paper grows on trees? Do you . . ."

Rowsell interrupts. "Brother Walsh, doesn't paper come from trees?"

Jawbreaker thinks he's being a wiseass, reaches across the aisle to Rowsell's desk and whacks him on the side of the head with the back of his hand.

"Not ordinary paper, boy, *toilet* paper. Don't be a smarty-pants, Mr. Rowsell."

We find this hilarious because Rowsell couldn't be smart if you paid him.

"And don't forget that there is an angel standing by each toilet keeping a record of the number of squares you use. Each time you use the toilet, boys, each time you tear off a square, it's recorded by your guardian angel. If you use more than six squares, it is an item for the confessional, to be revealed on the day of judgment. Unless, of course, you are absolved from the sin by the seal of the confessional."

Silence. Steam rushes from the classroom radiator like a snake hissing at the seriousness of it all. The room is getting unbearably hot. The classrooms are always too hot, and the dorms are always too cold.

"How many squares do you use, Mr. Murphy?"

"Four, Bruh, never more than four." Murphy licks his cracked lips and pushes back his shock of hair.

"Kelly?"

"Usually three, Bruh, sometimes four."

"O'Neill?"

"Three or four, Burr."

"Littlejohn?"

"Three or four, Bruh."

"Mr. Bradbury?"

"Four. Sometimes five."

"That's at least one too many, Mr. Bradbury, especially for someone your size. Someone your size should get by with one or two. Cut back. Pull up your socks."

"How many squares, Brookes?"

"Three, Brother."

"Good. Very good. It appears that, with one exception, you are not the boys who have to pull up your socks." Silence. He stares at the floor for a full minute. "Now, there are times, those rare occasions, when a boy may use more than four squares. If a boy is ill, for example. If a boy has the stomach flu or diarrhea, he may use twice the number of squares permitted per sitting. He may use eight squares, maybe even ten. Depending."

"Is that the only time, Bruh?" Bug asks, sucking up.

"Yes, that is the one and only exception. *Illness*. Then, and only then, may a boy double up. Only during illness may a boy use twice the number of allotted squares."

"Are there any other times you can double up, Brother?" Bug asks. "And when you do, is it a matter for the confessional?"

"No. It is not. And there are no other exceptions." Brother Walsh moves to the board and writes in very large capital letters: FOUR SQUARES. He turns and looks at the floor briefly and says, "But . . . But, boys, before you use even one square, before tearing off one simple square from the roll, you should simply sit. That is correct, boys. After you finish your business, you should sit for at least five or ten minutes. You will find, boys, that five or more minutes of sitting will help immensely."

Brookes raises his hand. "Brother, if I'm finished using the bathroom, why should I sit there for five or ten minutes?"

Silence. The radiator hisses softly again, a tiny steam leak.

Jawbreaker walks slowly to Brookes's desk and hovers over him. Brookes looks up sheepishly.

"To dry, Mr. Brookes. To dry. *Dry*." He turns to the class. "How many times have you been told, if you sit and dry for five minutes or more, boys, you will find, all of you will find, that you will not need to use even four squares. You would get by quite nicely with two, maybe even one. Remember boys, this is not Buckingham Palace. And toilet paper, *toilet paper*, Mr. Rowsell, does not grow on trees."

The buzzer jolts us. In the next class, McCann hunches his shoulders, tilts his head and stares at the ceiling. He's breathing so heavily we can hear the air whistling in and out of his nostrils. Monologues and Dialogues today deals with mortal and venial sin. This class, McCann has only one prop, a baseball. He rolls it back and forth between his palms. He has just read from the Baltimore Catechism that a mortal sin is deadly, entailing spiritual death, whereas a venial sin is not mortal. It is pardonable, not deadly like a mortal sin. He uses the game of baseball to explain. I close my eyes and fast-forward to the moment he drills the ball at some boy's head. I open my eyes and pray it does not happen. I stare at the ball and will it not to happen.

"Take this baseball," he says. "Just an ordinary object, a sphere, a simple geometric shape. Or is it? You have all watched professional baseball, boys. You all know who Whitey Ford is. Whitey Ford throws strikes and balls every time he stands on the mound at Yankee Stadium. Think of a strike, boys, as a mortal sin and a ball as a venial sin. If Whitey Ford decides to deliberately hit a player ... If in full conscience he decides to bean a batter because, say, that player hit a home run the last time up, or simply because he doesn't like him, and Whitey Ford beans that player and knocks him down. Out cold. *Kaput.* Maybe even out of baseball forever. Then Whitey Ford, class, has committed a terrible sin, a deadly sin, a *mortal* sin."

"What about if he just nicks him, Brother, and the batter only gets a slight headache?" Bug Bradbury shows his teeth he's so proud of his question.

"Ahh, good question. Mr. Bradburys is asking about *intent*. But the *intent* is to harm. Whitey Ford tried to seriously injure the batter. There is intent, Mr. Bradburys. Therefore it is a mortal sin. Clearly a mortal sin. The intent, you see, is everything, boys. The intent supersedes the act. Ergo, Whitey Ford would have committed a grave sin, a mortal sin."

"What would be an example of a venial sin, Brother McCann?" Bug asks, sucking up. "How could Whitey Ford commit a venial sin? And could you give us another baseball example, Brother?"

McCann smiles, tilts his head and stares at the ceiling. He taps his lips with his index finger. Tiny greenish white saliva spots dribble from the corners of his mouth.

"Well ... if ... say ... yes! If, say, Whitey Ford wanted to bean a batter, and just before he released the ball he changed his mind . . . But it is too late. He is finished his windup. The ball is released.

But Whitey Ford had clearly changed his mind. Then the intent is not to harm, even though he may have done so, may have harmed. Even killed the batter. The intent, which is all, at the last split second, is *not* to harm. Ergo, no mortal sin. One might even argue, boys, that Whitey Ford had committed no sin at all."

"No sin at all?" Oberstein says.

"Perhaps, Mr. Oberstein."

"Like a deathbed conversion, Brother," Bug shouts.

"Yes, Mr. Bradburys. Precisely!" The whites of McCann's eyes are visible as he rolls his head back and stares at the ceiling.

"But what if Whitey Ford just wanted to nick the batter, to just hurt him a little bit. But he hit him in the temple and he died. Would that be a mortal or a venial sin?" Kavanagh asks.

"What is the *intent*, Kavanaghs?" McCann growls. "Is the intent to kill? Or is the intent to wound? Killing is murder. Murder is a deadly sin. Ipso facto, it is a mortal sin. And if Whitey Ford died that day, he would go straight to hell."

"Unless he confessed on the way to the hospital or had a deathbed conversion," Bug cries out.

"What if you felt you *had* to kill someone, but you didn't want to," Ryan says. "That wouldn't be a sin, would it?"

"What kind of question is that? Killing is murder, Mr. Ryans. Plain and simple."

Silence. Another hiss from the radiator. Oberstein looks at Blackie, who stares at Ryan.

"Now where was I? Mr. Bradburys, of course. Deathbed conversion," McCann says. "Confession always obliterates the stain of mortal sin. Are there any more dialogues, class?"

Littlejohn says that last class we were told that it's a sin to eat anything before Mass. He asks if it's a venial or mortal sin.

McCann asks Oberstein, who says it's a venial sin.

"Correct!" McCann says.

"So if I don't eat before Mass," Bug says, "and I take communion and after Mass I get hit by a truck, I'll be so holy I'll go straight to heaven. Right?"

"Straight to heaven! That's correct. That is, if you have no mortal sin staining your soul, you are in a state of sanctifying grace."

Several hands go up, including Oberstein's. But McCann ignores Oberstein. He rarely calls on him because Oberstein's questions are too difficult. Oberstein could give a rabbi a hard time about the Talmud. If he does call upon Oberstein, McCann usually goes on and on, making no sense. He concludes by asking Oberstein what he thinks the answer is to his own question. McCann always agrees with Oberstein's answer, adding a few meaningless comments to make it sound like his own solution.

Oberstein, for example, might ask what if somewhere between the windup and the release Whitey Ford had doubts about whether to nick or injure the batter, and as he released the ball he definitely wanted to injure but not seriously maim the batter, and his footing slipped on the mound as he was thinking about this, and the ball got away from him and seriously injured the ump, who, many times, Whitey Ford had wished to injure because of his calls. Wouldn't that still be a mortal sin, ipso facto, given the history of his thought, even though the ump and not the batter got hurt?

McCann would get on with a lot of gobbledygook for a few minutes, and then ask Oberstein what *he* thought the right answer was. If Oberstein said it was a mortal sin, McCann would agree with him. If Oberstein said it was a venial sin, McCann would agree with that. But McCann usually avoids asking Oberstein to participate.

Ryan asks if these are the only two types of sins. McCann says no, there is one other kind of sin, the worst sin of all, the most vile of sins, especially for Romans.

"The *sacrilege!*" McCann shudders and stares off into space. "The unforgivable, the unpardonable sin! It is a sin against the Holy Spirit and cannot be blotted out. It is the sin of despair, the total rejection of the Almighty, the total rejection of God's holy light. The deliberate demonic alignment with darkness, the evil one, Satan. Only a Roman can commit such a sin. It is reserved for Romans, the true believers. Protestants and unbelievers cannot commit a sacrilege because they do not know the difference. Romans are enlightened, boys. Romans know the difference." He stares at the picture of Our Lady of Perpetual Help on the side wall. "Defamation of that picture of Our Lady by a Roman would constitute a sacrilege."

"Would Whitey Ford be able to commit a sacrilege?" Bug asks.

"If he is a Roman. Most certainly."

"Couldja give us a baseball example of a sacrilege, Brother?" Kavanagh asks.

McCann moves his index finger slowly back and forth across his lips. He sighs, squints his eyes and furrows his brows so that we will think he is contemplating.

"Perhaps Mr. Bradburys could give the class an example."

"Well, if Whitey Ford is a Roman Catholic, he could commit a sacrilege in many ways," Bug squeaks.

"Correct! Name one," McCann interjects, spraying spit. "What would be an example?"

"Well, say Whitey Ford had a picture of Our Lady of Perpetual Help taped to his locker door in the club house during the season. And he prayed to it every day for protection and good luck, and one day he lost a big game, say the seventh game of the World Series. And he spit on the picture and cursed on it and tore it up into a tiny million pieces and threw it into the toilet and used the bathroom on it and flushed it down. Wouldn't that be an example of—"

"A *sacrilege!* Excellent example, Mr. Bradburys. Excellent!" McCann showers the front row. "A perfect example of sacrilege!"

Bug cocks his head, turns to the class and grins.

"What about if you burned a crucifix in the incinerator, one that is blessed with holy water by the Archbishop?" Anderson asks. The incinerator is an oversized barrel with gashes in it that the brothers use to burn old clothes and odds and ends.

"Sacrilege!" McCann shouts.

"Or a set of rosary beads blessed by the Pope in the Vatican?" Murphy says.

"Sacrilege. Another example of a sacrilege." McCann foams at the mouth.

"Or you stole a host from the tabernacle and buried it in the graveyard," Pat Fitzpatrick shouts.

"Oh, sacrilege! That too would be a sacrilege." McCann is almost out of control.

The examples are fast, one after the other, like gunfire, each one forcing from McCann a more frenzied response. I look over at Oberstein, who sits with his arms folded tightly, his eyes glued to a paperback hidden inside the hardcover catechism he pretends to read.

"What if someone urinated in the chalice?" Bug Bradbury squeaks.

"Sacrilegious, oh yes, sacrilege . . . *Sacrilege,*" McCann cants, as the front row prepares for another shower.

There is a sudden pounding at the door, and Brother McMurtry rushes in. The classroom becomes a morgue.

Bug, scrunched in his seat, his fist jammed against the side of his mouth, becomes stiff as a board. Oberstein rubs his wrist against his hairline. Blackie's eyes nervously dart between McMurtry and McCann. Murphy bites his lower lip and picks at the hockey tape on his glasses. Rowsell's drowsy look changes as he stiffens, sniffs the sour classroom air and sits up in his seat. Father Cross rubs his acned jaw, hunches his shoulders and picks lint off his woolly sweater.

McMurtry never interrupts a class unless someone is gonna be punished. The silence is deafening. A shudder passes through the room. We all have goosebumps. My stomach tightens, the way the panic starts before the spells. McCann folds his arms across his black soutaned chest, unfolds them again and picks up a pen to jot things down. Brother McMurtry clears his throat and questions Ryan about his whereabouts the other night.

"I went to the bathroom, Brother."

"And then what?" McMurtry removes his glasses, bites the tip of an arm and stares at Ryan. Specks of dust float behind him near the sunlit window.

"I can't remember, Brother." For a moment the classroom is silent. Bug wipes sweat from the back of his neck. McMurtry stares blankly at the floor. A faint smile ripples across McCann's face.

"*You can't remember?*" The force of his words seems to push us back in our desks. "You weren't trying to run away again, were you?"

"No, Brother. I was sleepy, Brother. I fell asleep." Ryan scratches the veins on his skinny neck.

"You fell asleep?"

"Yes, Brother." A loud mocking hiss from the radiator.

"On the toilet?"

"Yes, Brother. On the toilet, Brother. I was drying. Like Brother Walsh told us to do."

A pause. McMurtry's face muscles stiffen. He asks Ryan if he fell asleep *before* he used the toilet or after.

"I can't remember, Brother. Before, I think. No, before and after. I used the toilet again after I woke up.

"And then what?" A grin, like a shadow, creeps across his face.

"Then I wiped myself, Brother, and went back to bed."

"Very well, Mr. Ryan. We shall continue this conversation later." He strokes his hair, which is white as the driven snow, as his wolf eyes scan the class. "Brother McCann and I shall be holding a series of, shall we say, interviews. With a number of, shall we say, suspects. You will be the first on the list, Mr. Ryan. It appears someone, not necessarily Mr. Ryan, not necessarily one of our suspects, but someone, some boy or two or, God knows, more . . . *someone* is responsible for stealing wine from the sacristy. It is our intent to find the culprit, or culprits. These thieves. These wine smugglers. These smugglers of holy wine. And punish them. Even if we have to strap the entire orphanage."

I can feel the back of my shirt dampen against my chair as McMurtry leaves the room. McCann stares at us, stone-faced, until the buzzer sounds.

After class Blackie calls an emergency meeting with the Klub executive and Ryan, out by the incinerator.

"Interviews, my ass," Oberstein says. "Interrogation is what the Nazis called it."

"What are Nasties?" Bug says.

"Stick to your guns, Ryan," I say. "They'll try to trip you up. Don't say anything new, for God's sake. Stick to your guns. Remember what happened to the guy on *Perry Mason*."

Blackie and Oberstein grill Ryan over and over until they're certain he won't screw up.

"Did you say anything else to Spook?" I ask.

"Don't think so. Not that I remember," Ryan says.

"They ask you who you knock around with, just say everyone. Say, just about everyone," Blackie says. "And remember. Interrogation's like a card game. Silence is your trump card. Understand? Silence."

"I understand," Ryan says.

"No information, 'less they ask," Blackie repeats.

When we finish the cross-examination, as Oberstein calls it, Ryan gets up and walks off, scratching his greasy black hair. He is dazed and worried. We follow him, silently. We are all dazed and worried. This is the sort of thing that makes a bout of spells get worse. Bug and Anstey are the only ones who never get the spells. You avoid Bug like the plague if you have them because he really gives you a hard time. "Sissy baby, got the spells. Nah-nah, nah-nah-nah." He just loves teasing and mocking anyone who has the spells. He pays criers with comics and marbles to shout it through the halls: "Oberstein's got the spells again. Sissy baby's got the spells. Oberstein's got the spells again. Sissy baby. Sissy baby." Once Bug teased me about not having a mother and father. "And you'll never ever have one in this world," he said, "for the rest of your life." The way he said it really hit me. I couldn't shake the spells for the longest time.

Last Sunday, after my sister, Clare, visited, they started up again. The minute she left, I could feel them coming on. The Great Panic, as Oberstein calls it. And I haven't been able to shake them. We're all so worried about the wine stealing, it makes it a hundred times worse.

I may have to talk to someone. Oberstein and some of the other boys say that talking to someone about the spells can give you a lift. I've never done that before, and I don't want to, but I don't think I have a choice. I'm considering talking to Blackie. He's the most sensible in many ways. He may say something that helps. Or maybe I'll talk to Ryan or Kavanagh. Or Oberstein. Oberstein is certainly the most intelligent. Any one of them would probably be a big help at this stage. No, I think I'll talk to Blackie. The others don't need to be reminded of the spells. Especially Oberstein. And Blackie only gets them once in a while, like the time he was watching the news on TV. A bunch of black students at a college in the States refused to leave a Woolworth's lunch counter after the waiter wouldn't serve them. They talked to them right there, live on the TV. The oldest said, "We ain't movin' for nobody. We stayin' till we treated same as white folk." The news announcer said it would probably spark sit-ins and race riots. It certainly sparked the spells in Blackie. "I don't get it," he said. "Not servin' someone a hot dog 'cause of the color of their skin." He turned off the TV and started to cry. I tried to perk him up, but he wouldn't speak for the rest of the week. That's how Blackie deals with the spells. He just doesn't talk. Oberstein gets sick. Kelly stops eating. We all have our different ways.

I might even talk to Rags. His face turned so sad last week when Brother McMurtry told him the U.S. Supreme Court was cutting out praying in schools. I was sure he was getting the spells. But I don't think the brothers get them.

Sometimes, the spells last a long, long time. I had them two years ago off and on all winter. It was a really cold winter, freezing all the time, and we were buried in snow, which made it worse. So cold nobody even wanted to go outdoors after school. And at night the dormitory was freezing. You had to slide under your blanket and breathe hot air to get warm. Spells are always worse at night. When I get into bed, I feel so empty, like I'm living outside my body, on the empty bunk above mine, looking down at myself.

To fight the empty feelings, and so I can get some sleep, I often close my eyes and pretend Clare and I are with Mom and Dad in Dad's big old blue bus, driving down to Torbay or out to Manuels for a picnic. Mom singing her favorite songs—"Let Me Fish Off Cape St. Mary's" and "Time Would Tell"—the ones Clare told me she loved singing and sang to her all the time. And Clare and Dad and me joining in. Mom had such a beautiful voice and sang to us all the time, Clare says. Even now when I hear a woman singing a beautiful song I think of Mom. I must have got her gift because the brothers always get me to sing the Gloria and the Sanctus at Mass. I'm not as good as Oberstein but I can carry a note in a basket, as Brother Walsh says.

We'd be bouncing along in the big old bus, and I'd be up in the driver's seat in Dad's lap at the steering wheel, pretending I was the driver the way he'd let me sometimes. In my mind, we'd race along, and Dad would be the tour guide commenting on just about everything, the way Rags does when he takes us on an outing. "Oh, there's Murphy's goats on the left. Best goat's milk around the bay. You can spot O'Reilly's horses further on in the meadow. Ladies and gentlemen, if you look to your right, you'll see the property of Mr. Willam Nash, who died last year trying to rescue four fishermen lost on the high seas. The story of Newfoundland, ladies and gentlemen, the characters change, but the ocean and the story always remain the same." As Rags says, it's the story "of doors held ajar in storms." And all at once Dad's face would turn sad, and his mouth would take on an odd shape, and tears would appear in his sad gray eyes.

I can picture everything so vividly it is just like watching a movie. Every once in a while I'd clear my mind of everything except the image of the four of us at a picnic in Manuels, out in the canyon, where the brothers take us to swim during the summer. And I feel the warm summer sun on my face and the hardness of the rocks, the big boulders where we'd sit with our picnic basket, eating sandwiches and watching the river. And I pray to them to help me get over the spells. I don't know if they could or not, but I pray hard to them and to Mother Mary that they hear me and help me. Sometimes it feel like they answer. For a little while. Once, it got so bad I was gonna run away to St. Martha's, to be with Clare, but Blackie and Oberstein stopped me.

Every now and then, I escape the spells by daydreaming

about running away, being the only boy from Mount Kildare to ever perform Brother McMurtry's impossible trick. In my mind, I would take up his challenge. I would hide out somewhere. In the shed at the Mount Carmel graveyard for a few days. It would be cold at night, but I would have blankets and an extra sweater and provisions stashed away and a friend, someone smart like Oberstein, to bring me reports every so often about where they were looking for me and when it was safe to change my hideout. When the time was right, I'd steal some money and head for the ferry terminal at Argentia or Port aux Basques and sneak on the big boat that sails to Nova Scotia. Over there I'd get a job in a garage, maybe, or a restaurant, washing dishes or waiting on tables. I'd do that for a year or so till I could save enough money to get to the United States. New York, maybe, or Washington, where Oberstein says there's a HELP WANTED sign in every window. I ask him if that's because it's where the president lives in the big white house, and he says no, it's because they have a special economy with special budgets that the other states don't have. It's really amazing the stuff Oberstein knows.

Pretty soon I'm thinking about how awful Oberstein's spells are, and I don't feel so bad. And by and by Spencer starts talking in his sleep about his brother Jimmy's hockey cards, or O'Connor starts rocking, or someone gives out a mournful sigh, and I'm reminded of how cold it is and pull the blanket over my head again and start blowing hot air everywhere. And when I am good and warm, my mind becomes clear, and I'm exactly where I was hours before, with nothing but my loneliness. Then I bury my head in the pillow and hope that sleep hauls me under.

It all started last week. Outta the blue. I was listening to Brookes talk about when his mother told him and his two brothers they would have to go into the orphanage for a while.

Brookes said he almost went insane. He threatened to run away, and would have if his mother hadn't cried so much and gotten sick. It was really tough listening to him talk about it.

It made me remember the worst day of my life. My trip to hell. The day I had to choose between my mother and father. I was five at the time, but I remember it as clear as day. Mom was upstairs in her room packing. When I walked in, she told me to go to my room and start packing my things, we were leaving. I started to cry and said I didn't want to leave. She was only a mouse of a woman, but she grabbed my hand and squeezed it so hard it hurt. She turned me around and aimed me toward my bedroom and marched me there. Then she took both my hands in hers and dragged me to my suitcase, an old brown cardboard one with long straps that went all around and looped into big brass buckles. I wonder what happened to that old suitcase. I had it when I came here. I must ask Rags about it. He'll help me find it. That suitcase must be stored somewhere. I'd really like to see it again. Anyway, we were almost finished packing when Dad came and stood in the doorway. He was so tall he had to stoop. He was wearing his blue bus uniform. I'll never forget his expression. He was smiling, and his face was the color of raw meat. He lit a cigarette and laughed and said, "I hope I'm invited on this wee trip." He used the word *wee* a lot when he was drinking. There was a long silence. I felt a real sinking feeling come over me. It was terrible. I remember it as if it happened yesterday. I'm sure it's the feeling you get if you go to hell. Only the feeling lasts forever in hell.

"I don't want to go away," I said, and ran to my father, crying.

He patted my head and said, "You don't have to. You can stay right here with me if you want to. Isn't that right, Maisie?"

There was that sinking feeling again and another long silence, during which my mother stared right through me.

"Yes, that's right. Your father's right. You may stay. It's your choice." She turned to my father. "But if he stays, I want you to know that he will never see me again."

I ran to her and cried harder than I had with Dad. She buckled my suitcase and took me by the hand. As we passed through the doorway, my father patted me on the head. "Be a good boy," he said, "a good wee boy."

I could smell the whiskey on his breath. I didn't know what the smell was then. I thought it was a smell like the one Mom wore every Sunday when she dressed for church, only a bit stronger. I looked up at his red, smiling face and said goodbye. My mother tugged my arm and raced downstairs and outside to an ugly brown taxi that was waiting with Clare in the backseat.

I only saw my father once after that. We moved into a small apartment on Prescott Street in St. John's. My mother got a job downtown at the Arcade Stores, and I started kindergarten at Mercy Convent School, and Clare was placed in grade six. One day Dad appeared in the kitchen. Mom was making supper, and *boom*, there he was, in his bus uniform, tall and thin and leaning on the refrigerator. They got into an argument really fast. And Mom threw herself into a chair and started to cry. All at once, my father's face turned sad, and his mouth took on an odd shape, and tears appeared in his eyes. Then he knelt down beside her and kissed her and stroked her long brown hair and put his head in her lap and started crying too. Then I started crying, and they both stopped. He said he wanted her to go for a ride in the bus so they could talk privately. Mom said okay and asked the neighbors to keep an eye on me and Clare. I remember looking out the window down into the street at the two of them. They were holding hands and laughing as they got into Dad's old condemned-looking big blue bus.

That's the last picture I have . . . I never saw them again. A while later a gigantic policeman with a lightbulb nose and a bald head came to the neighbors and told us that the big blue bus went over a cliff in Outer Cove and that my mother and father were dead and I would have to come with him to a place called Mount Kildare and that Clare would have to go to a place called St. Martha's. "Them's places what looks after children what got no parents," he said. I remember the exact words. And I remember crying and crying and crying. And listening to Clare crying and crying and crying.

I only get the spells once in a while. And I never get them as bad as most of the boys. I feel real sad sometimes and a bit blue, but I never feel as terrible as Ryan and Blackie and Murphy do. And never, ever like Oberstein, who gets them worse than anyone.

Anstey never gets the spells because his father comes to see him a lot. Mr. Anstey is huge, like the Friendly Giant on TV, only he has a much bigger head and a moonbeam smile. Anstey is gonna be just as big. And he's so kind. He's the kinda father, if you only saw him once a year, it'd be enough. He gives all of us great big bear hugs when he comes here. And he always bursts out laughing when he asks us if we're true Newfoundlanders. If we say we are, he says we have to prove it by standing stiff as a poker with our arms straight as arrows while he lifts us off the ground. Oberstein's the only one who buckles when he's lifted, but we think that's deliberate. Oberstein's so proud he's an American. So you can imagine what Anstey feels like when his father's around. He's lotsa fun. I'd never get the spells if I had a father like Mr. Anstey.

Lately I've been praying to the Blessed Virgin to help me shake them. I even made a deal. I promised her I would help O'Grady with his homework during study hall every night till Christmas if she helps me get over the spells. It seems to be working a bit. Whenever I'm helping O'Grady, I don't think about my moment in hell. Of course, O'Grady's so stunned you have to give all your time and energy just to teach him that seven divided by seven is one. He's slow as cold molasses. He can't remember much, and he's a terrible stutterer. When I'm working with O'Grady, there's no time for the spells.

So I shouldn't really complain. Study hall is the only time lately that I don't have the spells. I'm grateful to O'Grady and the Blessed Virgin for their help. I think working each night with O'Grady is helping me break out of it. So I may not have to talk to anyone after all. Or run away to St. Martha's so I can be with Clare for a while. Time will tell.

7

THERE ARE TWO homemade flashlights, which Father Cross pieced together with batteries, bits of copper, bulbs, and electric tape that Rags uses for the hockey sticks. They work beautifully. Blackie uses one, leading the first pack, which consists of Shorty Richardson, Murphy, and Kavanagh. I lead the second pack, which consists of Ryan, Brookes, and Father Cross. Bug was dropped from Blackie's group because he passed out during our first run. The only reason Blackie gave him a tryout is he feels sorry for him. Bug complained so much about being dropped that Blackie made him chief timer and promised him some money.

Oberstein coordinates the backup, as Blackie calls it. Blackie loves a backup plan. Oberstein calls it the contingency plan. That's the plan we're to use in the event that we're caught night running. We call it the Runners' Watch. We're usually gone about ninety minutes, depending on the weather. If it's really bad out, we return in less than twenty minutes. Oberstein starts the watch, and half an hour later he wakes Bug, who mans the watch for thirty minutes and then wakes Spencer or another designated Klub member. Only a few boys Blackie trusts get a turn in the rotation.

If Spook, the night watchman, or one of the brothers finds

out we're missing, the backup kicks in. Whoever is on Runners' Watch at the time of the discovery will tell Spook or the brother in charge that Shorty Richardson is a sleepwalker and that he went missing. The watchkeeper is to say that he got up to use the toilet and discovered Richardson's bunk empty on the way to the bathroom and immediately woke Blackie and a bunch of the boys, who are outside looking for Richardson. The watchkeeper is to say that he'd been looking for Spook since we left. The brothers all know that Spook frequently falls asleep while on duty.

Depending on the time of the discovery, the watchkeeper, who always has my Mickey, will say how long we've been gone. If we're scheduled to be back in fifty minutes, the watchkeeper will say we left a few minutes ago. And Farrell, who is a really good sprinter and is always on red alert, will head out to warn the pack. If we're to be back in ten or fifteen minutes, the watchkeeper will say that we said we'd be back in ten minutes. It is a great plan, and sometimes Blackie runs rehearsals in case we have to use it. Everyone has his part down pat, just like when Rags gives us roles in *Julius Caesar*.

We run late at night, well before daybreak. Usually around three o'clock, before the brothers get up for chapel, and when Spook is fast asleep. Blackie devised a system called "stringing" for running in the dark so we can avoid obstacles like pot-holes. He uncoils a rope, and each boy wraps a strand around his wrist at ten-foot intervals. Blackie always runs ahead of everyone by about five minutes, his head to the ground like a bloodhound, intent upon the beam of light ahead of him. If he sees a rock or a hole or a fallen branch, he doubles back and warns Murphy, who jerks his string, creating a domino effect for the interval runners, so that the others know there is trouble ahead. Shorty Richardson always runs in the middle of the pack for protection.

Sometimes, if the moon is really bright, instead of stringing, we play a game Blackie devised. The first one to the finish line gets eight points, the last one gets one point. Each pack adds up their points to see which team won. Shorty Richardson is always first, so we have to work really hard to win. And half the time we do, thanks to Ryan, who's becoming a really good runner.

Most nights, starting out is bitter cold, but ten minutes on we start to warm up. The sweat stings our eyes, and we wipe it off on our sweater sleeves. We move slowly, the flashlights throwing a jumpy glow on the ground. Past the outdoor swimming pool toward the soccer fields, on to Fort Pepperrell, Virginia Waters, and finally to Robin Hood Bay. When we reach Sugar Loaf, the halfway mark, we stop at the lake and lie on our bellies and drink greedily. On the way back we pass an empty cabin, and we all yearn to creep over and disappear inside, but instead we think of the big day, the Royal Regatta Marathon, and how Shorty Richardson must be prepared better than any other runner in the city, how he must prepare as if for a Comrades, a double marathon, just like in South Africa. Oberstein told us South African runners have a Comrades, a double marathon, every year.

And so we soldier on. Ahead of my group, I'm close on the heels of Blackie's pack, pushing them, Blackie urging his runners to beat yesterday's time, if only by a few seconds. Our lips are dry and cracked. Our heads are spinning. Our feet are bloody and sore. We all want to stop and lie down and rest, if only for a few minutes. But Blackie's voice is always ringing in our heads: *Believe. We're a team. A winning team. Believe. Believe.* Some mornings, when we get back to our dorm, we are so dog-tired we barely have the energy to take off our clothes and wash, which Blackie always insists we do before falling into bed and sleeping the deepest sleep for a brief while. When the brother on morning duty sounds the buzzer, we do not want to get up. We lie there, exhausted, without will, until we hear McCann or Madman call our names, and we jump, fearful of what may happen if we are not dressed in time, to move with the herd toward chapel, where we will snatch a few minutes sleep here and there between the long prayers.

•   •   •   •   •

Winter coats in your dormitory. Winter coats in your dormitory.
Winter coats. Winter coats.

The weather is turning a bit. It's cold. But I know the criers are wrong. It's still too early for winter coats. Despite the cold, I'm glad we ran last night. I love running. I'm even looking forward to doing it during the winter. The leaves are almost gone now. There aren't as many robins around, and the pigeons seem to be spending more time in the big stone arches. I haven't seen Nicky for days. I really miss him sometimes. One night I woke up in a sweat, thinking he had flown away.

The dormitory is colder than usual in the mornings, and it's still dark out when we walk single file to chapel. The brother on duty turns on the dorm lights until we are washed and dressed. Winter is only a month or so away. When the first snow falls, the brothers will drag out the big cardboard boxes with the mothballed winter coats and stocking caps and thick mittens. It's a time when every piece of clothing, even socks, will be important. In winter, rarely a day goes by when I'm not cold. Even the classrooms turn cold. The building is so huge, and its only heat comes from a few radiators. Only the corridors are warm, and they always smell of the heated air that comes from the radiators, where we love to compete for a spot to warm our rumps during the time between meals and classes. More than a few drops of blood have fallen during a radiator scrum.

There's never a day when I don't wear odd socks. For a while, my nickname was Odd-Socks, but it never stuck. The rule is every night you must put your socks in the box over by the Rat Locker. The socks box is a big plywood box. Each night, the boy whose turn it is takes the smelly box down to the laundry room, and Rags washes every sock. Rags is a saint. I'm sure he's the nicest brother in the world. He has a great sense of humor. He's always acting and horsing around, and he's forever smiling. If he catches you running in the corridors, he stops you and asks where the fire is. Then he tells you it's okay to run, just don't go so fast, in case you bump into a little one. Rags treats us really well all the time, much better than the other brothers. And unlike them, he never asks you every five minutes if you think you have a vocation to the priesthood or the brotherhood.

Oberstein nicknamed him Rags one day when he heard him say that most Americans go from rags to riches, but he joined the Christian brothers and was sent to Mount Kildare and went from riches to rags. Blackie got the idea for the Dare Klub's motto from one of Rags' expressions—the glass half-full. It's written in Latin on a small plaque on Rags' classroom door: *Poculum semi plenum.* "Rags, Rags," Blackie always says. "He's the man to listen to." Blackie loves anyone who laughs, and Rags laughs all the time. Blackie says you can always trust a laugher. He refused to let some boys join the Dare Klub because they never laugh.

Another thing about Rags is he's always very fair. Unlike a lot of brothers, he doesn't have chosen ones, Oberstein's name for pets. And his classes are always exciting. He teaches science. Blackie gets a lot of his ideas from Rags. He's convinced Rags has black blood. "Don't need to be black to have some black blood," Blackie says.

"We all had black blood at one time," Oberstein adds. "Adam and Eve came from Africa."

Blackie and Rags like each other, and banter back and forth a lot during class. They're both from New York. Maybe that's why. Blackie's from Harlem, and Rags is from the Bronx. They're like father and son in some ways.

Rags is responsible for training the altar boys. You get up at six o'clock if you have to serve at the early morning Mass. About the only time you get matching socks, usually not your own, is when it's your turn to be an altar boy. If it's your turn to serve, Spook, the night watchman, wakes you about fifteen minutes before everyone else, before reveille, as Brother McMurtry calls it. You get washed and dressed and are almost awake as you rummage through the box for socks that look like yours. I hate waking up so early. It's one of the hardest things, morning beating at you like a board. I'm sure that's what causes the spells for some of the boys. If only we could sleep every day until seven-thirty. I think that would make a big difference for all of us. Bug is my altar server partner, and he's a sleepyhead like me. We usually fight over the few remaining socks.

We all love it when our turn comes round to serve Mass, because Rags usually asks the altar boys to stay behind after Mass and clean up, and we miss breakfast, so he takes us to the monastery, where we get bacon and eggs and orange juice and toast. There's always a fight over who gets to be the paten server and who gets to be the bell server. Everyone wants to be the paten server. The paten is a perfectly round gold plate, the size of a saucer, with a wooden handle. It is used during communion when the communicants kneel at the altar rail to receive the host. The altar boy holds the paten underneath the communicant's chin to prevent even a speck of the consecrated host, the body of Christ, from falling to the floor. After communion, the priest spends about ten minutes wiping the paten clean to make sure not even a smidgen of Christ's body is left there.

Everyone wants to be the paten server for two reasons. You

don't have to pay very much attention during Mass. Once you've recited the Confiteor, you can kinda doze off, drifting in and out a lot. You just have to mumble a few Latin responses once in a while, blasting out the last line or two so old Monsignor Flynn thinks you are paying attention and not goofing off. When you are the bell ringer you really have to be on your toes. There is a special way to ring the bells throughout different parts of the Mass, like the Sanctus, the raising of the host, the Agnus Dei. If you miss one, or screw up the way you're supposed to ring the bells, it's really noticeable and you can get into big trouble. You could even get strapped.

The other reason we all want to be the paten server is because you get to whack everybody in the Adam's apple. The paten is really sharp all around the edge, and it really hurts. Oberstein calls it the guillotine. The trick is to whack everyone, but hit your buddies the hardest without the priest knowing you're doing it. It gets really tricky when you're trying to whack a guy harder than he hit you the last time he was paten server. The chubby cherub holds the record at whacking boys really hard.

If you get caught, you're a goner. Once Murphy whacked Ryan so hard he gagged and coughed up the host. Old Monsignor Flynn, who's half blind and deaf, saw what happened and put down the ciborium and knocked Murphy up the side of the head. It was a really hard knock. It sent Murphy reeling.

If the host misses the paten and falls to the floor, it's a really big deal. During altar boy classes you're told that you are saving God from dropping into hell. "You all know what a circus safety net is, boys. The paten is God's safety net," Brother McMurtry lectures every new altar boy. When Ryan coughed up the host, Monsignor Flynn stopped the Mass. All the brothers raced to the spot where the host had dropped. Brother McMurtry bolted to the sacristy and brought back oils and holy water and starched altar cloths to clean and cover the consecrated spot. Chairs and altar kneelers were gathered and arranged into a circle of protection around the holy area for two days. It was a really big to-do. They did everything but call in McNamara's Construction to jack up the building.

I always fight with Bug over who gets the paten. For some reason, this morning Bug's nose looks longer, and he seems stuck on talking through it. Probably a touch of the flu. I really want the paten because I owe a big one to Oberstein, who nearly drove my Adam's apple down my throat last time he served. Getting to be paten server is resolved in one of the usual ways: it's purchased with a few cigarettes or canteen card IOUs or marbles or stamps or baseball or hockey cards. Or you fight for it by having a snap game of palms. I offer Bug a wrinkled Johnny Bower card, but he refuses.

"C'mon, Bug," I say. "I really want the paten. I owe Oberstein a hard whack."

He refuses again, saying he is too sleepy to take the bells.

"I'm really tired too, Bug," I say. "I feel like I'm gonna fall asleep."

So we play palms. Bug's good at it. He wins a lot. In snapper palms, you play odds and evens once to see who has upper and who has lower palms. This time I'm lucky. I get lower palms, which gives me the advantage. One or two finger teases, Bug draws back, and *wham* ... I nip him. I get the paten, and Bug gets the bells.

When Bug isn't an altar server, he always falls asleep. Sometimes he snores lightly in the pew, and the boy next to him has to poke him awake. He has never fallen asleep on the altar, until today.

Just before Mass starts, I say five Hail Marys for the success of the marathon and a few Glory Be's that we don't get caught for stealing the wine.

I glance over at Bug after the Introit, and he is looking kinda groggy. I point to the bells so he'll remember to ring them as Monsignor Flynn climbs the altar steps, chanting *Gloria in Excelsis Deo*. Bug gives me the finger. He's really tired and cranky. He picks up the bells and drops them before ringing them properly. Old Flynn turns and gives him an ugly look.

I don't pay much attention to Bug until the offertory, when he's supposed to join me in bringing up the cruets of water and wine. He's asleep, so I cough a few times, but he doesn't hear me. I get up and walk over to get the cruets, kicking his feet as I pass by. I figure he'll stay awake for the rest of the Mass, so I don't pay much attention until right before the Sanctus, when he's next supposed to ring the bells. He's out like a light. And he's swaying from side to side, slowly, like a ship at sea. Several times it looks like he's gonna fall, but he doesn't. But when I'm not watching, I hear a deep gurgle and turn to see him drop like a sack of potatoes, his head smacking against the linoleum floor. I race to him and bend over, pretending to help him up while whispering to him that he conked out and to keep his eyes closed and pretend that he fainted. Monsignor Flynn turns around and stares down from his perch as Brother Malone and Brother Walsh hurry to Bug's aid. They help him up and walk him off to the sacristy the same way they would've helped an injured baseball player off the field.

It is all very exciting. Bug is lucky old Flynn or one of the brothers didn't catch him sleeping, or he would've been a dead duck. Monsignor Flynn motions for me to take the paten and move to the bells' side of the altar. It is the first time I've ever served Mass alone. I don't mind. It's a bit of an adventure until we get to the Agnus Dei, when I remember I don't know all the words, so I half-cough and half-mumble my way through. Then I sing the Laudate to announce communion, pick up the guillotine, wait for Monsignor Flynn to descend the steps and walk to the altar rail to administer communion to my prisoners.

When Bug finally shows up at breakfast, white as snow, he gets razzed really bad.

"What happened, Bug?" Blackie asks. "Forget to take your wakeup pill?"

"Hey, if it ain't Bug the Slug," Murphy says. "He came, he saw, he conked out."

"Glory, glory, hallelujah," Oberstein sings. "The Bug keeps marching on."

"Keep it up, keep it up, four eyes," Bug says. "Your day is comin.'" And the whine of injury is louder than his words.

·   ·   ·   ·   ·

St. Martin's in the choir room. We're doin' a play by Skatespear.
Martin's in the choir room. Rags is doin' a play by Skatespear.
Martin's in the choir room.

The crier is Benny Long. He's in grade six. Rags has sent him to get us. We're doing a drama for the Christmas concert. Rags' favorite play, *Julius Caesar*. One of the drama teachers from Holy Cross, which is way out in the west end of the city, is coming to the Mount three days a week to help him out.

Today we're practicing on the stage, which we love, because we horse around in the wings. Usually, the choir gets the stage, but lately, because we're doing a play, we've been getting it a lot. Rags is a good director. He's patient, and he puts up with a lot of shenanigans. Like the other day we were horsing around on stage, waiting for him to show up, and just as he did, Oberstein was booming out, "I'm a Yankee doodle dandy . . ." If it had been any other brother, Oberstein would've been a dead duck. But Rags just laughed and said, "Okay, okay, silly season's not for another month. We have work to do. Act two, scene one, draw the curtain."

Father Cross is Julius Caesar, which is a good choice for the part, I think. Blackie is playing the role of Brutus. Bug is the soothsayer and Casca. He's the only one with two parts. "That's because he has a split personality," Oberstein says. Murphy is Mark Antony, and Oberstein is the stage manager, which Rags says is the most important job in the whole show. I'm playing the part of Cassius, which is a very important role. "Type casting," Oberstein says. "You have that lean and hungry luck."

Today we're practicing the stabbing scene, which we all love because we get to beat up on Father Cross. As we crowd in on him with our wooden daggers, we stab and punch and knee him until he falls to the floor. Once O'Connor grabbed him by the nuts, and he shrieked like a banshee. He's usually in agony by the time Rags yells, "Wunnerful, wunnerful. Excellent blocking. Great stuff." The conspirators do such a job on Murphy that Rags congratulates Father Cross every time. "Fabulous, Cross! You're terrific! Just terrific! You keep getting better and better. Good stuff!" Each time the scene ends, it takes poor Cross about five minutes to get up off the floor and fix himself up, while we're all in the wings howling with laughter.

Murphy is really good as Mark Antony. He'd be really good in any part. He has only one serious flaw, according to Rags. He keeps pushing back his hair all the time. Rags says, not to worry, it won't be a problem opening night because he'll have a Roman crew cut. Murphy gets to give the famous "Friends, Romans, Countrymen" speech. Rags goes over the opening with him again and again, because the way Murphy speaks, it sounds like "Friends, Romans, Cunt-tree-men." The first time Murphy delivered the speech, Rags stopped him dead in his tracks. He put his hand over his eyes and kept repeating, "Omigod! Omigod!"

As Murphy delivers today, we are crowded in the wings directly in his line of vision, mouthing each word, trying to get him to screw up or crack. When he says, "Lend me your ears," we all grab our ears or someone else's and mime handing them to him. All except Bug, who reaches for his dick, which cracks us up so much that Ryan falls to the floor in fits as Rags yells, "Quiet in the wings, *puh-leeze.*" Bug's as foolish as a capelin, but Murphy doesn't waver. He stares straight ahead and rattles away, moving about in the pulpit. Only once does he almost lose it. Each time he says Brutus is an honourable man, Bug drops his pants and moons him. We crack up, but Murphy doesn't miss a beat, which is really quite amazing. He's a really good actor. He delivers a perfect speech. "Terrific, Murphy! Fantastic! Well done!" Rags is clapping his hands hard from the back of the hall. Murphy is beaming with pride as we all roll on the floor in fits of laughter.

We all love play practice so much we ask Rags if we can have it every day. The time whizzes by. And we have such fun. One of the craziest things about practice is we all remember everyone else's lines. Every day now, in the dorm or the TV room, during recess, before study hall, at meals, everywhere, even in chapel, someone's always playing with lines from *Julius Caesar.* Bug's favorite is, "How should I know, it's all Greek to me." Blackie's is, "'Tis very like he hath the spells." And Father Cross says of Oberstein, "He reads much; he's a great observer and looks quite through the deeds of men." Oberstein's always saying to Kavanagh and Skinny Ryan, "Let me have men about me that are fat." There's no end to the quoting going on.

Tomorrow we are all being measured for costumes. Opening night is only three weeks away. Rags is taking photos of the lead actors and placing them outside the hall on a big bulletin board so everyone can see who's playing what part. He says that's the way the professionals do it on Broadway. Everyone is getting really excited about opening night. We're all taking it very seriously. Bug's stealing a couple of onions to peel just before Murphy's Mark Antony speech so he'll look like he's really crying. Father Cross says he's figured out a few more tricks so the makeup will look professional. Blackie has promised Murphy that Bug won't moon him during the performance, and we've all promised not to stab or knee or punch Father Cross too hard when the audience is present.

·   ·   ·   ·   ·

On the way back to McCann's class, Oberstein talks to me about the Talmud. He says it's written in the Talmud that every blade of grass has its angel that bends over it and whispers, "Grow, grow." Oberstein's gone mad over the Talmud. That's sort of like our Bible. He quotes it all the time. But everything he says is all Greek to me.

When we are all seated, McCann asks if anyone knows anything about limbo.

"Isn't that the name of a movie?" Rowsell asks.

"No!" McCann shouts. "It's not a movie. Good God!"

He says it's a place for lost souls and he'll teach us about it in a minute. But first he wants us all to understand an important difference between praying to Mary and praying to Jesus.

"You must never forget," he growls. "Mary always comes second. Jesus is always first. Remember Jesus is God. Mary is *not* God."

"Jeepers, isn't your mother the most important person in the world? I thought Mary ..."

"Mary is *not* God, Mr. Bradburys. Now, are there any further dialogues? Murphys?"

"Brother, remember the other day when you said that a child who isn't baptized goes to limbo? Well, what about if you are in the desert, and your wife had a baby, and the baby is only a few days old and dying from not having any water or food, and you really wanted to baptize the baby, but of course you had no water, and the baby died ... would it go to heaven or limbo?"

"Limbo," McCann snaps. "If a newborn is not baptized by water, and the spirit cannot be returned to its maker, it would go straight to limbo."

"But they had no water," Bug whines. "This is all Greek to me. They really, really, really wanted to baptize the baby but there was no water around anywhere. Not a drop."

"'Water, water, everywhere, but not a drop to drink,'" McCann giggles. "My Japanese brother's favorite poem." His brother is a Jesuit priest in charge of a parish in Osaka. He gets such a big kick outta his "Japanese" brother. We met Father McCann once. He looks a lot like Brother McCann, but he doesn't seem as crazy.

"And who was the founder of the Jesuit order, boys?"

"St. Ignatius Loyola, Brother."

"And its greatest member?"

"St. Francis Xavier, Brother."

"You know of his accounts of the Buddhist monks in the mountains of Japan, boys. About his reaching the peak of Mount Hiei to meet with the monks and being refused an audience. As the Holy Father reminds us, we are a small church in a large world, boys. What are we?"

"A small church in a large world, Brother."

"Why was he refused an audience, Brother?" Bug asks, trying to suck up.

"How the hell do I know that?" McCann barks.

"Is there no exception to the baptism by water rite, Brother?" Oberstein, sensing a storm, switches the subject.

McCann stares past Oberstein, his eyes closing as if in sleep. "There is a possibility that the newborn could go to heaven. You will recall from a previous class how Holy Mother Church makes two exceptions. Only two." He opens his eyes and pauses for dramatic effect. "One, baptism of fire. And two, baptism of desire. The latter happens when God believes you did everything within your power to find water, everything within your power, but were absolutely unable to."

"Could you use soda pop?" Kavanagh asks.

"Most definitely not, Kavanaghs. Soda pop is not water."

"Couldja use wine?" Rogers asks. Rogers is not a member of the Klub. Blackie and I look at each other and freeze.

"No. And most certainly not holy sacristy wine." There is a long silence as he scans the class.

"Couldja use spit?" Brookes asks. "Spit is water, isn't it?"

"Good God! *No*, you could not. It must be pure water."

Oberstein raises his hand. "What's so impure about spit? It's only H_2O." We all perk up. Oberstein asks such interesting questions. McCann gives him a long-winded senseless response that leaves us totally confused. When Oberstein rebuts him, McCann ignores him and says, "I'm sorry, Mr. Obersteins, but I cannot make it clearer than that. These are God's little mysteries."

"Brother, water is a compound of oxygen and hydrogen, of liquid form, seen in lakes, streams, rivers, rain, even tears, sweat, saliva. Even urine. They're all basically water, Brother."

McCann ignores Oberstein, turns his back, goes to the blackboard and writes the words "fire" and "desire." As he is writing, Ryan turns and whispers, "You could pee on the baby's head."

The class giggles.

McCann wheels around. "Who said that? Ryans, was that you?" Two kangaroo leaps and he is at Ryan's desk.

"Yes, Brother. But I only meant in an emergency. I didn't—"

"Stand up, boy. Hands up."

"I never meant no disrespect, Brother."

"Never meant no disrespect! Good grief, the grammar around this place." McCann sprays spit bullets as he pulls his leather roll from inside his soutane. We watch the snake slowly uncoil, like a yo-yo. He gives Ryan two whacks on each hand, jumping off the floor with each whack. "Now, there'll be no more shenanigans when it comes to the teachings of Holy Mother Church. None, do you hear? None! Save the shenanigans for the hallways. Now open your catechisms and read numbers eighty-seven to one hundred and one. You will learn that baptism by desire happens when God feels that your desire to baptize the infant is greater than if you actually had the water in your presence to perform the baptismal rite."

Bug flaps his hand. "Yeah, 'cause God knows what's in your heart," he says, really sucking up. "The good and the evil . . . of the just and the unjust."

"Very good, Mr. Bradburys. That is correct."

"And what about baptism by fire, Brother?" Bug asks. "How do you get that?" Bug is such a suck.

"Yes. Excellent dialogues. Baptism by fire occurs when an unbaptized person gives his life for God. You do not need water, because the individual in question is baptized in blood, his own precious blood."

"Could you give us an example, Brother?"

"Certainly. You will recall little Pundhu Ghanga, from an earlier class. Had he died from his wounds, he would have been baptized in his own blood. A little martyr! Martyrs experience baptism by blood. Another example is the Crusades. Or any holy cause. Many unbaptized Romans died in battle, fighting for the cause of Christendom. Those brave soldiers were instantly baptized. And, I might add . . ." He raises his index finger, turns and points to the crucifix above the blackboard, ". . . instantly *confirmed*. They became instant soldiers in the army of Christ. That would be an example of double grace."

Kavanagh raises his hand. "Just like a double in baseball, wouldn't it be, Brother? You know, two bases on one hit?"

Silence. McCann frowns, thinks for a few seconds and says,

"Yes, I suppose so, Kavanaghs. Like a double in baseball. Yes."

O'Toole's hand shoots up. "What if a guy wanted to kill himself, and he jumped outta the Empire State Building, and on the way down, just before he went splat, in his heart, he had a change of mind—he had the desire to be baptized. Would he be? Would that be an example of baptism by desire?"

McCann's brow wrinkles again. He squints and closes his eyes, opens them and frowns as if he has been asked a trick question.

"Yes. Yes, that would be such an example. If, in his heart, the penitent wanted God's grace . . . there being no water around . . . he would receive the Holy Spirit . . . and be baptized by desire."

"What about if he happened to have some water? Say he was drinking some on the way down," Bug says.

McCann squints, closes his eyes. "He would have to use it. He would have to baptize himself with it," he says.

Oberstein raises his hand.

"Enough dialogues, Obersteins," McCann says. "Open your catechisms, class. Numbers eighty-seven to one hundred and one. That's your homework. Get at it."

◆   ◆   ◆   ◆   ◆

Study hall in ten minutes. Study hall. Study hall. Ten minutes.
Study hall. Study hall.

Formal study always takes place downstairs in our homeroom. The brother on supervision gives us a stern warning about being quiet and usually leaves after a few minutes, popping in and out at long intervals, which is great because we get a chance to whisper and exchange notes. Maybe play X's and O's.

I sit opposite Oberstein, and I can't wait for study hall so I can chat with him. I think I'm going crazy. I'm not kidding.

I think I'm hearing things. And worse, seeing things. Like Joan of Arc and Bernadette Soubirous. I think I might've had a vision. Either that or I'm gonna wind up in the Mental. That's what everyone in St. John's calls the nuthouse. It must be the spells wearing me down. They can do that if they get really extreme. I'm reading another book about Floyd Patterson. Blackie gave it to me after I talked to him about the spells. It's called *Victory over Myself*. It's a really good book. He used to get the spells a lot. Only he didn't call them that.

The vision happened a few days ago when I was doing my chapel duty for Advent preparation. In the weeks leading up to Advent, the brothers appoint a boy every few hours to spend vigil time in the chapel, right up until lights out. I was kneeling in front of the statue of the Virgin Mary, just staring at her for about an hour, watching the glow from her beautiful face, asking her for protection. That's what Rags told us to do every night before going to sleep and every morning after we get out of bed. Pray to Our Lady of Perpetual Help for protection and guidance, first thing every morning and the last thing every night.

Mary is a really big gun at the Mount. Everyone's always praying to her for something or other. Brother McMurtry comes round to each classroom during the feast days of Mary with ice cream and potato chips and soda pop. He calls them wingdings. If it is the feast of Mary, Queen of the World, or the Seven Sorrows of Mary, or Our Lady of Lourdes, or Fatima, or the Assumption, or Mary, Queen of Peace, we have a wingding. We used to pore over religious books, looking for anything named after the Mother of God to get another wingding. Once, Bug read in a magazine the name Our Lady of Guadalupe, but Brother Walsh said that feast day didn't count, for some reason. But when a feast day did count, we would make candles and paper flowers and decorate the statue of Mary in our classroom, and Brother McMurtry would come by and stop class and inspect the statue and give a little speech about Mary's feast day, and then we'd have our wingding. He'd always finish up his speech by telling us that the first thing we should do each morning is hit the hard, cold floor on our knees and ask Mary to beg Jesus for forgiveness for our sins.

The brothers are always telling us stories about the lives of the saints, and how they had visions and apparitions of Jesus and Mary. My favorites are Bernadette Soubirous and the miracle at Lourdes and St. Joan of Arc burning at the stake. Rags used to tell us that we didn't have to say any prayers or anything if we didn't really want to, that it was fine just to kneel there and stare at the statue, that Mary would know our thoughts and our needs. Almost all of the boys at some time kneel before a statue of Mary or Jesus or one of the saints and ask for something. We're supposed to pray for protection against evil, or for the poor souls in purgatory. Ryan once told a few of the brothers that he did seven novenas asking Mary, Queen of Heaven, for a hockey stick, and one miraculously appeared at the foot of his bed the next morning. We've all been praying our brains out ever since.

Anyway, I was kneeling in the chapel in front of the blood-red candles at the base of the statue of the Virgin Mary, staring at Mary's long and graceful body and her beautiful face, which is polished to a butter-smooth sheen, and all of a sudden the glow disappeared. The swinging chapel doors creaked open, and a breeze rushed through, flickering the candles and seeming to rustle the folds of her sleeves. And her face suddenly turned dark, a sort of stormy dark. Even her golden hair turned fuzzy-looking. She looked more Halloween than holy. Outside, a light rain tapped at the stained glass windows. Her outstretched hands seemed to open wider, and her fingers extended as if to receive the rain. She seemed to stir, bend almost. And she spoke. It might have been my imagination. I don't think so. I was asking her for protection, and I heard her speak. I didn't see her mouth move or anything. I just heard her voice. It was a soft whisper. "*Felix culpa*..." She said the words in a sort of singsongy way, her lips seeming to curl in a bow of delight. It was all so strange.

The reason I'm sure I heard a voice, that it isn't my imagination, is because of the Latin. I hardly know any Latin words. I remember these words, though. How could I forget them? It was the first time I ever heard them. And she spoke in such a strange way, like in an Alfred Hitchcock movie, a really slow whisper, like she was singing all four syllables: *Feee-lix cull-paaaa* ... Maybe that was her way of proving that it's real, that it isn't my imagination.

We head into study hall just in time to see McCann leaving the room. When we're sure he's a safe distance away, the rustling silence is broken by boys coughing, the lifting and closing of desktops and my soft whisperings with Oberstein. He doesn't want to talk about my vision. He's giving Blackie a hard time about his writing, using tiny circles to dot his *i*'s, like Amos in *Amos 'n' Andy*. Then he wants to talk about our next night run. He's keeping all the times and is getting really excited about Ryan's progress. But I won't let up. I ask him again about the words. "You're the Latin scholar, Oberstein. C'mon, what's it mean?"

"O happy fault. It refers to the Garden of Eden. Original sin. It's the Church's way of saying Adam and Eve's fall was okay. It's called a paradox."

I tell him about my experience with Mary.

"*Felix culpa*. It's used a lot during Lenten services. Never during Advent. You sound pretty confident. Are you sure she spoke Latin? It's all Greek to me." Oberstein giggles and shakes.

"Chrissakes, Oberstein, get serious. Was it a vision? Did I have a vision?"

Oberstein covers his head with his hands in mock distress. "It probably wasn't a vision," he says. "If it was, you may have to become a priest. You may be getting *the call*. You could be like James Cagney in *Fighting Father Duffy* or Spencer Tracey in *Boys' Town*." He giggles and shakes again and says, "Don't sweat it, everyone around here gets pretty excited about miracles and visions and the lives of the saints. It's all that church mumbo-jumbo. And we're all pretty spooked about the wine and getting caught. Besides, you were there a long time. It could have been fatigue. Have you had the spells lately? You were probably dreaming, half daydreaming. It's called a semiconscious state."

"I couldn't have dreamed it, Oberstein," I say. "You can't dream words. You can only dream pictures. This wasn't a picture. It was a Latin phrase—*Felix culpa*—and I don't know very much Latin."

"It's definitely odd. I don't think anybody in the Mount would have known that expression. Not even some of the brothers."

"Then how did it get in my mind if I didn't know it and nobody else does?"

Oberstein looks at me and shrugs.

"Was it a vision?" I ask again. "Like the saints have? Did I have a vision?"

"Don't ask me," he says. "I'm Jewish." He turns away and pretends to study.

I'll never know if it was fatigue or my imagination or if I'd heard the words long before and had since forgotten. Or whether it really was a vision and she really spoke to me. Next Saturday, during free time, I'm gonna walk to St. Martha's and ask Clare. She believes in miracles. She'll know.

I turn to Oberstein to ask again, but he's asleep, his glasses standing on their lenses beside him on his desk top, his face in his folded arms. I poke him and whisper, "*McCann!*" His body twitches, and he lifts his head, his blue eyes meeting mine. "It was a vision, wasn't it?" I say. He turns a page of his notebook just as McCann re-enters the study hall and paces up and down the aisles before coming to a halt near Cross's desk.

"Well, now, what's this, Mr. Crosses? Required reading, is it? *Lively Saints.*" It's a fat red book Cross always carries around. Cross is always reading about the lives of the saints. He always has a story or two to tell at the Bat Cave about some saint who was boiled in oil or forced to sit forever on top of a two-hundred-foot spike.

"Required reading, is it?" McCann is wheeze-breathing and spraying spit, as usual. He shakes his jowls in disbelief, opens the book and begins reading about St. Stanislaus, the patron saint of Poland. He reads aloud about how poor Stanislaus was defending a tower and took an arrow in the head. "Interesting, Mr. Crosses, but not what you'll find on your physics exam tomorrow. Hardly Boyle's Law, is it?" He orders Cross to stand up and put out his hands. He begins wheezing like he's gonna have an asthma attack before giving Cross a whack on each hand. But they are only half-hearted whacks. You can hardly hear them. We all know that McCann doesn't want to strap him, that if we weren't around, Cross would be spared the strap. McCann is doing it to save face. Cross sits down, folds his arms, lowers his head and cries silently. We all feel pretty bad for him. It's really mean if you think on it. Strapping a boy who wants to become a priest and who is reading about the saints.

I know I'll never be able to look at Cross the same way again. When he gallops around the Mount in his Lone Ranger outfit, I'll only see the image of him weeping at his desk. From now on, he'll always be a weeping ranger to me. It's a very sad thing, and it really hardens me against McCann. We all feel he shouldn't have strapped poor Cross. We all know McCann isn't playing with a full deck, as Murphy puts it. We knew it even before he beat up Blackie. McCann always has this insane look about him. Out for the weekend, Blackie always says, referring to the Mental. It's nothing for him to flip out, even after a minor incident like the one with Cross. As if to try to undo the strapping, he strides up and down the aisles, foaming at the mouth while lecturing on study hall rules. He shouts that if he ever catches another boy with a book that isn't required reading, he'll strap him until the boy can't stand. He repeats the phrases over and over in his high-pitched, asthmatic voice, and each time he shakes his jowls. Then there is a long silence, and he says he has to leave the study hall for a few minutes, and heaven help the boy who isn't studying when he gets back.

Blackie looks around when he knows McCann is gone and whispers, "He got so excited he gotta snap the lizard." Most of us laugh silently. Leave it to Blackie to take such a chance. About five minutes later, McCann returns and launches into another speech about study hall rules and the subject of discipline. He sprays spit bullets everywhere, raging that when boys misbehave they deserve but one thing and one thing only— a royal strapping. Writing out lines is no good. Extra chores are no good. A royal strapping is what is needed, he says. I glance at his face as he walks by my desk and notice the ever-present greenish white foam in the corners of his mouth. As he walks up and down the aisles, we can feel his eyes on our backs. He continues to shout wildly, seeming to find new energy as he roams the room. That is the only way to discipline such a scoundrel, the only way to teach him a good lesson. A bloody good strapping until the boy is black and blue. He says he will take great pleasure in being the brother who will administer such discipline. I glance sideways at the black soutane that stops by my desk. My heart is pounding with fear that he might ask me something, my opinion on what he said. And that I might blurt out the wrong thing and get strapped. So I don't dare budge. I can feel his eyes burning into my back, daring me to move, and I stiffen and recall what Oberstein told me about his grandfather, who had been in the German concentration camps during the war, how he had seen a man get shot in the head for taking a step. One step. Just for moving, Oberstein said. And *bang*. He was dead.

8

MCCANN HAS DECIDED to have a sumo wrestling team. He says it will help us better understand our separated brethren, the Romans of the Asian persuasion, thus helping us to be more ecumenical, which is the wish of the Holy Father.

"The Church is changing, boys. There's talk of a Second Vatican Council, Vatican Two." He looks at us as if he expects us all to cheer. "The Holy Father has informed us that our Church rejects nothing that is true and holy in the other great world religions. Less than 1 percent of the people of China and Japan are Christian, boys. And only 2 percent of the people of India. What percent, boys?"

"Two percent, Brother."

"We are, I repeat, in the words of our Holy Father, a small church in a large world. Repeat that now, boys. A small church . . ."

"A small church in a large world."

"Very good. But we look with respect on these other ways of life, those teachings, which, though differing in many ways from what Holy Mother Church sets forth, nevertheless often reflect a beam of that truth which enlightens all peoples. That's what Vatican Two will be all about, boys. And we must follow the will of the Holy Father. Now, many of you know that my brother, Father McCann, works in Japan. Some of you met Father McCann on his last visit to Newfoundland. A Jesuit in the tradition of Loyola and Xavier. The Jesuits have made great gains in Japan, boys. *Great* gains. And we, boys—you and I—will do our little bit to help out."

McCann is always talking about his Japanese brother. He giggles whenever he says the words. His brother sends him tons of stuff from Osaka—kimonos, fans, chopsticks, cushions, origami kits, woks, Japanese comics. There's no end to it. McCann has become as fanatical about the Japanese as Brother Malone is about the Irish.

He reads from a huge hardcover book entitled *Zen and the Art of Japanese Wrestling*: "Japanese wrestling is an art which evolved from a primitive style of combat into a religious ceremony, before becoming a method of military training; it eventually emerged as sumo, a form of wrestling still practiced in Japan today. Its long tradition is highly revered and has been faithfully preserved."

He tilts his head, which appears to be growing like a mushroom out of his black soutane. He listens carefully and stares at the ceiling as if expecting to hear a voice. Then he returns to the book. "Prior to the 1600s, wrestling was a form of combat, using lethal kicks and blows. It did not differ much from European styles of wrestling."

"Does Father McCann have a black belt in karate?" Bug interrupts.

"In 1570, however, the ring ... *dohyo* ..." He ignores Bug and points to the tumbling mats on which he is standing. The mats are arranged inside a fifteen-foot circle marked out with masking tape. "The *dohyo* was introduced, and with it, basic rules. The *dohyo* is a holy place. In this sacred ring, the ancient pageantry and combative spirit of Japanese wrestling unfolds in the centuries-old sumo style. Sumo wrestling is ritualistic. It is part of the Shinto religion." He holds the book against his chest and shouts, "Today's sumo wrestlers are powerful men selected for their size and then trained through discipline and diet. The most powerful of these is the grand champion, the *yokozuna*."

His head droops to the side as he rolls his eyes again toward the ceiling, lost in thought. Then he stares at us, then back at the ceiling. He taps his finger on his lower lip. "Naturally, boys, I shall be your grand champion. I shall be your *yokozuna*." He lowers his head. "Of course, you will have to wear loincloths, boys, to be proper sumo wrestlers. I shall provide loincloths, *mawashi*. All the way from Japan. From Father McCann, my Japanese brother." He giggles as he raises the book and shows us a picture of a straw rope with white zigzag paper strips. "*Mawashi*. And I shall instruct you on the proper wearing of such."

He reads, "All *sumotori* wear the classic silken belt around the loins which tradition attributes to the exploits of Hajikami, a wrestler of such strength and skill that in a tournament held in Osaka eleven hundred years ago any opponent who could merely grab a rope tied to his waist would win."

"Needless to say, no one could do that." He shakes his head. "Besides loincloths, boys, you will be expected to wear your hair according to the traditional sumo styles. *Oichomage* for the grand champion and *chommage* for all other sumos." McCann closes the book and drops it. It lands on the floor with a loud thud. "The sound of one hand clapping," he shrugs, stares at the ceiling and hums to himself. He then claps his hands sharply and shouts, "Who wants to be on the sumo team?"

When nobody raises a hand, McCann says that to be a sumo wrestler, you have to put on a lot of weight. "About two hundred pounds," he says, "and this means every boy who joins the sumo team will receive extra meals each day and double servings. As well, all sumos will be released regularly from class for special trips to the canteen. Sumo wrestlers will receive special canteen cards."

Every hand in the class shoots up.

"You may dialogue among yourselves about the advantages of becoming a sumo." McCann walks to a chair, sits down and lowers his head. The class becomes a beehive.

"I put my hand up, but I wouldn't be caught dead walking around with a diaper stuck up me arse," Ryan whispers.

"Fuck the loincloth," Murphy says. "I'm in it for the grub. Extra meals and free trips to the canteen's good enough for me." Unlike poor Ryan, Murphy doesn't need the extra weight.

Oberstein looks downcast, the way he does when he gets the spells.

"What about you, Oberstein? You in?" Murphy says.

"I dunno," Oberstein says. "The Japs bombed Pearl Harbor. My president declared war on them for that. I dunno if I can promote their rituals."

Blackie urges Oberstein to join. "Oberstein, there's two kinds of people in this world. Them that says, I'm gonna make it happen. And them that says, What the hell's happenin'?"

"You're an American, Blackie," Oberstein says.

"One hundred percent. Stars and Stripes forever," Blackie says.

"What about Pearl Harbor?" Oberstein says.

"Ain't nobody from Pearl Harbor livin' in Mount Kildare," Blackie says. "We're POWs, Oberstein, POWs, and we're AWOL, just like in the movies."

I look at Oberstein and imagine him two hundred pounds heavier.

McCann claps his hands twice. "There are seventy sumo moves. You must master all seventy. The first tournament of the Mount Kildare Sumo Wrestling Team will take place tomorrow after school. Besides the grand champion, there will be junior champions and pre-champions. These will be followed by senior wrestlers, contenders, beginners, and recruits. Right now, you are all recruits. After tomorrow's tournament, you will be ranked. And who knows? Maybe there will be tournaments in town. Against other schools. The Protestants. Maybe there will be Protestant sumos. But Mount Kildare sumos will be the best sumos in the province. Just like our band and our choir and tumblers. Please show up half an hour early for hair and loincloth demonstrations, *chommage* and *shimenawa*. And remember, boys, once you come to the ring, you always refer to me as your grand champion, your *yokozuna*. Your what, boys?"

"*Yokozuna*, Brother."

He claps his hands again, sharply, like a Chinese mandarin, raises them palm to palm, says "*Gassho*," bows a deep, slow bow and leaves.

"I don't think we really got a choice." Murphy nods his head in McCann's direction.

Bug rolls his eyes and cocks his head. "*Yokozuna*," he mocks.

"Yoko loco," Blackie says.

•   •   •   •   •

There are twenty-seven boys on the sumo wrestling team. Each practice Brother McCann begins roll call by shouting the number one in Japanese, *ichi*. Each boy shouts his number in turn—*ni, san, shi, go, roku*—until twenty-seven is called. McCann refuses to allow numbers four and nine to be called out during the same class. They must alternate, he says. *Shi*, number four, has the same pronunciation as "death." And *ku*, number nine, has the same meaning as "to suffer."

"*Kurushimu*, four and nine, a very bad combination, sumos. Very, very bad. Forty-nine, as you know, is the worst mark you can get on a test. A *limbo* mark. Better to get one or zero.

Forty-eight means you definitely failed. Fifty means you barely passed. But you passed. Forty-nine means you almost made it. You're in a sort of limbo. It's the worst mark a student can possibly attain. Also, 1949 was a very bad year, sumos, a very bad year. You are all students of Newfoundland history. You all know your *Dictionary of Newfoundland*. You all know what happened to our great country during that fateful year, 1949. That was our Pearl Harbor, sumos. The year we joined the Canadians. April Fool's. Ha ha! A terrible, terrible year. We might as well have become communists. We surrendered our souls, our independence. Shameful. We gave up everything, our government, our stamps, our Bank of Newfoundland, our currency, our ambassadors, our pride, sumos. Our pride. Forty-nine . . . *a very bad year.* Four plus nine equals thirteen, unlucky thirteen, sumos. Never ever let me hear *shi* and *ku* called during the same class. Never, ever, ever." He is extremely angry.

I am number nineteen, *ju-ku.* We all shout our numbers. For some weird reason, McCann thinks shouting is synonymous with being a Japanese sumo wrestler.

"Kavanaghs-san, you're over the line," he screams. "Review your seventy sumo moves. Murphys-san, bow deeply before your bout." During sumo sessions he always adds *san* to everyone's name. Bradburys-san, Ryans-san, O'Connors-san. He has an English–Japanese dictionary his brother sent him and he's always looking up Japanese words and shouting them at us.

"Sayonara, Kavanaghs-san, you're over the line again. Westcotts-san, Ryans-san, all sumos, straighten your *shime-nawas.*" As he sprays, a strand of slime sticks to his chin.

Ryan and Kavanagh never get their loincloths on properly. They're always half falling off. Poor Kavanagh's droops so low you can usually see his pubic hair. But it's not just Ryan and Kavanagh, all of us, one time or another, have difficulty with our diapers, as Oberstein calls them. We all look pretty foolish.

Brother McCann wants every sumo to be properly loin-clothed and haired for the opening tournament. He has arranged the competition according to weight. The winners will receive prizes in the form of extra canteen privileges—bags of chips, candy bars, Tootsie Rolls and soda pop. Everyone wants to win. All matches will be fought in the *dohyo*, and McCann instructs us to gather in a circle and clap our hands over and over, while bowing to each other, until our necks are sore.

"The match begins," he shouts, "when two sumos enter the ring." But first, he has to explain the *chiri-chozu* ceremony, which we call the Cheerios ceremony. "Squat at opposite ends of the ring, extend your arms, clap your hands once." Then he performs the foot-stamping ritual, which is like a war dance the Apaches do in the movies. "Next, the purification ritual," he shouts, and takes a handful of salt from a bowl Kelly passes him and throws it into the *dohyo*.

Finally, he teaches us the glare-off. "The glare-off is high noon with Gary Coopers," he says. He pulls Kavanagh and Ryan, the scrawniest sumos, aside and tells them to crouch down at marked white lines. "Clench your fists and glare at each other. Try to break each other's concentration. Glare as hard as you can. It's like a faceoff in hockey." As he turns and tells us the importance of keeping our focus, Kavanagh bares his teeth at Ryan, who sticks out his tongue. "The glare-off takes four minutes, sumos. You may lunge at any time during the glare-off."

Every day now, McCann has a new Japanese item, as he calls it. Mostly clippings taken from papers and magazines sent by Father McCann. Yesterday, he read to us from a newspaper clipping sent from Tokyo on the Japanese Noh theater about a Mr. Tetsunojo Kanze, who was born into a family of Noh actors. Today, he asks who Mr. Kanze is.

"Head of one of five major troupes of Noh, a six-hundred-year-old form of musical dance drama that uses measured chants and movements," Oberstein answers.

"Mr. Kanze is very famous. In Japan he is considered a living national treasure, and he is extremely well known world-wide. He made his first performance at the age of three and currently performs with his two older brothers, Hisao and Hideo." Today, McCann catches Rowsell daydreaming and asks him to properly pronounce the names of Mr. Kanze's older brothers. Rowsell can't pronounce his own name. He keeps stuttering the word Kansas until McCann gives him a whack on each hand.

Mr. Kanze stages performances for peace and the abolition of nuclear weapons because of the horror of the atomic bombing of Hiroshima, which I like to remind Oberstein about when he mentions Pearl Harbor.

Today at practice, McCann reads a piece from a book called *Essays in Idleness* by Yoshida Kenko, a fourteenth-century Buddhist priest. It's about how the Japanese imperial bed-chambers always have the pillow facing east in order to receive the influence of the light. McCann asks Oberstein, who is a crackerjack in geography, what direction the east is, and when Oberstein says Virginia Waters, McCann tells us all to change our pillows before bedtime so that all sumo pillows face east.

When he finishes reading from *Essays in Idleness*, he reaches for a game box and holds it high above his head. "Another Japanese item," he shouts, "from Father McCann. Samurai Sabres, a game of high adventure, which all sumos must master." He is extremely excited, shouting and spraying spit everywhere. "The time: Sixteen hundreds. The place: Feudal Japan at war. The challenge: Command an army of samurai warriors, battle for provincial control, eliminate your enemies and become shogun. It is a game of strategy, secrecy, diplomacy. Plan your moves in the cafeteria, during recess, before going to sleep, everywhere, except chapel. Cloak your campaign in secrecy by hiring temporary mercenaries or the ninja to spy and assassinate. Form mutual bonds of loyalty with an enemy warlord. But be constantly wary of the knife in the back."

"So, what's new?" Bug whispers.

McCann passes the game to O'Neill. "This is a game for sumos, all sumos, to master." He chops his hands sharply, drops his jaw and stares at the ceiling.

Before the tournament tomorrow we must all memorize a Japanese Zen meditation, which we're to recite before every wrestling match. And Brother McCann has talked Rags into teaching us the art of Japanese haiku. That's a form of poetry that has strict rules: three unrhymed lines totalling seventeen syllables, with a pattern of 5-7-5. But Rags says you don't have to stick to that strict pattern. Haiku written in the States usually ignores the rules. Rags says not to worry about the rules, just have fun. He wrote a couple of examples on the blackboard. They're short and cute and fun to write. Most of us really like them. We trade them like baseball cards. My favorite is:

> *In the old stone pool*
> *a frog jumps:*
> *splishhh*

We are told to write a haiku to read out at our next sumo wrestling class. Bug passes one around during study hall:

> *Cloud sails by Kavanagh's crotch*
> *loincloth slips:*
> *fuck*

We crack up. Study hall quickly turns into haiku madness, dirty haiku being passed around hand over fist.

* * * * *

We are all a sight for sore eyes. Buck naked except for our diapers, and with our hair oiled and bobbed on our heads like Pebbles from *The Flintstones.* We've arrived early for McCann's demonstration class. He asks for a volunteer to demonstrate various Western techniques and positions that are unacceptable in sumo wrestling. His special lessons, as he refers to them, can last for up to fifteen minutes. Today he wants us to see the leg sweep, the leg hold, and the head-and-arm throw, all illegal. "No hair pulling," he shouts, "no fist punching, no eye gouging, no kicking in the privates."

Nobody volunteers for his special lesson, so he nabs McBride and lies on his side on the mat, locking his legs around poor McBride's skinny waist. He tells us that this is the scissors hold, and no sumo would be caught dead using such a primitive technique. Then he flips poor McBride and jumps on his back and grunts and growls something about arm throws and body braces and why they are illegal. Poor McBride is gasping for air, pinned beneath McCann's throbbing weight. McCann makes a high-pitched moan and looks up. We can see the whites of his eyes. The veins in his neck stick out, his face is reddish purple.

"Jesus," Bug says.

"What?" Ryan whispers.

"Jesus," Oberstein repeats.

Instantly, we all understand what's happening. McCann reminds me of one of the aliens in the horror movie we saw last week. He's snorting and drooling and shouting Japanese words while humping McBride and rocking him to and fro.

"What about all that gasping and moaning?" Murphy mocks, during break.

"I don't see why Yoko Loco needs to give special lessons," Blackie says.

"He sounds like McGettigan doing the scales in choir practice," Bug says.

"Special lessons, my ass," Ryan says. "We all know what he's up to."

"Whaddaya mean?" Rowsell asks.

"He isn't just humping McBride," Oberstein says.

"Omigod!" Rowsell says.

"He's getting his rocks off," Murphy says.

Rowsell turns pale. He looks like he will throw up. "Oh, boy," he says.

The first match is between Kelly and Kavanagh. Kavanagh couldn't pin a mosquito. Kelly will easily win. He's not called the King of Pain for nothing. He grins his horsy grin, turns his hand into a gun and says, "Stick 'em up!" Then he shoots Kavanagh. *Bang! Bang!* Kelly's always doing that lately. Ever since we saw a movie about a bunch of bank robbers called *The Story of the Ned Kelly Gang*. Rags says it's the oldest movie in the world, made in 1902. Kelly wants everyone to call him Ned. He gets really pissed if you call him by his real name, Phonse. He even asked Brother McMurtry if he could change his name to Ned. McMurtry poked him in the side of the head.

Kavanagh doesn't have a prayer against Ned, who's about a hundred pounds overweight to begin with. He's one of the fattest guys in the Mount. And Kavanagh's definitely the skinniest. Kavanagh's new nickname is Sumo Toothpick, he's so skinny. Even his Roman nose is thin. And so is his wavy orange hair. He's the exact opposite of what a sumo wrestler should look like. If you were looking for a guy to play the role of someone on a hunger strike, Kavanagh would be your man. But a sumo wrestler, not in a million years. Brother McCann started him on extra meals right away. But I don't think twenty extra meals a day would help poor Kavanagh get fatter. Knobby Knees is such a rake. As he's doing the sumo bow, he usually squints his eyes and bucks his teeth while giving his opponent the finger. Or during the glare-off, he crosses his eyes and screws up his face and looks so hilarious that his opponent usually cracks up, which enrages McCann. And, of course, everyone cracks when Kavanagh hits the mat. But we're all so scared to death of McCann that we hold our laughter inside, which makes it ten times funnier.

McCann in a loincloth is a sight to behold. He's really hairy. Oberstein says he looks like a gorilla in diapers. Blackie says he looks like a retard. He's the referee of every bout. He jumps around, spraying spit everywhere, screaming out Japanese phrases that make absolutely no sense to anyone. Once he stopped the Kelly–Kavanagh match and yelled *Kee-Koo-Yu* about fifteen times at the two of them. They just froze there, like frightened animals, until McCann finally realized they didn't have a clue what he was saying and blew his whistle, karate chopped both of them on the shoulders and shouted for them to continue wrestling.

We all know Kavanagh is gonna lose every match he ever fights, but in our hearts we all want him to win.

"Poor Kavanagh," Blackie says during break. "Everything's goin' wrong for him today. Seems like some days everythin' goes our way, everythin' falls together, everythin's so easy. Other days, just the opposite. On a bad day we're all thumbs. Gonna be a lotta bad wrestlin' days for Leo Kavanagh. Willie Mays got it right. 'Say hey, it ain't hard. When I not hittin', I don't hit nobody. But when I hittin', I hit anybody.' Kavanagh ain't hittin' nobody today, or tomorrow, or the next day. Kavanagh's headin' for a loooong slump." Blackie shakes his head and laughs harder than I've ever seen him laugh. He gets such a big kick outta Kavanagh.

And it's true. Knobby Knees can't do a thing right. If he isn't being pinned to the mat or knocked outside, his loincloth is slipping. We can see his pubic hair or the crack in his ass, and we howl. But Kavanagh's a mystery. He's always in trouble, but he's always smiling. And he has the widest smile you've ever seen. Rags always calls him FDR, because he says they have the same smile. He's an amazing character. He gets pinned, he laughs. He gets knocked down, he gets up and laughs. His loincloth slips, he giggles. McCann belts him for no apparent reason and he's laughing as he tells us about it. He bows and chants the Zen meditation, and there's a broad grin on his face. And he doesn't just laugh with his mouth. He laughs with his whole body. It's like he accepts whatever comes his way, good and bad alike. And this gives him a special kind of freedom, the freedom to always move ahead, always leaving room for the good things. "Kavanagh's always gonna survive the hard times," Blackie once said. "He's one helluva laugher."

•   •   •   •   •

We look like a scrawny lot for sumos. We're eating a lot more, but the running is keeping the weight off. Except for Oberstein. The chubby cherub is starting to look like the ballooning Buddha. He's really packing on the beef. Today, before wrestling, Brother McCann teaches us about Buddhism and the Eightfold Path. He says it will help us to become better sumos. The first step of the Eightfold Path is the "right knowledge" of existence. When we are all dressed in our loincloths, he calls us to the tumbling mats and lectures us on right knowledge. He reads from a paperback entitled *Zen and*

Mind over Matter, which he keeps tucked in his loincloth when he is not reading from it.

"Attention, all sumos. All sumos, attention. Today, sumos, we will learn a Japanese version of Zen, which teaches that the mind is kept imprisoned in the lower region of the abdomen and must be freed, since such imprisonment prevents the mind from operating anywhere else." He reads, "'The power generated by abdominal centralization ...' This power will permit a sumo to push another over the circle's rope without touching him. Pay close attention, sumos, to the following: 'The runaway mind must be stabilized and unified.' What are the key words here, sumos?"

"Stabilized and unified, *Yokozuna*."

"Excellent, sumos, excellent. 'The runaway mind must not be localized, but permitted to fill the whole body. Allowed to flow throughout the totality of your whole being.' Listen carefully, sumos..." McCann's face becomes very intense, and his voice drops to a whisper. "This is the great sumo secret. The *power pack*, sumos. The mind, in accordance with its nature, must be free to exercise its functions ... unhindered, uninhibited."

"The power pack?" Murphy says.

"Quiet, Murphys-san. It will meet your opponent as he moves about trying to strike you down. When your hands are needed, they are there for the mind. So too with the legs. When ordinary thoughts are quiet enough, the higher mental center receives grace. God's grace. When energies are balanced through meditation, they produce an intelligent awareness that is located in the belly. Where attention and breath meet. Where, sumos?"

"Where attention and breath meet, *Yokozuna*."

"It is the *power pack*, the place where energy is transformed." McCann repeats the words again, and then tells us to assume the lotus position and meditate on the message.

"Oh no, not the lotus position," Oberstein says.

After five minutes or so, he orders us to stand and resumes his lecture. "The mind, sumos, must be left to itself, utterly free to move according to its own nature. This type of mental freedom, sumos, is spiritual training, religious training, *ecumenical* training. The Holy Father's wish. Like the spiritual exercises of St. Ignatius Loyola. Properly trained, a Zen master can skilfully neutralize sword attacks with a fan. That's right, sumos, a fan. No matter what technique a warrior or swordsman uses. And some of you young sumos may be called upon one day to fight a swordsman with only a fan."

Oberstein looks at me and turns white.

"Nothing, *nothing*, can put honor right as the thrust or cut of a sword. During the Tokugawa Period, *rikishi*," he joins his hands in prayer and bows when he says this word, "sumo wrestlers were regarded as being of sufficient social status for permission to wear the *daisho*, a combination of long and short swords, normally reserved for warriors. Next week, sumos, we shall look at the art of swordsmanship known as *iaido*, the way of the sword. Iaido is a mental discipline, sumos. Also, sumos, it is based on the proficient use of the traditional Japanese sword. Iaido is an art that contrasts the idea of 'life' with 'life worth living.' Next week, sumos, you will all learn the formal etiquette of iaido, the ten basic steps. And you will learn also the character of the sword itself. The choice of sword, proper costume for iaido and all other essentials."

"Iaido voodoo," Bug whispers.

"Now the first step in freeing the mind, sumos, is meditation and concentration in the still posture known as *zazen*, perfect for abdominal breathing. What is the posture known as, sumos?"

"*Zazen, Yokozuna.*"

"Excellent! All sumos must now learn the art of *haragei*." He tells us to take the lotus position again on the mats and practice our abdominal breathing. He takes a ski pole from the equipment rack, calls it a *ski-o-saku* and walks around shouting orders on breathing technique and whacking wrestlers on the back and shoulders with the ski pole if they are not breathing properly.

"We Westerners are soft, we do not train our athletes properly," he yells after belting O'Rourke. "Do not swell your chest out with pride, O'Rourkes-san. That is the wrong way, that is the Western way. Be a Roman of the Asian persuasion. Breathe from your belly. Your soul is in your stomach, sumos. Remember that. Your stomach. Where attention and breath meet. The power pack. Repeat that."

"The power pack, *Yokozuna*."

He allows us to meditate a while longer, then yells for every sumo to halt his breathing and pay attention to a demonstration of how tremendous power can be generated by freeing the mind from the lower regions of the abdomen. He orders Kavanagh to stand up and prepare to give him a stiff karate kick in the stomach at the sound of the whistle. It is the only time Kavanagh doesn't laugh. He doesn't even grin. The last thing in this world Kavanagh wants to do is kick McCann in the gut. McCann tells him he must breathe deeply and concentrate, preparing to kick him with all his might.

"Aim for the belly button, Kavanaghs-san," McCann says.

"But, Brother . . ." Kavanagh stammers, stroking his skinny arms and legs, which are covered with a light blond down.

"The belly button!" McCann shouts, and crouches with his legs slightly bent and his hands resting on his knees. There is a terrible strain on McCann's reddish purple face. The veins in his neck are popping. He looks like he's going to use the toilet. "Almost ready, Kavanaghs. Steady now. Pay attention, sumos. This is the art of *haragei*. No more swelling chests. Sumos must develop the bellies and the tremendous power needed to compete. At the sound of the whistle, Kavanaghs will kick his hardest at my belly button, and I will heave my abdomen forward with all my might, hurling him backward and to the ground. Ready, Kavanaghs-san? Pay attention, sumos."

McCann steadies himself, breathes madly for a few seconds, puts the whistle in his mouth and blows. Kavanagh leaps into the air and sends his bony right foot smashing into McCann's huge belly. There is a deafening ripping sound. McCann screams in agony and falls flat on his back. Kavanagh crashes on top of him, jumps up and hops around the gymnasium on one foot. McCann spits and coughs and gurgles. He is in extreme pain. He rolls on his stomach and gasps, drooling and appearing to be about to throw up. We all think Kavanagh, who is crawling back to join us on the mats, is a goner.

"Sayonara, Kavanaghs-san," Bug whispers.

After several minutes of gurgling and snorting, McCann pushes himself to his knees. He gasps and stutters Kavanagh's name. "K-K-Kav-Kavanaghs..." Kavanagh races to him and hovers over him. We can see the fear in his eyes. "Too . . . too high, Kavanaghs. Too close to chest . . . Missed . . . Missed the belly buttons . . ."

Kavanagh apologizes and asks if he should try the kick again.

"No!" McCann can only whimper. He is still in tremendous pain. "Tomorrow . . . next class . . ." He stands, dazed, stares at the ceiling for a full minute and says, "Lockers, sumos . . . Over . . . Class is over . . . today."

Everyone heads to the lockers at once. En route, we laugh about Kavanagh's kamikaze kick. With a disgusted huff, McCann hobbles off. Still hacking and spitting, he waves to Ryan and Oberstein and me to roll up the mats.

As McCann disappears through the door, Oberstein points to the pale brown spots on the backside of his loincloth.

"He shit himself," Oberstein says, when McCann is safely out of sight.

"I think he only farted. It was a giant fart," Ryan says.

"No way! Didn't you see the brown spots on his diapers?" Oberstein says. "He shit himself."

•   •   •   •   •

We're only back in class a few minutes when Brother McMurtry pounds on the door. It's clear from his sour expression that we're not in for a surprise wingding. He walks the aisles silently for a minute before removing his steel-rimmed glasses and biting the tip of an arm.

"The culprits will be exposed. It's just a matter of time. You understand that, do you not, Mr. Ryan?"

"Yes, Brother." The gap between Ryan's front teeth seems wider.

McMurtry asks me if I understand.

"Yes, Brother," I say. I want to tell Ryan to stop biting his nails.

"Mr. Kelly?"

"Yes, Brother," Kelly says.

"We accept, Mr. Ryan, that you fell asleep on the toilet and were missing from your bed for a period of time. What happened to you can happen to anyone. We all get tired. We all need sleep. Isn't that right, Brother McCann?"

"That is correct, Brother McMurtry."

I'm starting to feel weak.

"We are not accusing you of anything, Mr. Ryan. Every boy is innocent until proven guilty. Now, what do you know of the wine missing from the sacristy?"

"Nothing, Brother." Ryan coughs and keeps rubbing his sweaty palms on his knees, which he always does when he's nervous. He looks as guilty as sin.

"Nothing?"

"Honest to God, Brother. First I heard of it was the time you mentioned it in class."

"There has been no talk of it among the boys? Not a hint of it?"

"No, Brother."

"No talk of boys drinking stolen wine on the weekend?" McCann interjects.

"No, Brother. Honest." Ryan's really nervous. His baby face is getting paler by the minute.

I cough to try to break the tension. They look at me.

"First I ever heard of it is when you mentioned it in class, Brother." I stare at McMurtry's swollen forehead.

They are silent. Then McCann turns to me and says slowly, "Mr. Carmichael, would you place your hand on the Holy Bible and swear to it?"

I'm so scared I'd swear to anything. "Yes, Brother."

"By all the saints? Would you swear by all the saints?"

"Yes, Brother."

"And you, Mr. Ryan? Would you swear by all the saints?"

"Yes, Brother."

They seem to believe us. Ryan sits silently. I can see the sweat on his forehead. He's really frightened, and the tears are beginning to come into his eyes. I'm worried that he might crack, so I invent a story about how I hate alcohol because my sister told me that it is the devil's poison and that she saw my father and Uncle Will Carmichael get so drunk one night they nearly burned the house down. I tell the story so quickly and with such speed that I almost believe it myself.

Ryan stares at me. He believes every word. Brother McMurtry seems to believe me too, but there is doubt in McCann's eyes.

"It is surely demonic, a tool of the devil," Brother McMurtry agrees.

McCann asks if we've ever seen any of the altar boys taking a sip of wine, from the bottle or from the cruets when they are filled up for Mass. We both say no.

Brother McMurtry scans the class.

"Does anyone have anything to say?"

Silence.

Blackie and Oberstein and Murphy have been staring straight ahead the whole time.

"Now, before you leave, I want you boys to promise me that if you hear a word about drinking you will report it to me or Brother McCann right away. The minute you hear it, is that clear?"

"Yes, Brother," we all say in unison.

"I want you to promise me, Mr. Carmichael. Do you promise?"

"I promise."

"Mr. Ryan?"

"I promise, Brother," Ryan says.

"Mr. Spencer, Mr. Kavanagh, Mr. Brookes? Do you promise?"

"Yes, Brother."

McMurtry looks at his watch. Class is almost over.

"Very well, you may go."

As we leave, he passes each boy a holy card of the Sacred Heart. It's a picture of Jesus standing on a globe. He has long hair, and there's a perfect gold circle around his head. From his exposed burning heart, rays of light pour out. In the background is the moon, and a million stars.

"Say the prayer on the back of the card every night when you go to bed. Say a special prayer that we find the wine culprits."

"Yes, Brother," we say as we leave. Our heads are bowed as we walk away. And we are thinking the same thing. How much longer can we hold out? I can feel the pressure. And I know that Ryan is feeling it too.

Daydreaming in study hall that night, waiting for the altar

bells for rosary and Benediction, I think about the wine stealing. Blackie and Oberstein are right. It hasn't been a bad week.
At least, not as bad as we expected. There was only one close
call, when Rags asked Blackie and Ryan why they were doing
laps around the soccer field and running around the grounds
so much. Ryan shot back that they were getting in shape for
the hockey season, and Rags laughed and said they'd be in better shape than Gordie Howe. That's always best when you're in
a jam like that. The simplest answer is always the best. The
brothers still have no idea about the wine stealing, and all we
have to do is stick to Blackie's advice and play dumb. Only the
Klub members know anything about our wine raids. A Klub
member would never squeal. If we just continue to play dumb,
they'll have to give up questioning us eventually. But I'm really
worried about Ryan. He may crack. He's so nervous. Out of
nowhere, Blackie's words come back to me: "Ryan's a lot
tougher than all of us." I think of the terrible strapping he got,
and only days later he was on his first wine raid. And as the
buzzer sounds for chapel, I come to the horrible realization
that I might crack. If it comes down to taking a beating or
spilling the beans, I don't think I'll be as brave as Ryan.

•   •   •   •   •

Lights out takes place at nine-thirty. By ten o'clock we're
usually all asleep. Oberstein and I plan to stay awake as long
as necessary tonight to find out who the night walker is.
Oberstein thinks it's one of the older boys, stealing from our
lockers. We know for certain it isn't Spook, the night watchman. He's always asleep.

I am starting to drift as I squint at my Mickey around midnight, when I hear the footsteps. It isn't one of the older boys.
The steps are heavier than a boy's. This is the sound of soft
shoes, squeaking now and then along the hardwood floor. A

boy would be barefoot, his steps lighter. I tense up, straining with all my might to listen. The sound of the footsteps is heavy and measured, stopping, starting, stopping. The night walker moves slowly and confidently, a few heavy, squeaking steps, then stopping to drink in the silence. The walker has to be one of the brothers. But which one? I pray Oberstein is still awake. I want so much to talk to him, to compare notes later on, when the night walker has gone.

The footsteps start again, five even squeaks that stop on my side of the wooden lockers stretching the length of the dorm. I pull the bedsheets up to my chin, snap my eyes shut and pretend to be fast asleep as I wait to count the night walker's squeaky steps again. After what seems like forever, the heavy steps pause by my bed. I think of the death camps and Oberstein's grandfather. Auschwitz and the Nazis. Late at night. A guard's creaking steps patrolling the sleeping quarters. I clench my teeth and count: one ... two ... three ... four ... Stop. . . five ... six ... seven ... Stop ... eight ... nine ... Eighteen footsteps, followed by a deadening silence. I reckon about three to four steps per bunk, which means the night walker has stopped about five bunks away, at Nowlan's bed. Nowlan has the top bunk, but the bottom one is empty. Nowlan is a tiny boy with a small pointed face. He has dark brown eyes, dreamy-looking eyes that make him look innocent and sad.

I turn ever so slowly onto my side, careful not to make my mattress squeak. Ever so slowly, I lean my head out over the side of my bunk, but all I can see is the night-light at the far end of the dorm, as usual, blinking madly off and on. There is a deep silence for a while, and I hear a bedspring squeaking and a soft, sweet moaning down Nowlan's way, as if he is sighing in his dreams. I freeze. Someone snores gently on the opposite side of the dorm. Someone else tosses quickly.

Then, silence again, before the sweet sighing gets louder and quicker, becoming a weak moan, turning into what sounds like a strange cry. Followed by long silence before the sound of the squeaking footsteps starts up once more, moving in my direction. As he walks, his soutane whispers. I freeze again and hold my breath until he passes. When I am sure the fading steps are far enough away, I lean out over my bunk to see a black soutane disappear through the doorway. I snap back into my bed instantly, as if I've been burned. And wait a long time. To be sure the footsteps will not return. Before I get out of my bunk and tiptoe to Oberstein, who's sound asleep.

"Obee," I whisper.

When he doesn't answer, I shake him.

"Oberstein, Oberstein," I say. "He was here. The night walker was here. Did you see him?"

"'And Isaac's mother said go . . .'" Oberstein mumbles in his sleep. "'Go into the fields . . . take your brother . . .'"

"Y'wake, Oberstein?" I say, shaking him.

"Tryna sleep. What the hellya doin'?"

"Whaddaya mean, what the hell am I doing? We had a plan. Did you see the night walker?"

"McCann? Is it McCann?" he asks.

"Dunno," I say. "He stopped by Nowlan's bed again. Only Nowlan's."

Oberstein sits up in his bunk and rubs his eyes. He reaches for his norph glasses, which he keeps in his sneakers at the foot of his bed, and puts them on.

"I thought as much. Does anyone else know? Did you tell Blackie?"

"No. Nobody else knows."

"You'd better get back to bed," Oberstein says, "in case he comes back. We'll talk to Blackie in the morning."

The next morning at breakfast we tell Blackie what happened, and he says he isn't surprised there's a night walker. And he isn't surprised that he stopped at Nowlan's bed either. He said he knew as much. "Nowlan's goin' to the infirmary a lot. Always sick. No, not sick, *sad*."

"But if Nowlan isn't sick, if he's just sad, why's he go to the infirmary all the time? Does he get the spells?" I ask.

"Nowlan's always sad," Oberstein says. "That's a kind of sickness, always being sad."

"It's deep . . . deep inside him," Blackie says. "It's soulful, a different kind of sickness, the sadness sickness."

"He's come twice now. First Friday of the month," I say. "Only First Fridays, always around midnight. I know him by his footsteps. He stays around ten or fifteen minutes, no longer. I counted his footsteps. And the seconds. It's creepy."

"You best be still. Don't count nuthin' next time," Blackie says. "And keep your eyes shut. Ain't a good idea to be awake when the angel of death passes by."

Winter 1960

9

IT IS LATE NOVEMBER. And freezing cold. Frost is on the ground. It's beginning to look like winter. Light snow is falling on the naked trees. Long, dark winter days are ahead. Soon the ground will be completely white, and the gray stone buildings will be painted with thick swirls of white. There will be snow on the blinking Celtic cross high above the Mount, and all the windows will be frosted over.

The sky seems to be bleak and gray all the time now. And some of the fading grass is almost the color of the buildings' gray stone. The yard is icy, and every pothole has frozen over. Running, especially night running, will be more dangerous with snow on the ground. This time of year is always hard. The next few weeks there will be extra study hall in preparation for exams. There will be an exam in every subject, and they will be long and hard. Even Oberstein doesn't like them. It'll be especially hard for Rowsell and O'Grady. They'll have that daydreamy look for weeks. The dormitory will be freezing most of the time. It will still be dark when we get up and wash and dress for chapel. And even the chapel and the classrooms will be cold. Looking forward to Christmas is the only thing that saves us all from getting the spells.

• • • • •

Sumos on the soccer field. Sumos on the soccer field in ten minutes ... Ten minutes ... Sumos on the soccer field.

McCann has chosen a few sumos to practice Japanese calligraphy. They made a sign for the dedication of a Shinto shrine at the far end of the soccer field. All week, Father Cross has been doing *kado*, the art of flower arrangement. It's the day of the dedication, so we dress in full sumo attire and march single file to the field. When we arrive, McCann bows several times and invites us all to sit on wooden benches in front of the Shinto shrine. It's so cold there's even frost on the benches. Murphy's teeth are chattering as we sit on the cold hard benches in our flimsy outfits, compliments of a Tokyo friend of McCann's brother.

"Might as well be in our PJs. It's enough to freeze the balls off a brass monkey," Murphy says.

Kamikaze Kavanagh is rubbing his hands and blowing on them like a maniac. The frozen grass on the field looks like silver hair.

The shrine consists of a raised platform constructed with clay and sand, onto which a fifteen-foot circle is marked out using half-buried bales of hay. Like the *dohyo* in the gymnasium, only that's marked out with masking tape. Suspended above the wrestling ring is a wooden structure that resembles the roof of a Shinto shrine. Attached to the roof is the huge Japanese sign made by the sumo calligraphers. Nobody seems to know the meaning of the words on the sign. A whisper ripples along the benches. Bug says it means How's your left nut?

When we are all seated, the calligraphers serve us tea, which is ice cold. Eventually, a procession of sumos comes out and stands beneath the big sign. The leading figure is Father Cross, who periodically covers his partly painted white face with a huge fan. Today, his acne seems a bit worse, even though a big hat shades his face. He is dressed in a spectacular brown ceremonial outfit, which he has spent weeks making. Blackie had Cross tell McCann about his sewing skills in the hope that it might gain him access to the sewing room. And it worked. McCann gave Cross his own key.

"You make the costumes of the world, Soup," Blackie says, watching Father Cross's face turn a deeper shade of red. "Batman, Superman, Captain Marvel—you make 'em all."

We all nod in agreement, because it's the God's truth. Last week we saw a Zorro movie, and a day later Cross was tearing around the Mount wearing a Zorro costume that looked like it had been stolen from the movie set. He's amazing. Nobody else could've painted the great big bat on the wall inside the Bat Cave and the beautiful golden lion over the trophy case. We never know where he gets all the materials for his costumes. Some of it comes from the sewing room, but not much. The rest is a mystery. A fashion designer with unlimited supplies would never match Father Cross's work. He can work magic with a sheet off a bed or an old discarded curtain.

Blackie says the marathoners can now look forward to some decent running gear. We know Cross can make any costume in the world, and in jig's time. Because he finally has some decent supplies to work with, this costume is the best he's ever made. It has big wide pant legs and a huge round purple hat. "Father Cross looks very impressive," Murphy says. Bug tells us he's a crackerjack, and he should catch the next flight to Tokyo.

Cross is in complete control of the shrine dedication. He removes his hat, and his face is extremely stern looking. "I've never seen Cross look so cross," Oberstein whispers. He

chops his hands and directs his assistants, who wear colorful attire with richly embroidered silk aprons. They bow like
crazy to each other, and the ceremony begins. It's all very
elaborate, with cups and vases that have fine black branches
and richly colored flowers painted on them. A small group
of sumos dressed in black outfits with silver yin and yang
signs on their backs moves toward Father Cross, forming
a circle around him. He lights the incense in the thurible
and swings it around so that there's smoke everywhere. The
smell is sweet. As he passes the thurible to Crosbie, a coal
falls out. Father Cross stamps on it, and a million sparks fly
into the sky. A cheer goes up from the benches. Brother
McCann smiles. He thinks it's part of the ceremony. Large
snowflakes drop gently from the sky as the sumos sword
dance about, waving their arms gracefully and singing ever
so slowly: "*Eyo! Eyo! Eyo!*"

We're all enraptured watching the performers. It's all so
amazing to see, especially Father Cross, who seems like a
totally different person—elegant but severe, almost frighten-
ing. Suddenly, we're mesmerized by a series of elaborate
flowing gestures he makes with his arms. Out of nowhere,
McCann appears in front of us, taps Oberstein on the shoulder with his fan and gestures for him to follow. Oberstein
nudges his way slowly through drawn-in knees. They disappear behind the raised platform and re-enter from the
opposite side just as the dancers finish their sword dance.
McCann makes a loud speech in Japanese that nobody
understands: "*Untano utusini doi jinchi Oberstein-san . . .
Unakano . . .*" He bows and points to Oberstein, and urges him
to speak in Japanese. Oberstein speaks Japanese like a Spanish
cow, but he fakes it, speaking in pig Japanese for almost a full
minute. We politely listen as if we understand every word.
Rowsell nods his head the whole speech. When he's finished,

McCann claps softly and motions for us to join in. We all clap halfheartedly as Oberstein bows, rolls his eyes and returns to his seat.

McCann then motions to Father Cross to light the incense in front of the shrine as he moves to the center and makes several slow bows. He instructs us to stand and do the same. Then he shouts madly in Japanese for a few seconds, bows sluggishly several times, turns to us and says, "Sayonara." The shrine dedication is over. Father Cross and his sword dancers lead the assembly single file to the gymnasium.

"What the fuck was that all about?" Murphy asks on the way back.

"Yoko Loco's losin' his mind," Blackie says.

"What's left of it," Oberstein says. As we walk, he and Blackie linger behind, chatting about maps in the library and something about the Argentia ferry. I slow my pace, but Oberstein puts his hand over his mouth and I can't make out what he's saying.

"Jesus, it's cold," Ryan says. "Don't think I'll ever warm up again."

"Put your hands down by your nuts," Bug shrills. "That's what they all did in Scott's *Voyage to the Antarctic*."

"I don't remember reading that," Oberstein says.

"So get your eyeballs checked," Bug growls.

"My eyes are fine," Oberstein says.

"They should of had Clare and Tokyo Rose in that ceremony," Bug says. "It was missing the female touch. Clare and Tokyo Rose would of added a lot."

Bug has taken to calling Clare's friend, Rose MacNeil, Tokyo Rose, because she's collecting mission stamps for Father McCann's parish. It's a name he got from a movie we saw. Clare is at the Mount for a month, part-time. She and Tokyo Rose have been sent over to work at the bakery. She came a few days ago. The news was all over the Mount in two minutes. I heard about it from O'Connor, who was tearing around the building with a couple of criers, screaming out at the top of their lungs: "St. Martha's girls in the bakery. Martha's girls in the bakery." Clare really likes Bug. But she's worried that he's losing his faith because he has so many doubts. Brother McMurtry has given her permission to give Bug extra catechism lessons. She says the same thing about him that Blackie says. Bug has a handicap, so we have to be extra kind to him.

Clare and Tokyo Rose are going to become nuns. Silver crosses hang from silver chains around their necks, gifts from the Mother Superior. They have been told they have to work in the bakery as part of their obedience training. Tokyo Rose is tiny. She's only slightly taller than Bug, who's three foot nothing. She's thick-waisted, with cropped black hair. And she has very round cheeks and is always silent. Too silent. And what's really weird for someone who doesn't talk, is that her lower lip always quivers slightly. And she looks serious all the time, so serious that when you look at her, you want to turn away. Bug often says if she wasn't so serious and flat-chested he'd put the make on her. Which makes us roar.

"Let's pick up the speed," Bug says. "If we get back before next class, Clare and Tokyo Rose might have a few toutons or some hardtack for us."

Clare is always giving us stuff. She sneaks us toutons and cookies, mostly, and sometimes a full loaf. And she gives us holy pictures and prayer cards and rosaries, which Bug always chucks in the garbage when she's out of sight. He calls it voodoo. But when Clare gives it to him, he smiles and thanks her and says he'll carry it around with him forever.

She and Rose are always asking us about saying our prayers and memorizing our catechism, which really gets to me, but I do it for Clare. I'd do anything for Clare, I love her so much. I'd even try to get Bug to pray for her. But I think Bug really is losing his religion. He told Oberstein the other day that McCann is wrong to tell us we're going to hell for masturbating. "You're right, Oberstein," he said. "It'd make more sense to go to hell for *not* snapping the lizard. It's only natural to get a bone-on. And what's a guy spoze to do, stare at it? No, McCann's wrong, and I aim to tell him one of these days."

The other day Father Cross tried to get Bug to say a novena before exams, and he got really angry. "I don't get on your case about praying, so why do you get on mine about *not* praying?" he snarled.

"Because we all need God in our life," Father Cross said.

"Oh, fuck west, Cross," Bug said. "I'm an *atheist* and you're a *beaut.*"

And that was it. Father Cross never bothered him again about religion.

Back at the bakery, Clare gives us all a few toutons, which we devour like we are starving to death. Two older boys, Edward Harvey and Evan Cowan, are working with Clare and Rose at the bakery. They do all the lifting and heavy stuff, like cleaning the big mixers. Evan's nickname is Guns because he's King of the Hop-Along Cowboys and wears Cross's big black Hop-Along Cassidy hat. All he's gotta do is toss his head back or tip that big black cowboy hat, and you're in a Western movie. You should see him when he mounts up and lashes his rump, tugging the invisible reins as he races around the building. He's just like Rory Calhoun. Every kid in sight mounts up and follows. Once I watched a posse of about fifty chasing after him, slapping their rumps as they rounded the big stone buildings in full gallop, stampeding toward the Rio Grande. There's only one thing more thrilling than watching, and that's being one of the riders trying to keep up with the golden palomino of the King of the Hop-Along Cowboys. And he has the best toy gun collection at the Mount.

The four of them get along really well. Whenever I go to the bakery for a loaf, they're usually horsing around or chatting up a storm. They love poking fun at each other and cracking jokes. Even Rose, who is so serious, horses around sometimes. I think Evan flirts with Clare and Rose. Once I heard him ask Clare if she would like to go berry-picking up near Major's Path. Another time, I arrived at the bakery unexpectedly and they were alone there, behind the big tray racks. They had their arms around each other, and Evan was whispering something to her. I was startled and slipped away. Later on, I made up my mind that it was a beautiful thing to see. Clare with her thick blond hair in the arms of the tall and handsome King of the Hop-Along Cowboys. And I was happy for her, happy they'd found a time and a place to be alone together. And I hoped she would not become a nun but instead would run away with Evan. Mount up and ride off into the sunset, just like in the movies.

It's so nice to get to see Clare every day. Sometimes we sit at the long stainless steel table in the bakery, eating fresh bread and talking about baseball. She loves Ted Williams. "Home run kings will come and go," she says, "but Ted Williams will be remembered as the greatest hitter who ever lived." Or we talk about when we were a family, living together in Kilbride, just outside St. John's. If the weather's nice, she takes a break, and we grab some toutons and walk around the grounds and chat or go to her room, which is just a cubbyhole with a bed and a dresser over in the cook's quarters. We have a big old chat about Mom and Dad. She was almost twelve when they died, so she remembers a lot about the Kilbride days, as she calls them. I've learned a lot about my Mom and Dad from her. She said the memory that hurts her most is the day after Mom and

Dad died. A social worker took her down to Water Street to the Big Six to buy a dress for Mom and a suit for Dad, and she didn't know their sizes. She started to cry, and the social worker told her to pick out the colors, he'd find out the sizes. Clare says it's very important to hold on to all your memories, even sad and secondhand ones, because memories can be more real than things you see and touch. I believe that. And I believe it's true of dreams as well. I told her about my vision, and she smiled and said it was probably fatigue. "You've been through a lot," she said. "It's probably taken a toll on you."

Clare is so glad we're together for a while, because it's her last chance to tell me things about Mom and Dad. In the winter she's entering the convent at Corpus Christi, and I won't be able to see her for a very long time. She's becoming a postulant, and then she'll get to be a nun. On weekends we often walk to Water Street, where all the stores are. Clare gets a few dollars salary for working in the bakery, and she's allowed to keep some of it to spend. We go to Marty's and have a big feed of fish and chips and gravy. They have really great french fries, always chunky and golden. Clare has promised to buy me a school jacket when she saves enough money. Last weekend, after we ate at Marty's, we went to the Sport Store, which has tons of sports stuff, and there was a beautiful black baseball glove there with my favorite player's name, Phil Rizzuto, written in silver inside. I was gonna ask her for the glove, but I knew it would be more expensive than the jacket. Clare says that if I dream hard enough I might find it one morning under my pillow. "Dreams have a way of coming true," she says. "I believe in miracles. And *visions*," she adds. I love Clare. I really, really love her.

When we finish the toutons, Bug asks for more. I poke him, as Evan hollers, "Don't be so greedy, Bradbury."

Clare tells him too many will spoil his lunch.

"Pistil, I'm underweight, and I got a hole in my heart," Bug says. "And I wanna be a champion sumo, so I gotta eat as much as I can."

"Have you mastered the seventy sumo moves yet, Brendan?" Clare asks.

"Pushing, slapping, hoisting, tripping, throwing, pinning . . . 'I can do all things through Christ, who strengthens me,'" Bug says, as he turns and rolls his eyes. "I'd like to grapple with Tokyo Rose in the ring," he whispers. "Even though she's flat as a board."

Clare smiles and slips him two more toutons, which he gobbles up in jig's time. Clare gets such a kick outta Bug. I think she really likes him a lot because of his handicap. She sees him as one of the poor. We all do, I guess. And in his own way, he really is very loveable.

∙   ∙   ∙   ∙   ∙

I saw Evan and Clare touching again today. When I arrived at the bakery, the wooden doors were swung open. I stopped before entering and watched her oiling a row of freshly baked loaves with a paintbrush. She was whistling away, which she always does when she works, and brushing the loaves of bread, when Evan appeared out of nowhere. I thought she was alone, but he must've been helping another senior, Egbert Wall, dump the big bags of flour into the mixer at the far end of the bakery. He towered over her and smiled. Then he leaned into her and slipped his arm around her waist. She shoved it away, but he replaced it. She looked around shyly but did not move his arm.

Later, while I was tearing into a fresh loaf, I asked her what it meant to be a bride of Christ, an expression she uses when talking about her vocation to become a nun.

"It means you're married to Jesus, and as His spouse you commit yourself to a lifetime of simplicity, celibacy, and service to the poor."

"What's the difference between a bride of Christ and a bride of Evan?" I teased.

She was startled, and looked at me like I'd just torn her dress off and she was standing there naked. She stopped brushing the loaves of bread.

"A bride of Evan would mean a different commitment," she said. "It would mean a vocation to the married life. Children. Motherhood. Raising a family. A very different commitment."

"Sex," I said.

She began brushing a loaf.

"Is it a tough choice?" I asked.

"Not really," she laughed. "When you have a vocation, you are called. That's what the word means. *Vocare*. From the Latin. 'To be called'. If Jesus calls you, you hear his voice. You have no choice. Jesus said, 'I know mine and mine know me ...'"

I knew what she was talking about. Vocations was once the subject of Monologues and Dialogues. I told Oberstein after the class that I was worried I might get called. "Don't worry," he said. "Nobody would ever call you."

"Have you heard Jesus call?" I asked her.

"Yes. I think so." She stopped brushing.

"Think so?" I laughed.

"I know so," she said firmly.

I could see I had upset her, so I switched the conversation to baseball. "The Braves are playing next weekend. Warren Spahn's pitching."

"Spahn and Sain and pray for rain," she laughed and was silent.

"The Rex Sox traded Pete Runnels last night," I said, knowing it wasn't true but wanting to keep her mind off religion.

"You're cracked," she said. "Sister Kevin told me he's batting .320."

"Shows you how much I know," I said.

"But the Tigers traded Harvey Kuenn to Cleveland for Rocky Colavito."

"I know less about baseball than I do about religion," I said.

"Close your eyes," she said. Which means there is a surprise in store. "Imagine a picture of something you'd really like for your birthday." As I'm imagining the colors green and white, the colors of the Mount Kildare Lions, she tells me she has permission to take me to town. My birthday is in a few days, and she has saved enough money from working at the bakery to let me buy something at the Sport Store.

"You can have whatever you like," she says, "whatever you want in the store."

I throw my arms around her. "You're kidding," I say. I really need a pair of runners for the marathon, but my heart is set on something special. "Can I have a jacket? A school jacket? A Mount Kildare green-and-white jacket?"

I love school jackets. On weekends, when we go to town, I stare a lot at the blue and gold of St. Bon's, the green and gold of St. Pat's and the beautiful navy-blue and red of Prince of Wales. Almost everyone seems to have school jackets except for the boys at the Mount.

"Of course you can have a school jacket," Clare says.

On Saturday we go to the Sport Store on Water Street. The store owner, a tall, thin man with a long, wrinkled face and a neat moustache that looks penciled on, leads us to the back of the store, where there are racks of school jackets. He is wearing a blue blazer with the Newfoundland coat of arms on the breast pocket. He carries a beautiful pair of white runners, which makes me think of Shorty Richardson.

"There is every school jacket and uniform in Newfoundland on these racks," he says proudly, sliding a hand along a double row of coats. "Whatcha looking for?"

"A Mount Kildare jacket," Clare says.

"Mount Kildare? The orphanage ..." he says. "What colors might they be now?"

"Green and white," I say.

"Green and white," he repeats. "Don't think we've ever carried those." He turns to his stocky assistant. "Melvin, we ever carried green-and-white jackets?"

"Nope, never," Melvin says.

"Then you don't have every school jacket in Newfoundland," Clare says sarcastically.

The stocky clerk turns his back to us. The owner looks at the floor, toys with an empty coat hanger and pushes several coats along the rod.

"Would you be interested in another jacket?" he asks.

Clare looks at me, and the tears start to come.

"I want a Mount Kildare jacket," I say, " I want a green-and-white one." And for some reason, the thought of getting caught for stealing the wine enters my head and I cry harder.

"Shhh. There are lots of other nice jackets," Clare says. "Lots of other nice colors." She bends down and whispers that they don't make Mount Kildare jackets and that the red-and-white one is close to green-and-white. She urges me to try one on. Reluctantly, I do so.

"That's perfect," she says, "a perfect fit. And it will remind you of Christmas."

"That's a Bishop's College jacket," the owner says.

"Those are Christmas colors," Clare says, ignoring him. She tells me that if I like the jacket I can have it, and she will sew my Lions baseball crest on the sleeve. That makes me feel good, so I thank her and ask if I can wear the jacket right away.

We look at the owner, who shrugs and says, "Sure, why not?"

Clare pays him and asks where the jackets are made.

"Montreal," he says.

"You should order Mount Kildare jackets," Clare says.

"They don't make green-and-white ones, ma'am," he says.

"If they use red-and-white fabric, they can use green-and-white fabric," Clare says.

The man shrugs and says nothing.

"It wouldn't hurt to have a few green-and-white jackets in stock, would it?"

"No, ma'am, I guess not," the owner says, looking at the floor.

"Then you should order some," Clare says.

Outside, I thank her again for my birthday gift. She passes me a tissue and tells me to wipe my face and blow my nose. As I do so, she watches and says, "I have numbered all your tears . . ." I ask her what she means, and she says it's from the Bible. Like Oberstein, she's always doing that, saying lines from the Bible and refusing to explain them. "You'll read about it when you get older," she says.

We walk along Water Street for a while, commenting on how nice the jacket is, and how good it will look with the baseball crest on the sleeve. Clare says it's a perfect fit, and it will keep me nice and warm during baseball playoffs next year. She tells me not to be upset that they didn't have green-and-white jackets. "At St. Martha's," she says, "they don't even have school colors. The girls wear white blouses and black skirts and saddle shoes."

I tell her I don't mind. But deep down, I do. It just doesn't seem right that a store would have jackets for every school in Newfoundland except Mount Kildare.

10

ONE OF THE THINGS I hate most is shunning. It's worse than the spells. Shunning can last for weeks. Or months. Once a boy was shunned for almost a year. Lately, since we've been on our guard about the wine stealing, it seems more cruel than ever. Brother Mansfield does it to Brookes one day when he catches Brookes wearing Whelan's sneakers. He marches all the junior dorms, including St. Dominic's, the five and six year olds, to the gymnasium and has us stand with our backs to the four walls. Brookes stands in the middle of the gym, looking at the floor. It's a sad sight. I feel awful for him. Brookes has that monkey face that always looks happy. But this day he looks really sad. Brother Mansfield walks over and stands next to him, sticking out his little potbelly. Brother Mansfield is very small, small and wiry, with a long crooked nose and a long chin. He has crooked gray eyebrows, like a child painted them on, and he gets a new haircut every few weeks. But no matter how often he cuts his hair, in jig's time it's a thatch of gray, spiralling in a thousand directions. Bug says he should get it mowed. His haircut makes his chin look longer. He wears a hearing aid, which he's forever tapping and rattling because it never seems to work.

He's always called for when two boys are caught fighting. He has a terrible reputation for being mean. His nickname is Moody Mansfield. You never know what mood he's gonna be in. He could just as easily give you an ice cream from the canteen as the tweaks. The tweaks is when he pinches you by the sideburns and pulls hard. It hurts so much the tears come to your eyes. You don't wanna get caught in Moody's line of fire. Every boy at the Mount does his best to avoid the snake. That's Moody's strap.

"I want every boy here to look at Mr. Brookes's sneakers." He orders Brookes to take them off and hold a sneaker up with each of his index fingers. "These sneakers are not Mr. Brookes's. They are Mr. Whelan's sneakers. Mr. Brookes has stolen them from Mr. Whelan's locker. That makes Mr. Brookes a thief. And thieves must be punished. Thievery will not be tolerated at Mount Kildare. You all know the ten commandments. Commandment eight: Thou shalt not steal. Thieves must be made an example of. We shall all participate in Mr. Brookes's punishment by shunning him. That is, by completely ignoring him. Every boy in this gymnasium will shun Mr. Brookes until the end of the month. This means, boys, that Mr. Brookes does not exist until that time. Until the end of the month he has become invisible." Brother Mansfield turns to the St. Dominic's boys, tapping his potbelly. "Do you all understand? When you see him, you must pretend he does not exist. If you see him in the cafeteria or coming down the hall or outside on the playground, you are to close your eyes and cover your ears until he goes away. Is that clear? This boy is a bad boy. He is being punished. We are punishing him for stealing. We are punishing him by not speaking to him and by not seeing him. That's what we call *shunning.*"

He turns to the older boys and raises his finger and continues to lecture. "When you shun a boy, if he comes near you, you ignore him. If a shunned boy, like Mr. Brookes, appears in your path in the cafeteria, say, walking along with his tray, do not veer away from him. Do not stop in front of him. Do not move away from him. Prove to him, prove to me ... most important, prove to your fellows and to yourselves that this shunned boy does not exist. Prove that he is invisible. Walk through him. That's correct, boys. Walk straight *through* him, as you would walk through thin air. The only thing real about a shunned boy should be the sound of his tray crashing to the floor. Or the sound of his body falling to the floor. You will not be punished for such behavior. Quite the contrary! Boys who shun properly will be rewarded. Boys who refuse to shun properly will be punished. You do not have a choice in this matter, boys. Shunning is very serious stuff. There is an expectation here. And you must measure up. For the good of all."

"Do you have to shun him even in chapel?" Bug's hand is a propeller.

"Certainly, Mr. Bradbury. Shunning takes place twenty-four hours a day. There are no exceptions. Shunning should take place *everywhere*, everywhere, especially in chapel. A thief is being punished. Where better to do justice than in the House of the Lord?"

Poor Brookes keeps staring at the floor, holding the sneakers until Brother Mansfield orders Whelan to come and retrieve them. Then he commands Brookes to stand by the exit as we pass by in single file.

"Do not look at him, boys," he shouts. "Ignore him. *He does not exist.* He is a very bad boy. A thief. And thieves must be punished."

As Wilson, who weighs twice as much as Brookes, approaches the exit, Brother Mansfield orders Brookes to step forward. Littlejohn walks into him, knocking him to the floor. Kavanagh, rather than step on Brookes, hops over him.

"Do not hop, Kavanagh. Walk on him. He does not exist. It is his business to get out of *your* way. Not the other way around.

Remember, he is being shunned. He does not exist." The next boy, O'Connor, walks on Brookes's leg as he squirms along the floor, moving out of the path of the steady stream of boys.

"Well done, O'Connor. That's the stuff. Extra canteen privileges for you. Carry on, boys. Do not look at him. *Shun him.* He does not exist until the end of the month. Until the end of the month, Mr. Brookes is invisible."

As I walk by, I sneak a glance. Brookes sits on the floor with his head on his raised knees, crying.

"That's a taste of what we're in for if they find out about the wine," Ryan whispers on the way out.

"Or the marathon," Murphy adds.

"Shuddup!" Blackie says.

Blackie gets really upset when anyone is shunned. So does Father Cross. Oberstein hates shunning. "By mercy and truth and fear of the Lord is iniquity purged," Oberstein says when anyone is shunned. Oberstein seems to have a Jewish saying for almost everything these days. Blackie has taken to calling him Rabbi. We learned in religion class the other day that it means "teacher." Oberstein has really started taking his Jewish roots seriously. He's reading all kinds of Jewish stuff. He's a library prefect, so he gets to order books occasionally. He ordered *The Young People's Jewish Encyclopedia,* and he keeps it under his bed and reads it all the time. He also has books about the Second World War, the Holocaust, Auschwitz and Dresden and Bergen-Belsen, the German concentration camps, which he reads a lot because his grandfather was at Auschwitz.

"Hitler murdered six million Jews," he reads from the big encyclopedia. "Just imagine—that's almost half of Canada. He tried to kill every one of us. He tried to kill us all." He looks downcast and sad as his silky hair falls in front of his eyes, which are hazy with the horror of history. And you feel sad just looking at him. He purses his lips, blinking a tear, the way he did the day when Brookes was shunned. He closes the big book and flops into a chair, twisting his arms tight around himself as if constricting into a knot. His chubby face is the soundboard of silence. After a long time he says, "They've booted us out of everywhere. We were booted out of Spain and Portugal in 1497. That's when Cabot discovered Newfoundland. Maybe we came here. We wound up wandering everywhere. That's why there's the expression Wandering Jew and Wandering Gypsy. The gypsies were booted out of everywhere too. Hitler killed off a lot of gypsies in his concentration camps too. Somehow we wound up in Germany in the 1700s and began speaking German instead of Hebrew. When we were thrown out of Germany, we were scattered all over Europe. We kept the German language. But we wrote it in Hebrew characters. It's neat. It's called transliteration. It gave us a new language. Yiddish, which is German written in Hebrew. That's so amazing." His face lights up, he is so proud of what his people have done.

And he's really taking prayer seriously. "The world exists for the sake of three things, and three things only," he says, "charity, study of Torah, and prayer." He says this matter-of-factly, the way you'd say the Mainline bus will take you to Victoria Park via Elizabeth Avenue and Water Street. And he's forever quoting from the Old Testament: "Whatsoever is lofty shall bow down before thee . . ." His favorite when he is angry: "The Lord shine His face upon you and be gracious to you. The Lord turn His face toward you and give you peace."

He prays like crazy, about everything. Before meals, before bed, before study hall. He has a Popsicle, he says a prayer. Different prayers for different occasions. Before eating, he quotes David, before a game of frozen tag, Jeremiah, before study hall, Isaiah or Job. He has prayers of thanks and prayers for good luck and bad. And before every night run he places his hands upon Blackie's head, pressing his afro ever so gently—like it's a soft sponge—and prays, "And now I'll speak as the Lord spoke out of the burning bush on Mount Sinai. Let my words enter your hearts. Give them wings, Lord, that they may fly."

In a weird way, Oberstein's prayers seem more meaningful, more real, than the hurried litanies that pass for prayers during Mass and rosary and Benediction at chapel. Something special happens when Oberstein prays. I don't know what it is. But we all feel it. Maybe his getting religious is wearing off on us.

We were at the Bat Cave last Saturday, and Blackie asked Oberstein to tell us a story, and Oberstein started talking about creation. It wasn't really a story. It was kinda dull. It was the Jewish idea of creation, which he'd just read about. He was really excited telling us about it.

"Since God is all—*everything*—and He is *everywhere*, omnipresent and omnipotent, as it says in our catechism, he had to create a space that didn't exist in order to make something different from Himself . . . A big, special, empty space! What the Book of Genesis calls *the void*. It's like clearing off your desk in between periods. To get ready for the next class."

Blackie looked at me and shrugged.

"It's simple," Oberstein continued, "like cutting a circle in a piece of paper and taking that white circle and cutting it into a million tiny pieces and dropping them back into the hole. Dontcha get it?"

Blackie slouched in his chair and yawned.

"Sounds like *Alice in Wonderland*," I said, having just finished the comic.

"It is!" Oberstein shouted. "It's like we learned in science about the stars. A star collapses in on itself. That's what God did. Only he blew back some of himself. What the Bible calls *light*, into the void."

"Come off it, Oberstein," I said. "We don't know for certain that's what happened."

"We don't know for certain that's what happened," he mimics sarcastically. He rolls his eyes mockingly and sneers. "Maybe it's not scientific, but what's amazing is that the Jewish rabbis thought all about this thousands of years ago. *Thousands of years*, Carmichael."

Blackie yawned and closed his eyes.

"It's so simple. An idiot could understand. God created the world by stepping back from himself and making a void and then pouring himself into the darkness.

I looked at Blackie, expecting a sarcastic comment, but he was asleep.

"I dunno, Oberstein," I said. "That sounds pretty crazy to me. It isn't like the questions and answers in our catechism. It's more like Rod Serling's *Twilight Zone.*"

He just laughed and said, "What can you expect from a Gentile?"

And he's taken to wearing a yarmulke. Father Cross made it for him out of black crepe. If he forgets to wear it, Bug always drawls, "Forget yer yam-ah-kah?" Once Oberstein lost it and paid a crier to announce a canteen reward if anyone found it. And it worked. Brother McCann calls it his beanie. "Take that beanie off in class, Oberstein," McCann says.

He's learning an awful lot about the Talmud. There's all kinds of stuff about it in the *Encyclopedia*. The Talmud has really big pages, and in a little square in the corner of the page is the original Talmud. There's an L-shaped margin, and all around this square are comments written by different people. Really smart Jewish guys. It's a really important book. It has been passed down through the ages and discussed to death. Oberstein says he wishes there was a synagogue, that's a Jewish church, so he could go there and talk Talmud with the rabbis.

There are no modern comments on the Talmud. The comments stopped in the olden days, the Middle Ages. It sounds like a wonderful book. Oberstein would love to get his hands on a copy. It contains hundreds of questions on lots of topics, even meaningless stuff. And it has really wise sayings, like "Better blind of eye than blind of heart." But the Talmud has never been completely translated, which is strange for such an important book. Oberstein was really surprised to find out that it hasn't been fully translated. He's trying to find the address of a rabbi, so he can write a letter asking why. He says he'd love to meet a rabbi and talk Talmud.

"I'd love to add a question or two," he says.

"Like what, Oberstein?" I say. "You're just a kid. What could you possibly add to the Jewish holy book?"

"Well, let's talk Talmud. For one thing, it says we should not work on the Sabbath, the day of rest. I would like to know if playing frozen tag or going fishing is considered work. And if it is, what if I got you to hold my fishing pole, would that be the same as me working?"

"Would I bait the hook?"

"Yes."

"Would I cast the line?"

"Yes."

"Would I reel in the fish when we caught one?"

"'Course," Oberstein says, "but it would be my fish."

"Then I don't know why it would be considered work for you if I'm doing the baiting and casting and reeling in the fish when we catch one."

But Oberstein says it's not that easy. That's why his people have the Talmud. He says it's a question of *ethics*.

"What's ethics?" I ask.

"Right and wrong," Oberstein says. "Is it right for a person to pay another person to do something wrong for him? Would it be right for you to hire Murphy to steal something from Ryan for you, for example?"

"No. That wouldn't be right. That would be wrong. It would definitely be wrong."

"Then why would it be right for you to work my fishing pole to catch my fish and for me not to consider it working on the Sabbath? Work was done. A fish was caught."

"Because I was working the pole, Oberstein. Not you ..."

"But it was my pole and my fish," Oberstein says. "I would gain from your work the same as if I had done the work. Which would make it my work, wouldn't it?"

It doesn't matter what I say, Oberstein makes minced meat of my words. I think I am being very logical, and *wham*, he lowers the boom. He starts arguing like he's been writing commentaries for the Talmud down through the centuries. So I give up and say, "Oberstein, you're right. I might be holding the pole, and I might be catching the fish, but you're getting the reward, which is why we work for the fish in the first place. So I agree. It would be considered work." Then Oberstein pushes back his little black yarmulke and says, "Not necessarily." And he begins with the opposite argument.

It's nerve-wracking. You can't win for losing when Oberstein gets into one of his Talmud moods.

●　　●　　●　　●　　●

It's a cold morning as we wait for Blackie out by the incinerator, longing to fire it up. We're like breathing dragons. The air is so cold you can reach out and touch the next guy's breath. Soon we will be running through snow-covered fields. The sun is about an hour from rising, and the feeling of first light is a force that draws us together. Murphy lights a cigarette and passes it around. We all take a puff even though Blackie has forbidden smoking during training. There is little difference between the cigarette smoke and our breathing out the morning air. Murphy passes around a blob of Vaseline he has stolen from the infirmary. We all scoop a few fingers full and rub it on the insides of our thighs to prevent chafing. We huddle together smoking as Ryan cracks a few jokes. He's in a good mood, which is rare for him at this hour. Perhaps it's his new canvas sneakers. Blackie appears in the distance, a shadow swimming toward us, waving his arms, telling us the coast is clear. Murphy flicks the cigarette into the incinerator, and we begin the morning running ritual. As we break into our groups, Blackie hands Brookes a bit of hardtack. Everyone's being extra nice to Brookes now that he's being shunned.

Shorty Richardson takes out the coil of rope, and we position ourselves for stringing. Blackie takes a flashlight and the lead. We begin lurching along, eyes intent upon the worn path, searching for holes or other obstacles beneath the light dusting of snow.

The silence is broken by the sound of our feet moving on the frosty ground. Five minutes in, there are bird sounds off in the woods. I glance at Brookes. He grins that monkey grin of his. We share the same thought. We'd like to be in the woods now with a few precious stones. Brookes knows every rabbit hole and bird's nest from the Mount to Sugar Loaf.

The branches of the evergreens are spotted with powdery snow. We can feel our nostrils sticking as we run. The air is so cold it almost tastes bitter. We're glad Blackie advised us to wear extra layers.

Every face is intense, even though the race is nine months away. We've only just begun our training, but every face reads the same: This is it. The Comrades! I first learned about the Comrades from Oberstein when I heard him telling Blackie he read about it in a book he found in the library on marathon running. They were poring over a map, not an ordinary map, a geological map. They were really excited. Oberstein was telling Blackie that the marathon would make a perfect decoy. I looked the word "decoy" up in the dictionary right away. I know what it means, but I didn't know what Oberstein meant. The Annual Comrades takes place every year at the same time in South Africa. Fifty-two miles. A double marathon. Oberstein said that South Africa is the only place in the world where it happens. Blackie decided we'd do a Comrades as soon as he heard about it.

"If we train for two marathons, we'll sure be in shape for one," he said.

We know that a special time has arrived. We feel it in our blood. A oneness. It's in our veins, our hands, our eyes, this special feeling that has come over us all. It is knowing that we are preparing for a double marathon, the awareness of the Comrades, that makes us feel this way.

As we run along Logy Bay Road, someone whispers that Blackie has scabbed a fresh loaf for when we return. Thinking of tearing into the fresh bread when we finish gives us new energy.

"Do you think he's scabbed a bit of butter?" Kavanagh asks.

Ryan shrugs his shoulders.

We're panting hard as we reach Sugar Loaf, the halfway mark. There's a thin burst of flame in the sky. We're tired and not yet in shape, but we all think the same thing: *How beautiful!*

"Jesus, look at that," Ryan shouts, as we lie on our bellies and smash the thin layer of ice with our fists, greedily drinking from the pond. As each of us finishes, we stand and run on the spot while waiting for the rest.

When he finishes gulping the water, Ryan asks Murphy about the hockey scores. Murphy has the only transistor radio in the Mount. It is a tiny thing that he stole from Burns' Music

Store. It has a cord running from it with a metal clip like a small clothesline pin that he attaches to the steel frame of his bed to get a station. He's always up on the baseball and hockey scores.

"Beliveau scored again last night."

"What about the Pocket?" Ryan asks, his breath coming in little puffs.

"An assist."

"Boom Boom get one?" Blackie asks.

"Two," Murphy says. "First period and the last. Missed a hat trick."

"He'll get over fifty this season. Dickie Moore play?"

"Scored on a power play in the second."

"Fantastic."

"Plante getta shutout?" Brookes asks.

"Mahovlich scored in the third. Four–one was the final score. Leafs dropped to fourth place."

Blackie hoots, pumping his fist like a champion.

"Bower musta been pissed," Ryan says.

Shorty Richardson is the last one to finish drinking. There is more hockey chatter till he gets up. When he joins us, Blackie smiles and we start out again. I shiver as we run, letting thoughts of Shorty Richardson crossing the finish line at the St. John's Royal Regatta Marathon drift through my mind. Halfway home, Cross jerks our lifeline. A rock pile peeks through the new layer of powdery snow. Ryan and I jump the obstacle. Too late for Brookes, who stumbles and falls. Anxiously, we backtrack and help him to his feet. He's in pain, but he's okay. Only a bruised knee. He makes a joke of his fall and runs harder than ever.

It's at times like this that we are no longer running alone. Our heart's desire is one. We are brothers-in-arms, all at once together. Knowing that blood loyalty and teamwork will help us run to victory. Our shivering ceases as the great silhouette of the Mount appears in the distance. We think of getting back to the dorm and dividing up the fresh loaf and getting into our bunks under the warm covers for an hour or so before the ugly buzzer sounds for chapel.

* * * * *

Canteen's open for the feast of Saint Ray-field.
Canteen's open ... Canteen's open for Saint Ray-field ...
Canteen's open ... Canteen's open ...

Canteen criers are racing through the halls during recess, screaming with delight. There's always more criers than you can count when the canteen is open.

I look at my Mickey and head for my locker to get my canteen card. The brother in charge of your dorm hands out canteen cards at the end of each month. I close my eyes and see the first canteen card I ever received, a sky-blue index card. Along the top, typed in black, a row of four quarters. On the bottom, two rows of five dimes each. Along the left side, eight nickels. Along the right, ten pennies. In the middle of the card, typed in black, is my name, and in brackets my number: Aiden Carmichael (291).

A canteen card has a value of two dollars and fifty cents. Blue money, Oberstein calls it. You can use your card anytime the canteen is open. The brother on canteen duty will add up your bill and punch holes through the numbers on your card, totalling your purchase. The money has to last you the entire month. Needless to say, many cards are stolen, the name and number efficiently erased and replaced with another boy's. There's a rumour that Farrell, a member of the Dare Klub, counterfeits a few cards each month, but I don't believe it. For one thing, the thick blue paper is unavailable. Canteen cards are as good as gold. Boys exchange IOUs for cigarettes, chore swapping, and even clothing and food. I remember Murphy giving Father Cross his entire canteen card one month for his black cowboy hat. I thought it was a pretty good deal. Everyone argued for days about who came out on top. Blackie controls the canteen card trade, as Oberstein calls it, especially since preparations for the marathon began.

The canteen is opened most nights, and on Saturdays between one and two o'clock in the afternoon and Sunday night before we watch *Walt Disney* or *Bonanza*. Once in a while, the canteen opens at odd times. The PA crackles, and there's an announcement that the canteen is open. Or some half-crazed criers, like the ones running around now, race through the halls yelling, "Canteen's open for the feast of Saint Ray-field!" And the canteen can open on a whim, if a special event takes place, like when John F. Kennedy won the election. "Wingding for the first Catholic President. Wingding for President Kennedy! Wingding! Wingding!"

I'll never forget King Kelly's excitement when Brother McCann said Senator Kennedy was elected president. "C'mon everyone, the canteen's open for the first Catholic President. Betcha Oberstein and Blackie'll get extras cause they're Americans."

McCann's gone nuts over President Kennedy. We have special prayers between classes for President Kennedy. He reads every day from a book on President Kennedy's life. Bug says if he hears one more story about the PT *109*, he's gonna throw a baseball at McCann's nuts. Even when he's teaching diagramming sentences in grammar class, every sentence has Kennedy in it: "John F. Kennedy hit the ball." "Senator Kennedy, who has a bad back from a war injury, walked spryly to the store." "John Fitzgerald Kennedy, who is the first Catholic president, loves vanilla ice cream." "President Kennedy, a Catholic, is the thirty-fifth president of the United States because he beat Richard Nixon, a Protestant."

All the brothers, even McMurtry, have become really nutty since the election. Every morning, Mass is offered up for President Kennedy. Rosaries are being said. And novenas and benedictions. Bug calls it voodoo time. But it doesn't seem to have affected Rags much. He's the only one not cranked up about President Kennedy. Oberstein says that's because he's a Republican.

When the canteen is opened for a wingding, you don't have to use your canteen card. Everyone receives free ice cream and pop. We all really like canteen surprises.

There are a million stories about our canteen cards. You can just imagine the stuff that goes on. Once Rowsell paid fifty cents, blue money, to Bug to cut his hair. Rowsell's fussy about his hair. It's always slicked back in waves with a greasy ducktail. Bug put a bowl on his head and chopped away with a pair of old rusty scissors. Rowsell was a sight for sore eyes. Everyone called him the monk from Mars. He looked pretty goofy with his bowl cut. When he looked in the mirror, he was spellbound, his jaw hanging.

One of the best stories is about Ryan charging Murphy twenty-five cents for three one-cent stamps. Stamps are hard to get. You have to steal them from the post office, which is only open on Saturdays. And you need an insider to pull it off. Murphy had taken a boot in the balls playing soccer one day, and Blackie told him he'd never be able to get a hard-on again.

"You're probably ruptured," Oberstein said.

"What does that mean?" Murphy asked.

"You don't have to worry about an heir to the throne."

Murphy raised both his big hands and gave an exasperated look, indicating he knew he'd been successfully teased but couldn't think of a comeback.

"How do you know? How can you be so sure I'm ruptured?"

"You can't. Not 100 percent. But the pain you got means you probably are."

"You could try the stamp test," Ryan said. "That's one way to find out for sure if you're ruptured or not."

"What's the stamp test?" Murphy asked.

"It's a surefire way to find out if you can still get it up."

"How's it work?"

"Easy. You take three new stamps, joined. They gotta be new and joined. You lick 'em and put 'em on your dick when you're going to bed." Ryan was brimming with excitement. All you could see was the gap between his teeth. "In the middle of the night, if the stamps break, you know you can still get it up. If you wake and they're still joined, well, you gotta big problem. Let's put it this way, there won't be any little redheaded Murphys running around. You might not even snap the lizard again."

"'Course, if you don't get it up, it could all be in your mind," Oberstein said. "A sort of hypno-suggestion 'cause Blackie said you were ruptured. It's called self-fulfilling prophecy. Like when Rowsell gets a hard-on 'cause we tell him he's gonna get one. If it's all in your mind, the only way to overcome it is through the power of positive thinking. Through thinking positively."

Murphy agreed to pay Ryan twenty-five cents from his canteen card if he would lift the three stamps from the post office so he could try the test.

"It'll take a few days," Ryan said. "If you get it up in the next day or so, lemme know. No sense takin' a chance on a shit-kickin' for nothing."

Murphy didn't get a hard-on for the next few days. He was really worried. We all rallied round him and told him not to worry, to think positively, that everything would be okay, that he would pass the stamp test through the power of positive thinking.

"You're gonna bust them stamps to bits," Blackie howled, as we all placed our bets.

Saturday came, and Ryan got the stamps, and Murphy did the test Saturday night. He woke us all up early Sunday morning, running around the dorm yelling, "I passed. I passed the test. I'm not ruptured. I passed the stamp test."

At first we didn't know what was happening. We thought it was Brookes, who not only looks like a monkey, but acts like one all the time. Some Sundays he gets us up early, jumping from bunk to bunk, whacking us with a broom handle, which he calls his *ski-o-saku*, and chanting, "Rise and shine. Come on, my lads. You know what lads I mean. Up. Up. Let go of your cocks and pull on your socks. Up. Up. Rise and shine."

But this time, it was Murphy, running around like a lunatic, screaming that he'd passed the stamp test.

"Oh, that power of positive thinking!" Oberstein boomed out in his best opera voice from his bunk bed.

At breakfast, Blackie howled, "You passed the test all right, Murphy. You busted them stamps to pieces."

For a while, we all called Murphy The Postman. But like the stamps, it never stuck.

●   ●   ●   ●   ●

The next Saturday afternoon, we're on our way back to the Mount from Bannerman Park. Me, Murphy, and O'Neill. Two sea cadets carrying tags and tin cans pass us. They're so tiny O'Neill thinks they're midgets.

"Whatcha got, boys?" Murphy asks, putting his big hands around the tin can.

"Tags. It's Tag Day," they both say, in unison, their voices hoarse.

"I'm Petty Officer Wilson. This is Able Seaman March. We're with RCSC *Terra Nova*." He points to the gold lettering on his cap.

Able Seaman March, who is missing a front tooth, explains that Tag Day is used by the sea cadets to raise money for their cadet corp.

"Last year we raised over a t'ousand dollars," he says.

"How?" I ask.

"Just stands around supermarkets mostly and asks people if they'd like to support the cadets by buying a tag. If they says yes, we gives 'em a tag and they puts money in the tin. That's all's to it. Then we brings our money back to our Chief Petty Officer, and he counts it all up and tells the Corps how much we collected at the next sea cadet meeting. Last year I brought in over a hundred dollars."

"Can I have a tag?" Murphy asks. "But I got no money."

"That's okay, we got tons. Here, take one. We're finished for the day," the deeper voice says.

"Will you be selling them tomorrow?" Murphy asks. "Mind if I try on your hat?"

He passes Murphy his hat. "Nope. Not sellin' tomorrow. Tag Day is only on the last two Saturdays in November. Next Saturday's the last Tag Day for this year." Murphy's jug ears look juggier with the flat hat on.

When we get back to the Mount, Murphy tells Blackie about our encounter with the two little sea cadets. "It'd be a great way to raise money for the Klub," he says, his freckles standing out as he speaks. Blackie agrees and sends for Father Cross.

"Soup, you make the costumes of the world," Blackie says, watching Father Cross blush. "Zorro, the Lone Ranger, Geronimo . . . You make 'em all." Today, Cross's acne seems less pimply than usual.

"He can work magic with a sheet off a bed or an old curtain," Blackie reminds us.

"You're gonna turn Big Murph into a sailor," Blackie says.

"Only got till next Saturday. Tag Day begins at nine o'clock. Gotta get goin.'" And immediately he puts Cross on the payroll to do a uniform for Murphy. Father Cross says to put the money toward the marathon, that it will take a day or so, and he'll get started right away. He finishes the gun shirt in jig's time, white with a sky-blue trim across the square neck. He needs to dye the blue trim, but it looks beautiful. He is working on the bell bottoms when he gets really sick. Rags says he has the mumps and puts him in the infirmary. He says nobody is allowed near him, that he's contagious. We're all at a loss as to how to finish the uniform. Nobody but Father Cross can make costumes. Murphy says he'll give it a go, and Blackie tells him to get right at it.

"Father Cross will direct you from sick bay. Tomorrow's Friday. That uniform's gotta be ready."

He orders everyone in the Klub to pitch in and make tags, small white squares with a blue profile of a cadet. Each tag has a hole at the top, and a piece of white thread is attached so the buyer can tie it to a button.

After lights out at nine o'clock, when we know the coast is clear, we watch Murphy work away. We are surprised. We knew he wouldn't be as good as Cross, but we can't believe how quickly his big hands cut and sew the material, stopping only long enough to run a hand through the shock of hair that keeps falling over his forehead. We all help out. "Santa's little elves," Oberstein keeps saying. Everyone is excited, except Bug, who's a pain. He stands around, smoking and joking about how ugly everything looks and how we'll never finish in time. When Murphy gets stuck and doesn't know what to do, Blackie orders one of the elves to sneak down to the infirmary and ask Father Cross for directions. Ryan or Kavanagh returns and tells Murphy to use this or that shirt or to steal a piece of material from the laundry room or the sewing room. Or to create color by mixing blueberry jam with lard stolen from the kitchen storeroom. Fitzpatrick returns with measurements and directions for cutting and sewing. A triangle here, a few rectangles there. We are dog-tired at the end of the night. My head has hardly hit the pillow when the buzzer sounds for chapel.

I don't know how to describe what Able Seaman Murphy came up with. Everything about him is perfect. His cadet cap with the black ribbon round it and the gold lettering—RCSC *Terra Nova*—made from the gold leaf chipped from a statue of Mary in the chapel. The bell bottoms, the gun shirt, the navy blue collar, the white lanyard, even the black boots we stole from the marching band. Everything is there. It's the perfect uniform. But it's all faded. Even his freckles look duller. Murphy in faded full blues is a sight to behold. When he puts the uniform on for us he looks sad, like a shadow of the real thing. Even his tin can looks like it's been used for a thousand years. The paper is pale, the letters so faded you can hardly read them. Blackie tells Murphy to be at the Dominion Stores as soon as chores are over on Saturday morning. He gives him the fifty tags we made and says we'll have another fifty by the afternoon.

"Anyone asks about your uniform, say your mother washed it wrong," Blackie shakes his head. "They'll believe it. No worry. You'll get sympathy. Maybe sell a hundred tags."

Blackie tells him to put the uniform in a brown bag and change behind the supermarket. I'll never forget watching big Murph in his faded sea-cadet uniform standing outside the Dominion Stores selling tags. He looked like somebody had cut him out of cardboard and stood him up by the door. People gave him the weirdest looks. But almost everyone gave him a dime or a quarter. A few people gave him a dollar bill.

Tag Day comes and goes, and Saturday afternoon we all head to the Bat Cave to count the money. We're all pretty excited, thinking we'll be divvying up some of the cash among ourselves. But Blackie waves the speaking stick.

"Richardson needs a few pairs of sneakers and other things. And Ryan's runnin' real good. Maybe a pair for him too. All that money's for the marathon fund."

Blackie waves the speaking stick again and extends it toward the pile of money on the tree stump where we're counting. "How much's Able Seaman Murphy collected for the Dare Klub?"

"Sixty-three dollars and forty-two cents," Oberstein says. Everyone cheers.

"We'll need a seconder to bank it for the marathon," Blackie says.

"I'll second," Murphy says.

It isn't what we want to hear. But we all know Blackie's right, so nobody says a word.

"Oberstein's gonna take three dollars for Father Cross, two for Murphy. The rest is goin' in the Bank of Newfoundland." Blackie points to a huge boulder near the far wall of the cave. We gather up the money and put it back in Ryan's socks, which he donated for the cause. We hand it to Blackie, who orders us to roll back the big boulder that covers the hole that contains the homemade vault Father Cross made out of cement and scraps of iron. In it we keep all our valuables—money, tin food, the stolen wine and things we need for the marathon. The vault is almost as heavy as the big boulder. When six of us have the boulder cleared from the hole, Blackie opens his shirt and removes a key from a chain with a medal of Our Lady of Perpetual Help that he keeps around his neck. We watch him put the money into the vault and snap the padlock shut. Four of us lower the vault back into the three-foot hole. Then we roll the boulder back in place over the hole and lock the door to the Bat Cave before heading back for a feed of pea soup and dumplings and a slice of cold Diefenbaker meat, which is what we have every Saturday night before study hall.

After supper, we have half an hour free time before study hall, so Blackie orders us to do laps around the soccer field. He's always doing that. Every bit of spare time we have, he's got us running or working out. Murphy jokes that Blackie's training so hard because he plans on running away and wants to be in perfect shape.

The late November weather is cold, like winter, but as we run we quickly begin to sweat. Past the halfway mark, with Ryan outdistancing Richardson for the first time, a wind comes up that has a terrible bite to it. The sun is starting to go down, and soon it will be dark and unbearably cold, so we run all the harder. The days are getting shorter now. Another year is almost over, and winter is on its way. After the laps, Blackie calls us together and says, "Brothers askin' why we're runnin' so much, just say we're playin' a game. Say it's called who lasts the longest."

Most Saturday study halls, McCann has us exchange composition books to speed up the marking. All the guy next to you has to do if he wants to give you a break is mark a few mistakes correct. It's nearly impossible to get caught. And everyone in class turns a blind eye to a few mistakes once in a while. Everyone, that is, except Bug. He wouldn't turn a blind eye for love or money. Every spelling mistake. Every grammar error. Minus $^1/_2$, Bug writes in the margin in red ink for every mistake. He sits directly in front of me, so I have to exchange composition books with him a lot. And even though I always turn a blind eye for him, Bug never gives me a single break. He always has a spelling mistake or two or a capitalization problem or a misplaced modifier. He isn't that good a writer, but he's a great reader. When he reads out loud you would think there wasn't a single mistake in his composition. I cornered him once and asked him why he wouldn't give anyone a break.

"Can't chance it," he whined.

"C'mon, Bug, for God's sake, a single spelling mistake. Couldn't you just give me one spelling mistake? I give you at least two or three every time I get your composition."

"Your problem," he said. "I can't chance it. Might get caught. What then? You gonna take my whacks? Not likely, brother."

"C'mon, Bug, be a sport. You won't get caught. What's a half mark?"

"Not takin' a chance on gettin' the shit kicked outta me for your spelling mistake," Bug said. "It ain't worth it."

"I'll give you ten cents on my canteen card," I begged.

"Nope. I'm resolved," he said, using Brother Malone's favorite word, folding his arms and pursing his lips the way Malone does when he refuses to let us stay up past ten o'clock to watch the last period of *Hockey Night in Canada.*

"Bug, you'll never get caught," I argued. "Nobody ever gets caught. McCann always sits behind his desk and records the mark you give. There's no way he's gonna come to your desk and check the number of mistakes. All he ever asks is for you to read the composition out loud. You can correct a mistake or two as you read. He'll never know."

"He might, birdbrain. Might just be the one time he comes to a desk to check. While I'm reading. What then?" Bug said.

"But I always turn the blind eye for you, Bug."

"That's your problem, brother."

"Do it, Bug," I said. "If he catches you, just say you didn't see it. Say it was an honest mistake. Say you thought the word was spelled right or that you didn't think the word was supposed to be capitalized. He won't question you. He never has. Not once."

"It only takes once," Bug snapped. "Once, and I get caught. I'm a dead duck. No thanks, brother. I won't be taking any chances. Forget it. I told you, I'm resolved."

I argued with him until I was blue in the face, but he never gave in. I even threatened to stop turning a blind eye. And once I did exactly that. He misspelled the word *gravel*, and had four other mistakes, and I took off two and a half marks. When it came time to call his grade, I smiled across at him and announced "Seventy-five percent." But it didn't change a thing.

"Don't be such a prick, Bug," I yelled at him one day in the gymnasium. "It's only a few lousy marks."

"Fuck if I care. You do what you gotta do, brother," he said. "I'll do what I gotta do. Like I told you, I'm resolved." He folded his arms and pouted. So I gave up. I didn't wanna push him too hard in case he threatened to squeal about the wine or the marathon.

I can never figure Bug out. He's a puzzle with a lot of pieces missing. He won't take a chance on something as foolproof as turning a blind eye to composition mistakes, but he sneaks to the bakery during the middle of the night to steal a fresh loaf at the drop of a hat. Or he steals from the canteen or the post office when he's on duty. Or from the collection box during a wedding or funeral Mass. He'd even take a chance on stealing cigarettes from one of the brothers, all of which are much more likely to land him the strap than giving me a few extra marks on composition day.

Bug can be strange sometimes, especially when he gets a notion in his head. When he becomes resolved, as he calls it, not even a bomb could move him.

·   ·   ·   ·   ·

Ten minutes to the movie. Ten minutes to the movie.
It's a Western. Western. Western.

The criers are right about the ten minutes. They're probably wrong about the movie being a Western. But when study hall is over we are all excited. We never know what the movie will be until the reel is on the projector. Lotsa times the name on the can is not the same as the movie inside. Once, we had a can that read *The Kid*, starring Charlie Chaplin, and it turned out to be *The Blob*. Another time, a can marked *Night Train to Terror* turned out to be a movie about slavery and the American Civil War. Blackie really liked that one. He said to Oberstein after the movie, "A slave is somebody who waits to be free."

Rags tacks bedsheets to a wall in the TV room, as we bet on whether it will be a Western or a thriller. Most of us hope for a Western, especially Anstey, who always says, "I wants a Western, and no small guns either," which cracks us up. A few weeks ago we saw *Fastest Gun Alive*, starring Glenn Ford, and Anstey loved it. Ever since, when someone gets his dander up, Anstey turns into Glenn Ford. He whips his hand off his thigh and says, "No matter how far you ride, no matter how many towns you run to, there'll always be somebody faster." And he sounds just like Glenn Ford in the movie. He's very convincing.

Most of the time the movies are really good, like *Fastest Gun Alive*, but once in a while we get a real boner. Usually the brother in charge watches the movie with us, so even if it is boring we're all pretty quiet. There's usually the odd bit of whispering, but that's all. Sometimes the brother on duty leaves one of the older boys in charge while he disappears for a while. Tonight, after about five minutes, Rags has to go somewhere. The movie gets pretty boring. It's about the Germans sending a trainload of Jews across Europe during the Second World War. And everywhere they go, no town will take them in. The Nazis had set it all up so nobody would take them. It's pretty boring, but sorta sad too. It's called *Night Train to Munich*.

There are three dorms watching the movie, including St. Gabe's, the grade fours and fives. They're the youngest group watching, and they're pretty bored with it all. Most of them begin chatting and fooling around almost right after Rags leaves. Everyone is half-watching the movie and half-talking. Only Oberstein seems to be interested. He moves right up to the front row with the younger kids who are making the most noise, chatting and poking each other and horsing around. Oberstein tells them to be quiet every now and then, and once or twice he slaps a couple of them. He really wants to see what will happen to the Jewish refugees. The hero in the movie is named Jeremiah, and Oberstein is really taken with him. As the noise gets louder, Oberstein almost goes out of his mind telling everyone to shut up. Eventually it gets really noisy, and Oberstein, who almost never curses, goes crazy.

"You little fuckers better shuddup, or I swear I'm gonna throw every fucken one of you little fucken runts out the fucken window. Do you under*fucken*stand?"

The noise dies down a bit, and Oberstein throws his yarmulke into the air and yells, "Halle*fucken*lujah! Mar-ve-lous!"

When everyone's settled down a bit, Rowsell chews away on a Popsicle stick as he walks over to the younger boys and whispers to them to be quiet.

"Rowsell, you're abso*fucken*lutely useless," Oberstein says, "you block, you stone, you worse than senseless fucken thing."

The noise increases, and it becomes a bit of a free-for-all until toward the end of the movie, when the Jews take over the train and take it to a town run by Americans where they think they'll be allowed to stay. When the Jews take over the train, everybody starts to clap and cheer. Even the younger ones stop their shenanigans and cheer and clap.

When Rags returns, one of the little ones tells him that everyone was horsing around except Oberstein, so Rags cancels canteen for everyone and gives us all an assignment. We have to write a paragraph about the movie explaining the part we liked most and why. Oberstein writes a paragraph even though he doesn't have to. He says that the best line in the movie is when one of the women on the train said that nobody should have to die for a war.

Before we go to sleep that night, I ask Oberstein if he's still upset about not being able to watch the movie in peace. He says he is, but that when everyone started to cheer and clap when the Jews took over the train he was really happy. He says he hasn't been as happy in a long, long time. He says he felt like he was there on the train with all the refugees.

"Even the little ones know the difference between right and wrong," he says. "It was wrong to put them on the train, and it was wrong for the different towns not to take them in. It was so nice to hear everyone clapping. When you get the spells, remembering a moment like that, when everyone started cheering, that's the sort of thing can bring you around."

11

IT'S A WINDY NIGHT. And it's bitter out. Cold enough to skin a cat. The moon casts our long shadows on the glistening snow. Before heading out, I stare at the beauty of the ice-glazed windows and the snow-streaked stone walls. Far off, a dog barks. We're all afraid. Afraid we will be caught for stealing the wine. Afraid Blackie might do something we'll all regret. Afraid we'll get caught night running. That one night we'll return to find black-cassocked men with straps waiting for us. Oberstein wants Blackie to tell Rags about the marathon. He says Rags won't mind, he'll let us participate. Oberstein thinks Rags will even help us out. Blackie disagrees. He says if we tell Rags, one of the brothers will be put in charge, and that will spoil everything. Everything will change. It will all go down the drain. But Oberstein doesn't think so. He says involving the brothers will make it better. I think Blackie's right. We have to do it Blackie's way, or we won't have a chance of winning. There's no guarantee our groups will be picked to run, that's for sure. Blackie's right. We can't take a chance on the brothers finding out.

We strain to keep up with Blackie's group. They're keeping a fast pace. We're soon sweating and breathless, but we're keyed up and eager to knock off a few seconds from our last run. Suddenly the string jerks; there's a hole up ahead or a rock. My hands and feet are freezing. My whole body feels raw. It's the coldest night run yet. The tips of my fingers feel like they've been cut off. I long to race ahead to Blackie and beg him to turn back. But I think of the fishermen in their little boats out on the high seas, and what I'm doing seems nothing compared to those brave souls. And I know Blackie would think I'm crazy anyway. Blackie would never turn back.

I run a little faster, hoping to warm up a bit. I notice Brookes and Father Cross moving faster than usual too. Unlike most other runs, Cross isn't grunting with the effort to keep up. I long to make contact, just to say how cold it is. But I know speaking will somehow make it worse. It's even too cold to speak. Silently, we run. And silently, we endure the bitter cold.

The pack is almost one this morning, with Ryan, Richardson, and Blackie in the lead, only yards ahead. Perhaps it's the cold that keeps us close. Blackie is mumbling something, but I can't make out what he's saying. The wind is so strong it whistles through our clothing. I regret now not having added another layer. It's so cold my nostrils stick together and my cheeks sting.

"This must be what it's like running on the moon," Brookes whispers. His voice is raspy. He spits the words, like they taste bitter.

The sky seems to brighten as we pass Bally Haly Golf Course. Perhaps it's the whiteness of the rolling fairways. Car headlights beam in the distance. We slide down a bank and lie flat on the snow. It's cold and crisp. We lie low till Blackie gives the all clear. My feet are so sore they feel like they're on fire. As we climb the bank, Kavanagh is bent double, sucking snow. Brookes flicks his rump, and Kavanagh goes flying down the bank. We can hear him laughing as he climbs it again.

We're almost near the Sugar Loaf turnoff when we hear a

loud noise in the distance. Everyone is tense, but we keep moving. It's a deep groaning sound. Ice cracking in one of the nearby ponds. Or, deep in the woods, a tree breaking. Somewhere a bird chirps, readying itself for dawn. As I run, I have only one thought: What if we're caught? I take off a mitten and remove a nugget of hardtack and put it in my mouth. It tastes good. As always, I'll let it melt slowly in my mouth. The wind is still howling, but it's getting brighter as Brookes hurries past me. I'm about to pick up the pace when I hear the sound of shallow breathing. Father Cross pulls even. He gurgles and hawks. He breathes hard as he runs. Every breath is an effort. He offers me his big woolly mittens.

"Take 'em for a while. They're lined. I padded them."

I wave them off, but he passes me one mitten.

"Switch one till Sugar Loaf," he begs.

I feel bad for not sharing my hardtack. I pick up the pace. I've never finished behind Father Cross before. My eyes fixed on the leads, I decide to stay with him until the long stretch to the pond, when I know I'll outdistance him. Cross gurgles again, hawks and spits. The stretch appears sooner than I think. I kick hard and move ahead of him.

At the pond, Blackie and the others have smashed rocks through the new ice to make drinking holes. After we drink, I check my Mickey. We're a full two minutes ahead of our last time. And we can probably add over a minute for our slide down the bank. Blackie waves us on. I race to catch him and point to my Mickey. "Best time yet," I shout over the wind. His mouth is half open, but he says nothing, kicks hard and catches Ryan. My eyes are fixed on them. The wind is now at our backs. It feels warmer. Brookes's footsteps hurry past me, and then Cross's hawking reminds me that this could be our best time ever. Cross pulls up opposite me and spits. I look across at him. The strain on his face startles me. I want to speak, to egg him on, to tell him that this will be his personal best, but he gurgles and hawks again. He removes a mitten and passes me a candy.

"Sugar for the final stretch," he says. "This is our best time ever."

I nod and point to my Mickey and give him the thumbs-up sign, like the pilots do in the movies. His breathing becomes hard again.

"Oberstein is waiting for us with a fresh loaf," I say.

He nods a painful smile.

Away off in the distance, two black dots, Richardson and Ryan, move down the long, white road toward the massive stone shadows.

·   ·   ·   ·   ·

I wake in the morning long before the buzzer sounds. I do not talk. I do not rouse Blackie to hatch some scheme or Oberstein to sing a song or tell me a Bible story. There will be no dormitory antics today. I just lie there, in my bunk, stretching and feeling good, the good aching that comes from a long, hard run, the aching you can feel in every joint. I smell the cool light breeze flowing through the dorm, and I take it in, like a menthol cigarette, as I stretch and yawn and wake to the world, rolling onto my side, staring at the canvas sneakers by each bunk bed and the raggedy towels hanging on the ladders and the stack of comics Rags has left on top of the lockers.

I think of all these sleepers who are such a part of my life. Closer to me than Clare. We may be norphs to everyone in St. John's. But to each other we're family. And I think of each of them in turn, Blackie, Oberstein, Bug, Murphy, Ryan, Brookes, Kavanagh, Cross, Rowsell. I realize what I love most about each of them: that I never have to pretend anything with them, that I can always say whatever it is I feel, no matter what it is. That I never have to be on my guard, and I never have to be afraid. And I am happy knowing they will always be a part of my life. Even years and years from now. When we've all flown the coop, as Rags says. Nothing will ever change that. Not sickness, not sadness, not distance, not old age. I know I'll always carry something out of this marvellous, terrible place that will join us like glue forever and a day. And realizing that for the first time, I start to cry. Knowing that no matter what happens, I'll always be one with everybody here. The runners, the criers, the altar boys, the tumblers, the actors, the kings of the castle, the Dare Klub. And the tears pass and give way to other feelings until I am wide awake to my world.

I lie there remembering, my hands locked behind my neck, as a strip of light breaks through the crack in the curtains and hits the lockers, making the turpentined wood look golden. I think of Nicky and wonder if he's awake in his pigeon coop. I lie quietly and let the movie reel roll, remembering what happened at the cave during Blackie's last trial, how he ruled against Murphy and in favor of Brookes. I lie as still as I can, stretching and feeling the hardness of my body, thinking of Ruthie Peckford. Then I think for a moment about Floyd Patterson, and what Blackie said about my essay and me becoming a writer, and I feel good.

Someone coughs. A bed creaks. The curtain blows lightly from the open window, and another single bar of light crosses the lockers. Soon they'll all be awake. Brushing their teeth and washing their sleepy eyes, putting on their school uniforms and lining up for inspection in front of the bunk beds. I think of the marathon, and how Oberstein said that the first guy who ever ran one dropped dead of exhaustion. I say a Hail Mary that that doesn't happen to any of us. I close my eyes and watch Richardson crossing the finish line, with nobody near him for a mile. And I think of what the brothers will say when they learn that a Mount Kildare boy has won the Royal Regatta Marathon. I smile and put my hands behind my head again and stretch some more.

And in the golden silence I think back to what Oberstein said that day in the yard about how the place grows on you. And I try to imagine what it will be like years from now when these sleepers are no longer in my life. I block the thought. They will always be with me ... Blackie and Oberstein and Bug and Ryan and Murphy and Brookes and Kavanagh and Father Cross and Rowsell ... even O'Grady ... everyone.

I look at my Mickey. The buzzer will sound any minute. I stretch some more and shiver and crack my fingers and let my leg dangle over the side of the bunk and wish I could feel like this every morning, the way a baby must feel when it wakes.

* * * * *

There's a new guy. There's a new guy.
New guy ... There's a new guy.

O'Connor's shouting echoes through the corridors like gun shots. *There's a new guy* ... He came last night after we were in bed. Such news always creates intense excitement among us. Who is he? How old is he? What's he look like? Does he have any brothers? Where's he from? Is he a townie or a bayman? What dorm will he be in? And, of course, Blackie wants to know if he's a runner. Blackie has devised all sorts of games to test a new guy's running skills.

New guys are extremely vulnerable. They usually have money and clothing and food, and are easy targets. Even new brothers are easy targets, especially if they are young. During the Christmas and summer holidays, new brothers, usually young novices, as they're called, fill in for the regular brothers for a week or two. The Boot-Camp Boys, Murphy calls them.

They are innocent and green and easy to take for a ride. For example, on Sunday nights our dorm always goes straight to washup and bed after watching a movie or *Walt Disney*. It's always the same, every Sunday. There is never an exception. When there's a new brother, Ryan or Murphy will pipe up that the regular brother always gives us an extra hour on Sundays. Once, Bug Bradbury convinced Brother Hefferton, a dopey young brother with a mole on his nose, that we were allowed to be in town on Saturdays until eight o'clock. I remember Hefferton squinting his big, dumb eyes and straining his turkey neck. "Is that the rule, boys?" he asked. "Oh, yes, Brother, eight o'clock if you're in St. Martin's or St. Luke's dorm. St. Mark's gotta be back in by six," Bug said.

"Okay, okay, you people know the rules. Martin's and Luke's by eight. Mark's by six. Don't be late," he said in a tone that was a pathetic attempt at sounding like he was in charge.

The last new boy came just after Thanksgiving. His name is Lionel Chafe. He's from England. Liverpool. His father was a sea captain in the British Navy. Lionel's father died at sea. That's all Lionel knows about his death. A bunch of us were talking about it. It's pretty sad. Anstey almost started crying. He started thinking of his own father and how easy it is to die at sea. He started befriending Lionel right away, which was really good because Lionel is a skinny little runt and Anstey is the size of a barn door. Lionel was placed in the Mount when his mother got sick. She has a disease that keeps her in bed half the time and in a wheelchair the other half. Lionel has a really nifty accent and some very strange expressions. The brothers are always asking him questions in class just to hear him speak. The other day, in Newfoundland geography class, Madman asked Lionel to recite the names of all the coves along the northern peninsula near the Strait of Belle Isle.

"I say, you've got quite a few," Lionel chimed. "Blue Cove,

Seal Cove, Black Duck Cove, Deadman's Cove ... I say, jolly interesting, that lot. Bear Cove, Flowers Cove, Nameless Cove. I say, rather odd, that, Nameless Cove. Savage Cove ... Oh dear, are there savages there? I must remember not to travel along that route. Sandy Cove, Shoal Cove, Payne's Cove ..."

Everyone loves his accent and his odd little expressions. But it puts him in a tough spot, because he's always being called upon to read the morning prayer or say the grace or answer questions in class. And some of the boys laugh at him a lot. It's a tough spot to be in for a new guy, especially a skinny little guy.

The rumor is that the new boy is an American. But later we find out that his name is Merrigan and someone confused the sound of his name with his being an American.

It's really sad to see a new guy, especially if he's all alone. Lots of boys who come to the Mount come with a brother or cousin, which makes it a bit easier on them. But it's really bad if a boy is all alone. He often has the spells for a long, long time. Poor old Whelan had the spells for about a year. We all felt really sorry for him. Every Thursday, he'd start. "My Auntie's coming for me this weekend," he'd say. And he'd pull out the old wine-colored cardboard suitcase and fill it full with his clothes. "I gotta be ready for when she comes." His big round face would shine like the sun. "I can't afford not to be ready the minute she gets here." And he'd stare out the big dorm window for hours waiting for her car to pull into the long gravel drive-way outside. I used to feel so sad for Whelan, but I never let on. I would even help him pack. It never did me any harm to play along. So I did it. And I think it helped him a lot. It gave him hope in a way. To have somebody else also believe that his aunt was coming to take him home to Stephenville.

Every new guy goes through it, at least for a few weeks. His first bout of the spells. "I'm not in here for very long. Just for a little while. Then my uncle's coming to get me. He promised he'd come and get me in two weeks . . . two months." It's always the same story. Different voices. But always the same story. The weeks give way to months, and the months give way to years, and suddenly Merrigan or Pittman or Walsh is sixteen, and Brother McMurtry arrives with a brand new suitcase and new clothes and a new wallet with twenty freshly minted dollar bills inside. And there is a Mass and a Benediction and a rosary, after which Brother McMurtry gives a little speech about the boy who is leaving, how the Mount has prepared him with the tools to survive in a hard world. Brother McMurtry's speech is always the same, ending with that predictable conclusion: "And don't forget to come back and visit us once in a while. You know where to find us. Even in the dark. Sure, you can see the Celtic cross at the top of Mount Kildare from anywhere in St. John's. It's always lit, seven days a week, fifty-two weeks a year."

Unfortunately, when Randy Walters left that's not what happened. Brother McMurtry was sick, and McCann filled in for him. McCann announced that all dorms from ours to the seniors' were to go to the gymnasium. He singled out Walters and said, "I've only got two things to say to you, Walters: One, don't ever show your face around here again. And two, if you've got any high hopes leaving here, forget 'em." Then he gave Walters the customary letter of reference and saw him to the door. He didn't even get us to line up and shake Walters' hand, the way Brother McMurtry does when a boy leaves for good.

Walters is a cocky kid with straight floppy hair and oversized glasses. He just shrugged and curled his lip. I guess he was just as happy to be getting rid of McCann. Blackie found out later where Walters was staying and called an emergency meeting of the Brotherhood and had a collection and sent Walters a note and some money. Father Cross made a card out of cardboard with a sketch of everyone in the Klub on it. It was a really good card. The sketches were really lifelike. We all signed our names and wrote a comment beneath our sketch. We got a really big kick outta what O'Grady wrote beneath his sketch: "Brother MucCan is a big count." O'Grady can't spell his own name. Blackie delivered the card one Saturday afternoon.

"Walters was a good egg," Blackie said. "McCann shouldn't of treated him like that. It ain't fair what happened."

12

Two weeks to Christmas. Choice cards at the post office.
Two weeks to Christmas. Fill out your choice cards.
Choice cards at the post office.

WE JUST LOVE CHRISTMAS. As Rags says, it's the best time
of the year. All through December, everyone is always happy.
We spend a lot of time making wreaths for all the doors in the
Mount. And making the two cribs, one for the chapel and
a huge one for outside by the front gate. The brothers pick up
a lot of money during the Christmas season. People come
from all around to see the beautiful big crib and to say a prayer
at it. And they always throw a coin inside for a norphan.

We decorate all the dorms with red-and-white streamers
and Santa Clauses and candy canes. And all the statues are
spruced up. We hang lights all over the place, inside and out.
The older boys cut down a great big tree up in Major's Path and
drag it home and stand it up in the cafeteria. It takes days to get
all the bulbs and lights and decorations on it. And it looks
wonderful when it's finished. At supper time we eat with only
the Christmas tree lights on. And at night, in the dorms, the
brothers light candles. Rags always tells special Chop-Chops
stories during the twelve days of Christmas. We always look

forward to what Chop-Chops will get for Christmas. It's such a great time. And there's no school for two whole weeks.

The food is better all during Christmas week. It's the only time we don't have Diefenbaker meat. No Diefenbaker meat for a whole week. The businessmen on Water Street donate money and gifts. And the American soldiers bring us tons of food, and a group of women from town comes and cooks up a storm. We have midnight Mass and light candles, and afterward we sing carols all the way to the cafeteria, where we stuff ourselves while we open our gifts.

At the beginning of December every year, members of the Dare Klub meet and draw names. Whatever name you pick, you have to give that boy a little gift. Blackie's made one rule. It has to be something you own. Everyone gives something simple but nice. Once I gave my five little pebbles for playing jacks to Kavanagh. You can give a used comic book or a bag of marbles or some used stamps to start a collection. We meet at the cave on Christmas Eve and open the gifts in front of a raging fire. Sometimes the gifts are funny and we have a great laugh. Last year, Father Cross gave Murphy a pair of girl's underwear. We got a big laugh outta that. He said they were Karla Doyle's, but we all knew he made them.

Christmas day we have turkey dinner with dressing and gravy and mashed potatoes and carrots and turnips and beets and pickles and even dessert, plum puddings and fruitcakes. There's always tons of food. And an endless supply of treats, such as Purity syrup and peppermint knobs. We stuff our pockets and our lockers.

Everything is usually great until the day after Christmas. Boxing Day. At the Mount that has a special meaning. There are usually a lot of fights because lotsa boys don't get what they asked for and lotsa gifts are stolen. My first Christmas, I got a Lone Ranger set, toy guns and a mask and cowboy hat.

Somebody stole the set on Christmas night. I cried for a week.

Even Madman Malone puts his strap away at Christmas. If he wasn't such a lunatic, Madman's nickname would've been Baldy. He has a shiny bald head, and his eyes are slightly crossed and set deep into his red face. Really deep, like they're abnormal. And they're just narrow slits, so narrow that they sometimes look closed. Like a makeup artist did him up for a movie. And he has little puffy sacks under each eye and wrinkles all around them, like wild chicken tracks. Whenever he sits down, he props his feet upon his desk.

Even during Christmas, he has a St. Patrick's Day concert. He's always making references to Ireland. The Old Sod, the Emerald Isle, the Land of Saints and Scholars. "Ah, sure, where would we be without St. Paddy?" he's always saying. "Sure we'd be heathens, the lot of us." On Christmas Eve he makes all the little ones in St. Dominic's dorm dress up as leprechauns. And he parades them into chapel and seats them in the front pews. They look really cute. He's an Irish fanatic. Irish football and Irish poetry. Irish sayings and Irish songs. Irish monks and Irish castles. County Cork and County Kilkenny. He's from County Kilkenny. Sometimes, right out of the blue in the middle of class, he bursts into song: "Now in Kilkenny, it is reported, sure they've marble stones there as black as ink..." And he has a pretty good voice. For some reason, the gravelly sound disappears whenever he sings. He's no match for Oberstein, but he isn't bad. Only he sings the same song most of the time. He might be on supervision in the study hall or walking around the cafeteria during meal duty, and he'll start singing, "Now in Kilkenny, it is reported..."

"He sings in his sleep," O'Connor says. He calls O'Connor the last of Ireland's high kings. He brought a big picture book to class once on Irish castles. One of the pictures was the castle of the high kings of Connacht, whose family name is O'Connor.

"Your family's castle has been in ruins since Cromwell destroyed it, lad," Madman said to O'Connor, throwing the open book on his desk. "Hold it up for all the class to see, now. Show off your castle, King O'Connor."

O'Connor held up the open book and showed it around. It was a beautiful Victorian-Italian mansion. It was made of cement and stone and looked an awful lot like Mount Kildare.

"And why wouldn't it, Dumbos?" Bug snarled after class. "The guys who built this place were the Christian Brothers of Ireland, not Singapore."

With Christmas coming, it's hard to concentrate, and Madman has given our class a tough assignment. He wants us all to know more about our roots. We have to find out everything we can about where we came from and write an essay about the place. But before he gives us the final details, he lectures us on sliding down Tracey's Hill. We love sliding there every winter. Going down lasts forever, and it has a thousand bumps. We ski down on barrel staves or slide on homemade toboggans or hubcaps or by the seat of our pants. It's so exciting when it's icy. Mr. Tracey, the owner, always chases us off the hill, but we always return. He has come to see Brother McMurtry, who has laid down the law. Madman is playing policeman, forbidding us to use the hill ever again. The sun streams through the windows as he speaks.

"It's a very dangerous thing, to be sliding on that hill, very, very dangerous, indeed. Do ye hear me, now?" His Irish brogue is hard and serious and seems more Irish than ever. He is trying to frighten us. "A very, very dangerous thing for a young lad. Several years ago, a lad—not a Mount Kildare lad, a lad from town—a young lad your age was severely injured when he hit a bump, flew through the air and landed on a broken stick that was lodged in the snow. The lad landed ... well ... on his backside ..." ("Arse," Ryan mouths to the boys in the opposite row.) "...and the stick...the stick came right out his front. It was a terrible, terrible thing, a very dreadful injury, very dreadful. Do ye hear, now? He was rushed to the General Hospital in an ambulance. Do ye hear me, now?"

"Do you mean his stomach, Bruh?" Kavanagh asks.

"No, I do not mean his stomach," Madman says. "And the word is Brother, not Bruh, Mr. Kavanagh."

"His leg, Brother?" Littlejohn asks.

"No, not his leg, you fool." Outside the classroom window, the orange-red sun lingers for a moment in the sagging icy branches.

"Then where?" Bug Bradbury squeaks.

"There are other organs, boys, other parts of the anatomy." Madman looks slyly at his fly.

We all look at each other. Bug's jaw drops to his knees. Murphy looks at his crotch and cringes.

"Did he die, Bruh?" Kavanagh asks.

"No, he did not die, Mr. Kavanagh. But his sliding days were over, I can tell ye that. There were no more sliding days for that young lad, I can tell ye that, now. That young lad's sliding days were over—for good."

"So were his baby-making days," Ryan whispers.

Bug slips me a note: Helluva way to snap the lizard.

"Now for the new geography assignment," Madman says. "Remember boys, we live on a rock, seven hundred miles out in the cold Atlantic. Where do we live, now, Mr. Kavanagh?

"On a rock, Brother, seven hundred miles out in the cold Atlantic."

Madman says the new assignment will teach us a lot about Newfoundland geography and history. Poetry memorization is bad, but nothing's as dreadful as Madman Malone's geography tests. We sit in a circle around the room and he calls a random

place name and a random boy's name. "Mr. Murphy, the
Avalon. We are sailing north, due north from Harbour Main."
Poor Murphy has to name every nook and cranny along the
Baccalieu Trail until he's told to stop because of a mistake or
because Madman wants another boy to continue.

Murphy answers, "Harbour Main, Bacon Cove, Collier's
Point, South Point, Brigus, Cupid's, Bareneed, Port-de-Grave,
Ship Cove, Hibb's Hole, Mercer's Cove, Bishop's Cove, Spoon
Cove, Upper Island Cove, Southside, Bryant's Cove, Harbour
Grace—"

Madman interrupts, shouting, "Hands up, Mr. Murphy. You
missed Feather Point. Feather Point, sir, is after Bryant's Cove,
before Harbour Grace. Hands up, Mr. Murphy."

He checks with the class recorder, Adams, to see if Murphy
has any credits. Credits are points you get from Madman for
doing a cleanup in the classroom, or for doing well on a test,
or for anything, really, that Madman decides. Once, he gave
Pittman two whacks, thinking he'd misspelled the name
Ferryland, but Oberstein pointed out that Ferryland didn't
have a hyphen, so Madman gave Pittman a credit. Needless to
say, Adams is a very popular guy. Everyone sucks up to Adams
because he can get away with adding a point to your name
every once in a while. Madman gives Murphy a whack for each
word missed. Had he missed Upper Island Cove, he would've
gotten three whacks.

After the strapping, Murphy squeezes his big hands underneath his armpits and continues: "Bristol's Hope, Carbonear,
Freshwater, Flatrock, Blow-Me-Down, Salmon Cove..." until
he reaches the tip of the trail, Grates Cove, and Madman calls
on another boy. Another time, Murphy might be told to continue down the trail on the Trinity Bay side, listing another
twenty or so names. Or Madman might stop Murphy in his

tracks and call another boy's name and say, "Let's do the Cape Shore or the Burin Peninsula."

We all hate geography class. Only Oberstein seems able to avoid the Rocket, Madman's two-foot strap, which he keeps rolled up in his pocket under his soutane when it's not in use.

At the library, I've been studying my grandfather's home, Swains Islands, a bunch of islands in Bonavista Bay, near Wesleyville. Most of the islands were settled years ago, but eventually everyone left to go to Wesleyville. Tiller's Island, where my Dad's father, Jonathan Carmichael, was from, was the first place settled. It was one of the best spots to get to the fishing grounds. Clare told me Dad's father's father sailed a schooner. He used to catch seals. Anstey and Lionel were pretty happy to find out there's a sea captain in my family. But the truth is, if you go back far enough, there's one in every Newfoundland family. That's our history—fishing and sealing.

Studying your heritage is all pretty interesting, I guess. I'm really enjoying finding out about the early settlers, especially the skippers who braved the cold Atlantic in the stormiest seas. We're supposed to find out all we can about the place we're from, if there is a fish plant there or nearby, if there's a church, if there are roads, if you can only get there by boat. All the information we can find in books or from maps or from writing our relatives. After we've gathered enough information, we're to organize it under headings: Place Name Origin, Geography, History, Biographies. Stories about people from there, maybe your aunts or uncles or cousins.

Oberstein is sullen.

"What's wrong?" I ask.

"I can't find any information about my father. Or his father."

"That's okay."

"No, it isn't. I need to know my ancestry. I don't think I'm a typical Jew."

"You seem pretty Jewish to me," I say. "Jeez, you even know how to talk Talmud."

"But I don't look Jewish. Most Semites are dark. I look albino compared to most Jews. Look at my hair. I must of gotten my mother's genes. Her great-grandfather was Scandinavian. Either I got her genes, or my father's father was a convert."

I tell him it doesn't matter. All that matters is if you feel Jewish in your heart. "If you feel Jewish, you *are* Jewish," I tell him. That seems to cheer him up.

"The heart is half a prophet," he says. "Thanks, Carmichael. You'd make a good Jew."

Hynes is from Queen of Maids Cove on the Port au Port Peninsula. It's on the west coast of the island. He's beside himself because he can't find a shred of information on the place. It's not even on the map. There isn't a thing in the library on Queen of Maids Cove. And Hynes is a real norphan. He has nobody in the whole world to ask about his roots. Oberstein told him Queen of Maids Cove is like a lot of Newfoundland communities: the names change as people resettle. Brookes is helping Hynes make up stuff about the place in exchange for half his next month's canteen card. Under the heading Place Name Origin, Brookes told him to say the name came about as a result of two fishermen who got into a big fight during a game of cards, and one claimed the wind blew his Queen of Maids overboard and he could see it floating toward the cove. "If Madman asks you for your source," Brookes says, "tell him your dead Uncle Ned told you about it when you were little. He'll believe you. He has no choice. He doesn't know if you had an Uncle Ned or an Aunt Bessie."

Brookes is a lot braver since his shunning ended. By the time Hynes passes in his assignment, he'll believe everything he's written. Brookes looked up a bunch of names in the telephone directory and some information on the neighboring towns and is helping Hynes write a pretty convincing essay. "You'll have the best paper in the class," Brookes says. "You'll be so proud of your mark, you'll swallow your Adam's apple. Just like Rags."

．　　．　　．　　．　　．

"Only McMurtry was there," Murphy says between classes, pushing back his hair with his big hand. He's really jittery. He was called to McMurtry's office during geography class.

"Not McCann?" Oberstein asks.

"No. Only McMurtry. Brother Walsh came into the room once, but it was just to tell McMurtry that supper was delayed 'cause the older boys weren't back from Signal Hill." Murphy licks his index finger and dabs his parched lips.

"Only McMurtry. Strange." Blackie goggles his eyes.

"What did he say?" I ask.

"It was weird. He went on and on about how good boys have it at the Mount, how we all have three good meals every day and a bed and books and teachers and a place to study and organized games and so many opportunities. He said millions of children around the world have nothing. Half the world goes to bed hungry, he said. But every boy in Mount Kildare is blessed. He gave me this weird look and asked me why anyone would want to steal. He said it's like stealing from yourself. He asked me if I had a baseball glove or a hockey stick. I said yes and he asked if I saw any sense in stealing my own hockey stick. I said no. He wanted to know why anyone would steal from the chapel. Stealing from God, he called it. God's house, of all places, he said. He was pretty upset. He looked pretty pale, paler than usual. He was walking around the room. He interviewed me in the TV room, and at times he walked from one end to the other. He was pacing the whole time. He wasn't angry though, just upset. Every now and then he would take off his glasses and nibble on an arm tip."

"What did he say about the missing wine?" Oberstein says.

"He just kept asking me over and over why anyone would want to do it. Steal from the chapel. From himself. From God."

"You *say* anything?" Blackie asks. "Screw up?"

"No, nothing. I'd say nothing, and he'd keep pacing and saying how he couldn't understand it, how he'd never be able to understand it. He stood still a couple of times and stared at me and said, 'Would you please explain it to me, Mr. Murphy?' Finally he said, 'Maybe someday someone will be able to explain why people do things like that, steal from themselves, steal from God.' Then he just shook his head and left. I was sitting all alone in the TV room for about ten minutes, waiting for him to come back. I thought he'd gone to get McCann to ask me more questions. After a while I figured he wasn't returning, so I came back to class."

"It wasn't an interrogation," Oberstein says. "Or an inquisition. It wasn't even an interview."

"Was it a soliloquy, like in *Julius Caesar?*" Murphy asks.

"He'll call you again," Blackie says.

"I don't think so," Murphy says. "I got this feeling he doesn't want to talk to anyone about it anymore. It was like . . . like he's come to a dead end, just thinking about it."

"He'll come to a dead end when he catches us, not before," Blackie says.

"Maybe he's trying to trick us, set us up," Ryan says.

"We'd better not let our guard down," Oberstein says. "Ryan's right, it might all be a big act."

"Maybe," Murphy says, "but I don't think so. I think he came to a dead end."

"Still, we'll keep our guard up," Blackie says. "Like Floyd Patterson. In case Ryan's right."

We don't have to worry about keeping our guard up for very long. During lunch they call Kavanagh to the TV room and question him for twenty minutes. When he returns, he tells us they offered him a reward, a puck and a hockey stick, if he finds out any information leading to the thieves. Blackie and Oberstein are starting to really worry.

·   ·   ·   ·   ·

Sometimes, at the end of the school day and on weekends, myself and Blackie help Rags with his experiments in the science lab. Rags lives in the science lab. A few years ago he made a Santa Claus and reindeer that moved on a track around the roof of the main building. Everyone in St. John's came to see it. He's always experimenting with something or other, especially around Christmastime. We mock him that he's trying to find the formula for invisibility like the mad scientist in the movie *The Invisible Man*. He just laughs and says, "How'd you know that? How'd you know that?"

He's a really good science teacher. Lotsa fun. He's full of crazy ideas. Like the Mount Kildare Christmas Raffle board, which he created last year. It's a big circular piece of plywood with a map of Newfoundland painted on it. And tiny colored bulbs, each with a number, stuck in the middle of each outport. The bulbs are attached to a long cord that holds a switch. When you press the On button, all the bulbs blink madly off and on until all the raffle tickets are sold. When we work the raffle, we never tire of the blinking map of Newfoundland. The map of many colors, Oberstein calls it.

When the brother on the microphone presses the Stop button, one colored bulb remains lit, blinking slowly off and on while from behind the big circular board a member of the Mount Kildare Choir sings a solo or the whole choir sings a

Newfoundland song. Or a few members of the band play Christmas carols. If the choir gets tired and takes a break, the brother in charge of the raffle, usually Rags or Brother Walsh, puts a forty-five record on the small phonograph he keeps nearby and switches the microphone on so that everyone, including the Christmas shoppers out on the sidewalk, can hear some accordion music. It's always a lot of fun, and if Littlejohn is around it's a laugh and a half because he dances a jig while selling tickets on the next spin. Usually, though, the choir sings the whole time.

Here's how it works. Number nineteen, for example, is a green bulb stuck on St. Mary's–The Capes, and when it lights up you will always hear Bas Belbin singing solo:

> *Take me back to my Western boat,*
> *Let me fish off Cape St. Mary's.*
> *Where the hagdowns sail and the fog-horns wail,*
> *With my friends the Browns and the Clearys.*

It is such fun because Oberstein has a contest with Bas Belbin to see who can drown the other guy out. Oberstein usually loses because Bas Belbin has the microphone. But Oberstein always gives him a good run for his money. Oberstein has the most powerful voice in the world. Rags calls him Caruso. Once, on a bus going to summer camp, he out-sung a whole busload of boys. They all quit from exhaustion. When we got back to the Mount, Oberstein was still singing.

The best time of all is when bulb number 108 lights up. Tickle Cove Pond. It's a beautiful mournful song about a mare named Kitty and her master taking a shortcut across an icy pond and falling through, and all the neighbors coming to help them out. It's got wonderful lines like

She turned 'round her head, and with tears in her eyes,
As if she were saying "You're risking our lives."
The very next minute the pond gave a sigh,
And down to our necks went poor Kitty and I.

But it isn't the mournfulness of the music or the wonderful lines in the song that make us so look forward to the flashing blue bulb marked 108. There's another reason. It's Bug Bradbury. Bug turns his back to the brother at the microphone and using the crowd as a shield he grabs himself by the crotch and wiggles his bum while the choir is singing.

Everyone, except the brother at the microphone, howls. And we try to hide our laughter, which makes it all the more hilarious. We all love seeing Bug boogie, as Blackie calls it.

There are so many beautiful songs that working at the Christmas Raffle is never ever work. It's our favorite time of the year. The choir sings lines from "The Badger Drive" whenever a community in the central region of the province lights up. There are tons of Newfoundland songs, and they are all so beautiful: "Merasheen Farewell," "The Star of Logy Bay," "The Northern Lights of Labrador," "Feller from Fortune," "The Cliffs of Baccalieu," "Petty Harbour Bait Skiff," "Wedding in Renews." And at the end of each raffle day, when the last bulb has lit up and the last winning ticket is sold, we all sing "The Ode to Newfoundland." It gives me the goosebumps every time we sing it. I guess it's because we were a country once, and now we're a country no more. No matter who's at the raffle, young and old alike, they all join in and sing the Ode:

As loved our fathers, so we love,
Where once they stood we stand,
Their prayer we raise to heav'n above,
God guard thee, Newfoundland . . .

The only day we don't have raffle is Sunday. And we would all work on Sunday too, if the brothers asked us, even though it's a mortal sin to work on Sunday.

Another thing that happens around Christmastime is bowling. "We're all going bowling. We're all going bowling." The halls come alive with more Mount criers than you can count, just before Rags makes the announcement over the PA. In that New Yawk accent, Oberstein always mimics. "All raffle workers proceed to the bus and board for St. Pete's Bowling Alleys . . . *click.*"

After the announcement, there's intense scurrying and a mad frenzied rush to get a good seat on the bus. Bowling at St. Pete's Alleys is a real treat. The brothers at St. Pete's own the alleys, and they donate a full day to the raffle boys for working so hard to raise money for Mount Kildare. It's a goofy-looking place, an old gymnasium converted into bowling alleys. It has four lanes of five-pin with the old-fashioned stand-up pins that you have to fix upright each time you finish a frame. One of us has to go down to the end of the alley and perch on a ledge above the pins, wait till the frame is finished, jump into the pit and reset the pins. The boy who winds up doing this is called the pinhead because each bowler tries his best to smash the pins as hard as he can in the hope that one will fly up and hit him in the head. On the bus we pick teams and put names in the hat to draw for the pinhead. Whoever wins the draw gets the day named in his honor.

The last time we went bowling, it was Bug Bradbury Day. Bug hates being pinhead, but he's really good at it. Probably because he's so tiny and he's as quick as a hare. He's really hard to pick off. Bowling's good fun because there's always two games going on at the same time, five-pin and the competition to pick off whoever's the pinhead. If a boy gets a strike and picks off the pinhead during the same roll, which is rarely done, each boy on either team must surrender fifty cents from his canteen card. The unwritten rules are clear and carefully followed. The bowler is allowed to stand, bowling ball in hand, while the pinhead arranges the pins and the timer counts out ten seconds from my Mickey. Once the ten seconds are up, the bowler may fire the ball regardless of the number of pins standing. Or, once the last pin has been reset, the bowler may rifle the ball down the alley, attempting to hit the pins as well as the pinhead before he makes it back to his perch. If picked off by a flying pin, not only does the pinhead have to suffer the hit as well as the taunting of all the bowlers, but he also has to give twenty-five cents from his canteen card to the boy who lands the lucky blow. If the hit is from the bowling ball, the pinhead forfeits his entire canteen card.

Bug Bradbury is rarely hit. Because he's so short, he's permitted to bring a wooden Pepsi crate with him into the pit because otherwise he would not be able to reach the alley to reset the pins. He's the only boy allowed to use a crate. From his wooden crate, Bug appears like a jack-in-the-box, popping up and down while resetting the pins. Every now and again, when he can't get up in time, he remains in the pit. Actually, it's the pinhead's only choice if he fails to rearrange the pins before the ten-second count ends. It's much safer to lay low in a corner of the pit if you see that black ball coming than to try to get back up on the perch. Bug always knows when to lay low and when to fly high. He's very clever and is almost never hit. For this reason, and the fact that he taunts the bowlers with his shrill squeaky voice—"Another gutter ball, cross-eyes . . . You're worse than an old woman"—he's the favorite target of every bowler.

His survival method is to rearrange all the pins but one very quickly, in five or six seconds. With a few seconds to spare, the last one is placed at lightning speed. You can see Bug's hand shoot out with the pin. Then, flash, his whole body rockets through the air. Kelly always yells, "Blast-off! Here comes Bug, the human bowling pin." Blackie calls him the kingpin. It's a sight to behold. We're always amazed to see it. And it's always the same, every time: Bug flying through the air like an over-sized, fully clothed bowling pin, the red-and-white pins flying everywhere the instant he rockets out of sight, everyone in the alleys holding his breath to see if Bug will make it back to his perch.

I've only seen him get hit once. Blackie caught him in the shoulder with a pin. "That didn't hit me," Bug squeaked. "That didn't touch." Two days later, in the shower, Blackie claimed his twenty-five cents when he spotted an ugly purple streak along Bug's shoulder blade.

It wouldn't be so bad for Bug, he'd get a break every now and then, if he wasn't such a pest. But safe on his perch, he taunts the bowlers to no end with shrill, saucy barks. When a boy is finished rolling, he waits patiently for the crashing noise to subside. Then he breaks the silence by accusing the bowler of having arthritis or squeaks at him to go get his eyes checked or yells that he is slower than his crippled grandmother. He is incredibly saucy, which makes everyone want to pick him off even more. But we rarely do, thanks to his size, his speed, and his Pepsi crate.

Bug is always a big hit at the bowling alleys, but he isn't allowed to be a member of the Christmas tumbling team. He wasn't even allowed to try out. Because of the hole in his heart. We were all pretty upset about it. We wanted him on the team with us, because we get to travel during the holidays and we get gifts and treats, even special meals. But it was pretty obvious at our first tumbling practice that Bug wouldn't be a Mount Kildare tumbler. He'd get so out of breath after the first roll that Blackie would have to help him. He was allowed to stay in the gym and watch. Once he fainted just watching us.

During the Christmas holidays, and on special occasions like the opening of a new school, the Mount Kildare Band and the Mount Kildare Choir often put on a concert. Sometimes Brother Walsh and Brother Malone will do an Irish play or a few skits like "Aunt Martha's Sheep" or recitations like "The Smoke Room on the Kyle." They're usually big events, and if you get to take part, you usually get some kind of special treat, like a really good meal of cold cuts and salads and all the soda pop you can drink. If the choir or band goes to a place like St. Patrick's Mercy Home, a seniors' home, or the Mental, the Mount Kildare Tumblers usually go along too.

If you're in St. Martin's dorm, you are automatically a member of the Mount Kildare Tumblers. Every Christmas, the twenty-seven boys in our dorm go to the barbershop for crewcuts and then get their tumbling uniforms: green boxer shorts and white singlets.

At the concert, we unroll the tumbling mats, which we pack on a big yellow bus, and tumble away to our heart's delight while the Mount Kildare Choir sings a song, usually "Teddy Bears' Picnic," and the Mount Kildare Band plays along. The tumblers are usually first on the program. We roll out the mats in front of the audience, either on the floor or on a stage, and line up single file in front of the first mat and wait for Brother O'Reilly, the tumbling coach, to give the nod to Brother Walsh, the band conductor, to strike up "Teddy Bears' Picnic," which the choir sings over and over until Brother O'Reilly can't see a smiling face in the audience. That usually takes a long time because, for some strange reason, at every concert the tumblers are adored. People love us to death just because we tumble. They clap their hands and stamp their feet as the band plays and the choir sings over and over:

At six o'clock their Mummies and Daddies
Will take them home to bed
Because they're tired little Teddy Bears.

"Another retarded audience," Oberstein says at each performance. It never fails. We're always the favorite. We can't
believe it or understand it, but it's true. It really pisses off the
band, because they practice morning, noon, and night. We
never think we're doing anything special. Certainly nothing
like playing in the band or singing in the choir. Those boys
practice for hours every day. We don't even practice. All we do
is get crewcuts, dress in green boxing shorts and white singlets, line up in a straight line and tumble until we run out
of mats. Then we bounce up and race to the end of the line
and repeat the exercise until the band and the choir stop
playing. It's the oddest thing you've ever seen. Twenty-seven
boys with crewcuts in boxers and singlets tumbling endlessly.
Brother O'Reilly stands at the head of the tumblers, his stern
face never once cracking a smile, giving each boy a little poke
in the back, the cue to begin, as if we are skydivers jumping
from a plane.

Occasionally Kavanagh, because he is so high-strung, will
tumble beyond the mats, often not stopping till he hits a wall
or goes flying into the wings of the stage. This causes confusion and breaks the flow of the tumblers. Brother O'Reilly has
to hold back a tumbler or two until the boy after Kavanagh
arrives on the scene to help Kavanagh up. We thought at first
that Kavanagh was doing this intentionally, because the audience loved it. They'd point to him and howl with laughter,
completely ignoring the other tumblers. But Kavanagh wasn't
doing it for attention. Tumbling off the mats along a hardwood
floor is no picnic. He just had a ton of energy. He couldn't help
himself. He really got into it. And he forgot where he was. One

time, at Mary Star of the Sea, instead of a wall at the end of the mats, there was a curtain draped in front of a set of stairs, and Kavanagh tumbled through the curtain and down the stairs, breaking his leg. Brother O'Reilly motioned to Brother Walsh to continue the music, as he raced to assess the damage to Kavanagh. It was hilarious to see O'Reilly emerge from behind the curtain to thunderous applause carrying a smiling Kavanagh in his arms.

"I guess he's a *tired* little teddy bear," Oberstein said.

* * * * *

It's well past ten o'clock. There's not a sound in the dormitory. I'm lying awake with a headache, anxious about our early morning run. We are running much farther now, and Blackie wants tonight's run to be our longest and our best time yet. He wants us to run as far as Marine Drive.

I lie awake thinking about what I overheard between Blackie and Oberstein after study hall. They were in the geography room, trying to figure out the distance from St. John's to Argentia. They were looking at the geological map again and arguing about a logging road. Oberstein was using the word "decoy" a lot. Maybe Blackie plans to run away. To New York, to find his mother. I'm worried to death. If he's caught, he'll be killed. Maybe that's why we're training so hard, doing a Comrades. So Blackie can be in perfect shape to run most of the way to Argentia, to catch the ferry to Nova Scotia. We're training for Blackie. Blackie's escape. Maybe that's what Oberstein meant by decoy. The summer marathon is a decoy for Blackie. Shorty Richardson's a decoy. Ryan's a decoy. We're all decoys. For Blackie.

They put the map away really fast when I came into the room, and pretended they were doing an assignment for Madman. But Murphy told me he's heard Blackie and Oberstein talking about it a few times. "We're decoys alright," he said. "Blackie's wooden ducks." He wasn't really angry about it. He was just mad that Blackie hadn't confided in us. I don't want to believe him. I make up my mind not to tell the other runners. But maybe I should. They have every right to know about Blackie's plan. And they'll want to help. It'll make them train harder. We all want Blackie to get to New York to find his mother. I'll tell them tomorrow. I gotta tell them. They should know.

My head spins as I think about Blackie getting caught. I see Ryan's strapping again, clear as a movie. And Rowsell getting strapped. And Brookes being shunned. And Clare and Evan touching. And then Blackie wandering aimlessly around New York, with no home and nothing to eat. Like Chop-Chops. The ferry to the mainland is so far away, much farther than a Comrades. And New York . . . New York is a galaxy away.

I think about Oberstein's mother's hands and little Jack. Like Oberstein, I wish he was there to look after her. I say a few Hail Marys that her hands will get better, and I say a few for little Jack, that one day Oberstein and little Jack will be together again. I think of Blackie and Oberstein and all their secret meetings. And I worry again about Blackie getting caught. I pray that when that time comes, he doesn't get caught. I close my eyes and think of nothing for a few minutes. Hoping I don't get the spells. A bout that could be the worst ever. I'd rather get in the ring with Floyd Patterson than face this bout. I just know it's gonna be awful.

Finally, I think of the run and how fast we're getting. Our time gets better and better every race we run. We're so excited for Shorty Richardson and for each other. There's a special feeling, almost a vibration when we run together now. I try to sleep, because Blackie has warned us of the danger of not being in shape for the marathon. Red Kelly, who plays for the Maple Leafs, once said during intermission on *Hockey Night in Canada* that young athletes must get eight to ten hours sleep every night. "You kids need that," he said. "It's the most important thing." But Mickey Mantle is in my mind, then Yogi Berra, then Casey Stengal, then a scene from *The Fly* where the cat is prowling around. *The Fly* is the scariest movie I've ever seen. Bug still has nightmares about it. Finally, I remember Oberstein's advice and give in. "It's the only way I can get any sleep when I have the spells," he once said. "I just give in and try to stay awake and somehow that manages to get me a few hours sleep."

I pretend Clare is sitting on my bunk telling me to close my eyes and sleep as she clicks her heavy black rosary beads.

"You need sleep too," I say.

"I'll sleep when I finish the rosary. Shhh."

I sit up. "We're gonna win the marathon, Clare. Sure as Ted Williams will win the batting title this year. It will be another first for the Mount. Like the time we beat the Salvation Army Band. It might be close, but Shorty Richardson will win. And Ryan will come second. Ryan's getting so fast. Blackie thinks he has a shot at beating Shorty. We're up to fifteen miles now, and our time gets better every run. The night running is working out great. Every night out we knock off a few more seconds."

She clicks her beads and then asks softly, "Aren't you afraid of getting caught?"

I laugh. "No, Clare, we know how to cover the bases. We're like a team of Phil Rizuttos..."

"Be careful. Don't get cocky. You still could get caught. And you'd all be strapped. Worse, you wouldn't be allowed to run in the marathon."

"Ah, don't worry, we're not stupid. We'll be fine. We won't get caught. Blackie and Oberstein have a foolproof plan for every night we run."

"But you must be very careful. Especially when you are

the lead runner. It's dark and icy, and you could fall, break your leg . . ."

"Clare," I interrupt, knowing she's worrying too much, "why aren't there any nuns here? At Mount Kildare?" I laugh and mimic little Jimmy Burns: "'How come there ain't any female brothers?' Wouldn't it make sense to have a few nuns around here? It's great having you and Tokyo Rose working in the bakery once in a while, but I don't see why some nuns couldn't come here too."

"What a good idea," she says. "I'll ask Reverend Mother about that tomorrow."

She sighs. Her face is a ghostly gleam in the darkness.

"Now, you must sleep. Close your eyes." I lean forward and kiss her cheek. "And you must eat more—you're too skinny."

"I'm not skinny. I'm gaunt. That's what Oberstein says runners are spoze to be."

She strokes my hair and chuckles. "My, my, whatever am I to do with the chubby cherub?" she says. Clare loves Oberstein. I think it's because they're both religious. As I close my eyes, she says hastily, "I almost forgot. I have a pair of woollen socks for you, for night running. They'll keep you nice and dry during your winter runs."

Clare is so thoughtful. I want to sit up and throw my arms around her, but I'm afraid we'll both cry, so I just close my eyes and say good night.

"Good night, and God watch you," she says.

The dorm is pitch-black. Outside, the wind is whining. I hope it's stormy, but not too stormy to cancel the run. We all love running in bad weather. Somehow it makes us feel better. I check my Mickey. Midnight. At the foot of my bed, under my mattress, is my running gear. In a few hours, Oberstein will give us the all-clear signal. I toss and turn, and say a few Hail Marys that I will sleep.

The wind has died down when Oberstein rouses me a second time. I've overslept.

"Blackie's pissed. Get a move on." His whisper is gravely and harsh.

Instead of running our regular route—behind the pool, across the soccer field and past Virginia Waters to Sugar Loaf—Blackie heads toward Quidi Vidi Lake, home of the Royal Regatta. On the way, we pass a parked snowplow. The operator is asleep in the cab. We kill our flashlights. Blackie motions toward the driver and then points to a side street. In bad weather, we run in one pack, with Richardson in the middle for protection. It starts to snow really hard, and Murphy tells Blackie we may have to cut our run short, as it looks like a storm's brewing.

"Keep movin'," Blackie barks.

"Blackie, what if a cop car comes by? We're out in the open."

Blackie stops so suddenly we bang into each other. "Side streets," he says. "Side streets to the lake and back. Run fast. Gonna be a short run."

We make slow progress in the soft, wet snow, which is getting thicker by the minute. Now and then someone slips on the greasy pavement. There's the occasional stumble, but nobody falls. It's freezing cold, and I can see the breaths coming, like smoke, from each runner's nostrils.

Kavanagh's face is always the same, no matter the weather: an intense grin that looks like he's about to break into laughter. The scrawniest guy in the Mount, he's strong and generous, always looking around to see that everyone's okay. In history class, when we were doing the great Newfoundland sealing disaster of 1914, where so many brave Newfoundlanders were stranded on the ice and died, I thought of Kavanagh and how if he'd been there he would've made it. And when Brother Vincent asked the class who among us would be most likely to survive, I thought of Blackie and Kavanagh. I don't know if anyone else in our group would've made it, but I know Kavanagh would've. With that silly grin on his face. And he would be giving everyone a friendly slap on the back, passing a cigarette and joking and telling us the sun was coming up soon. Giving us hope minute after minute. It's like Kavanagh was put in this world just to laugh. Everyone knows Blackie would survive anything, but it's Kavanagh who would be the one to egg us on, the one to give us constant hope, the one who would save a few others. Kavanagh's smiling even when we're running against the wind.

Coming off Berteau Avenue, we head to the bottom of New Cove Road. The wind is a banshee, howling down a line of parked cars, and the snow is swirling furiously. A million tiny snowflakes fly toward us.

"We're in a storm, Blackie." Father Cross is nervous. "Looks like a northerly squall."

Blackie nods and points in the direction of Kenna's Hill, which means the run is cut short.

"Two-minute hill," Blackie yells above the storm. He means he wants us to take Kenna's Hill in under two minutes. From Memorial Stadium it's impossible on a good day. I check my Mickey when we reach the traffic lights at the base of the hill. The pavement is thick with greasy snow now, and I'm sure nobody will make it through the sleety wind in less than four minutes. But we will give it our all. For Blackie.

Halfway up, there are headlights in the distance, so we duck behind Conway's old stone house until the car glides past. Ryan keeps running. At the top of the hill he waits by the cemetery. He's in high spirits, pumping the air with his victory fist, thinking he's done the hill in less than two minutes. But while he is well ahead of the pack, he's a full two minutes beyond the mark.

The final leg, we stay close to the houses on Torbay Road in case we need to duck a vehicle. Blackie blasts Ryan for not ducking behind Conway's. "Fool, fool, fool," he keeps saying. Ryan apologizes and falls behind, sheepish the rest of the run. Unobserved, we arrive at the soccer field, the beginning of our property, each runner scooping up a mittful of sweet snow to suck on as we finish the final yards. Blackie directs us to make a wide arc toward the back of the swimming pool so we can enter safely through the yard. Off the streets, giant snowflakes are gently drifting down, creating a peaceful, easy feeling. Blackie orders us to stop near the cement porch by the handball courts before scooting across the yard.

Inside the building, we crouch down and are perfectly still. We're hardly breathing in the dull light, like little animals. About to head to the dorm, we hear footsteps and dart inside the washroom. Our timing is off because we have returned early. The footsteps come nearer, very close to us. It's Spook. We hear his grunting, and the rattle of his night watchman's clock and chain. As the footsteps descend the stairs and disappear, we remove our sneakers, and Blackie nudges us off to the dorm in pairs. Kavanagh and I are first. We're so tense, Kavanagh laughs. In the morning Blackie will curse him and Ryan for their foolishness. But for now, all that's important is our safety. Oberstein is sitting at the top of the stairs reading as we take the steps two at a time.

"Chrissakes, where were you?" he whispers. "I was worried to death; there's a terrible storm ..."

I put my finger to my lips, and we head off to the dorm. Within minutes everyone's tucked away, listening to Murphy's five long snores, the signal that we're safely in bed and the coast is clear.

My bunk is freezing, so I bury myself beneath the blankets and start breathing hot breaths. As the bed warms up, my eyes close and I see Marilyn Monroe. She's pursing her lips and putting on lipstick. I love looking at her doing that. I think of her in the movies and just recently on TV, a storm of confetti falling on her and DiMaggio as they leave the church. I try to hold the happy couple in my mind, but Jolting Joe won't stay. I stare at her beauty mark, her beautiful blond hair, her gorgeous smile and again her pouting lips. She's definitely the most beautiful woman in the world. I look at her for a long time. As I fade, she's wearing a low-cut dress, and she's seated on a rock wall, leaning forward, with Niagara Falls roaring in the background. She speaks but says nothing as I press my pillow into my face and imagine her there with me, wrapping me in her arms and smothering me with her breasts.

13

MADMAN KICKS HIS YARDSTICK. We're being quizzed on Newfoundland place names. It's morning, the period before recess. The coldest day of the year. At Chapel you could see your breath as we said prayers, and there were icicles hanging outside the stained glass windows. We are cold and tense. Colder than usual. And more nervous than ever. Oberstein has made a mistake, a terrible mistake.

"What year did Cabot discover the New found land, class?"

"1497, Brother."

"Very good, class. And the capital, St. John's, was named by the Franciscans for what great saint, class?"

"St. John the Baptist, Brother."

"And how old is this great city, boys?"

"The oldest city in North America, Brother."

"Well done, class. Now, it's time for nomenclature. And what is nomenclature, Mr. Oberstein?"

"Refers to the system of names used to identify geographical features, Brother, including the names of settlements. Toponymy, derived from the Greek words *topo*, place, and *onama*, names, is the study of geographical names, or toponyms, Brother."

"Excellent, Mr. Oberstein. Mr. Kavanagh: Aguathuna . . ."

"Aguathuna. Western, Brother. West of Stephenville. Port au Port. Used to be called Lineville. No, no . . . Limeville. Limeville, 'cause of all the limestone there. First named Jack of Clubs Cove by sailors of Her Majesty's Royal Navy 'cause they thought the limestone cliffs looked like the playing card. October 24th, Brother, the feast of St. Raphael, patron saint of Mount Kildare . . . October 24th, 1911, the residents changed the name to Aguathuna, replacing Jack of Clubs and Limeville. Aguathuna is Beothuck, Brother. *Aguathoonet* means great white rock."

"Thank you, Mr. Kavanagh. Well done, lad. Mr. Brookes: Angel's Cove."

"Angels Cove. Avalon, Brother. On the eastern shore of Placentia Bay. Corruption of 'Angles Cove,' used in 1910 by the historian Reverend M. F. Howley as a name for the community. The *Dictionary of Newfoundland* lists 'a curved inlet' as one defi-nition of angle."

"Thank you, Mr. Brookes. Let's see now, Mr. Ryan: Cape White Handkerchief."

"Labrador, Brother," Ryan answers correctly. "At the entrance to Nachvak Fiord. So named for a large square of light-colored rock . . ."

Oberstein is tense. Blackie is tense. We are all tense. Agitation is evident everywhere. Oberstein made his mistake during an interview with McMurtry about the wine stealing. Fidgeting is the order of the day. Oberstein thumbs the edge of his *Dictionary of Newfoundland* and stares at the floor. Blackie sits with his arms crossed tightly against his chest, waiting for Madman to drop his dictionary, his usual signal that the quizzing is over.

"Mr. Hynes. Let's see, now, we've had none from central. Gambo, Mr. Hynes."

"Gambo. Central. Northeast of Glovertown, Brother. On

October 3rd, this year, the communities of Dark Cove, Middle Cove, and Gambo were joined together to form the town of Gambo. Origin, Portuguese, Baie de les Gamas, Bay of Does . . ."

Murphy twists in his seat, turns, and rolls his eyes toward Rowsell, who is white with fear. Rowsell has studied only the names of the central region of the island. It's unlikely Madman will ask more than two or three place names from central. Rowsell slouches in his seat.

"Lester's Field, Mr. Yetman." Madman drums his *Dictionary of Newfoundland* with the yardstick. It's always a horrible sound, but today it's unbearable.

"Avalon, Brother. Used as an airstrip on June 14th, 1919, by Captain John Alcock and Lieutenant Arthur Whitten Brown for the beginning of the first nonstop transatlantic flight from St. John's to Ireland . . ."

"Ireland?"

"Clifden, Ireland, Brother."

"Part of the city, lad. Part of the city of St. John's, Mr. Yetman. You neglected to say it was originally named for its owner."

Surprisingly, Madman does not give Yetman the traditional two whacks for screwing up.

"Mr. O'Toole: St. Alban's."

"St. Alban's, Brother. Eastern, on Bay d'Espoir. It's pronounced Despair, Brother."

Madman smirks. "Well done."

"First known as Ship Cove, Brother. The name was changed in 1915 by the Reverend Stanislaus St. Croix, the parish priest, who wanted a Catholic name for his Catholic parish. St. Alban was a third-century martyr, Brother, who was murdered on the site of St. Alban's Cathedral, in the city of the same name in Hertsfordshire, England."

"St. Patrick would have been a more appropriate name, don't you think?"

"Yes, Brother."

"Well done, Mr. O'Toole. Well done, lad."

O'Toole beams as Madman drops the *Dictionary of New-foundland* to the floor. There's a mad scraping of desks and a bustle of body movement. Madman always picks the boy he thinks is slouching the most. Again, Rowsell is odd man out. Madman kicks at his yardstick while strolling toward Rowsell's desk.

"You have a choice, Mr. Rowsell. One of life's many choices, sir. You may take your two whacks now, or you may opt for double or nothing. Do you understand double or nothing?" Rowsell nods. "Very well, the final place name for the day ..."

Rowsell's eyelids move at lightning speed. His body stiffens. He looks to Oberstein for help.

"We'll make it a little more interesting now, shall we?" He opens his dictionary. "We'll give you a little hint now, Mr. Rowsell. The last name for the day will be from ... let's see, now ... from the eastern. No ... no ... from Labrador. Unless *you* have a suggestion. Do you, Mr. Rowsell?"

It's an old trick. Rags told us once that it's used in the US military all the time. He said he had a friend in the navy whose commanding officers asked if he'd like to be stationed in the Atlantic or the Pacific. His friend said he'd love to go to the Pacific, and they sent him to the Atlantic for five years. We're all on to it, all except slowpoke Rowsell. Madman wants Rowsell to name a region, and he will choose a place name from a completely different one. We all bristle, certain Rowsell will say central. Rowsell shrugs, purses his thin white lips. He does not know what to do or say, whether to take the two whacks or gamble on all or nothing. Madman licks his lips as he kicks his yardstick. "Time's up, sir. Newtown."

"Newtown, Brother. Central. On Bonavista Bay. Used to be called Inner Islands. Changed in 1892 by John Haddon. He owned a lobster business. In November 1929 Captain Job Barbour, travelling from St. John's to Newtown in his schooner, the *Neptune*, went adrift in a storm. Barbour's journey took him to . . . to Tober . . . Tobermary, Scotland. It's all in his book, *Forty-eight Days Adrift*. Used to be known as Inner Islands. Changed in 1892, Brother."

Oberstein realizes that Rowsell has forgotten to mention that the Barbour family of Newtown produced several generations of prosperous sea captains. His hand shoots up.

"Yes, Mr. Oberstein."

"I've read *Forty-eight Days Adrift*, Brother. It's in the library. I was wondering, Brother, the author, Captain Barbour, refers to his Queen Anne–style family home, which he opened for the public. As a museum, Brother. I was wondering, Brother, why would a sea captain open his home like that? Was that a common thing back then, Brother?"

Madman kicks at his yardstick as he moves toward Oberstein's desk. He laughs.

"A good question, Mr. Oberstein. The outport aristocracy. The Brits again, with their snobbery and cajoling. Outport aristocracy of the sea, Mr. Oberstein. Do you understand the meaning of the word 'aristocracy'? A bright boy like you should know that."

"Oh yes, Brother. It means the ruling class, the nobility. Now it makes sense, Brother," Oberstein says, sucking up.

"That's it for today's *Dictionary of Newfoundland*. Now for your homework . . ."

Rowsell has been spared four whacks. He glances over at Oberstein, purses his lips and nods. Oberstein removes his glasses. His eyes are red. He wipes sweat from his forehead with the palm of his hand. He's still upset about his big mistake. He looks at Rowsell, blushes, and lowers his head, his silken hair falling in front of his eyes.

• • • • •

"Take it easy, Blackie, we all make mistakes," Father Cross says during recess.

"Yeah," Murphy says. "We all make mistakes, Blackie."

We're all in the library, searching the bookshelves. Ryan, Bug, and Kelly are rifling through the *Encyclopædia Britannica*. Father Cross is looking through magazines. We're all in a sweat.

"Trump card's silence. You should of taken the fifth."

"They didn't suspect anything," Oberstein says.

"Don't matter. Red flag's gone up."

"I'm sure they didn't ..."

"Maybe. Maybe not," Blackie says.

Oberstein is worried about how he handled his interrogation, as he calls it. He has given us a play-by-play of what happened. Blackie thinks Oberstein made a mistake. Somehow, during the questioning, Oberstein got sidetracked and said the word hangover. When McCann asked him how he knew anything about a hangover, Oberstein said he read about it in a book. When Brother McMurtry asked him the name of the book, Oberstein said he couldn't remember, but it was in the library. Blackie insists that was a big mistake and urges us to root out a library book with something on hangovers.

Oberstein doesn't think he's sent up a red flag. But he doesn't dare challenge Blackie.

"You're probably right, Blackie. I guess I say too much sometimes."

"No shit," Blackie says. "And you're in the Brotherhood." He's really pissed off.

"But I don't think we have anything to worry about ..."

"Maybe. Maybe not."

"The way I said it, they won't suspect anything ... I'm sure ..."

"Can never be sure about any little thing. Never. Can be sure about death, that's all."

Oberstein shakes his head and runs his nervous fingers through his silken hair. He knows Blackie is right. He has made a mistake. He feels terrible. "Red flag," he says to me. "Most unkindest cut of all."

"Check the index for alcohol effects or drunkenness," Oberstein tells Ryan. "You won't find anything under hangover. It's slang."

"If we find somethin', Oberstein's gonna talk to McCann right away. Cover things up nice."

Blackie calms down a bit. He thought Oberstein would play the silence card better than any of us. He keeps telling Oberstein he should've known better, being an American. He says Oberstein should've taken the fifth. The fifth means the Fifth Amendment. We all know what he's talking about because we saw Jimmy Cagney do it once in a gangster movie. He kept grinning and saying Fifth Amendment over and over to every question. We all went around for weeks saying Fifth Amendment to everything. Someone would say, Hey got a smoke? And the answer would be Fifth Amendment. Luckily, it didn't last very long, just a few days. It drove everyone crazy.

Murphy finds a reference to moonshine and bootlegging in a ratty old encyclopedia, but Blackie says it's no good. Oberstein needs a book that describes a hangover, or at least gives a few details about it. We've poked through the shelves for ten minutes when Kelly yells "Bingo!" He has found an old medical journal with a full page on the unpleasant aftereffects of alcohol consumption. Oberstein is so happy he gives Kelly a big kiss on the top of the head.

"I'd rather have a cigarette," Kelly says.

Bug clicks open his little silver case. "One," he barks.

"I'll bring the book to McCann right away," Oberstein says.

Blackie grabs Oberstein's arm and snatches the book from him. "Tell him you just remembered. Like it just came to you. Outta the blue."

"Good idea," Ryan says. "Tell him you remember reading about it in a medical book in the library. Let McCann hunt for the book."

"Seek and ye shall find," Father Cross sings.

"Oh, he'll hunt for it. He'll hunt for it, and he'll find it."

Blackie puts the journal back on the shelf where Ryan found it, and we head out, feeling a whole lot easier than we did when we came in.

On the way to our next class, Oberstein is downcast.

"You okay?" I ask.

"Yeah," he says.

But I know he's not. He feels he has let Blackie down.

.   .   .   .   .

McCann approaches the front of the classroom and shakes the chalk dust from his soutane. Another session of Monologues and Dialogues is about to begin. He has two props: *Missions Magazine* and a poster of a red maple leaf on a white field. He tapes the poster to the front of his desk, shakes his head slowly and stares at it for a long time. He turns, rolls the magazine slowly and taps it on Tracey's desk.

"A leaf. A simple maple leaf. Worn by our Olympic athletes since 1904. Or is it? Is it a mere leaf?" He squints, drops his jaw and stares at the ceiling.

Brookes raises his hand. "If you look at the whites around the two leafs, Brother, it looks like two angry men."

"I . . . don't see . . . any men."

"You gotta stare just at the whites, Brother."

"Quiet Brook!" McCann can't see the angry men. "Today,

class, there will be a new twist to Monologues and Dialogues, a one-time-only Monologues and Dialogues session. A special event, if you will. During today's Monologues and Dialogues, there will be no Dialogues. That is correct, class. No Dialogues. Only Monologues." He unrolls the magazine and opens it. "With talk of Vatican Two, the Holy Father has asked all Romans to take a keen interest in the culture of our foreign brothers and sisters. Remember, boys, we are a small church in a large world. What are we?"

"A small church in a large world, Brother."

"You've been told that we are to enter into dialogue and discourse in order to discover that ray of truth to be found in other world religions." He eyes the magazine. "In the current issue of *Missions Magazine*, Father Yukio Basho, a converted Roman from the Asian persuasion, a Japanese Roman, has written a koan, as it's called, not to be confused, class, with 'cone' as in 'ice cream cone.'" He giggles foolishly. "My Japanese brother loves both kinds of koans. In his recent letter he informed me that in Japan the study of koans begins by investigating the koan *Mu*, pronounced Mee-oo in Japanese. Let me hear that now, Bradburys."

"Mooooo," Bug bellows.

McCann reaches over and smacks him in the side of the head. "Meee-ooo, Bradburys. Like a cat, not like a cow. Let's hear it, everyone."

"Meee-ooo!"

"Excellent, sumos. When Master Chaochou was asked if a dog had the Buddha nature, he said, *Mu*. All sumos must practice the *Mu* sound. Repeat it inwardly over and over during the day, everywhere you go. Let it be your mantra. Chant it during meditation. This is very important, sumos, most important. *Mu* is associated with the power pack—breathing from below the belly button. Concentrate on locating the *Mu* in the belly button and become one with it when you chant. Later, we will take the lotus position and practice.

"Yikes, the lotus position," Oberstein sighs.

"Now for an example of a Japanese koan: You know the sound of two hands clapping . . . but what of the sound of one hand clapping?" He giggles again. "This koan is spelled with a K. . . . *K-O-A-N*." He is dead serious again. "Will you remember that, Kellys?"

"Yes, Brother. Koan with a K, Brother."

"Very good, Kellys. K-E-double-L-Y. Kellys, with the green necktie. Father Yukio Basho's koan, which you shall hear momentarily . . . This koan, like all Japanese koans, is not meant to be discussed. It is . . ." He pauses and stares at the ceiling, searching for a word. He snaps his fingers. "Yes, it is an enigma. No. More than an enigma. It is an enigma wrapped in a conundrum. And conundrums aren't meant to be discussed, class. They are beyond the reach of the ordinary intellect. They are meant to be contemplated. Meditated upon. You see, that's what the Japanese Romans your age do, boys." He is extremely excited. "They sit quietly, contemplating their koans."

"'Scuse me, why do they count their koans, Brother?" Rowsell asks.

"Not counting, Rowsells. Contemplating. Thinking, man, thinking. Something foreign to people like you, Rowsells. These Asian Romans contemplate, boys, to gain understanding and enlightenment. All sumos will contemplate koans privately, under my guidance. I will assign koans to each sumo. You will meet with *Yokozuna* to present your answers for my approval or rejection."

"Brother, where do koans come from?" Murphy asks.

McCann rolls his head toward the ceiling. "Who's to say? Nowhere special. Everywhere and nowhere. Listen to koans in your daily life. All around you. Brother Walsh muttering, 'Canteen card, please.' One of the little ones singing, 'Catch me if you can.' A Newfoundland fisherman saying, 'Far as ever a puffin flew.' A sumo saying, 'Come in out of the rain.' Koans are everywhere . . . and nowhere.

"Now then, to our Monologue, our koan from Father Basho's sermon. Pay close attention now, boys, close attention. This is Oriental wisdom. As there will be no Dialogues, you will be expected to sit still for the remainder of the class, contemplating the koan. Here it is, boys. Listen carefully, now."

He reads from the magazine:

The wind was flapping the temple flag and two monks were having an argument about it. Monk number one said, "The flag is moving." Monk number two said, "The wind is moving." They argued back and forth but could not reach the truth. The sixth patriarch said, "It is not the wind that moves. It is not the flag that moves. It is your mind that moves." The two monks were struck with awe.

Silence. Oberstein slips me a note: What of the sound of pigeon droppings?

Brother McCann raises his forefinger to his lips. "Shhh," he whispers. "No Dialogues . . . Shhh . . . Conundrums are beyond the reach of the ordinary intellect." He turns and tiptoes back to his desk and sits down. He puts a finger to his lips. "Shhh," he whispers. "Contemplate. As the Holy Father has requested." He points to the maple leaf, smiles foolishly and closes his eyes. Then he tilts his head and listens as if straining to hear some distant music.

I look at Blackie, who rolls his eyes, raises a finger to his ear and spins it rapidly. Murphy glances at me, shrugs his broad shoulders and closes his eyes. I look around the room. Everyone except Blackie has his eyes closed. I look at my Mickey. Thirty minutes left. Thirty minutes to stare at the two angry men in the maple leaf or contemplate Father Basho's koan.

·   ·   ·   ·   ·

McCann jumps to his feet. He has dozed off contemplating Father Basho's koan, and the buzzer jolts him.

"Composition books, boys. Double period. Take out your composition books. Today's essay topic is an ecumenical one. And there is a big prize for the boy who writes the best essay." McCann smiles, tilts his chair and lolls his head, looking upward, as if searching the ceiling for a hairline crack he knows is there.

We all look at Oberstein, who will not only win the essay contest but during the double period will write some of ours. Oberstein keeps detailed records of how many spelling and grammar mistakes he deliberately places in the essays he writes for Kavanagh and Bug and many of the other boys. "It's important to have the same pattern in each essay," Oberstein says, "but not the exact number of mistakes each time." I write essays for some of the boys too. But I'm not as picky as Oberstein. I guess if I want to be a real writer I should be more like Oberstein.

"The boy who writes the best essay will receive a big prize. A suitable prize."

"What's the topic, Brother?" Kavanagh asks.

"Today's topic is ..." McCann straightens his chair and smiles his stupid smile, "If Jesus Were Japanese."

Bug looks at Blackie and rolls his eyes.

"Break into groups, class. You have ten minutes for dialogues."

"What a topic!" Oberstein says. "Why Jesus Is Jewish would

at least make some sense. Why couldn't he at least give us a sensible topic?"

"If Jesus Were Japanese is pretty dumb, if you ask me," Murphy says.

We break into groups and discuss writing an essay about Jesus being Japanese. We all agree to call him Jesus-san. We are permitted to chat for ten minutes before writing. Most have pretty ordinary ideas: describing Jesus-san wearing a kimono or Jesus-san eating Japanese fish, something called "sushi," or Jesus-san going around bowing a lot to Peter-san and Andrew-san.

Kelly's is really interesting. He writes about the boy Jesus-san in the temple at the age of twelve. Instead of Jesus-san mesmerizing the Pharisees with his knowledge of Scripture, Kelly has him jumping around as a sumo showing the Pharisees all kinds of new moves.

Oberstein writes about Jesus-san wandering around a Shinto garden the night before he is crucified. He has Jesus sweating blood in a Japanese garden while contemplating an original koan about nature spirits. Then he has him fall asleep and go to Shinto heaven with Peter-san and James-san and John-san, where he dreams they are skipping on rose-petal water while playing a game called H_2o-ku, which Oberstein made up, and which is a half-assed combination of water polo and box-ball.

Halfway through the second period, McCann asks each boy to read what he has written. Oberstein's essay is chosen as the best in the class, which doesn't surprise anyone. McCann says he awarded it the big prize for its creativity and realism, which makes Oberstein roll his eyes and jab his fingers in his mouth.

After lunch we are called to the chapel for the rosary and a special ecumenical assembly for the presentation of

Oberstein's big prize. Brother McCann and Brother McMurtry give brief speeches. Brother McMurtry talks about the importance of the universal church, the ecumenical movement, and the coming of Vatican Two. McCann says we cannot pray hard enough for our separated brethren of the Asian persuasion. He then echoes what he says and adds a bit about the importance of reading and writing.

All the brothers go on about the importance of reading and writing. When I told Rags once that I might become a writer, he promised to take me to the Gosling Public Library. "I'll introduce you to the *New York Times* and the *New Yorker*," he said, "the best writing in the world."

Brother McMurtry agrees with McCann, and lectures us about how a boy will get nowhere in this vale of tears without knowing how to read and write. "When a boy leaves Mount Kildare and enters the real world he will need to know how to read and write more than anything else."

When he finishes his speech, Brother McMurtry announces that Oberstein is the winner of the ecumenical prize and calls him up to the altar rail, shakes his hand, and urges us to give him a big round of applause. Then they ask Oberstein to read a sample paragraph from his winning essay. Oberstein reads the part about how difficult it is for Jesus-san to say sayonara to the disciples the night before his crucifixion. How it made Jesus-san weep tears of blood the color of rose petals.

When Oberstein finishes, Brother McCann urges everyone to clap again. Then he presents Oberstein with his prize. He snaps his fingers, and two older altar boys appear, each carrying something from the sacristy. One holds a large, colorful Japanese fan. The other carries a finely embroidered silk kimono. Oberstein looks oddly at Brother McCann, a vacant, slightly bored look. He squints several times, as if not believing what he sees, then glances at the altar boys, who stand dumbly, holding his prizes.

"Congratulations!" Brother McMurtry says.

Oberstein stares at the fan and kimono through his perfectly round glasses with a blend of curiosity and sad surprise. Brother McMurtry snaps his fingers, and one of the older altar boys helps Oberstein into his kimono while the other boy unfurls the oversized fan.

I'll never forget Oberstein cursing all the way to the dormitory after Chapel, Bug trailing behind us, bellowing, "Mooooo."

"What the hell am I supposed to do with a goddamn kimono and a fucken fan," he shouts, tossing them both into his locker, where they lie for months, until one day he gives them to Father Cross for materials for one of his costumes.

14

ATTENTION, SUMOS! Leverage against force ... The Japanese art of jujitsu was made famous by the samurai. Jujitsu uses the principle of leverage against force, redirecting an opponent's energy and harmony of motion. There are fifty-one arresting devices to help you do so. You will learn them all, like the seventy sumo moves. The object of the exercise is to disable, cripple, even kill an attacker by using his own momentum and strength against him."

Oberstein rolls his eyes. Bug cocks his head. Dark laughter.

"Today we will use *mondo* to discuss this subject. *Mondo* is Zen repartee, using questions and answers. It will replace Monologues and Dialogues. Now then, an attacker's great advantage is momentum, force, power, speed. The victim, sumos, is aware of his attacker's great strength. This awareness is his weapon. Leverage against force. In jujitsu, the attacked becomes the attacker. Think, sumos, you are on a dark street late at night. A car screeches to a halt. Your attacker races toward you with a hunting knife. What do you do, sumos?"

Silence.

"Kellys, fight or flight?"

Silence.

"Ryans, the knife is nearer. Fight or flight?"

"Flight, Brother."

"Wrong!" McCann's eyes bulge. He has fooled us again. *Arresting devices.* You use an arresting device, Ryans. There are fifty-one in jujitsu. We will learn them all— tumbling, throws, restraints, chokes, kicks—all. First, you must learn to use your tumbling skills. You are all members of the Mount Kildare Tumblers?"

"Yes, Brother."

"The hunting knife is coming toward you. The jujitsu sumo does not run. He is not afraid. He uses technique. What is your arresting technique?"

Silence.

McCann shakes his head. "It is simple, sumos. You use the first arresting technique. The tumble technique. You fall to your back, and at the last possible moment, if you are skilled, you take advantage of your attacker's strength by kicking your feet upward into your attacker's belly. Whose own force sends him crashing into his car, knocking him out. Or worse. It takes much practice, sumos, much skill."

"Like in baseball," Bug says, sucking up. "The faster a Whitey Ford pitch is, the more chance it has of being hit out of the park."

McCann ignores him and claps his hands. "Tumbling, sumos, is what we will practice before the break. The first defense against weapon attacks. The first of the fifty-one techniques in the Japanese art of jujitsu."

After the break, Yoko Loco—everyone calls McCann that now—appears in full sumo dress, his Pebbles hairdo off to one side. He is late. He waddles to the mats. Oberstein, who is the leader, the *hancho,* passes McCann a list of boys who are absent due to illness or who have assigned chores. McCann eyeballs the list and growls. "*Kiotsuke,*" he shouts, and we stand straight as arrows, holding our breath. "*Keirei,*" he screams, and we all instantly bow. Sometimes, if a boy doesn't bow properly, McCann sends him to the *dojo*, the far corner, to practice bowing for the entire morning. It's terribly boring. I had to do it once. Every second day, McCann orders Brian Carey to the *dojo*, and each time he calls Carey's name, Oberstein whispers, "Hurry, Carey," which cracks us up because hara-kiri is a form of Japanese suicide. Once, when Oberstein and I were in the *dojo*, Bug passed us a note: How do Larry and Moe like the *dojo*? And where is Curly Joe?

"Tear him for his bad verses," Oberstein said, "tear him for his bad verses."

"Sumos," McCann barks. "*Tenko*," which means roll-call. "*Ichi…*"

· · · · ·

One of our favorite runs is a sprint from the Mount to the Bat Cave. It only takes about fifteen minutes. And we love hanging around the cave after we've run. On the way up, my running time is terrible, and Blackie really razzes me about it. "Your worse time ever, Carmichael. Gonna need good sprinters during the marathon. To run special assignments during the race. To protect Richardson and Ryan. You gotta improve your sprints or you're out." I lie that I injured my foot and promise to practice. I almost cry, it hurts so much to hear Blackie scold me.

Ryan has scabbed a bag of toutons from the bakery, and we pass them around. Kavanagh and Brookes are playing a game in which they take turns burning holes with a lighted cigarette in a Kleenex that holds a dime suspended over a glass.

The Klub members who aren't in training for the marathon are sharing cigarettes. Rowsell's clicking his Zippo as he smokes, his moon face turning beet red with each puff. His big oily brown eyes could easily belong to a calf. He's tall and thin, a string bean. We're all teasing him about the bowl cut Bug gave him. "You got broom hair," Kavanagh says, "like Moe in *The*

Three Stooges." He squints and says, "Gosh, guys . . . Do I really?" He's always squinting and grinning. He's from Ship Cove, on the west coast. His father and mother were Salvation Army ministers. They were drowned at sea. According to Rowsell, they used to travel by dory to a hundred little outports like Ship Cove to do God's work, as he puts it. Rowsell's kinda religious. Not as religious as Father Cross, but almost.

"One morning, they got into the boat and rowed away. And that evening they never came back."

Rowsell was alone for two whole days, living on peanut butter sandwiches, until a neighbor brought him to the social workers in St. John's. The social workers brought him to the Mount.

Rowsell's a really bad reader. He says the letters keep jumping on him, the same way as the numbers in math class. He says he reads the Bible once in a while in honor of his parents. He's a really naive guy. He believes everything in the Bible is 100 percent true. And he gets really upset if you tell him something's not really true. If you tell him, for example, that Jonah probably wasn't swallowed by a whale.

"Oh, it's true," he says, his calf eyes bulging. "It's true. Yeah, Jonah was swallowed by a whale. If it's in the Good Book, it's 100 percent true. My mother and father told me if it's in the Good Book, it's the word of God, and you must believe it."

He's so naive you can get him to do just about anything if you keep at him. Bug sends him on a wild goose chase almost every day. If Rowsell's telling you the simplest thing, like the canteen's open or Blackie's calling a meeting, his big brown eyes get bigger and he stutters with excitement. And when you ask him a question, he beams and leans toward you and strains his skinny neck as if trying to see inside your brain. One day, we used Oberstein's power of positive thinking on him. We kept telling him he was getting a bone-on until he got one.

We knew he was really naive when Bug tried to teach him to blow farts, and he said, "Gosh. Gee, guys . . . I don't think I can possibly do that. Mother wouldn't . . . Oh boy . . . She wouldn't approve of my doing that."

There are two ways to blow loud farts. Well, three if you count the normal way. But you can't control that. You can create a loud farting sound by blowing on the bare skin of your arm, and you can create a really loud fart by cupping your hand under your armpit and pumping your arm like you're playing the Irish bagpipes. Bug couldn't even get Rowsell to blow a fart on his arm. When we all started in on one of our fart contests—softest fart is out—Rowsell covered his ears with his hands and repeated, "Gosh, guys, golly, that's really loud."

Murphy hands him a touton and says, "I don't believe you ever read the Bible, Rowsell. You can't *read*." He winks at us.

"Oh, yes. Gosh, golly. I can so. It's true. Father and Mother taught me to read when I was only four years old."

"Don't believe it, Rowsell. Reading a few words in the Bible every now and then is not really *reading*. Let's see if you can read from a book you've never seen." Murphy pulls a paperback out of his pocket. The cover has a black-and-white sketch of a man in a top hat and cape chasing two housemaids. Stamped at the top in Gothic red letters are the words *Sam the Ram from Notterdam*. "Here, start reading from the top of page seventy-eight." Murphy passes Rowsell the paperback and winks at us as we crowd around Rowsell's chair.

"Okay. Sure, sure. From the top of the page . . ."

"Top of the page," Murphy says. "*Read*, Rowsell, *read*."

Rowsell reads:

Sam bristled at the thought of the housemaid, Louise, telling Lady Wentworth of their secret meetings. But he pushed the thought to the back of his mind and replaced it with a picture from the previous evening—the first time his eyes drank in the sight of her . . . ample naked bosoms . . .

"Ahh . . . Gosh, guys. Gee, gosh, I dunno if I can read this. Oh, boy . . ."

"Sure you can," Murphy says. "You're a good reader, Rowsell. You can do it. Can't he, guys?"

"Sure. Yeah. Of course. *Read*, Rowsell." The voices can barely contain their laughter.

"Well, gosh. Okay, guys." His big eyes bug out as he reads: "'He remembered how her . . . cleavage had caused him to stiffen.' Gosh. Gee, guys, I dunno."

"*Read, Rowsell, read.*" Murphy leads the chant, and we all join in. A loud chorus. We are in stitches.

"Gosh, okay, guys. 'Her hard brown . . . nipples . . . reminded him of bullets.' Oh, boy."

"Read, Rowsell, read!"

"Gosh . . . 'He could feel his member . . . throbbing again . . .' Omigod . . . 'as it had the night before . . . when he . . .' I dunno about this, guys. Oh, boy."

"Read, Rowsell, read," howls the chorus.

"'When he buried his head in her . . .' Golly . . . 'bare bosoms.' Gosh, I don't think I can . . ." Rowsell's face is turning really white. He doesn't know whether to laugh, shit, or go deaf.

"Enough, Rowsell," Blackie laughs. "Rowsell reads better than all of us." He takes the paperback from him and tosses it to Murphy. Too late. Our laughter is out of control. Ryan and Bug are on the ground. Bug's about to have a seizure.

"Gosh. Golly, guys," Rowsell repeats, his big innocent eyes growing wider than ever.

We're all having a pretty good time laughing it up, and Blackie settles us down by asking Oberstein to interpret a dream. Oberstein started dream analysis, as he calls it, after reading the story of Joseph and the coat of many colofrs in the Old Testament. He just loved the part where Joseph tells the pharaoh that the seven lean cows eating the seven fat cows means seven years of plenty followed by seven years of famine. Every time he tells someone about it, his eyes turn into big blue saucers. When he finishes, he shakes his blond hair like crazy and says, "I had no idea there was another world you could go to. One more real—and safer, more reliable—than this one. The world of dreams." He wants to know every detail of everyone's dreams. He's even analyzing one of Rags' dreams about meeting President Roosevelt.

Oberstein is going on about how Bug's dream of being stuck in an elevator with Marilyn Monroe, which we all know is a lie, didn't have anything to do with Marilyn Monroe.

"Had to," Bug insists. "She's there in the elevator with me. Plain as day."

"Dreams don't usually mean what they seem to," Oberstein says. "In fact, they usually mean the opposite, or something very different."

"Tell me mine, Rabbi," Blackie says, and goes on about how he's in Africa in his dream, training to become chief of an African tribe, and the medicine doctor who's training him dies from drinking one of his own potions. "What's it mean, Rabbi?" Blackie asks. "And it better be good, or it'll be just like in the movies. Off with his head." Blackie flashes a cutthroat grin and karate chops his neck.

"I'll need some time to think about that one, Blackie," Oberstein says. "Straight off, it sounds like it might have some-thing to do with the marathon, a warning maybe." He looks at

Blackie, and Blackie's eyes bug out. "Or it could be an omen of some special scheme you're gonna dream up. Let me chew on it for awhile."

I know they're up to their secret talk again, but I don't let on. Then Oberstein asks him a bunch of questions about his dream, all the little details, like what color clothing is the medicine man wearing and what time of day is it and did he hear anything or smell anything or taste anything. Oberstein is really big on the small details. He carries around a little spiral notebook and writes down everything he can about every dream he's trying to figure out. Practice makes perfect, he says. Except for Bug's dreams, we all take his interpretations seriously because once he told us that O'Grady's dream about looking for his little sister in the forest meant she was going to die. A few weeks later, O'Grady found out that his sister had leukemia.

"I have another one besides Marilyn Monroe in the elevator," Bug says.

"Shoot!" Oberstein says.

"I'm lying in a hospital bed, and all these old doctors—they are all about a hundred and fifty years old and they look like Japanese sumos, but they have long white beards—they're examining my lizard, which is world famous 'cause it has grown down to my knees. And it keeps growing, like Pinocchio's nose. One of the doctors is laughing and showing the others a headline in the newspaper that says 'World's Most Famous Hot Dog.'"

Blackie laughs so much he falls off his throne. We all howl pretty hard.

"That's an easy one to interpret," Blackie says. "A case of wishful thinking."

"Did it grow when you told a lie?" Oberstein plays along.

"Nope, only when I went to confession," Bug says.

Even Oberstein laughs now.

Then we settle down again for a while and everyone is quiet. Just lazing—"cronking," Rags calls it during rehearsal breaks— and looking at Blackie nodding his head and twirling the speaking stick and surmisin', as he's fond of saying.

Suddenly, out of the silence, a small voice says, "I have a dream sometimes."

We all look at Nowlan, who rarely says a word he is so shy and so sad all the time. When he sees us all looking at him, he lowers his pointed face.

"Let's hear it," Oberstein says.

Nowlan starts describing his dream. It's Hallowe'en. It's dark. There's only a night-light on. He's in bed in the infirmary. Someone, a man, is dressed really weird; he's wearing a wig and red lipstick and a long black dress. Like a girl would wear, Nowlan says. And he's putting makeup on Nowlan's face, powder and lipstick and eye shadow. Then the light goes out, and there's only the occasional glow from the blinking Celtic cross. And the weird man sits on his bed and waits for a long time. What seems forever, Nowlan whispers. Then he removes his dress and leans over the bed and babbles something, and starts coughing and drooling like he's sick. He's wearing a black bra and white panties. Girl's clothes, Nowlan says.

When he finishes describing his dream, Nowlan's eyes light up as he waits to hear Oberstein's interpretation. There is a long silence before Oberstein starts going on about how the dream means that Nowlan is going to make a lot of money running a clothing store, or a costume house, or maybe even a restaurant. But we know that Oberstein is feeding him a crock. We all look at Blackie and then at each other. And everyone in the cave knows we're all thinking the same thing. That it's no dream.

To avoid saying any more about the dream, Oberstein starts to sing. He's so good at improvising. He's always taking songs like "Tumbling Tumbleweed" and "Camptown Races" and sticking in someone's name, so we all have a grand old laugh waiting for the next guy's name and to hear what Oberstein will make up. Oberstein's amazing voice just gets better and better. No wonder the brothers always pick him to sing solo at funeral Masses and Christmas and holy days of obligation.

Kelly starts making a feed of roasted spuds. A few boys have started playing cards, a few others stones—our name for jacks, because we use five smooth stones—when Blackie asks Oberstein to make up a new song. Oberstein starts singing a beautiful song called "Wilde Mountain Thyme," which we always sing whenever there's a concert. There are always a lot of requests for it. Only, Oberstein changes the chorus from "Will you go, lassie, go?" to "Will you glow, Blackie, glow?" We all perk up pretty fast. Everyone has the same thing on his mind. How will Blackie react? We all wonder if he will get angry, and maybe punch Oberstein. But he just laughs and says it's pretty funny, but not as funny as Oberstein's "Panis angelicus, don't pee on your mattress."

Blackie asks him to sing the chorus again so we can all join in. He says it will be a nice song to sing on special occasions. "Gonna make it our Klub anthem," he shouts. And as Oberstein booms out the chorus, Blackie stands up and takes a stick from the woodpile and starts directing us just like Brother Walsh does:

> And we'll all glow together,
> Through the wilde mountain thyme
> All around the bloomin' heather
> Will you glow, Blackie, glow?

Blackie looks very funny, and everyone sings and has a really good time of it. And the singing is right on key. And it gives us a big lift to be singing so powerfully. We smile to beat the band and have a grand old time watching Blackie mimic Brother Walsh as he directs us with his stick. And we sing as loud as we can and laugh like crazy even though it's a sad and mournful song.

After the singing and a feed of roasted spuds, Blackie changes the subject to girls. I pray Oberstein hasn't told him about Ruthie Peckford. Only Oberstein knows I like her. We only know a few girls. The Doyle sisters and Ruthie Peckford and her friends. They all hang out Saturdays at a planned spot, Bannerman Park or Quidi Vidi Lake, waiting for us with pop and chips and cigarettes. We have a lotta fun with the Doyle sisters. Blackie has even promised to let them come to one of our Klub meetings. Karla is the prettiest, tall and soft with dark eyes, and she loves to go grassing down by Quidi Vidi Lake. But her hair is always like a birch broom in the fits. Cathy is slim and stiff with golden hair, and she is always sniffling. Jane is different. She has the tiniest worm-shaped scar on her lower lip, the color of lightning. She is pretty, but short and fat with gorgeous brown hair that curls at her shoulders.

Bug makes us laugh when he says he'd like to smear chocolate all over Cathy's naked body and lick it off, real slow. Oberstein asks him if he would go to confession afterward for the big solution, which makes us laugh louder. Once Blackie conned Bug into believing that Cathy Doyle is wild about Old Spice aftershave. Bug gave up two canteen cards to get a bottle. He used the whole thing one Saturday, almost knocking out all three of the Doyle sisters. He stunk like a skunk. Nobody could go near him all week.

Pat Fitzpatrick starts bragging about how easy it is for him to get a girl. And it is. He is Hollywood handsome and could easily be in the movies. He has more moves than Kookie on *77 Sunset Strip*. And he's always snapping his fingers like a beatnik and combing his blond hair back, just like Kookie. When he pulls out his comb, we all sing, "Fitzy, Fitzy. Lend me your comb." Fitz always smells different than the rest of the boys. He's always fresh and smells of strong soap, aftershave, and Brylcreem. Nobody knows where he gets the stuff, but he always seems to have a variety. Unlike Bug, with his Old Spice, everyone likes the smell of Fitzy. We always return from chores or the gym sweaty and wet. Not Fitz. He refers to himself as a lady's man. He's going on about Karla being the prettiest sister. "A real looker," he says.

"When it comes to girls, you're a sleep-talker," Blackie jumps in. "Why you wanna gal in the first place, Fitz?"

"Toldja. A few feels and a marathon necking session in the woods behind the soccer field."

"You should wanna a gal for just one reason," Blackie says.

"What's that, Blackie?" Kavanagh says stupidly.

"Skin," Blackie says. "Girls know that. And the best looker ain't always givin' the best lovin'. Looks ain't everythin'."

Fitz slicks back his hair with his comb. "I'm all ears, Blackie," he says. A shaft of yellow light slips through the half-closed doors, making a small square on the ground.

"Forget looks. Looks don't mean diddly squat. How big or how small her nose or how straight or crooked her teeth. How tall or how short. Gangly or chubby. None of that matters a row of beans. Listen to the way she breathes. And watch for the tail end of her smile. See if it lingers. If it's *looks* you want, count Jane out right away 'cause of her acne. And she could be a tiger out grassin'. Forget about acne and warts and moles and all. That don't mean nuthin' when it comes to neckin' and pettin'. Don't be afraid to kiss her if she has pimples."

Bug says, "Only need to know one thing about girls. Their plumbing's on the inside. Ours is on the outside."

"If you wanna know which gal's the best necker, listen real careful to her voice. How light it is, how giggly, how bubbly. That'll tell you somethin'."

"Golly, whaddaya mean, plumbing on the outside?" Rowsell says.

"How high, how low the sound. Listen for whether she chews up her words when she speaks. And the speed, how fast she speaks. Most of all, watch how she moves. That don't mean she gotta be a Mexican jumpin' bean. Does she sit on that park bench just swayin' a little every now and then? Read a woman, Fitz. Read her like a book, page by page. Word by word. Like you're readin' a mystery novel. Study all them love crumbs. Study her like you're gonna have a big test the next day and your life depends on it. The length of her smile. The softness. A simple sway now and then. Maybe you'll see a river or Niagara Falls all pent up there, just waitin' to bust through and wash over you."

"Blackie's right," Oberstein says. "A person's face is like a book."

"What about makeup?" Bug asks. "I love lipstick. And nail polish. I love shiny red nails."

"Maybe a little," Blackie says. "Like Marilyn . . . But God gave you one face, why create another? Take Ruby Gosse. She wears enough lipstick to paint a battleship and enough powder to blow it up."

Bug almost chokes laughing.

"And a girl's smile is a love print. If her smile's a sort of grin, closing fast, hard at the corners—she's tough. Like Kelly at shortstop. You don't wanna mess with her any more than Kelly. A girl's smile is a powerful signal every time. It's like an X-ray. Like I said before, Kavanagh loves to smile. Watch how he bares his big teeth. And Rags has a perfect smile, his smile carries that comet's tail every time. But you take McMurtry, his smile's always lopsided, and he hangs on to it too long. It ain't natural. He learned it somewhere. A smile's a perfect gift from God. You can fake a lotta things. But never a real smile."

"I'm glad my plumbing's on the outside." Bug wolf whistles, grabbing his crotch and wiggling his bum.

That cracks us all up. As things settle down, Blackie gets that faraway look of his and says, "When I was six, seven, maybe, back in Harlem, the neighbors had a doggie. One day it got wet in the rain and shook water from its back, drops sprayin' in every direction, the way McCann does when he shouts. I saw a man take out a revolver and walk up to that beautiful white doggie and put that revolver to that dog's head and shoot it. *Bang.* Poor doggie just dropped. *Kerplunk.* And that man said, 'Two types of dogs in this world. Them with spunk and them without.' I was small, but I remember. I remember it same as if it happened two minutes ago. Now, that man thought he was killin' something beautiful. God maybe. But God's like the dandelions out in the baseball field. You tear them out, they keep comin' back somewhere else. Sure as the sun shines every day, they'll keep comin' back."

Fitzpatrick puts his comb back in his pocket without saying a word.

"If you quit 'cause of Jane's pimples, you're goin' nowhere *real* fast."

There's a long silence as we pass around the last of the toutons. Blackie is such an amazing guy. He's always saying stuff like that, stuff that makes you think hard and long. We don't say anything as we finish eating. We all just mope and think awhile and look at Blackie scattering the ashes from the fire. I get to wondering about what he said. I'm not sure he's right. Girls are awfully mysterious. But Blackie believes every word he says. And when Blackie believes something, he can be pretty convincing.

That night it's more difficult than usual to sleep. I think about Blackie running away and about Clare and Evan, and I hope they run away instead. Not Blackie. Then Mom and Dad pop into my head, and Oberstein's spells. And Brookes being shunned and Rowsell getting strapped all the time. And I think

of the hole in Bug's heart, and for some crazy reason I picture
the rabbit looking at his watch and saying he's gonna be late and
Bug falling through the rabbit hole. And I'm so sleepy I think the
rabbit's a decoy. Then Bug appears with rabbit's ears, bellowing
"Moooo." Then I worry about the brothers finding out about
the marathon or catching us for stealing the wine. And my head
starts to really pound. Like it's being hit with a board.

I fall asleep for a short while and wake and lie in my bunk
listening to the night noises: the coughing and snoring and
bedsprings popping and sleep-talking. And I watch the
nightlight dim off and on, down by Ryan's bed, until it gets
quiet and peaceful for a while. As I start to fall asleep again, I
think about the three Doyle sisters, and what Blackie said this
afternoon at the Bat Cave.

I do not sleep long. Everything's eating at me. The marathon,
the wine stealing, final exams, Ruthie Peckford. What Blackie
said the other day about my lousy time sprinting to the cave. I
sleep in snatches. Crazy sleep. Something's still eating away at
me. Ruthie Peckford maybe. Or the way Clare looked the last
time we met. Pale and sad and sickly. Or what Blackie said
about my sprinting time . . . I reach beneath my mattress for
my running gear. I suit up and head out alone. Sprinting
against my own best time.

The air is damp and tastes sweet as I run toward JD's pine
trees, their branches swaying against the gray sky. Spring will
be here soon. I can feel it in the air. And soon, the snow will all
be melted. I know I shouldn't be night running by myself. But
I need to. Not doing it would be worse. Maybe I'm trying to
ward off a bout of the spells. Blackie will kill me if he finds out.

The moon is bright. There's been no new snow for weeks.
But there's still plenty down. I won't run far. To the Bat Cave and
back. It won't take me long. Along the way, I listen to the silence.
As I head up Major's Path to the trail, the moon drifts behind a

cloud. At the cave, I sit on a tree stump and wait for the moon to reappear while gobbling up a candy bar I won from Brookes playing palms. I love the strange, deep silence of the woods.

So many thoughts race through my mind. That's one of the great things about running. When you're running, the thoughts come one at a time, slow and clear, and they hang with you for the whole run. You don't have to fight to hold a thought in your mind. But when you're alone, at times like this, or lying awake in bed, or in chapel or class, thoughts come so quick sometimes, like Whitey Ford fastballs. You feel like you're gonna have to duck. I think of the games we play. And what fun we have. King of the castle, which Blackie usually wins and Bug can never win because he's too weak. I remember the time Blackie told us to let him become king, but Bug figured it out and said he'd rather be the last king in the world than be a fake king of the castle. He said he'd rather be king of a bunch of lepers.

Remembering that makes me sad, so I think about Ruthie Peckford. I love her hair. The smell of it. I approach the door of the cave and try to lift the rusty iron bar locking the entrance. I don't know why. It always takes two of us to lift it off. I sit on a rock and think of the time we caught Father Cross getting his skin, and I wish I was inside the cave with Ruthie Peckford. Blackie's words race back to me. If you *believe* it will happen, then it *will* happen. I close my eyes and imagine her looking at me, smiling. I smile back. She is wearing a long winter coat with a fur collar and a soft felt hat. She is gorgeous. We are holding hands and walking along Water Street, looking for a restaurant. I have money and a job, and I'm looking forward to buying her a piece of jewelry or some flowers, a dozen roses maybe, to see her eyes light up, before taking her to dinner. I stop suddenly and touch her face with my fingers. "I love the way you touch my face with your hand," she says. She looks me in the eyes and lifts her hand to my face in a way that makes it seem as if the hand is not hers. I lean down to kiss her, just before exploding. I don't think about necking and petting for a single second. Sex is the farthest thing from my mind. I'd really hate that. To mistake my own pleasure for love. That'd be like a runner forgetting he's always alone, that there's only him and the road and the wind. I repeat her name over and over in my mind. I can see her, plain as day—thin lips, sky-blue eyes, turned-up nose, blond bangs. She is pretty.

I stand and open my eyes. Blackie's right. If you wish it hard enough, it happens. I wish I had a cigarette. Then a voice comes from out of nowhere: Thanks for the lovely roses. I smile and break the magic and race down the silvery path leading to the cave. The black branches and the bushes are getting wet. The moon has gone behind the clouds again, and for a second the sky is the color of dull steel. It's dark and cold and misty. I'm glad I have my flashlight. I turn it on. Everything in front of me is blackish white and wet. I don't have my Mickey. But I know it's my best time.

As I approach the yard, a chill runs through me. The light over the cement porch by the handball courts is on. It wasn't on when I set out for the cave. I do not think of Ruthie Peckford anymore. Or of playing king of the castle. Or of how rainy it has become. I say three quick Hail Marys that I won't get caught, and think of what to say if I am. I'll say that Oberstein went missing during the night after we all went to the bathroom. I'll say I was running around the grounds looking for him. I'll start to cry as I say, "I couldn't find him. Maybe he's dead." Oberstein is quick. If asked, he'll back me up. He'll say he went to his locker, or the chapel to pray. Oberstein will get me out of a jam if anyone can. The darkness deepens. My sweatpants are wet and clingy. There is no moon now, and the rain is coming down in buckets.

Dog-tired, I duck inside the porch and wait until my heart stops racing. I wish it was for Ruthie Peckford. But it's not. It is fear. Fear of the strap. Slowly, I make my way across the yard, enter the building and remove my sneakers and socks. I stand in the doorway, dripping wet, and listen to the silence before sneaking up the stairs. The dorm is still. No snoring. No tossing and turning. No sleep-talking. Nobody budges as I undress and put my wet clothes on the radiator to dry before slipping into bed.

Right away, I think of Ruthie Peckford, and the image of her thin wet lips haunts me until I give in to them. I imagine her waiting for me again near the birch trees by the Bat Cave. Nobody around. Her blond bangs blowing about. The night-light flickers madly for a bit and then goes out as if it knows my thoughts. And I see my hands remove her white woollen scarf, then her winter coat, then her heavy sweater. I notice a tiny patch of pimples on her shoulder and think of the Burin Peninsula on the Newfoundland map. I remember what Blackie said and start kissing the patch, light pecks, until I drift into sleep kissing the rosebuds of her milky white breasts.

Spring 1961

15

THE FREEDOM OF THE WIND in our faces makes us feel like we're flying. You can smell it. The cool air in your nostrils, the buds on the trees, the mud splashing on your shins. Everything new begins to appear. Everything has a new smell. The smell of first-time things. Even in the Sugar Loaf woods the snow is all but gone and the sun shines brightly on the yellowy grass. With the weight of winter behind us and the marathon looming closer, each run is different now. Special.

Spring, next to Christmas, is my favorite time of year. Everything is new and fresh and full. I just love the smell of the new earth. And I love watching Virginia Waters overflow its banks. And I love the rain. I love running in it when it falls so hard it hurts. We all love running in the rain. Seeing Blackie's drenched afro and Murphy's glasses splattered with mud. Seeing the final crusts of snow melt away each day until all of a sudden there isn't a patch to be seen anywhere, not even deep in the woods.

Soon we will be up to thirty miles. Nobody will beat Richardson. Blackie feels we may even take the silver medal, Ryan is running so well. Every run now is so important. Each time out, I look forward to tying up my sneakers. Sometimes I have butterflies in my stomach, the way I look forward to meeting Ruthie Peckford or the Doyle sisters. It's such a feeling. Like walking on air. Sometimes, finishing up a run, I imagine it's the big day, the St. John's Royal Regatta Marathon, and Ruthie Peckford is there, beaming as I cross the finish line, yards ahead of the second runner. But I know I'm dreaming. My role during the marathon will be to ride shotgun as a sprinter or a peashooter or a supplies carrier. Anyway, I could never beat Shorty Richardson. Nobody can. He's amazing. And he's getting stronger by the day. Blackie says he must have African blood, he's so good. "Yeah, Shorty, you got some black blood," Blackie always says, each time Shorty knocks off another second or two. Oberstein says all the great Olympic runners are from Africa. They win the Olympic marathon every time. I felt awfully good to hear that, because it's the poorest place in the world and running is the one thing you don't need any money for. All you have to do is put one foot in front of the other. It's pretty simple and anyone on earth can do it. Oberstein says some of the Kenyans run barefooted. When I heard that, my heart almost stopped. That is truly amazing. Imagine! Running twenty-six miles in your bare feet and beating every runner in the world. Wow! I'd rather have a hero like him than Rocket Richard or Mickey Mantle or maybe even Floyd Patterson.

This Saturday we're going to try to get permission to go to town a few hours earlier than usual. Blackie says he has a new route, which will take us out to the Trans-Canada Highway. He wants to check out a few of the logging roads. "Runnin' toward Argentia," he says, "where they get the ferry to the mainland." He's really anxious about the route. He and Oberstein were chatting about it again the other day after supper. But they stopped talking when they knew I was listening. "It's not a Comrades. But it's close," I heard Oberstein say. "Helluva good run." I got the feeling he wasn't talking about the marathon. Blackie's really going to run all the way to Argentia. In my heart I'm sure that's what they mean. And I think back to the time I heard Blackie tell Oberstein he would get to New York and find his mother after he performed the impossible trick. Then Oberstein began telling Blackie about hitting the wall. "You'll have to refuel by eating on the run," he said, "but you'll lose speed. You can't have both. Otherwise you'll hit the wall."

Later, they both lectured the runners on diet. "You have to be careful of your glucose. That's your blood sugar. Careful it doesn't drop too fast," they'd say, "or it'll be like banging into a cement wall. We'll stash bars along the route the day of the marathon so everyone will have enough sugar. Remember, fat for distance, sugar for speed." Blackie made us walk around in a circle chanting in unison fifty times: "Fat for distance, sugar for speed."

When Father Cross asks Blackie if it wouldn't be smart to eat a big meal before we race, Blackie laughs and says, "Mount Kildare Lions eat after the chase, not before."

We're all looking forward to Saturday. It's our longest race yet. And our most important competition. Blackie says there's a big prize for the winning pack.

"Dress right," Blackie says. "We're goin', rain or shine."

If we can get away right after lunch, stash our play clothes behind the Dominion Stores and head out, we should have lots of time. We're all edgy. There's a lot at stake. We've all got cards on the line. I've put my only Mickey Mantle against Ryan's Whitey Ford. If I lose, I'll just die.

·   ·   ·   ·   ·

We've just finished supper. Diefenbaker stew, which is thick as tar, with homemade bread and bog juice. I hate the bog juice, but I love the bread. And there's usually plenty of it. A fresh

Mount Kildare loaf is the best in the world, especially the fat slices that appear periodically on the plate with the other five regular slices. Fat slices are rare. They only appear when the bread cutter loses a blade. One boy stands on a chair behind the cutter and lines up five or six loaves and guides them through the blades while another boy turns the handle. Many a bread pusher has cut his finger by failing to keep ahead of the boy turning the handle. With three turns of the handle, a dozen fresh slices fall into the huge metal bread drawer beneath the blades. Every now and then a blade snaps, and a double slice from each loaf falls into the bin. When Blackie's turn comes to cut bread, we know there'll be fat slices. He uses his pen knife to remove a blade, cuts a few dozen loaves and replaces the blade. Blackie's the only one with guts enough to do that.

The stew wasn't too bad tonight, thicker and hotter, not as Diefenbaker-ish. But, as usual, there wasn't enough. There's never enough food. After supper we go directly to the chapel for the rosary. Sometimes there's Benediction too. But tonight there's only the five joyful mysteries. Very boring. I sit next to Murphy, and we play odds and evens and rock, paper, scissors. So there's a little bit of joy at least.

After rosary we have a fifteen-minute break before study hall. We aren't allowed to have phone calls. The telephone is off limits. There's only one phone, and it's in the monastery. One of the brothers might let you use the phone if someone in your family is really sick or dying or something. But that's the only time you're allowed to use it. So I'm really surprised when Rowsell comes looking for me to tell me I'm wanted on the telephone. Every once in a while a boy is given phone duty. He's told to sit at a desk in the monastery and take phone messages. Rowsell must not have known the rules. He must've thought we're allowed to take phone calls. It's a miracle he finds me right away. I'm playing blackjack with Rogers by the corridor leading to the gymnasium. It's even more of a miracle that Rowsell doesn't know the rule about phone messages. But Rowsell can be kinda stunned at times.

"Hello," I say into the black receiver.

"Hello, it's Ruthie . . . Ruthie Peckford."

"Hello," I say again. All I can think of is how she looked at Bannerman Park the last time I saw her. She had her hair in a ponytail, and she was wearing Minnie Mouse white high-heeled shoes, which she must've carried in her purse because McPherson girls aren't allowed to wear high heels with their school uniforms. Ruthie Peckford is the first girl I ever kissed, which is no big deal because every boy from the Mount dares every other boy to kiss any girl who comes within ten feet of us. That's how the Dare Klub started, on a dare to kiss one of the Doyle sisters. Ryan and Blackie dared me to kiss Ruthie one afternoon at Bannerman Park. After an easy chase, I caught her and drew her toward me and kissed her hard on the lips. She has really soft lips, so I felt kinda bad about kissing her so hard.

"I was wondering," she asked, "if you would like to come to the sock hop at McPherson Junior High. Last Saturday of the month."

"*Believe.*" Blackie's voice haunts me.

"Sure," I say, just like that, not thinking about what I'm saying.

"Great! I'll see you at the front door of McPherson around eight o'clock."

"Sure thing," I say and hang up the phone. I'm breathing like crazy, like McCann does when he goes nuts. I'm excited about what has just happened, and I'm scared I might be caught using the phone. We aren't even allowed in the monastery. You can get killed if you're caught in the monastery. I look at Rowsell, who's seated at the phone desk, picking his nose.

"Thanks, Rowsell," I say, and wonder how in God's name I'm gonna get to McPherson Junior High at eight o'clock the last Saturday of the month.

I don't mention to anyone that I have my first date. I have no idea what I'm gonna do. I think maybe I'll just pretend the phone call never happened. But that would be standing her up, and only a rat would do that. Then I start thinking of how soft her lips are, and I really want to see her again. Before study hall, I tell Blackie about the phone call.

"You *believed*," he says, his eyes popping, devouring mine.

"Yeah, I believed," I say.

"And now you're in a fix," he chuckles.

"No kiddin'," I say. "I really wanna meet Ruthie Peckford at that dance, Blackie. I wish Nicky was ready to fly messages."

Blackie tells me I can do one of two things. Tell the truth to one of the brothers, Rags, maybe, and try to get permission to go to the sock hop. Or I can lie. Blackie recommends that I do a bit of both. The wisdom of Solomon, as Oberstein says.

"Say you're invited to a friend's birthday party during Saturday free time, and you need extra time to stay out. You won't be able to sign the Doomsday Book by six. The party's at six and it's a few hours. Say your friend's father's gonna drive you home at nine. That way you'll have a half-hour at the sock hop, a half-hour to run home. That run's a snap for you. You're doin' a ten-minute mile now. You can do it in less than fifteen. Have a dance or two, then tell her you're sick and gotta go home. You're on medication. Say you're a diabetic. Tell her you'll see her Sunday at the park. She'll be excited 'bout all that. Girls love everythin' to be serious."

It's Wednesday before I get up the nerve to go see Rags.

"It's spring and a young man's fancy ..." he chuckles. "Do you need money?" He looks over the top of his glasses the way he does when he's checking our ears before bed.

I'm so stunned by his question that I don't know what to say. "No," I stammer.

"You'll need some money. For a birthday gift. Is your friend a boy or a girl?" Rags winks.

"Ahh . . . girl . . . boy . . ." I say, meaning to lie but getting all tangled up in my thoughts.

"Well . . . Which is it? Is it a boy or a girl?" he asks.

I don't say anything for fear my nervous voice will betray me.

Rags reaches under his soutane into his pants pocket and withdraws his wallet. He removes a crisp one-dollar bill.

"If your friend's a boy, cigarettes. If it's a girl, chocolates. Girls love it when boys bring them chocolates." He looks at me and smiles as if he knows everything that is in my head. I can't believe my good luck. I'm so happy I think I will die.

"Thanks," I say and turn away quickly so he won't see my tears.

•   •   •   •   •

Letters in the post office. Letters in the post office.
Blackie's got mail. Murphy's got mail. Carmichael's got mail.
Letters in the post office.

O'Connor sticks his nose inside the TV room, and we know we have mail. I have a letter from Sister Mary Leonard. She's the Mother Superior at St. Martha's. The last time I saw Clare, she told me she had applied to become a nun, a Sister of Mary. Part of the process is a trip to the General Hospital for a complete physical. She told me they found something wrong with her, but the doctors didn't know exactly what it was. Sister Mary Leonard's letter explained it. She has a cyst on her ovary. It scares me to read it. Here is some of what Sister Mary Leonard wrote:

Dear Mr. Carmichael:

I have good news and bad.

The good: Your sister, by the grace of God, has been accepted as a postulant into the Order of the Sisters of Mary. Pray that she may be worthy of her vocation to serve our Lord and Savior, Jesus Christ. As of today, your sister is no longer an orphan. She is now a member of the Sisters of Mary. During all correspondence with her from now on, you must refer to her as Sister Clare or Sister. From this time forth, you must never refer to her by her first name only. Next year she will take her religious name, at which time, of course, you will refer to her by her chosen name. That name will be either Philomena or Henrietta.

The bad: Your sister had a cyst on her ovary that needed surgery. Had she not, by the grace of God, been at the hospital for her physical examination, it might well have developed into something tragic. Mercifully, and by God's grace, she was successfully treated. Your sister has been recovering at the General Hospital for the past two weeks. She returns to St. Martha's tomorrow. If you receive permission from the Brother Superior, you may sit with her here at St. Martha's on Friday after school or during visiting hours on the weekend. Please have the Brother Superior contact me if this is permissible.

Everyone at St. Martha's is praying for your sister. Mass and communion are offered daily here for her. I shall be contacting Monsignor Flynn about having a special Mass offered at Mount Kildare. Be certain to urge your classmates to make a novena to the Virgin on your sister's behalf, and keep her in your daily prayers. We must never ever underestimate the power of prayer. Pray to the saints and the archangels to intercede to Jesus' Mother on Sister Clare's behalf.

I don't know what to do. I hope I don't get the spells. I want to put on my sneakers and race to the hospital and throw my arms around Clare and hold on to her forever. But I know I won't be able to see her until Friday. She was upset the last time we talked. She was nervous and said she had a sharp pain in her side, but that it wasn't too painful, just uncomfortable at times. I don't know what to do. I have to talk to someone. Blackie or Oberstein. Or maybe Rags. I miss her so much.

Rags tells me he'll drive me to see Clare on Friday after school. "I'll take you in the school van," he says. Waiting to see her seems like forever. When Friday finally comes, we drive to St. Martha's through the rain, drizzle, and fog.

Visiting hours at St. Martha's are always the same: Friday after school or Saturday and Sunday afternoons between two and four o'clock. Whenever you visit, you always have to go to the cafeteria, and the first thing you notice is a big sign on the wall that says NO TOUCHING.

The nuns have back-to-back chairs arranged throughout the room. Postulant and guest sit back to back, whispering, while Sister Mary Leonard, a shovel-faced nun dressed like a penguin, walks around the room praying the rosary. All of the postulants sit with their rosaries during visiting hours. There is a steady clicking throughout the room.

I sit with my back to Clare, talking about baseball. I tell her I'm thinking about becoming a Red Sox fan, betraying my beloved Yankees, which is a big lie but I think it might cheer her up.

"It's all because of Ted Williams," I say. "I've come to the conclusion he's the greatest hitter of all time."

"Nobody will ever touch him," she whispers. "I had a dream about him last night. Two nuns were fighting over his ball cap. Sister Kevin wanted to bury it in the cemetery behind St. Martha's. Sister Bonaventure wanted to put it in the freezer. Dreams can be so strange."

I tell her about Rabbi Oberstein's dream interpretations. "He's like Joseph of the coat of many colors," I say. She laughs, and says she can't wait to hear what the chubby cherub says about her dream. Then she tells me she has to go back to the hospital tomorrow because of an infection. For some reason, I think she might die, and I start to cry. I can't say a word. All I can do is let the tears fall. Finally, I ask her if she's in pain.

"Just a bit of sharpness in my side," she says. "Nothing to really worry about."

She asks me how play practice is going. I tell her that Rags likes everyone to be perfectly quiet in the wings, sitting still, waiting for their cues. But most of us horse around a lot. We're usually trying to prevent an actor from making an entrance by pinning him to the floor and sitting on him. We try to outdo each other at making loud farts by pumping our arms under our armpits. We deliberately give people the wrong cues, sending them on stage too early or too late. We fling spitballs the size of your fist at each other. We trip Father Cross every time he makes an entrance. We tape Kick Me signs on actors' backs. We can't help it. It's such great fun. Clare asks if I horse around. I lie, telling her I'm always quiet, sitting in the wings reading and listening for my cue to go on. I tell her that I'm the unofficial stage prompter, which is a terrible lie because I'm always stealing Oberstein's prompt book.

"Well, that's good to hear," she says. "Rags has his hands full with directing. He doesn't need any shenanigans." She says she's really looking forward to the performance. All the nuns are.

Rags is putting on a special matinee for all the nuns in St. John's. She gives me a little lecture about how important the roll of Cassius is and why I should take it seriously. She tells me how important theater is for building confidence and how it teaches cooperation. All I can think of is how much we cooperate when we're stabbing Oberstein in the wings. "Maybe you'll be a famous actor someday," she says. "Maybe you'll be the next Spencer Tracey."

"Or Mickey Rooney," I say, referring to my height, which Clare knows bothers me to no end. I want so much to be tall like Murphy and so many other boys at the Mount.

"Oh, you'll shoot up," she says. "There's plenty of time for you to shoot up."

She clicks her rosary beads for a while and sighs that Ted Williams is God's gift to baseball.

"Greater than Babe Ruth and Ty Cobb," I say. "His record will never be broken."

She gives a weak little laugh and tells me I'm finally coming to my senses. We chat about pitchers and catchers, Whitey Ford and Yogi Berra, the only Yankee Clare really likes. Out of the blue I start to cry again. This time, she hears me.

"Why are you crying?" she snaps.

"I dunno."

"There's always a reason."

"I've been crying a lot lately. Over everything. Oberstein lost his canteen card the other day, and when he told me I burst into tears."

She doesn't say anything. We just sit there in silence, except for the clicking of her rosary beads now and then. I know she's upset and afraid. I can feel the fear.

"Do you have your rosary?" she whispers. She's always telling me to pray the rosary whenever things aren't going well.

"Yes," I lie.

"Say one of the joyful mysteries whenever you feel sad. A decade of the rosary changes everything."

"Clare, this is crazy," I blurt out. "You could be dying of some weird infection, and we're sitting here back to back, whispering and counting beads."

"There are rules," she says.

"I hate the stupid rules," I cry. "Why is there a rule that says visitors can't touch each other? I'm your brother. I'm not some stranger." There's a silence, and I know I've upset her, and I start to cry again.

After a while she asks if I'm finished, meaning if I'm finished praying a decade of the rosary. When I say yes, she reaches her hand over her shoulder and strokes mine. I can feel how sweaty it is.

"All through your life, there will be rules. Most of them you won't like. Some you will hate. But you will always have to obey them. That's how life is. If you don't agree with a rule, offer it up for the poor souls in purgatory. You'll never learn anything in life unless you learn to say no to yourself."

I don't agree with her, but all I can think about is her sweaty hand and the sharpness she's feeling in her side. So I stick my tongue in the corner of my mouth and bite down hard, the way Murphy does when he's really angry, and just sit there crying silently, waiting for Rags to come and drive me home.

•   •   •   •   •

*Carmichael's goin' to the hospital. Carmichael's goin'
to the hospital.*

It's Sunday morning after Mass. I've been in JD's garden with Bug, planting Japanese cherry trees for McCann.

"His Japanese brother says their branches will weep pink blossoms," I told Bug.

"Not before they shit brown buds," Bug said.

Rags must've asked the criers to find me. I have permission to see Clare again, this time at the General Hospital, where she's recovering from the infection.

The criers find me in the dorm, changing into my play clothes. They tell me Rags says I must wear my Sunday clothes before I leave for the hospital. That means a white shirt and school tie, my gray flannels and my blue blazer with the crest of St. Raphael on the upper pocket. Visiting hours are between two and four o'clock. Without me even asking, Blackie tells Kelly, who's on telephone duty, to get a message to Ruthie Peckford to meet me at three o'clock at the hospital canteen.

"You see an opportunity with a gal, you gotta grab it," Blackie nods. "You only get so many chances. Grab every one."

At breakfast, I can't eat. I'm worried about Clare and anxious about meeting Ruthie Peckford. I keep drinking cup after cup of bog juice. I hate bog juice, but it's all there is to wash down the fried Diefenbaker meat. And this morning I drink more than my usual cup because my mouth is so dry. Oberstein looks more nervous than I am. He leans with his elbows on the table, his chin on his hands, staring at his empty plate.

"What's the matter, Oberstein?" I say. "Why are you so nervous? I'm the one with the date."

"It's not that," Oberstein says, looking around to find the brother on duty. "We may have to cancel the marathon. Bug's threatening to blow the whistle on us about everything . . . the Bat Cave, the bakery, the wine, the marathon . . ."

"Holy shit!" Murphy says, his eyes growing rounder as he stares at Bug, who has a face like a boiled boot.

"Blackie poked him last night for saying Americans are a bunch of braggarts. He hardly laid a finger on him, but Bug's really touchy lately about everything. And he's been driving Blackie nuts all week. Driving everyone nuts."

I look over at Bug's table. He's as cross as the cats. Sitting hunched and sulking, like someone peed in his porridge, tapping his spoon against his cup.

"He's acting really strange lately. Have you heard about his fire antics? He stole Rowsell's Zippo twice and lit paper fires. I think he's cracking up. He wants an apology from Blackie and financial compensation."

"What's that?" Murphy asks.

"Money," Oberstein says, "or he'll squeal."

We eat the rest of breakfast in silence. Oberstein doesn't eat or drink. After breakfast, we approach Blackie and ask him to apologize. He says he shouldn't, he hardly laid a finger on him. Oberstein says the stakes are awfully high, and Blackie asks us to tell Bug to come to the TV room. When we're all assembled, Blackie slams his fist against the wall and says, "Sorry, Bug, but you insult America, you take a big chance . . ."

"You shouldn't of *punched* me." Bug's voice twangs with injury, and he begins to cry. "You're twice as strong as I am. And I got a fucken hole in my heart." The tears start really rolling.

"I hardly touched you. It was just a gentle poke . . ."

"I want financial compensation or I'm tellin' McCann about everythin' right fucken now," he shouts, his whole upper body shaking with the emphasis of his words.

"It was just a love tap," Blackie yells. "For Chrissakes, Bug . . ."

"Five dollars. And your canteen card. The clock's ticking."

"Okay. Okay," Blackie says. "Jesus, you're touchy lately." Bug's lower lip curls as he bolts from the room like a singed cat.

"He'll be fine," Blackie says. "He ain't gonna squeal now."

"I'm not so sure about that," Oberstein says.

"I know Bug. I'll talk to him. He'll be fine."

"Talk to him *soon*," Oberstein says, as we race after Bug. His face is ghostly. He's worried. We find Bug where he always goes to sulk, the last stall in the washroom, which, as always, has a faint pissy smell. He's sniffling and sobbing and saying fuck a lot and kicking the stall door.

"Bug?" Oberstein says.

Silence. I can picture him in there, kicking at the door, outraged, sniffling between each kick.

"Bug, he shouldn't of poked you."

"*Punched* me."

"Okay, punched you. I'm an American too, Bug . . ."

"Yeah, and what ever happened to freedom of speech in the land of the fucken free? Blackie's a bully. A big bully. And he's a show-off. He thinks he's King Tuk . . . And he knows I got a fucken hole in my heart."

"*Tut*. It's King *Tut*, Bug." There's a strain on Oberstein's face, like he has to go to the bathroom. "Look, I'm sure he didn't mean to—"

"Stop trying to pawn it off," he interrupts. "Blackie's a prick."

Oberstein leans his head against the stall. His face twitches as he whispers, "He's sorry, Bug."

"He's a first-class prick. He's got no right to go around hitting people."

"You're right, Bug. Hundred percent!" Oberstein says. "He was wrong to *punch* you. Blackie's wrong."

"Fucken right, he's wrong." He sniffles and starts singing, but he's half-sobbing and not hitting most of the notes:

Yankee doodle went to town
Riding on a pony.
Stuck a feather up his ass
And called it macaroni.

Oberstein has to put his hand over my mouth to hold back the laughter.

Silence. The sound of Bug peeing and sniffling.

"You okay, Bug? Bug, you okay?"

"You're not snapping the lizard in there, are you, Bug?" I joke, trying to cheer him up.

"Fly the fuck," he says.

Oberstein's eyes pop. He strains his mouth and knifes his index finger across his throat. Another silence, followed by a loud *kerplunk*. Oberstein puts his hand over my mouth again.

The toilet flushes. Bug sighs and appears, faintly white, except for his eyes, which are red rimmed as if he's been rubbing them.

"What are you looking at, fuck nuts?" He pulls his pants up over his belly button and tugs at his belt. "I want compensation. I got a hole in my heart." He drops his jaw and cocks his head like a dog. And I almost burst out laughing.

"Blackie's agreed to that," Oberstein says. "He'll give you compensation."

I look at the pee stains on Bug's pants as he cocks his head again and pushes past us.

"Fucken well better," he says.

•   •   •   •   •

At lunch, Blackie asks if I'm all set for my big date, and tells Oberstein to give me fifty cents from the Bank of Newfoundland to buy something for my girl. "You don't wanna be a cheapskate. And give Bug five dollars and a pack of cigarettes," he says. "That'll shut him up."

After lunch, Oberstein and Kavanagh walk to the General Hospital with me, and we horse around by Quidi Vidi Lake until two o'clock, when it's time to go visit Clare. A sparrow of a nurse leads me to her room on the second floor, where Clare has one hand hooked up to a machine and the other holding her rosary. She looks sad and anxious, as if in a dream, and her thick blond hair is hidden by her new white novice veil.

"I miss seeing your golden hair," I say.

"It's cut off," she says. "You have to cut your hair when you take the veil. Thought I might as well get used to it."

"Big game last night," I say, examining the machine. "Canadiens clobbered the Leafs five to one."

"I'd rather talk about the greatest hitter who ever lived," she says. "About his records, which will *never* be broken."

"You mean Lou Gehrig?" I say, teasing her.

"Who's he?" she says.

I don't say anything. I'm amazed by the pole she's hooked up to. It looks like a lamp post. It's got a plastic bag attached to it, and there's a tube going from the bag to the back of Clare's hand. She sees me gaping and says, "That's called an intravenous. That's how the antibiotics get into my system to fight the infection."

"It looks pretty scary," I say. "And you look kinda weak."

"I'm not," Clare says. "And that's just fighting the infection. But you don't have to concern yourself with it. What's new at Mount Kildare?"

"Not much," I say. "I came fourth in a long-distance race last week. Shorty Richardson came first. Beat us all by ten minutes."

"He must be fast."

"Fastest boy in the Mount. Runs like the wind."

"I am never alone, Lord, your wings widespread and ready for flight," she says, her eyes becoming heavy lidded, as if fighting sleep.

"Give them wings, Lord," I whisper.

"What did you say?" she asks.

"Nothing, just something Oberstein always says. Do you really think Ted Williams' record will never be broken?"

She smiles and says nothing.

"Whatcha thinkin'?" I ask.

"My beloved Red Sox . . . If I had been able to go to his games, I would have had tears in my eyes every time he came to the plate." She looks at me like she's remembering a date she had with him, and I think of Evan. "During his senior year in high school, while pitching and playing outfield, he batted .406. On the mound, he was just as good, a sixteen-and-three record. Once, he struck out twenty-three batters. The Yankees offered him two hundred dollars a month to sign with them, but his mother said no. She wanted him to finish his schooling. So he played semi-pro for three dollars a week. Thank God for mothers. Ted Williams could have been a Yankee."

She laughs and drops her rosary, reaches inside her habit and withdraws a package of bubblegum baseball cards. I rip open the package and pull out the cards. Two Cincinnati Reds and one Yankee, Elston Howard. I throw my arms around her neck and give her a big kiss.

"Easy," she says, "you'll unhook the tube."

I offer her some bubblegum, which she loves, and we both sit there, chewing away and talking about baseball, mostly, and a bit about religion. She wants to know if I say my morning and night prayers. She says my first and last thoughts each day should be of God. I tell her I do, which is a lie, and add that I offer Mass up for her every morning, which is true.

"Thank you," she says.

Around ten to three I get kind of antsy, and tell her the brothers gave me a quarter to buy her something from the canteen. She says she'd like a hazelnut bar or a Tootsie Roll. We chat until my Mickey says three minutes to three and I bolt. The canteen is on the ground floor. When I get there, the first thing I see is the back of Ruthie Peckford's head, that beautiful blond hair. As usual, she is wearing a plaid skirt and high heels. She asks if I'd like anything from the canteen. There are no hazelnut bars, so I ask for two Tootsie Rolls, which she insists on paying for.

"I don't have much time," I say. "I'm visiting my sister on the second floor. She had a cyst on her ovary and after the operation got a bad infection."

"Jeepers, that's pretty bad luck."

"Yeah," I say. "And there's more bad luck. We only got about ten minutes. I'll tell my sister I got lost."

"Come this way," she says, taking my hand and leading me down an unlit corridor. The feel of her soft hand is beautiful, and I want to jump her in the corridor and kiss her like crazy for ten minutes.

"Have you ever gone steady?" she asks, stopping by a huge green door.

"No," I say.

"Wouldja like to?" she asks, pushing the door open and pulling me through to the other side.

"Like to what?" I ask.

"Go steady . . . with me," she says, kissing me hard on the lips. I start to tremble, and my knees get weak. I'm not sure if it's because of the question, her kiss, or the fear of getting caught.

"This is the linen room, where they store the clean sheets and pillow slips. There's no one here. I checked it out." She kisses me again, and her lips are as soft as marshmallows. "Now that we're going steady," she whispers, "we can neck." While we're necking, she shuffle-dances past the door and pins me to the wall, teasing my teeth with her tongue. In no time, I'm hard as a rock. Out of the blue, she starts a giggling fit and puts both hands to her mouth.

"What's so funny?" I ask, sure that she's laughing at my hardness.

Her giggles turn to laughter as she says, "I was just thinking, if you knocked me up, this would be the perfect place to be to have a baby."

I get the quickest reverse hard-on in the history of the world.

"Gog. Got. Go . . ." I mumble. "My sister's stuck to a pole." I look at my Mickey. It's three-fifteen. I wiggle away from her.

"Don't forget the sock hop," she yells. "Next Saturday!"

I race to Clare's room, arriving in a sweat.

"What took you so long? I was beginning to worry about you." Clare's eyes are strained, and her face flushes as she questions me.

"I got lost in the halls. They're winding. Full of turns, and it's really dark down there," I say, handing her a Tootsie Roll.

"It's a big hospital. It's easy to get lost."

"Did I tell you I got asked to the McPherson sock hop next Saturday?"

"You have a girlfriend?"

"Not really. She just asked me to the dance."

"Well, that's nice. Behave like a gentleman at all times. Do you have some money to buy her something?"

"Yeah, I have fifty cents," I lie, "from the last time you gave me money."

"Well, have a good time. And don't take cigarettes from anyone. It's a very bad habit." She unwraps her Tootsie Roll and gives me half. "Save yours for later," she smiles. "I only want a bite." We sit there, munching away on the sweet candy. When we finish, she smiles and passes me her rosary beads and says, "Close your eyes and say a sorrowful decade for my recovery."

I close my eyes and pretend to mumble Hail Marys, but all I can think about is Ruthie Peckford's blond bangs and soft lips and how long it will be before we have to get married, now that we're going steady.

·   ·   ·   ·   ·

Back at the Mount, Brother McMurtry has called a meeting of our dorm. Small and pale, he stands in front of us and wipes his swollen forehead with the palm of his hand. "I have decided to offer a reward," he says. "A reward for information that will help us find the culprits who stole the wine. Actually, there will be several rewards. A new canteen card for next month, in addition to your regular canteen card. The boy who supplies this information will have two canteen cards for next month. Two canteen cards to use at his leisure." He holds up a silver key and passes it to McCann. "Brother McCann will open the canteen three additional weeknights for the boy or boys with an extra canteen card. That's one reward. Another reward will be extra free time in town on Saturdays. And the best reward of all: a pass to a Saturday night hockey game at Memorial Stadium to see the St. John's Caps." Brother McMurtry steps aside, and McCann moves to the center of the classroom.

"Any boy or boys who would like to report information that may be helpful to us may do so at any time simply by slipping a note underneath the monastery door. Or my classroom door, whichever is convenient. If Ryans, for example, or Kavanaghs or Spencers wants to provide information, all you have to do is write a note and slip it under the door. Simple. Very simple. Are there any questions? Raise your hand if you have a question."

Bug propels his hand.

"Yes, Mr. Bradburys."

"What about if you want a different kind of prize? What about if you wanted to trade the hockey game prize for a Saturday movie at the Nickel? Would you be allowed to do that?"

McCann looks in Brother McMurtry's direction.

"Of course," Brother McMurtry nods his head. "A movie is an excellent idea for a reward. A movie downtown, at the Nickel, with popcorn and soda pop."

"That would be a better prize," Bug sulks.

"Thank you, Mr. Bradburys. Are there any other questions?"

"What if someone thinks he has information, Brother," Bug says, sucking up, "but it turns out to be no good. Does anything happen to him?"

"If you mean, will that boy be punished," McMurtry says, "the answer is no. Absolutely not. In fact, if he is sincere and thinks the information is accurate, that boy will most likely get a treat for trying to help us catch the culprits. Isn't that right, Brother McCann?"

"Yes, Brother," McCann says.

"Raise your hand if there are any further questions. If there are no hands," he says, staring sharply at us as if to see what we are secretly thinking, "Brother McCann will review the procedure for reporting information."

There are no more questions, so McCann reminds us once again where to put the note. "And be sure to sign it," he says, "so we'll be certain to know who gets the reward."

"Of course," Brother McMurtry says, "if you wish to provide information and do not wish to sign your name, you wish to remain anonymous, that will be fine. Your privacy will be protected."

"I don't like it one bit," Oberstein says after we're dismissed. "That's a pretty big carrot they're dangling in front of the Klub members."

"And that's a pretty hard birch stick we got at the cave," Blackie says. "If someone squeals . . ."

"But what if someone gets jittery and caves in?" Murphy says.

We all look at Blackie, who is tapping his gold tooth. Not a good sign. He is nervous.

"What are we gonna do, Blackie?" Ryan asks.

"Someone's gonna have to write a note," Blackie says.

"Sure ain't gonna be me, brother," Bug says.

"A note?" Oberstein says. "Whaddaya mean? What kinda note?"

"Let's think about that," Blackie says. "Let's think real hard."

. . . . .

When Oberstein tells me there'll probably be a door charge at Ruthie Peckford's school dance, I'm beside myself until Blackie tells me not to fret, I can take it from the Bank of Newfoundland. "Won't be too much," he says. "Fifty cents, maybe."

"I'm really, really nervous," I say. "I've never been to a dance before. What do I do? What if I can't find her? What if she's late or she doesn't show up? Or I'm late and she's already at the dance?"

"Relax," Oberstein says. "When you get to the dance, if you can't find her, just follow a bunch of people inside and walk around looking for her. She'll be there somewhere. Or just find a spot to sit down and talk to someone. Or stand around listening to the band. Just do what everyone else is doing. Nobody will notice you. Relax. Just don't squint your eyes a lot. You look kinda dumb when you do that."

"If you're really lucky, maybe some gal will ask you for a kiss and shove her tongue down your throat," Bug hollers.

The night of the dance, I'm as ready as can be. Father Cross has given me a really neat haircut and lends me his razor to clean up my peach fuzz. And Fitzy lends me his comb and some Vitalis. Murphy gives me his underarm deodorant. Everyone is really excited for me. Even Bug, who offers his Old Spice. Out of nowhere, Blackie and Oberstein come up with a shoebox that Cross has been painting all week. It's really beautiful. Every color in the rainbow.

"Open it," Blackie says. "Big surprise for the lady's man. For the big shindig."

I open the box and stare at a new pair of sneakers. Not the black-and-white canvas kind all the norphs wear. Real runners. Red Converse high-tops. They look magical.

"Give him wings, Lord, that he may fly," Oberstein chants.

As I take them out of the box, I start to cry.

"Hey, cut that out," Blackie says. "Predictin' an eight-minute mile tonight. Eight, could be seven if you kiss her long enough."

When I'm all laced up and ready to go, Father Cross steps back and examines me. "Cat's meow," he says, and starts splashing my face with aftershave. After he touches up my hair they each take turns teaching me how to dance. Bug shouts, "Chubby Checker got nuttin' on me, brother." He flaps his arms and puckers his lips and twists like a maniac. Watching Bug dance around, smooching his lips and wiggling his bum, cracks me up so much I can't concentrate. Finally, Father Cross shows me how to twist without being too noticeable. "It's all in how you hold your head," he says. "That's how Chubby Checker does it. Think of Chubby Checker when you're moving around. And don't worry about the slow dances. The slow dances are easy. But don't take jerky steps. Just get the girl to lay her head on your shoulder and hang on to her hips. Like they do on American Bandstand."

"Yeah, put your hands on her hips, but don't forget to pull her toward you." Bug wolf-whistles and makes panting noises.

Everyone laughs and wishes me luck. Before I head out, Blackie asks if I know how to kiss.

"Oh, I know how to kiss," I say.

"How do you do it?" Blackie says.

"On the lips," I say. "You just kiss her on the lips."

"Ain't that simple," Blackie says. "You gotta be careful when you smooch. You don't wanna look stupid, or worse, be taken for a sissy. And most important of all, you gotta be sure your noses don't knock. You gotta tilt your head at an angle so your noses don't knock."

He grabs Bug and demonstrates.

"Got it?" he asks. To a chorus of laughter, Bug yells yuck, and wipes his mouth with the back of his hand.

"Yeah," I say, "I got it."

"And don't forget to buy her a cola or something," Murphy says. "You don't want her to think you're a cheapskate."

As I leave, Father Cross tells me I've forgotten something. He passes me a wallet, which he has made from old scraps of leather. "The pièce de résistance," he says. "You won't get very far in life without one of them." I open it and find a one-dollar bill inside.

Oberstein and Bug walk with me to the gate. The smell of the unthawed earth fills the night. It is stronger than Bug's Old Spice.

"You look real pretty," Bug says, giggling and wiggling and bellowing like a cow.

"You smell like the whore of Babylon," Oberstein says.

Halfway across Elizabeth Avenue, I can still hear them laughing and shouting: "Don't forget to let her put her head on your shoulder ... Just like in the song!" Bug's shrill off-key voice is almost drowned out by Oberstein's boom: "Put your head on my shoulder ..."

At the entrance to McPherson Junior High, I search frantically for Ruthie Peckford, who's nowhere in sight. My heart's in my throat as I follow the plan and join a group of people entering the building. Inside, one of the parent chaperones, a skeleton with jug ears dressed like an undertaker, welcomes us. He stares at me oddly and says, "And what's your name, sonny?"

"Floyd," I say in my toughest Cagney. "Floyd ... Oberstein."

"Oberstein ... That's not a St. John's name. What does your father do? Does he work for the government?"

"Visiting," I whisper hoarsely, "from Toronto ..." I lower my head and stare at my new sneakers.

"Toronto? Whereabouts in Toronto?"

"Washroom," I squeak, grabbing my crotch and crossing my legs while straining like I'm gonna piss myself.

"Oh heavens," he says, "right this way, right this way." He escorts me to the boys' washroom.

Inside the smoky room, there's a hubbub of activity. Two guys in leather jackets puff hard on their cigarettes, while another guy fans smoke toward an open window. Guys are checking their ducktails in the mirrors above the long row of sinks. A beefy guy with a wart on his forehead is arguing with his buddy about stealing his date. I slouch inside a cubicle, lock the door and sit on the toilet. When the argument ends and the noise dies down, I check my hair in the mirror. The Vitalis is holding up fine. Pretty soon, the band starts up. There's chaos and hurry and girls squealing outside as everyone heads for the dance floor.

Ruthie Peckford's blond bangs are unmistakable. I love the way her hair hangs, mournfully, like it's begging to be touched. I spot her near the entrance, straining to get a view of the newcomers. She looks beautiful in a deep-blue velvet dress with a light-blue collar patterned with snowflakes. And she is anxiously looking for her date. I sneak up behind her, and in my best Humphrey Bogart accent say, "Hey sweetheart, would you like to dance?"

She turns and beams. "I knew you'd come. I just knew it." She hugs me like I'm a long lost friend. We head to the dance floor and dance for a while, but she's very pretty so everyone keeps cutting in and dancing with her. I keep waiting for a slow waltz to cut back in, but all the songs are fast and I'm really nervous about dancing fast. I stare around the gymnasium. Along the walls are fold-up chairs with girls who aren't very pretty sitting very straight and staring at all the lucky girls who've been asked to dance. I feel so sorry for the girls sitting around that I start to get tears in my eyes thinking how stupid and unfair it all is, so I approach one, a thin girl with Coke-bottle glasses, and ask her to dance. She springs forward like she's just been pinched. We're dancing away to a slow song, and Ruthie Peckford cuts in, which I later learn she's not supposed to do because it isn't proper. The thin girl stops dancing with a jerk, slaps a hand on her hip and huffs, before storming off. We dance for a minute, but I'm afraid someone's gonna cut in, so I walk her to the canteen and buy her a cola and a bag of chips.

"I can't stay past eight-thirty," I say. "I'm diabetic. I've got to be home to take my medicine."

"Oh, what a sin!" she sighs, like I just told her I had three weeks to live. "I'll walk home with you."

"That's okay," I lie. "Brother McMurtry's coming to pick me up."

We go back to the dance floor and stand there for a long time, not speaking, just staring at the dancers moving in the strobe light. Now and then a boy asks Ruthie to dance, but she says no. Then, out of the blue, she says, "You're really cute."

I don't say anything.

"Guess how long we've been going steady?"

Her best friend, Paula, who has wavy brown hair and long red fingernails, passes by with her boyfriend. She introduces me. When they're gone she says, "They're going steady."

"What's that?" I ask, pretending not to know.

"Dontcha remember? I asked you that day you were visiting your sister at the hospital."

"I don't remember," I lie.

"Well, it's been two weeks," she pouts. "Dontcha know? Dontcha know that when a boy and a girl really like each other a lot, and they don't want to go out with anyone else, the boy gives the girl a ring and they go steady. Dontcha know? Then a while later, they become engaged . . . then they get married. That's how it all works. That's how babies begin."

The band starts playing a slow song, the lead singer dragging out the words. To avoid talking about going steady, I ask her to dance. She leans her head on my shoulder and sighs like she's about to fall asleep. I put my fingers on her hips. They're so bony I pull back like I've been burned.

"What's wrong?" she says.

"Nuthin," I say and grab her hips hard, thinking back to what Blackie said about a girl's looks and size and shape.

As we're swaying to the music, I loosen my grip. And for a minute it feels like we're perfect together. When the song is over, she stares into my eyes a long time and whispers, "I love you."

"I gotta go," I say. "I gotta take my insulin."

As I start running home, I can see the big Celtic cross above Mount Kildare blinking on and off. The air smells of wet earth. I stare at my new runners and hope the last of the melting slush won't ruin them, and I know I'm making great time as I enter Elizabeth Avenue. It'll soon be bedtime. The feeling of love pounds in my runner's heart. I think of the marathon and pick up speed passing Rennie's River, which is raging from the spring thaw. I think of Virginia Waters, and how all the rain and melting snow must've created a roaring river by now. I love being by a river when it's roaring. It sounds alive. Like an animal. I check my Mickey and beam as I fly past St. Patrick's Mercy Home, my heart outracing me as I move closer to the blinking cross and my bunk bed and dreams of getting married to Ruthie Peckford.

16

*Interviews in the TV room. Interviews in the TV room.
Interviews. Interviews.*

THE NEXT MORNING, after breakfast, Brother McMurtry announces over the PA that all the boys in St. Luke's and St. Martin's dorms are to line up outside the TV room for individual interviews on what he calls "the facts of life" with the Brother Superior, who has just arrived from Rome. There will be another meeting later with the assistant to the Brother Superior for anyone the brothers think might have a vocation to the brotherhood.

"Gosh, what's the facts of life?" Rowsell asks.

"You know, world history and all that stuff," Murphy says.

"No, it ain't. Don't be such an idiot. It means having babies and all that old crap," Bug Bradbury says. Bug has seen the light. He's become a true atheist since an argument in class between Brother Walsh and Oberstein about the Church's official teachings. Oberstein argued that common sense is more important than ancient laws. Brother Walsh said we need the official teachings of the Church to prevent people from fooling themselves into doing whatever they feel like.

Otherwise, people would deceive themselves, he said. It was a really big argument.

"If Jeremiah or Isaiah had to depend on anyone, they wouldn't have been prophets," Oberstein said after class. "It makes more sense to be your own priest and prophet, rather than depend on somebody else." He convinced Bug that common sense is more important than any law. "If you lose your marbles, you're a dead duck. You're finished without common sense. You have nothing," Oberstein said. "You'll become just like a robot. Just like Gort in *The Day the Earth Stood Still*." Bug beamed. He'd seen the light.

"You're right on the money, brother," he said to Oberstein. "Why should I feel guilty about snapping the lizard all day? Shag that."

Bug's a new man. His attitude has completely changed about everything religious. He's an atheist, he says, and proud of it. He even lies in confession. He says it's fun, and having a few laughs is more important than trying to be a holy-holy. His last trip to the confession box, he told Monsignor Flynn that he's having a very serious discussion with the devil about getting to spend a night with Marilyn Monroe. Then he almost gave old Flynn a heart attack when he said he was having impure thoughts about sleeping with Marilyn and Jane Mansfield at the same time. Another time he asked old Flynn if he ever tugged the toad. Luckily, old Flynn didn't know what he was talking about. He thought he was confessing to blowing up a frog.

It's an odd sight. All the norphs leaning silently against the oak wainscoting outside the TV room, waiting obediently for an interview with the Brother Superior, a man we've never met. But we're sure he's very important because he has come all the way from Rome to talk to each of us about the facts of life. The long line stretches through the corridor and down the stairs leading to the cafeteria. The only other time we line up like that is when we have confession during Lent. A dozen priests from the Basilica come, and temporary confessionals are set up all over the place so that the hundreds of boys can fulfill their Easter duty. Which means you have to go to confession at least once a year to remain a Catholic. Which Oberstein says defies common sense, like eating meat on Friday.

Oberstein is behind me in the lineup. Ryan is in front of me, and Bug is ahead of him, driving everyone nuts, chanting "Mooooo" and running his knuckles back and forth along the wainscoting, acting like he's Liberace. When the Brother Superior calls for the next boy in line, you're supposed to go into the TV room and sit on a chair and ask this brother who's visiting from the head office in Rome any question you want about the so-called facts of life.

"I haven't got a clue what to ask," Ryan whispers.

"Neither do I," I confess.

"Just ask where babies come from," Oberstein says. "The Brother Superior will give you an explanation, and you nod your head and leave. There's nothing to it."

"Is there penance?" Ryan asks. "Will we be tested on it?"

"No, there's no penance, no test," Oberstein says. "It's not like confession or school. It's more like a private conversation."

"Omigod! I'm not askin' that. A two-year-old knows where babies come from," Bug squeaks. "I'm not askin' nuthin'. I'm gonna be *tellin'* Brother Hoity-Toity Know-It-All from Rome a thing or two. Not askin'. Those guys don't know nuthin' about girls. I'll be tellin', not askin'."

"Tellin' what?" Ryan asks.

"That masturbation's not a mortal sin, Mr. Smarty-pants. And that you're not goin' to hell for doin' it. That McCann's wrong about it. That Holy Mother Church is wrong. That the Romans are wrong. And another thing, brother, I'm gonna tell him that it's not even a venial sin to eat meat on Fridays. And anyone who thinks it is a sin is nuts, including Monsignor Flynn and Brother High-Falutin' Superior Know-It-All from Rome. And even the Pope, if you wanna know."

"Eating meat on Friday has nothing to do with the facts of life," Oberstein says. "The facts of life only have to do with the birds and the bees, sex-related issues."

"Okay then," Bug yelps. "I'll tell him it ain't a sin to get a hard-on thinking about a pretty woman. Like a movie star. Marilyn Monroe." Bug puckers up his lips.

"You'd better not say 'hard-on.' You'd better use a different expression. Say 'getting aroused,'" Oberstein says.

"Yeah. The Brother Superior might strap you for saying something like that," Ryan says.

"Naaah! He wouldn't strap anyone," Bug says.

"Why not?" Ryan asks.

"'Cause he's from Rome," Bug says.

"What's that got to do with the price of tea in China?" Oberstein says.

"'Cause he's over there in Rome with all the other holy-holies saying the rosary and going to Mass and Benediction and meditating all the time. They don't go around strapping anyone over in Rome. They're not like the clowns around here. They don't have the time for it."

"I wouldn't count on that," Ryan says. "A brother is a brother, no matter what, and he can strap anyone anywhere in the world, if you ask me."

"Who's askin' ya?" Bug shrieks and gives Ryan the finger.

"I'm not gonna tell the Brother Superior anything. I'm taking Oberstein's advice. I'm just askin' one simple question. Where do babies come from?" Ryan says.

"I'm not *askin'* Brother Smarty-pants anything. I'm gonna *tell* him where babies come from. And then I'm gonna ask him if he has any Italian cigarettes," Bug says, just as the door to the TV room opens for his turn to be interviewed.

The Brother Superior is a bullish man whose upper lip curls outward so that almost all his teeth are entirely exposed.

Bug cocks his head toward the Brother Superior. "Jerry Lewis," he says, and walks to the door.

"And what's your name, son?" the Brother Superior asks.

"Darby O'Gill," Bug says, recalling the name from a movie we once saw called *Darby O'Gill and the Little People.*

"Very well, Darby, my name is Brother LaForgue. Right this way, if you please."

The door closes, and everything becomes silent for a few minutes, and then we hear the Brother Superior screaming, "Because it *is* a sin, that's why. A sin is a sin."

There's silence for another minute, and then the Brother Superior's voice booms again, "I am not here, young man, to argue with you about what is and what is not a mortal sin."

Another brief silence. Again, the Brother Superior's voice, this time much louder. "No, I do not have any Italian cigarettes. I do not smoke."

And with that, Bug comes charging through the door, his head cocked to one side, proud as a peacock, looking as if he's just arrived at home plate after hitting a grand slam.

When my turn comes with the Brother Superior, I tell him my real name and sit on one of the straight-backed chairs he offers me.

"You know this young O'Gill fellow, yes?" he asks, with a humorless snicker. "He is a friend of yours?"

"No," I answer, not realizing he's referring to Bug.

"A very argumentative little fellow," he says. "Amazingly argumentative for such a young man. And amazingly arrogant for a norphan." He removes a snow-white handkerchief from the inside sleeve of his soutane and silently blows his nose.

"But it mustn't be easy, being a norphan. There must be many an argument among all you boys."

I don't say anything. He leans forward slightly, places his hands on his knees, drums his fingers and stares at his shiny black shoes.

"You are familiar with the facts of life, yes?" he asks shyly.

"Sort of," I say.

"You have some questions you would like answered?"

"I'd . . . like to know . . . where . . . babies come from," I stammer.

"You know something about this subject, yes?" he asks.

"Nothing, Brother," I lie.

"Very well." He lowers his voice. "When the man and woman, husband and wife, have intercourse, at the appropriate time, the man's penis becomes erect." His voice becomes a whisper as if he's sharing some great secret. And he forms a small circle with the forefinger and thumb of his left hand.

"The woman, at the appropriate time, receives the erect penis." He raises the index finger of his right hand, points it at me, accusingly, and pushes it back and forth through the circle, his brow furrowing with each push. "During the intercourse, at an appropriate time, the penis releases semen, which the woman receives. And voilá . . ." He throws his arms up, flicking all his fingers outward at the same time. "The recipe is complete. Nine months later, little Junior comes howling and screaming into this vale of tears."

He looks at me with a big stupid grin, and all I can think of is Jerry Lewis. I bite my tongue and squint my eyes hard, trying not to laugh.

"You now fully comprehend the facts of life, yes?"

I tell him that I do, and thank him for his explanation. I race past the blank faces to search for Bug Bradbury to compare notes and to get all the juicy details of Bug's encounter with the man who from that day forward would always be known as Brother Jerry Lewis.

* * * * *

"It's called the act of transference. That's what the assistant to the Brother Superior calls it." The assistant to the Brother Superior is having interviews as well.

"His name is Brother F. F. Lannon. It's how you become a man." Kavanagh's eyes glisten as he speaks.

"What's the F. F. stand for?" Ryan asks.

"Fuck Face," Bug snaps. "He's gotta mouth like a hen's ass."

"What'd he say to you, Blackie?" Murphy asks.

"Nuthin'. Just if I know the meaning of 'rite of passage.' Told him Brother McCann taught it to me, and he told me to leave."

"He asked me where babies come from," Ryan says. "I told him they come from a woman's backside."

"Lot you know," Bug says.

"He say anything to you?" Blackie asks Murphy.

"Well, I went to the monastery door at two o'clock and knocked, just like he told me to. He's got a really gray, wrinkly face. He's a spooky guy. He peeked through the glass cross in the door. Bug's right. He really does have a mouth like a hen's ass, and he's got really crawly skin, ashy colored. It reminds me of one of those mummy movies. He opened the door and told me to come in. 'You're Mr. Murphy. Come in. Come in,' he said. I felt pretty good because he recognized me right away. Probably because I was an altar boy for the Brother Superior's Mass. He led me to the parlor and sat down and straight off asked if I knew the difference between males and females, 'as God created them. It's in the Book of Genesis,' he said, the wrinkles on his forehead jumping up and down a mile a minute. I've never seen anyone so wrinkly. I told him I read the Bible all the time. He asked me if I have a girlfriend, or if I've ever dated a girl. I said no. I wasn't about to mention the Doyle sisters.

"Then he asked me if I'd like a soda pop—Coke or Pepsi. And I said, 'I'll have both,' just horsing around, you know, like we always do with Rags. Big mistake. He came over to where I was sitting and laughed this goofy laugh he's got, like he's coughing instead of laughing. And he sniffs like crazy—nff-nff, nff-nff. He sniffs a helluva lot. And, *whammo*, he clocked me one in the side of the head. 'You'll have *one*,' he said, 'just *one*, and don't get fresh around me. I don't have time for wise guys.' Then he went and got me a Crown Cola. As I took my first swig, he asked if I knew anything about the act of transference. I said no, and he asked if I knew where the stuff of life comes from. Have any of the brothers taught it to me? I wasn't sure I knew the answer, and I was afraid of getting another whack in the head, so I said no, I don't know anything about it. He did his nff-nff routine and asked my age. I told him I'll be fourteen in September. 'Nff-nff, you're into your teens,' he whispered. 'That means you'll be a man soon.' Then he just stared at me. He's got a really creepy stare; his wrinkly forehead puckers up and down like crazy. I got kinda nervous, so I started swigging my Crown Cola. After a while he said, 'Yes, nff-nff, you'll be a man soon, nff-nff, a man like all men. Do you know what happens when a boy reaches manhood, Mr. Murphy? When he moves through his rite of passage?' I wasn't sure what he was getting on with, so I said no.

"There was a long silence. I took a few more swigs of cola, and he started pacing. 'A man,' he said, 'has something that boys do not have. He has something only men have, something a boy can receive only from a man.' He stared that creepy stare again, and his forehead crinkled as he spoke. His skin looked more than ever like mummy skin. 'Do you know what that something is, Mr. Murphy?'

"'No, Brother,' I said.

"'Of course, why would you? Nff-nff. Why would you? You're a boy, a norphan boy. That something, Mr. Murphy, is spermatozoa. Do you know that it takes forty tiny drops of blood purifying in the body for forty days to produce a single drop of spermatozoa?'

"He started twitching like he was gonna give me another whack, so I asked him if that had anything to do with Jesus spending forty days and forty nights in the desert. Just so he'd think I was interested. But he ignored me.

"'This is how you receive the spermatozoon, the mature sex cell in your semen. Sperm, as your friends probably call it.' *Spunk*, I feel like saying. 'You are a teenager now. Soon you will have unlimited spermatozoa. But not until a few drops enter your system. After we have primed the pump, so to speak. Then you will produce endless spermatozoa. Like me. Like all the brothers. All adults. Like all the young men here. That's what makes you become a man. This happens during what is called the act of transference. Not to be confused with the act of transubstantiation. Do you know what that act is? Are you familiar with the act of transubstantiation?'

"'Yes,' I lied. I know it's got something to do with God entering the host during Mass. I'm not really sure, but I didn't let on.

"'Both are holy acts, the act of transference and the act of transubstantiation. The former, transference, is that special initiation time when a teen is inseminated and becomes a man. A man capable of producing his own spermatozoa.' He stared at me for a long time. I didn't know what to say, so I nearly drained my Crown Cola. The whole thing was getting pretty spooky.

"'The adult spirit is contained inside the adult seed. Do you know how spermatozoa first enters a young man's system?' I shook my head, and he said, "It's simple, very simple. This will be our little secret. From man to man. It is passed on from the adult to the teenager, from man to boy. That's how men have become men from the beginning of time, passing on their sperm, down through the ages. It's like entering the Sports Hall of Fame, only it's the Spirit Hall of Fame. It's spiritual, you see, nff-nff.'

"'Like Babe Ruth and Lou Gehrig,' I said. I was getting worried about being late for sumo practice and was trying to speed things up. 'Precisely,' he said. 'Huh-huh, clever young man. Every boy must endure his rite of passage, his initiation into manhood.' I could feel myself getting into a real sweat 'cause the whole thing was getting too spooky for words.

"'This is why I asked you earlier, young man, if you know the difference between males and females, as God created them. Females do not have spermatozoa. They have eggs. Females have menstruation. Males have masturbation. You know the difference? Women menstruate. Men masturbate. Necessary evils, so to speak. The first time a girl menstruates, she becomes a woman. The first time a boy masturbates, he becomes a man. But before he does so, a boy must receive spermatozoa. Have you received spermatozoa from a man yet, Mr. Murphy?'

"I almost choked on the last of my Crown Cola. When I told him I haven't, he said, 'Not to worry, you can have some of mine. You can take the spermatozoa from my system into yours. When my adult spermatozoa, the stuff of life, enters into your system, you will then become a man. The act of transference, the ritual act of masculinization will be complete. This is the only way a boy can truly become a man. Are you interested in experiencing the act of transference now? Would you like to become a man today? This very minute?'

"I told him I had sumo practice, and I was already ten minutes late.

"'Well, another time,' he said. 'Nff-nff.' But before letting me go, he told me that when I have my own spermatozoa, I must guard it with my life. 'It is your treasure,' he said, 'your sperm bank, nff-nff. Store it up. Store it through abstinence for your own spiritual profit. A young man must learn to say no to himself. No, no, no.' He kept repeating the word about a hundred times. He really worked himself up. 'In the Book of Genesis, Onan spilled his seed upon the ground and was struck down by God. Remember that.'"

"He wanted you to suck him off," Bug says.

"That's what he told me too," Kavanagh says. "That the ritual act must remain a secret."

"Secret, my ass," Ryan says.

"The act of transference," Oberstein says, shaking his head over and over.

"Bastard!" Blackie says.

* * * * *

"Today boys, while the Brother Superior and his assistant are here, I want to talk to you about a very serious matter, a very sensitive matter. The position of Holy Mother Church regarding conjugal relations."

Kavanagh thinks McCann means conjugation, and raises his hand.

"We do that in Latin class, Brother. When we list the different forms of a verb, we do conjugations."

"*Conjugal relations.* Not conjugations, Mr. Kavanaghs. Conjugal, from the Latin *conjux*, consort, of marriage or the relationship of husband and wife. Not the grammatical system of verbal inflection."

Silence. McCann tilts his head to the side and rolls his eyes toward the ceiling.

"Now, conjugal relations, boys, are . . . well, physical relations."

Bug Bradbury flaps his hand.

"Is that like the Brother Superior from Rome talked to us about? The facts of life?"

"Yes, that is correct, Mr. Bradburys. The facts of life, correct. But conjugal relations . . . Well, it involves more than baby-making. Such relations, between man and wife—"

Murphy's hand shoots up. "Brother, I was wondering. Why do they always say man and wife. Why do they never say woman and husband? It's always man and wife. Wouldn't it be more sensible to say husband and wife?"

"*Tradition*, Mr. Murphys. Tradition. The expression goes back many years. Now, I was about to say, boys, that such relations, well, exist for more than the purpose of procreation. God, in his infinite wisdom, has designed a great gift for those who enter into the sacrament of marriage. It is given for pleasure as well as procreation. Primarily, of course, for the purpose of procreation. But a secondary reason for its existence is pleasure between man and wife. It exists to bind the couple in their fidelity to one another. Yet, there are times when this gift can be misused, even in marriage. Today, class, I wish to make clear to you the times when Holy Mother Church has ordained it sinful to have conjugal relations. There are three main occasions during which conjugal relations are sinful. One: entering into such relations during menstruation."

"What's that?" Kavanagh asks.

"When the girl's having her period, isn't it, Brother?" Bug Bradbury squeaks.

"That is correct. When the wife is *menstruating*. That is the term, Mr. Bradburys . . ."

"Gee, I didn't think that would be a sin," Bradbury muses.

"Well it is!" McCann growls.

"Mortal or venial, Brother?" Brookes asks.

"Mortal, Mr. Brooke. All of these sins are mortal. The three examples I am about to give are *all* examples of mortal sin."

"Like eating meat on Fridays. Eating meat on Fridays is a mortal sin, right Brother?"

"Yes. Correct, Kavanaghs. And mortal sin cuts you off from what, class?"

"God's grace, Brother."

"Precisely. And that is why we have the sacraments. And what is a sacrament, boys?"

"A sacrament is an outward sign of God's grace."

"Precisely. Precisely. And no matter how many rosaries, no matter how many Masses, and Benedictions, no amount of holy communion or novenas will remove the stain of mortal sin, boys. You can eat so much holy communion you get sick. It won't help you one bit. You'll not receive God's grace. You'll remain in the state of mortal sin until you confess to a priest and receive absolution. Is that clear, boys? If you fail to confess, you'll go straight to hell. Where to, boys?"

"Straight to hell, Brother."

"Very good. Now, do you understand the dangers to your soul? Of masturbation, boys?"

Ryan turns in his seat and forms a circle with the thumb and index finger of his left hand while rapidly pushing his right index finger back and forth.

"Now, number two. The second occasion during which conjugal relations is sinful. Wearing a prophylactic. Instead of practicing the rhythm method. You all know about the rhythm method, which the Brother Superior explained during his recent visit. When a husband opts to wear a prophylactic during conjugal relations, it is a mortal sin."

Dead silence. We all wait for Kavanagh or Bug to pop the big question.

"For the benefit of those boys who do not understand the word, perhaps a synonym will help. Another word for a prophylactic is 'condom'. It is a contraceptive sheath worn by men who have conjugal relations outside marriage. The condom is worn to safeguard against disease."

"We call it a rubber, Brother," Bug Bradbury interrupts.

"It protects you against disease." McCann ignores Bug.

"Like VD, right, Brother?" Bug says.

"That is correct, Mr. Bradburys. *Venus veneris*, sexual love. To safeguard against venereal disease and other infections contracted by sexual intercourse with an infected woman. The third example of when Holy Mother Church deems sexual relations a sin is the deliberate wasting of seed during conjugal relations."

Silence.

Bug Bradbury's hands are propellers.

"Yes, Mr. Bradburys?"

"What if you're practicing the rhythm method with your wife, Brother, and you think it's the rhythm time, and you get inside your wife and you're about to, you know, procreate. And you realize you messed up on the calendar date. What would you do?"

McCann looks like he has been hit on the head with a hammer. He stares off into space for a minute and says, "You would do what a good soldier does when he is under heavy attack, Mr. Bradburys. You would pull back."

Oberstein turns white. Blackie is in shock.

"Wouldn't pulling back be like masturbation? And wouldn't that then be a sin? It's all pulling," Bug insists.

McCann looks like he's been hit with the hammer a second time.

Silence. McCann mumbles to himself. He sounds like someone talking in his sleep.

"I do not think that would be a sin," he says, finally.

"But isn't that the same as onionism, Brother?" Bug whines.

"*Onanism*," McCann corrects. "'And Onan spilled his seed

upon the ground.' It would not be a sin because you did not waste your seed for pleasure. Like Onan."

"Was Onan a norph?" Rowsell asks.

"You did not pull back *for pleasure*. Not like masturbation." He ignores Rowsell.

"But you *were* having pleasure," Bug insists. "At least, until you pulled back."

"But not *after*," McCann hastily adds, spraying spit. "There is no pleasure *after*." McCann is angry, but he's letting Bug get away with murder for some reason. It's very strange.

"Perhaps it's a venial sin, then," Bug squeaks.

"Possibly, yes. That would be a possibility," McCann agrees.

"Unless you touched it. You know, to pull back. Like in masturbation. Then it would be a mortal sin, wouldn't it, Brother?"

"Definitely, Mr. Bradburys. Then it would *definitely* be a mortal sin," McCann says. He sways to one side and stares into space again. He looks like a boxer who's on the ropes. He tells us to study our catechism and sleepwalks back to his desk.

During recess, we wander out by the incinerator for a smoke, and Murphy says, "I can understand why it's a mortal sin to have sex with a girl when she's on her period, but why would it be a sin to wear a condor?"

"*Condom*. The word is condom," Oberstein says. "A condor is an ugly bird with a great big head."

"Condom, as in a rubber?" Ryan says.

"Haven't you ever used a rubber?" Bug puffs out his chest.

"I don't get it. Why would you need an eraser to have sex with a girl?" Murphy says.

Bug laughs so hard he falls down. We're all in stitches.

"Murphy ever gets his tail, he's gonna have an ugly bird with a great big head on the top," Blackie says. We almost die laughing.

"I'll tell you one thing," Murphy says, after we settle down, passing some hardtack around. "When I get inside a girl, you'll never see me doing what a good soldier does when he's under attack. I'll never be pulling back, mortal sin or no mortal sin."

"I'm with you, Murph," Bug squeaks. "I won't be doing the good soldier thing either. And you can take that to the bank."

"Yeah, the sperm bank," Blackie says, chewing his biscuit.

And we all howl with laughter again, louder and longer than before.

Back in religion class, we're sure Bug is a goner again. He's really pushing his luck. McCann picks up where he left off last class, the difference between a venial and a mortal sin. Everyone is asking idiotic questions like, Is picking your nose a venial sin or a mortal sin? Or, Is it a venial sin or a mortal sin to think about a naked woman? Ryan wants to know if it's a mortal sin to hurt an animal, like blowing up a frog with a straw. McCann says it's a venial sin, but Oberstein argues that it is a mortal sin because an animal is alive just like a human. Life is life, Oberstein says. But McCann says we're not like animals, that animals are lower life forms, and have no souls, and God created them to be killed and eaten. That settles things until Bug asks if it is a mortal sin to steal from a church. We all turn white, praying Bug won't mention the wine. But McCann just shrugs and says place doesn't matter, it is the nature of the sin that counts. Then he turns and writes the word "masturbation" on the blackboard. He draws a long horizontal arrow opposite it and scrawls in large capital letters: DEADLY SIN.

Bug raises his hand and squeaks, "It's not, Brother McCann. It's not a mortal sin. I don't think it's even a sin."

"Oh, but it is. What's a mortal sin, class?"

"A mortal sin is a grievous offense against the law of God."

"It's not a sin," Bug insists.

"Oh, but it is. It's a terrible sin, a deadly sin, a mortal sin," Brother McCann says. "Holy Mother Church—"

"It can't be," Bug says. "It's too natural to be a sin. It's how God made us."

McCann grabs the Baltimore Catechism and says, "Page sixteen, question number nine. 'What is a mortal sin? A mortal sin cuts the sinner off from God's grace.' And masturbation, Mr. Bradburys, is on the list of mortal sins. It's on the list." There is spit everywhere. "What are the chief sources of sin, class?"

"Pride, covetousness, lust, anger, gluttony, envy, and sloth. And they are commonly called deadly sins."

"You see, it's on the list."

"Whose list, Brother? Who makes the list? Who says it's a deadly sin?" We all look at each other as if to say "Bug's gone bonkers."

"Holy Mother Church's list. *Lust,*" McCann growls. "Lust . . . Lust is a deadly sin."

"But I masturbate, Brother. All the time. I can't help it. Every time I think of Marilyn Monroe and Jane Mansfield. I think it's only normal. Everyone does it some time or other, including brothers. Only animals don't do it. Do you want us to be like animals? I think even priests do it."

"Priests! You should be saying what you're saying to a priest. Not to me! To a priest. And in the seal of the confessional box. Not to me. And certainly not to your classmates." McCann's voice becomes soft. It takes on a strange tone, almost defeated, as if he's becoming embarrassed.

"Brother McCann, if God is a loving God, why would he be mad at me for masturbating when I can't help it? It's natural. That's the way He made me."

McCann's eyes seem to be wondering what Bug means. "Masturbation is on the list of sins deemed by Holy Mother Church to be mortal. And a mortal sin deprives you of . . . of what, class?"

"God's grace, Brother."

"Precisely. And no sacrament, no amount of holy communion, will help you. You'll not receive God's grace. You'll go straight to hell. Now do you understand the danger to your soul caused by masturbation, boys?"

"Yes, Brother."

"That's why it's a deadly sin, boys. Why it's on the list. One of the seven deemed by Holy Mother Church—"

"The Church is wrong!" Bug shouts. He's saucier than we've ever seen him. We're all amazed. Ryan shudders at the punishment to come. Blackie looks at me and goggles his eyes. We're sure McCann will knock Bug's head off any minute. He's strapped us for a lot less.

"The Church is right," McCann says.

"Wrong," Bug says. "It's stupid. The Church is wrong about masturbation. Or we're all going to hell, every last one of us. You included."

There is a long silence. We know Bug's a dead duck.

McCann turns to the blackboard, picks up an eraser and begins erasing the words "DEADLY SIN."

"Perhaps . . . perhaps, Mr. Bradburys, you are right. Perhaps God . . . Perhaps God meant for us . . ."

He finishes erasing the board and tells us to study questions twenty to twenty-five on the sacraments. Then he sits down behind his desk and stares off into the distance, like a boxer who has been stunned by a blow. Nothing happens the rest of the class. He doesn't say anything to Bug. He doesn't strap him or punch him. He just sits there in a daze until the buzzer sounds. Then he leaves the room, and Brother Walsh comes in to teach Latin.

After supper, we ask Bug if he's lost his marbles. Blackie and Murphy say he's lucky he never got his head handed to him. Bug grins and calls us a bunch of chickens, and says he knew McCann wouldn't do anything to him. When we ask why, he says because the night before he caught McCann in the act.

"Whaddaya mean? What act?" Ryan asks.

"Caught him down in the laundry room. Snappin' the lizard. By the big dryers. I was talkin' to *him* during class. Not anyone else. And he knew it. He's happy I said he ain't goin' to hell. I was tellin' him it isn't a sin. I *knew* he wouldn't hit me. I knew, because I was tellin' him that I *saw* him, caught him red-handed in the act."

"You got more balls than I have," Murphy says.

"Like Oberstein says. It's common sense. Oberstein's right about that. Common sense is more important than Church rules. I know it. And McCann knows it. I knew deep down he'd be glad to hear me say what I said. That the Church is wrong, that it's not a sin to snap the lizard. And he needed to hear it more than anyone. He needed to hear that it's normal. It *is*. You're not goin' to hell for that. Nobody's goin' to hell for that. Not even McCann."

"You took an awful chance," Oberstein says.

"Don't think so," Bug grins. "He won't ever bother me again."

"You're lucky," Blackie says. "Could of turned on you."

"Don't think so," Bug says. "And you wouldn't either if you'd seen his face when I walked in on him down in the laundry room."

"He's gonna getcha. Tomorrow, maybe next day. You're walkin' on thin ice. You're gonna get it," Blackie says.

"You didn't see the look on his face," Bug brags. "He won't be botherin' me anymore."

"You got balls, Bradbury," Murphy says.

Bug puffs out his chest.

"'The sorrow of death compassed me,'" Oberstein says, "'and the pains of hell got hold of me. I found trouble and sorrow.'"

"You're in deep trouble, Ladybug," Blackie says. "You better fly away home."

Summer 1961

17

THE MARATHON is getting so close. Blackie and Ryan and Richardson ran over thirty miles last Saturday. Our times have never been better. Ryan almost beat Richardson last time out. He's gonna be a great runner one day. Maybe even better than Richardson, Blackie says.

Summer's on the way. We can't wait. Like Christmas, there's no school. Only this time, for two whole months. No study hall, no homework. That alone is enough to put you in seventh heaven. The outdoor swimming pool is open every day, and we have a lot more free time. We spend a lot of time at the Bat Cave, and in the woods building bough huts. We fish and have boil-ups at Virginia Waters. There are picnics at the canyon at Manuels River. The brothers pile us into a big yellow school bus and take us there, or to Power's Court, where we fish and swim and light fires to roast hot dogs. There's always plenty of hot dogs every time we go anywhere. And we get an increase in our weekend allowance this summer. We'll all get fifty cents each Saturday for free time. That means we'll be able to buy the famous Newfoundland Spruce Beer. I've never had it. Murphy says you can get drunk on it, but Oberstein says you can't. It has the same froth as beer, but it stinks to high heaven and tastes like branches from a tree. It costs twenty-five cents a bottle.

The best parts of the summer are the regatta and the camping trip. The regatta is always the first Wednesday in August. It's six weeks away. We're all counting the days. That's when we're allowed the most free time of the whole year. The regatta starts at nine in the morning and goes till nine at night. It ends with an hour of the most amazing fireworks. You can see it from anywhere in the city. The regatta is the only time during the year that the brothers have off. They meet up with brothers from the other schools and spend the day at a cabin on Hogan's Pond. The senior boys are given money to take the little ones to the regatta. The little ones have to be back by six, but we can stay out till nine, after the fireworks. There are boat races all day, and games of chance, and clowns and cotton candy and hot dogs and hamburgers and chips and candy apples. The older boys always buy spin tickets to try to win teddy bears for the little ones. Sometimes they steal one.

The regatta marathon starts at noon. The regatta is cancelled only if there are high winds. The marathon is never cancelled. Oberstein and Blackie have been arguing a lot lately about how many runners should enter. Oberstein wants everyone to run. But Blackie wants just Richardson and Ryan to run. He wants the other runners to ride shotgun, as he calls it. He's set up specialty teams for running supplies, and he's dreamed up schemes for slowing down the really good runners who might get too far ahead. The peashooters have been practicing for weeks. Father Cross made them tiny straight tubes out of copper for spitting their darts. Blackie says he read that in Africa a pygmy can bring down a lion with a peashooter. If the St. John's runners get too much of a lead, Blackie wants to have obstacles in place to slow them down, even knock them out of the race.

Our summer camping trip takes place the last week of August. We go to Ferryland, a small fishing village on the southern shore, and stay at the Holy Cross Cadet Camp for a

whole week. It's the best fun you could ever have. We stay in
bunkhouses, six to a house. And the food is amazing. Dick the
Dutchman cooks all our meals. And just like Christmas, no
Diefenbaker meat for a whole week. Breakfast is bacon and
eggs every morning. And Dick the Dutchman lets you eat as
much as you want. In fact, he gets kinda upset if you don't eat
a lot. He makes big vats of black coffee. And you can have all
the orange juice you can drink. There's toast and real butter
and partridgeberry jam. Murphy and Oberstein eat a loaf of
toast every morning. And you can have your eggs fried, boiled,
scrambled, or poached. And there's always sugar and honey
and salt and pepper and ketchup and mustard on the tables.

We play softball and baseball and soccer. And we get to go to
the Ferryland Garden Party, which is always great fun. We
build forts and go mountain climbing and hiking and fishing.
And we swim in the ponds nearby. And every now and then,
on a bet or a dare, someone swims in the freezing ocean. And
we borrow the cadet boat, an oversized dory, and row outside
the bay and catch tom cods and flat fish and even sculpins. It's
always such fun. Last year we built a sail and sailed the dory
around the bay for hours. Oberstein used an old goalie stick
for a rudder. Blackie says that when he dies, if he gets to the
pearly gates, he's gonna ask St. Peter to send him straight back
to the Holy Cross Cadet Camp forever. "That's my idea of
heaven," he says.

Bug has the best time of any of us at camp. He spends all his
time chasing the girls up the shore. One night last year, after
supper, he brought three girls and a few bottles of spruce beer
to the bunkhouse, and we played strip poker. But the girls
wouldn't take off their underclothes. Bug deliberately lost
every game of blackjack so he could strip down fast, which
made the girls giggle a lot. "Oh no," he'd say, "I'm busted again.
There goes another sock."

If he keeps up his shenanigans, Bug might not make it to camp this year. We're all getting really worried about him. Ever since he caught McCann in the laundry room, he's acting really crazy. Blackie was right. It was too good to believe that Bug wouldn't get strapped. McCann said he was strapping him for what he said in class. But Blackie says he got it for blabbing about catching McCann in the act. He's starting to act weird. Oberstein thinks there's something seriously wrong with him. A disorder, Oberstein says.

The first time it happened, we couldn't believe our eyes. "Firebug," Murphy howled with delight. Bug clicked a cigarette out of his case, lit it, put the lit end in his mouth and kept it there while I counted out a full twenty seconds on my Mickey.

"He eats fire," Kavanagh said. "He actually eats fire."

"The incombustible man," Oberstein called him.

The next incident was out behind the soccer field. We were at the incinerator, roasting potatoes on hangers, and Bug bragged that he could pass his hand through the fire without getting burned. Blackie told him not to do it, but we all dared him, and he did it as we chanted four Mississippis. He got a bad burn. Soot blackened his skin, but he just laughed and squeaked that it didn't hurt him one bit. But we all knew it did. We were all thrilled at first, then upset. Blackie brought him to the infirmary, where Rags bandaged his hand in gauze and salve. Rags was really concerned. He said it was a pretty bad burn, and asked them a lot of questions. Bug said he did it playing by the incinerator. Rags said Bug would have to go to the hospital for a checkup if it didn't heal quickly.

"I'm fireproof," Bug bragged all week.

"You're mad," everyone said.

All week we told him he was crazy. But he just laughed at us, craving all the attention and getting saucier by the second.

Then it happened again. At the Bat Cave. He tried the

cigarette trick again and burned the inside of his mouth. "The most unkindest burn of all," Murphy said. It musta really hurt because Bug was hell to live with all week. When we told him he was really gonna hurt himself, he taunted us by taking off his shoes and socks and wiggling each bare foot close to the flames. He put them so close, the skin around his toenails became an ugly red. Oberstein insisted he had acquired some abnormality. The more attention we gave him, the cockier he became.

"You can roast a wiener while I put my foot in the fire," he boasted. "I'll keep it there till the wiener's done. If my foot burns, I'll stick my own wiener in the fire." He wanted to try it, but we wouldn't let him.

"Gotta stop playin' with fire, Bug," Blackie almost begged. "You better not let the brothers know about it. The brothers find out about it, you'll go to the Mental."

"How can you even think of putting your hand over a flame?" Ryan said. "*Christ.*"

"I told you, Einstein, I'm like the superheroes. *Invincible!*"

"Jesus, this'll be a real problem for all of us if the brothers find out," Blackie said.

It was a while before Bug played with fire again. Dared by a few doubters at the Bat Cave one day, he took a hunting knife and heated it until it scorched the wood. Then he stroked his arms with the red-hot blade. He dropped the knife after a few seconds, but got another bad burn.

With each new gamble with fire, he became more arrogant and smart-assed, looking down his nose at the dumbos, as he calls us.

Blackie has started protecting him more than ever. Anything his heart desires, all Bug has to do is hint at it and it is his. Blackie treats him like a prince, even though his sauciness never changes one bit. In fact, it has gotten worse. Bug takes advantage of our kindness. If there is an extra slice of bread on the plate at mealtime, in unison we ask him if he wants it. He curls his lip and sneers and says, "Naw! Gimme Ryan's. He's got the fattest one."

It's an odd situation to be in. One minute you want to punch his lights out, but every other minute you're looking over your shoulder to make sure he isn't trying to play with fire.

Worst of all, Oberstein's worried that Blackie's spending too much time worrying about Bug. "It's taking his mind off the race," he says. "It's getting close. We gotta concentrate 100 percent on the marathon."

*   *   *   *   *

Bug Bradbury's out on the window ledge. Bug's on the window ledge. Bug Bradbury's gonna kill himself. Bug's on the window ledge. Bug's gonna kill himself.

The most criers I've ever heard. The word spreads fast. Bug's out on the second-floor window ledge of St. Luke's dorm, threatening to kill himself.

At first, I think it's a dare. Our new game, madman of the mount. Lots of summer days, after swimming in the pool, we change into our play clothes and play games in the big yard. Lately we've been playing a lot of madman of the mount. Bug usually wins. The way it works is somebody makes a crazy dare, like climb up on top of the fire escape and jump off. Once Ryan dared everyone to strip to their underwear and race around the yard yelling, "The British are coming. The British are coming." Bug was buck naked before you could say Jack Robinson. Another time he jumped down the long flight of stairs by the chapel on a dare from Blackie and bloodied his head on the archway. *Boom!* Right in the forehead. Knocked him cold. We thought he'd never get up. But Bug's tough as nails.

I race to the window ledge and can tell right away it's not a game. Bug is there, plain as day. And he's dead serious about jumping. Nobody knows what got into him, why he went out on the ledge. Oberstein says he flipped because Madman Malone strapped him for telling lies. Bug has taken to telling a lot of lies lately. He can't open his mouth without shooting the shit. And he's become a Mount crier—the worst we've ever had. *Canteen's open. Canteen's open. Canteen's open.* His favorite chant is always a lie. And he's started stealing too. He steals things out of pockets and desks and lockers, but if you catch him in the act he yells "Fifth Amendment" and argues with you till he's blue in the face. If you insist long enough, he hands the thing back to you, always shouting the same expression: "That's your right. To have it back. Take it, it belongs to you. That's your right." It's like a game, and everyone except the brothers plays along.

Murphy says Bug told Madman that Brother McMurtry wanted to meet him in the infirmary, it was an emergency. Madman raced to the infirmary for a meeting with a few empty beds. He's become a compulsive liar, Oberstein says. He can't help it. You might be walking to the cafeteria and bump into him, and he'll tell you that Kelly's been looking for you all day or that there's mail for you, Ryan has it in his locker. Or he'll tell you he saw a rat in the washroom. Or he'll ask, dead serious, "Where are you goin'? We're all spoze to be goin' to the gym. C'mon, hurry up. Brother so-and-so just announced it on the PA when you were outside playing."

He lies like a trouper. One Saturday afternoon Ryan and Murphy were headed to Virginia Waters, and he gave them a couple of cans of beans and a loaf of bread and tea bags for a boil-up. He told them Brother Foster allowed him to take the supplies from the kitchen stores for a camping trip, and that they could take whatever they wanted. They took a ton of stuff and went off to Virginia Waters. When they got back, they got strapped for stealing.

He not only lies all the time, he does crazy things. He's constantly licking his hands. He has a really long tongue, and he licks one hand after the other. Starting with each wrist, he goes all the way to his fingertips. We're all worried there's something really wrong with him. Once he showed up for Chapel wearing only his shoes and socks. And he's always burping in people's faces. He told Oberstein that he burps because he got his tonsils out, which is a lie. He says before he got his tonsils out the gas bubbled up and used to go to his tonsils, hit them, and go back down. Now it just goes straight up and out through his mouth and into people's faces.

Bug almost never gets away with lying to Blackie. He might try to lie to Blackie that he left his paperback in the gym, and Blackie will just smile, and Bug will giggle and say, "Okay, okay."

Whatever Bug does, Blackie almost always approves of it. About a week ago, I was chatting with Bug about my baseball cards, and he was really bugging me about trading me a Mickey Mantle if I gave him one of my two Phil Rizzutos. Just to get him off my back, I said I'd think about it. That night, when I was asleep, he stole one of my Phil Rizuttos from my locker. I told Blackie about it, and he just laughed. "You should know better," Blackie said. "And besides, you should of given him one. You have two. And giving something like that to Bug means a lot more than giving it to anyone else." I told him he was crazier than Bug. He just shrugged and laughed. But in a way I knew he was right.

When the others hear Bug is out on the window ledge, they all run to the front of the building, where a small crowd has gathered. Everyone's staring up at him. He's about fifty feet up, standing there, his hands outstretched, like a crucifix. And he's soaking wet from head to toe. He looks as cute as a drowned rat. He must've taken a shower for some reason before going out on the ledge. He's barefoot and wearing a tumbling outfit. I'm terrified of the height. I close my eyes and wish it wasn't summer. I wish it was winter, and there was a mountain of swirling snow that rose almost as high as him so he could jump into it and scream "I'm king of the castle" and get up laughing and do it all over again.

"Jump!" O'Connor heckles. "Jump, Bradbury, you chicken-shit. You won't even break a leg from that height."

Everyone laughs and moves closer, the thawing mud caking their sneakers.

"Jump, Bug, jump!" someone yells. And everyone joins in, laughing and chanting, "Jump, Bug, jump!" The chorus is reaching a feverish pitch when McCann and Madman Malone arrive on the scene. McCann hops through the crowd whacking heads and spraying spit everywhere, shouting at everyone to be quiet and to move the hell back away from the wall. When the chanting stops, he yells up at Bug to stay put, one of the other brothers is coming to get him. He orders several boys to run to the infirmary to get blankets to use as safety nets in case Bug jumps. While we wait for the boys to return with the blankets, Brother Malone moves closer to the wall. He looks up at Bug and speaks softly, "Brendan, be careful. Don't move. You could really hurt yourself if you fall."

"I hate you. You shouldn't of strapped me." Bug is sobbing, his shoulders bobbing up and down. He's out of control, and it looks like he could fall any minute. I pray he won't fall or jump or say anything about the wine stealing or the marathon.

"You were strapped for telling lies, Brendan. You must learn to take your punishment like all the other boys do when they misbehave."

"Shuttlecock. Pistil . . . Pistil-cock and shuttlecock. I hate you. *Hate you.* Hate . . . hate . . . hate . . . you. You just wanna act the big shot all the time. You think you're King Tuk . . . But you're not, you're only King Shit . . . You shouldn't of strapped me. You didn't strap O'Grady when he clawed *me.* You're *baaaaad.*"

"No, Brendan. You were bad. You told a lie. And lying is sinful."

"I hate you. Hate . . . Hate . . . Hate . . . Get back . . . Get back, or I'll tumble."

And we watch in disbelief as Bug unzips his fly, pulls out his pecker and pees down on Brother Malone. We all rush madly away from the building.

"There. That's what you get for strapping me. You deserve it. You're *baaaaad.*"

As Brother Walsh arrives, teeth bared like a mad dog's, Madman steps back from the building, removes a white hand-kerchief from his cuff and begins slapping at his soutane.

"Gabe is up in the dorm," Brother Walsh says. "He thinks he can get an arm around him and pull him in. He wants you to keep talking to him. Keep his attention away from the window."

"Get back and stay back," Bug roars. "I can last longer than a shower. I've been drinking water all day. And I'll pee on every one of you if you move any closer." He shakes his pecker. "Ha-ha-ha-*haaa*-ha." He tries to sound like Woody Woodpecker. The crowd draws back again.

Brother Walsh looks up and says, "Brother Malone is very sorry, Brendan. He should not have strapped you."

"Well . . . that's not good enough. And don't call me Brendan. I'm *Bug.* B-U-G, moron."

Malone says, "Okay, Bug. I can only say that I'm sorry. I can't undo the strapping, Bug."

"You can undo *something.* Make it up to me *somehow.*"

"How? What can I do, Bug? How can I make it up to you?

Tell me what to do, Bug. Whatever you think is fair, I'll do, Bug."

It's sickening to hear Madman sucking up to Bug by using his nickname all over the place. Sickening and sad. And at the same time, exciting to see Bug having some power over him for a change.

"I dunno. Something . . . anything."

"What? What would you like me to do, Bug?"

"Canteen card," Bug says.

"Canteen card," Brother Malone repeats, clutching a straw. "Another canteen card, Bug? An extra one? You can have an extra one, Bug."

"No . . . No . . . I want to . . . to strap you. I wanna strap you as hard as I can. Till it stings your hot dog. Just like you strapped me."

"Okay. Okay, that's fair. That sounds fair to me."

"And I wanna use *your* strap to do it."

"Fine, Bug, you can use my strap. That's fair."

As they're talking, Brother McMurtry leans out the window, grabs Bug and pulls him inside. All we can hear is squealing and screaming. My heart breaks for him.

Nobody tells us what happened to Bug. The brothers won't say. There's a rumor he's gone to the Mental. All I can think of is Christmastime and the choir and the tumblers performing at the Mental. We were all frightened to death. Babbling drooling patients kept trying to join the tumblers. Men in white suits kept taking them back to their seats. One old hunched-up guy made it to the middle of the line and screwed everything up so much we had to start over. I hope that's not where he is. A lot of us will have the spells if that's the case. Oberstein's sure that's what happened to him. He's really upset. He has that same downcast look he always has whenever he gets the spells. I try to perk him up by telling him Bug will be fine and that we've gotta spend all our time now on the marathon. It's getting so close. "Don't get the spells on us, Oberstein. We need you. The regatta's only a few weeks away."

"If he's there, we're gonna bust in," Blackie says, "and bust him out."

"Jesus, breaking into the Mental," Murphy says.

"Gosh, can you really do that?" Rowsell asks.

"They shouldn't strap people like Bug," Oberstein says. "It's not fair. He's not like the rest of us. He's upset, and he has a hole in his heart. And he doesn't know what he's doing half the time lately."

"He'll be a lot worse off in the Mental than at the Mount, that's for sure," Brookes says, and starts to cry.

Oberstein puts his arm around Brookes. "'Weeping endures for a night, but joy comes in the morning,'" he says.

"We're gonna bust in, and we're gonna bust out," Blackie says. "Just like in the movies."

"Gosh, are you gonna use guns?" Rowsell asks.

•   •   •   •   •

Bug Bradbury's not around anymore. Who wants to hunt for Bug? Come out, come out, wherever you are.

Our worst fear is true. The criers are right. Bug's not around anymore. He's been sent to the Mental. Five long days to Saturday free time before we can get to him. The days pass like years. But mercifully, as Clare would say, the waiting ends.

It's two o'clock when we arrive at the Mental in search of Bug. The Mental consists of two huge red brick buildings opposite Bowring Park, where we often go on Saturdays to watch the ducks and swans and to climb the Fighting Newfoundlander, a beautiful statue dedicated to the Royal Newfoundland Regiment of the First World War. Brother

McMurtry told us the Newfoundlanders fought like lions during the Battle of the Somme.

The four of us—Blackie, Oberstein, Murphy, and me—scramble through a thicket of alders, climb a long-hedged bank and struggle through the sudden green-and-yellow shock of summer to the big parking lot in front of the buildings. Blackie tells us to wait in the lot while he cases the joint. As he heads for the side entrance, an ambulance arrives, its red light flashing. Men in white uniforms shuffle a struggling man wearing a straitjacket toward the ambulance. He has a square pink face and sleepyhead hair.

"Another fighting Newfoundlander," Murphy says.

Patients gather in the doorways and windows, bluebottle flies buzzing around their heads. Those at the back stand on their toes to watch. Somebody screams from an open window, "Hence! Home, you idle creatures . . . Mooooo . . . Get you home. Is this a holiday?"

"Bug!" Oberstein says. "Second floor, last window over."

"Friends, Romans, St. John's cunts, lend me your tears . . ."

And sure enough, there's Bug, bigger than on a movie screen, leaning out a window and squawking, "I have come to straitjacket Bernie, not to praise him. Bernie, you forgot your smokes."

A fat cook comes out in his apron to have a cigarette and to see who's causing all the racket. He is joined in a few minutes by a thin man with a walrus moustache who wears a white uniform.

"Poor bastard," Oberstein says. "Wonder why they put him in a straitjacket?"

"Hope it doesn't have anything to do with Bug," I say.

Blackie returns and tells us that getting in is a piece of cake. "No security guards. Geared to keepin' people in. Guess they don't care 'bout keepin' people out. There's an open window on the second floor," he says. "It's not too high up."

"We spotted Bug," Oberstein says. "Last window, second floor." Blackie looks in the direction Oberstein is pointing but Bug's no longer there.

"Gonna need a human ladder to get through the window," Blackie says, looking at Murphy. "We should be able to get in standing on his shoulders."

"Jesus, never thought we'd ever be breaking into the Mental." Murphy strains as he lifts Blackie onto his shoulders.

Once inside, Blackie and I head straight for the corner room on the second floor. The door has BRADBURY stamped on it. We push through the heavy door. The room is painted a glossy white. It's tiny and plain, with a bed and a night table. The walls are bare and lonely. On the table is a stack of Classics comics that Oberstein collected and sent. Bug is sitting up in bed, smoking a cigarette and reading *Alice in Wonderland*.

"Took you long enough," he says, without looking up from his comic. He burps loudly. "Gas keeps bubbling up." He licks his arm.

"How'd you know it was us, Bug?" I ask.

"You kiddin' me, brother? Pretty hard to miss." He snaps his fingers, jumps out of bed and goes to the window. He's wearing a pale-white gown, the kind the patients wear on *Ben Casey*. "You guys are real dopes. Hanging around the parkin' lot like a crowd of crooks. Looked like hoods from a Cagney movie. *Dumbos*. Wonder someone didn't lock you up."

Blackie laughs. "How's the world's most famous hot dog?" Blackie asks. We crack up.

"Still getting longer," Bug giggles. "Got a ruler?" He scratches his crotch and says, "I'm some glad my plumbing's on the outside."

I ask Bug about the guy they took off in the straitjacket.

"Ahh, that's just Bernie," he says. "Thinks he's the Bird Man of

Alcatraz. Jumped out a window. They're takin' him to the General for an X-ray."

Blackie laughs again. "They treatin' you okay, Ladybug?" he asks. "What've you been up to?"

"Hangin' out with headshrinkers, mostly. Puttin' the make on a few nurses. There's a really cute patient from Labrador on the third floor. Name's Wendy. I tell her she's Wendy the good little witch. I sneak up to her room a lot. We smoke cigarettes and watch TV and do lotsa heavy necking. But she won't pet. She says it could lead to twins. She has twin brothers. She's got a really wet tongue. You should see it, it's longer than mine. Almost got caught red-handed in bed with her once. There's another old guy from Hare Bay who fell off a ladder and landed on his head. He thinks he's Joey Smallwood. I tell him I'm Julius Caesar. We have some pretty good chats. But it's all Greek to me. He wants me to join the Liberals. Think Cross can make him a pair of Joey glasses? This guy's a whiz at playing crib too. Beats me at every game."

"You seeing a shrink, Bug?" Blackie asks.

"Almost every day. He thinks I'm okay. But he's nuts. He wears a magnifyin' glass that he keeps on a string in his top pocket. You know, like the Planter's Peanuts man. I call him Mr. Peanut. He's only a tiny guy, but he doesn't seem to mind bein' called that. He can't ask a question without hauling out his magnifyin' glass and lookin' at you through it. He keeps buggin' me about my relationship with my mother. I told him she gave me cigarettes and coffee when I was still in a high chair. And that I think about her when I snap the lizard. That got him off my case for a while."

"How's the food? You eatin' good? Betcha miss the Diefenbaker meat."

"Food here's pretty good. They don't serve bog juice. Real tea and real coffee. Ice cream, pop, chips. The whole shebang.

Every day's a wingding, brother." When he finishes, he takes short, squeaky breaths. Then he murmurs to himself and moans softly and sits down on the bed.

"I've been getting winded a lot lately. And I fainted in the shower the other day. Mr. Peanut told me he's gonna get me a wheelchair if I keep fainting. Guess what, I been fainting twice a day. I'd love a wheelchair."

Blackie and I look at each other. We're not sure if he's bullshitting.

"Gotta get you outta here," Blackie says. "We're gonna bust you out, Bug."

"Don't need any help. 'Bug from bondage will deliver Bug.' Besides, it won't be necessary, they're sending me home Monday."

Blackie's so happy he gives him a big hug.

"That's great, Bug," I say. "It'll be good to have you back at the Mount. I was worried you might miss the marathon."

"You kiddin' me? This place is *paradise*. I'd rather stick around here, any day. Lotsa cigarettes. TV whenever you want. We're allowed to stay up till midnight to watch wrestling. Like I said, food's a lot better. And tons of it. No fucken Diefenbaker meat in here, brother. No rules. No class. No study hall, Mass, rosary. Perfect place for an atheist."

We laugh. Then there's an uncomfortable silence. Bug looks as if he's trying to remember something. Blackie's eyes jump, taking in the room.

"'If it were so, it would be, and if it was so, it might be . . . but seein' how it isn't, it ain't.'" He rolls up the comic and bops himself in the forehead. "It's all in *Alice*," he says. Then he takes out his little silver cigarette case and snaps the cover open and shut a few times.

"Ole Flynn was here to see me the other day. Tried to give me holy communion. I told him to stick it where the sun don't shine. Asked me if I wanted to go to confession. I didn't go, but I told him we stole the wine."

Blackie's jaw drops, as we stare in disbelief.

"Relax. Just kiddin'. Gettin' yer pee hot, weren't cha?" He laughs himself into a coughing fit, choking and sending spit everywhere, the way McCann does.

Blackie's eyes twitch madly. He races to Bug and smacks him on the back.

"Everyone misses you, Bug," I say.

He lets out a long, squeaky, doleful sigh.

"I don't miss anybody. *Nobody*. Except, maybe . . . Rags. Yeah, I guess I miss Blackie too. Blackie and Rags." He whimpers and stares blankly at the clock on the wall. His eyes fill up, and we know he misses everyone. He closes his eyes. There is another doleful squeak. He can't say anything. For the first time in his life he seems to have lost the power of speech.

We don't say anything. It's a really dense silence, the kind that invites the sort of thoughts that can give you the spells. "Ladybug, Ladybug, fly away home" comes into my head, and the words won't go away. They play over and over. Like when the needle's stuck on a record player. Blackie reaches into his pockets and brings out fistfuls of Tootsie Rolls and suckers.

"For the Bug," he says.

"Jeez, thanks, Blackie," Bug lets out a wild little yelp.

"Do you need us to bring anything else?" I ask. "More comics . . ."

"Bottle of wine. And Tokyo Rose, *naked*."

Blackie howls. More silence. Bug stares blankly at the clock again.

"I mean it. You can have anything you want, Bug. Just name it."

"I wanna be king of the Mental," Bug says and stares blankly at the clock again. Then we listen to him reciting lines from *Julius Caesar*.

"The Doyle sisters been asking about you, Bug," I lie.

"Didja get your skin yet?" Bug asks. "Didja jump Ruthie Peckford?"

I can feel the blood running to my head.

"Didn't think so," Bug laughs. "They'll be coming with my medicine soon," he says. "You guys better vamoose."

Before we leave, Blackie tells him about the marathon training. "Over thirty miles now, Bug. Only two weeks to the big race. Everyone's gonna be ready."

"*Shuttlecocks*, Richardson won't win it," he groans. "And don't waste your money on Ryan. He's too scrawny. Nick the pigeon would beat him in a race. Besides, scarecrows don't win marathons. He's too skinny."

"He's got a little muscle now," I say. "He's not as skinny, and he's still light. And he runs faster."

"Would that he were fatter," Bug says.

"Gonna win it," Blackie says. "And Ryan's gonna get the silver."

"And pigs fly." Bug pushes his nose up so he looks like a pig.

"Are you really coming back to the Mount on Monday?" I ask.

"So Mr. Peanut says," he moans. "But I'm doin' my best to stay right here in paradise with Wendy. Faintin' as much as I can." Each time he says paradise I think of what Rags said to Oberstein about making a heaven of a hell. And in his own way, with all his lying and cheating and bragging and stealing, I know that's what Bug is trying to do. What Rags once said about all of us. He's looking from behind bars, trying to see stars.

"Be seein' ya Monday, Bug," Blackie says.

"Beware the ides of August," Bug shrieks. "Neither one of those jokers will win. Betcha fifty bucks."

The public address system clicks on, and a voice asks Dr. Peterson to report to the front desk.

"Peterson the pest," Bug says. "Better vamoose, amigos. And

don't forget what the Cheshire cat told Alice." He pops himself with the comic.

"What's that, Bug?"

"'We're all mad in here.'" He yelps and laughs, and is quickly out of breath.

"See ya Monday," I repeat.

But he's not listening. He's back in bed, propped up on his pillow, a sucker in one hand, his comic in the other.

All the way home we argue about whether Bug will be back on Monday. As we sign the Doomsday Book we're still placing bets. Blackie and Oberstein are sure he'll be back. Murphy and I are convinced he won't be. I hope they're right. Things are sure a lot more lively with Bug around.

* * * * *

Bug's got a wheelchair. Bug's got a wheelchair.
Wheelchair. Wheelchair.

Bug's got a wheelchair. He's supposed to spend all his time in it. He's only supposed to walk once in a while—going to the bathroom at night or walking from his bed to his locker. The rest of the time, he has strict orders from the doctor not to do any exercise and to stay in his wheelchair. It's a really neat wheelchair. It's got a black leather seat and big chrome wheels. The Americans at Fort Pepperrell donated it. Two handsome servicemen dressed in white uniforms showed up with it one day. They both had crewcuts and black moustaches. They were really nice soldiers. They sent for Oberstein and Blackie, and asked if there were any other American orphans. They gave them each a brand new baseball glove. I thought that was pretty nice of them. Americans are like that. They've got really big hearts. The soldiers beamed like little kids when Bug sat in the chair.

"There, you'll be fine from now on," the tall one said.

"No, I won't, Colonel," Bug squeaked. "I got a bad heart. This stupid thing'll kill me. I'll strain myself every time I wheel around in it. It's useless 'less you put a motor on it."

The soldiers smiled and said they'd see what they could do. And they took the wheelchair away and rigged it up with a motor that worked off a battery beneath the seat. They brought it back a few days later and gave Bug instructions on how to use it. They beamed again when he sat in it, saluted them, and roared off.

From that moment on, Bug Bradbury became the scourge of the Mount. Dennis the Menace has nothing on Bug Bradbury. He flies through the halls like he's at the Indianapolis 500. Father Cross makes him a rubber horn that squawks like two crows fighting over a scrap of bread. He races madly through the halls as fast as the machine will go, always intent upon wiping someone out. He's wiped himself out a few times, and he almost killed himself playing chicken in the gym one day when he turned too fast and flew out of the chair and into a cement wall. He had an ugly bluish yellow bump on his forehead for a week.

When we hear Bug's horn squawking, or the mad whirring of the motor, we all bolt for cover. It doesn't matter if we're sitting around playing jacks or cards or marbles, when we hear him coming we clear the decks. Everyone, that is, except Kavanagh, who's already been hit twice. Kavanagh gets really excited and always stands in the middle of the hallway, daring Bug to hit him, jumping away from the speeding wheelchair at the last possible second, just like in the movies. Bug got the idea from a Jimmy Dean movie. Blackie teases him that he'll be able to win the marathon now that he has a wheelchair.

Bug has created bumper pads, as he calls them, by tying Eaton's catalogs to the sides and the upturned footrest. He refers to the wheelchair as the tank. He wants everyone to call him General Bradbury. Father Cross made him a green beret like the US army wears. Bug gave it back and told him to put five stars across the front. He wants to be a five-star general.

"Bumper pads are for the sooky-babies, afraid to take a little knock," he teases.

With the exception of Kavanagh, the sound of Bug's horn strikes terror in every boy, including Blackie. It scatters us in every direction, the older boys pulling the tiny ones to safety. Boys run everywhere, through open doorways and up the nearest flight of stairs. They jump up on window ledges and climb on top of hot radiators. They'd hang from the light fixtures if they could reach them.

After Bug wiped out Kavanagh for the second time, spraining his leg, Rags told him he would lose his wheelchair if he got caught speeding in the halls. So Bug hired a few scouts, offering nickels and dimes from his next month's canteen card, to make sure the coast is always clear of the brothers before he goes on a tear. As each scout reports back to him, he races off through the hallway, squawking his horn and screaming as loud as he can, "Arrr! Norphs, ahoy! Clear the decks, me hardies! Arrr! Clear the decks!" This is an expression he got from a pirate movie we saw about a month ago.

•   •   •   •   •

"That's a suicide mission," Oberstein says.

"Suicide squeeze," Blackie says. "Got no choice. Marathon's too close. Only weeks away. Can't chance them findin' out now."

Blackie's just informed us that he's gonna confess to stealing the wine. He says someone has to take the fall. He wants the investigation to end. The questioning is getting too close for comfort. They're beginning to interrogate some of the weaker members of the Klub, and Blackie's sure that one of them will crack and say something about the Bat Cave or the Klub. Or worse, he's afraid that if it continues much longer the brothers will find out about the marathon, which is only a week away. "Gettin' too close. Not gonna take much for someone to squeal now. Pack of cigarettes might do it."

"They'll crucify you," Ryan says.

"'Gonna rise on the third day . . .'"

"Fun-nee," Oberstein says. "I'll write a note saying I confess to stealing the wine. I'll say I didn't want them to punish the wrong person. I'll take the whacks. I'll write the note, so they'll go easier on me. I'll tell 'em little Jack's sick, and— "

"Forget it." Blackie taps his gold tooth.

"I'll go," Father Cross says. "I don't mind the strap or being shunned."

Blackie is stone-faced. He wipes his glasses on his shirt.

Ryan volunteers. Then Brookes. Then everyone wants to take the fall.

Blackie raises his hand, as if stopping traffic.

"'A friend should bear his friend's infirmities.' Captain's always last off the sinkin' ship. The leader makes sure everyone's safe."

There's a long pause. He looks at me and tells me to get my pen and paper.

"Rabbi, we'll need help writin' that note. Gotta be mighty careful with the words."

We're all in shock. We know Blackie will be severely punished. We stare at him, amazed, thinking the same thing. Blackie's our leader. But we don't deserve him.

The next day the bottom falls out.

"Bug iced it for them," Oberstein says. "He knocked down one of the little ones, and McCann threatened to take away his chair. He could of killed someone. I saw the whole thing. I was there when he squawked."

"He squealed?" Murphy says. "Jesus."

"He *plea bargained*," Oberstein says. "There's a difference. Blackie's taking the rap. He gave the confession note to McMurtry. He doesn't want anyone else involved. He says there'll be hell to pay if anyone else claims to be in on it. The marathon's the most important thing now. Nothing else. We're counting the days. That's why he confessed."

"'Cowards die many times before their deaths,'" Murphy recites from *Julius Caesar*.

"*Damn* you, Bug," Ryan says. "*Damn*."

•　　•　　•　　•　　•

I'm with Father Cross in the dorm, only minutes before he's caught. We are gabbing about what might've happened to Bug if he hadn't squealed.

"He almost got strapped for nicking Kavanagh a few days ago," I say. "Knocking down one of the little ones was the last straw."

Cross rolls back the mattress on his bed and snatches up a package of Viceroy cigarettes he has hidden there. "Shouldn't of strapped him," he says. "Bug's not playing with all his marbles lately."

"You're not spoze to smoke in the dorm, Cross," I say as he lights up. "It's five whacks on each hand if you're caught."

He ignores me, turns to the open window and watches the curtains stirring in the breeze. I push them back and look into the yard. A few older boys are playing become the batter as the sun sets through JD's pine trees. There are pigeon feathers on the windowsill, and I wonder if they are Nicky's.

"I'm not worried about the ten big ones," he says. "If we're caught, you say that you just got here. I'll back you up. Don't worry, I'll take the rap."

"McCann smells your breath," I interrupt.

"McCann's giving special sumo lessons to O'Connor and McBride." He lights a cigarette and inhales deeply. I watch his acned face get redder with each puff. He passes the cigarette to me.

"Thank God they didn't offer a carton of cigarettes as a reward," I say.

"Yeah, would of been tough for Bug." We pass the smoke back and forth for a while. "McCann shouldn't of threatened to take his chair away," he says.

"Little Matthews got a pretty bad knock," I say. "I saw the bruise on his neck. It's pretty ugly. Oberstein says Bug was really flying."

"Bug's not playing with a full deck. Besides, that little kid always stands in the middle of the hallway and dares Bug. You don't dare Bug. Nobody dares Bug."

"But McCann didn't know that. Bug should of told him. If Bug hadda told him, he wouldn't of threatened to take his chair. And Bug . . ."

"McCann should have more sense. Bug's pretty weak. He's got a fucken hole in his heart. They should protect him, not strap him. And that chair means the world to Bug. McCann's gonna burn in hell."

I can see Cross is really upset. I want to bring up our last-minute plans for the marathon, but I decide against it. He is really red, a lot redder than usual. He looks at the incident the same as if someone squealed on Bug about smoking. I know he's getting angrier by the second. He's dragging on the cigarette really hard. I've never seen him so angry. I'm getting uncomfortable, and I want to get away from the dorm. I'm afraid of getting caught, so I take a few more puffs and pretend that Blackie and Murphy are waiting for me in the gym for a game of frozen tag.

"Thanks for the smoke. I gotta go."

"See you later," Cross says. "Say a few for Bug, okay?"

"Yeah, sure," I say.

I don't hear about the strapping till later that evening, after supper. Ryan tells me. He acts like he is sorry for Cross, but he is beside himself telling me about it. That's always the way it is when someone tells you a boy's been strapped. Deep down, the teller wants to feel sorry for the guy, but his voice is so excited it betrays the truth about how he really feels. How happy he is that it's not him. And how excited he is to be reporting the news. And when Ryan's the messenger, he's a nervous Nellie, and it sounds like he's telling you the prime minister was shot and he's getting a million bucks for breaking the news.

He says he walked into the dorm just as Father Cross was putting out his cigarette on the bottom of his sneaker. That's how it's done. If you have a smoke in a forbidden place, you put the butt out on the bottom of your sneaker and then store it inside until you have a chance to dump it down the toilet later. Ryan watched Brother Walsh watch Cross putting out the cigarette butt. He knew right away Cross was a goner. When a boy is caught smoking, the brother always asks if any other boy is involved. If there is, and you squeal, it means you get half the whacks. Plea bargaining, as Oberstein calls it. It's very rare that anyone squeals about anything. A new boy who doesn't know the unwritten rules and the consequences of breaking them might squeal. But that's about the only time. Cross told Brother Walsh he was the only one smoking and took his ten whacks.

When Ryan finishes his story, I go straight away to Harris, a senior boy, and borrow a few cigarettes. I offer them to Cross after study hall.

"Keep 'em," he says.

"I want you to have 'em, Cross," I say.

"It's okay. It's fine. Keep 'em."

"But, Cross. You . . ."

"It doesn't matter. Don't worry about it," he says. "You would of done the same."

I think about it later that night in bed. I think Cross was right. I don't think I'd squeal. But you never know. Things are never the same, as Blackie says, when you're looking down the barrel of a gun.

18

BUG BRADBURY IS DEAD. The building is silent. There is no shouting in the halls. Not a crier in sight. No fire through dry grass. Nobody wants to announce Bug Bradbury is dead.

He died in his bed. It's a date we'll never forget. Wednesday, July 25, 1961. Oberstein found him on the way to Chapel, crumpled in a ball beneath his blanket. The only boy to die in the seventy-three-year history of the Mount. We all have the spells. Even Anstey, who never gets them.

Bug lies in a coffin in the chapel for three days, with his mouth sewed shut. The first time he ever shut up, Ryan says. It is kinda spooky when Old Flynn anoints him with oil. He walks over to Bug in the coffin and presses his oily thumb on Bug's cold forehead and says, "I am the resurrection and the life. He that believeth in me, though he were dead, shall never die." I look over at the sheen on Bug's forehead and shiver. The whole thing gives me the creeps. It reminds me of Vincent Price in *House of Wax*.

Each day for the three days before he is buried, we have morning Mass and the rosary at noon and Benediction in the evening. During sumo classes, we can be excused to go to the chapel and pray for the repose of his soul, which is great because we can escape a few scheduled matches. Bug's little gift to us, Oberstein says, getting us outta the box for a while. All of us ask to be excused at one time or another, not just to get out of sumo class but to be a little closer to Bug. Blackie asks to be excused from class several times. He's taking it pretty hard. He's really down. The brothers ask us to pick a boy from Bug's group to speak at the funeral Mass. And we all choose Blackie, who says it's hard on him because he wasn't all that close to Bug and isn't sure he can say the right thing during the funeral. Which is crazy. Truth is, Blackie was the closest Bug ever got to having a real brother.

Old Monsignor Flynn's gray wisps of hair seem grayer. He tells us that our lost classmate, our brother, has become a little cherub and is looking down on us from heaven. "What a crock," Murphy says. Monsignor Flynn coughs his way through the gospel according to John. Chapter 11. The story of Jesus raising Lazarus from the dead. After the gospel he gets the thurible and goes to the coffin and pumps incense all over the place. So much incense we almost choke. Then he gives a brief sermon about how we're all like Lazarus, and how Jesus loves us all so much that he will raise us all from the dead, including Brendan Bradbury. He says Jesus isn't only a great teacher and healer, he is a great magician, a magician who can raise not only others but himself from the dead. He says if Jesus hadn't risen from the dead he would've been just another prophet. He wouldn't have been God. Rising from the dead proves he is God. Clare says the same thing every Good Friday when we go to the Basilica for the stations of the cross. That's why he's God, Clare says. Otherwise it's all a big joke.

After the sermon Oberstein stands up, and out of the blue chants the Kaddish. He tells us it's the Jewish prayer for the dead, for the one who left the community, he says. We all think the brothers will go nuts. But they don't say a thing.

Brother McMurtry puts down his breviary, removes his

glasses and rubs his eyes. Then he speaks. He gets on with a lot of old crap about the Last Day and Judgment. He speaks too long and bores everyone to tears. He never mentions poor old Bug once. He just drones on about salvation and redemption and the Judgment Day, with nobody paying him one bit of attention. Only a few of the brothers are listening to him, or pretending to. Madman Malone sleeps the whole time McMurtry speaks. Most of us are staring at the floor and stealing odd looks at the coffin, at Bug's pointed chin jutting out. More than ever it seems. And his black glossy hair cropped across his forehead as if the undertaker used the same bowl Bug had the day he cut Rowsell's hair. And his mouth sewed shut. It all seems so weird as we steal glances at his green-and-white school sweater and the tiny black bowtie Cross made for him. We're all so sad we're beside ourselves. I look at the sad faces and know that from now on we'll all have holes in our hearts.

Once, while McMurtry babbles on, Murphy puts his hand to his mouth and squeaks, "Shuddup, you jerk. You're boring us to death with your bullshit." I almost start to laugh. "That was Bug," he whispers. "Look at his face; he's getting ready to say something else." I look over at Bug—his coal-black hair all slicked like the kid in *The Little Rascals*, his sallow complexion—and I swear Murphy is right. I would've bet my whole canteen card Bug was gonna bark out something saucy.

McMurtry finishes and says that the occasion is such a special one that the boys in Brendan's class—it is the only time he has ever called Bug by his first name—have been asked to choose a classmate to say a few words. He says that the boys have chosen one of Brendan's best friends to speak on their behalf. And he asks if Mr. Neville will step forward and come to the altar rail to speak for a minute or so on behalf of the boys in Brendan's dorm. Blackie stands up and ignores Brother

McMurtry. In fact, he ignores all the brothers. He walks straight to the coffin and stares down at Bug. And the tears come before he speaks, and when he speaks. I'm so upset. We all are. And so are the brothers. Even Brother McMurtry's eyes are really red. And Rags . . . poor Rags. The redness around his eyes will last forever. Some of the boys are so moved by Blackie's tears that they cry out loud. As he speaks, Blackie keeps one hand on Bug's shoulder.

"Well, Ladybug, you're gone now . . . Flyin' home. And with no warnin'. Nobody knew you were so sick. Don't wanna talk about the Judgment Day or Jesus and Lazarus. Nor the Holy Ghost. Nothin' like that. Just wanna talk to you, like you're still here, listenin'. 'Cause, in a way, you are. I believe . . . *believe* . . . you are. Let's talk like you're in the cafeteria, washin' cups and shinin' plates. Like you're fightin' with Ryan for the first extra slice. Or saucin' someone between classes. Or askin' Father Cross for help with homework. Or yellin' at us from your wheelchair or that high perch at St. Pete's Bowling Alleys . . .

"You're the sauciest one ever to come through the Mount, Bug. The sauciest of the saucy. That's why we'll miss you so much. That shrill tongue was always speakin' the truth. That squeaky voice . . . always teasin', always saucy . . . always there. It's gone now. Gone."

Blackie lifts his curly head up, flashes his gold tooth and chuckles, "We all got moments we had with him. Bug Bradbury moments. The one I remember most, my best Bug moment, hit me yesterday. Like lightnin'. It was a rainy day. We were playin' baseball. We were in the dugout lazin' during a break. Remember that old gray chair in the dugout at St. Pat's Field, the one Bug loved to stand on so much? That day I pulled the pegs outta that chair, and when Bug stood on it . . . *bang* . . . like the walls o' Jericho, he came tumblin' down. I laughed so hard. Bug stared at me with blinkin' eyes. I thought I was in for somethin' real saucy. Thought he'd say somethin' mighty mean. But no, he just sat there with his head cocked and said, 'Blackie, how come black people don't have no money? Whites have money . . . the English, the French, the Italians, the Russians. The Asians got money. The Chinese, the Japanese, the Koreans. Even poor Newfoundlanders got money. But not black people. How come there's no Bank of Africa, and nobody in Africa ever has any money?' I was stunned. I said, 'Bug, that's a good question. But I dunno the answer.'"

Blackie looks down at the coffin, then looks up at us and says, "Bug was always squawkin' about the good times." He looks at Ryan and says, "What 'bout you? What was your best time with Bug?"

Silence.

"Ryan?" Blackie's voice is thin and raspy.

Tears fill Ryan's eyes. "The fires . . . at the Bat . . ." Ryan starts to sob, and rests his head on the pew in front of us.

"Yeah," Blackie says. "Old Bug loved makin' the splits as much as he loved makin' the fires blaze up. What 'bout you, Oberstein? What was your best with Bug?"

Oberstein's eyes are glassy, and he looks at Blackie dreamily. Then his cheeks flush redder than I've ever seen. Blackie knows he can't speak.

"Your best, Murphy?"

"Once, he asked me if I was lost in the woods for a week, just me and my dog, would I kill him for food? I said yes, and asked Bug what *he'd* do, and he snapped back at me that he never would. He said I should be ashamed of myself for even thinking of hurting an animal, 'cause you can always depend on an animal, especially a dog."

Blackie shakes his head in agreement. "Your best, Kavanagh?"

Kavanagh laughs as if he's competing for a prize. "The time

he lost his socks at Virginia Waters, and we almost drowned trying to get them back," Kavanagh almost shouts the words. His jaw hangs wide open when he finishes, waiting for Blackie's approval.

"Yeah. We all got our Bug moments . . ."

Without being asked, O'Grady's voice sings out. "I loved watching him take a cigarette out of that little silver case he had. It was always so cute the way he slipped it out with one hand and tapped it on the case. And I loved watching him smoke it right down to the filter. He smoked harder than any of us."

Blackie looks around the chapel. His thick lips tighten, and he smiles painfully. "Yeah, he smoked them suckers hard," he says.

There is a rushing of hot steam from a radiator, like a faint cheer. Then Blackie looks at me. I think of telling a lie, but know it will be too hard to make something up, there in the chapel with the coffin so close I could reach out and touch Bug's face. And the memories flood back. I feel really bad, worse than I did at the beginning of the Mass. All I can think about, *my* Bug Bradbury moment, is that time in the gymnasium during the examination of conscience when Oberstein and Murphy and me beat Bug until he could hardly breathe.

"Sumos. Sumos and bowling," I stutter, and rest my head on the pew in front of me as Ryan had done.

"Gonna miss you, Bug," Blackie says. "Fly away home, Ladybug. Never gonna be the same." Then he whispers, "Goodbye . . . Goodbye, saucy boy."

We all just about die on the spot. I look at Oberstein, then at my Mickey. The seconds that go by are death-row ticks. Three long minutes before old Monsignor Flynn starts coughing and gargling and starts up the Mass again. And then Oberstein starts singing the Laudate and there isn't a dry eye in the chapel.

We couldn't have picked a better person in the world to say what we all felt. Jesus himself couldn't have done any better. And that's a fact. Blackie's the best. We'd all follow him to the moon and back. We are all so stung by him, by what he said, we stay frozen until communion time, when Brother McMurtry has to remind us to approach the altar rail to take the host.

Everyone at the Mount feels really bad after the funeral. A collective case of the spells, as Oberstein puts it. Every boy dresses in his school clothes, even the little ones, and we walk down Torbay Road to Mount Carmel Cemetery, where we bury Bug. Then we walk back. Nobody says a word going or coming, not even the little ones. To get my mind off Bug, I think about the big race. It's a bad time to get a collective case of the spells, with the marathon only a few days away.

"Bug sure picked a bad time to die," Murphy moans, raking his hair with his big fingers.

I can't seem to hold the good memories at all. The times we fished Virginia Waters, the boil-ups at the Bat Cave. The nights we stole a fresh loaf or sneaked out for a smoke. The walks to Bannerman Park on weekends to meet with girls. Bug, the fire-eater. Bug, the human bowling pin, in full flight at St. Pete's Alleys. The Mount Kildare Raffle. Bug racing around the floor in his white apron, a fistful of tickets high above his head squeaking out the prices: "Two for five, four for ten, ten big chances for twenty-five cents . . ." I can't seem to hold a single picture in my mind for any length of time. And I don't think I will for a long while to come. All I'll ever be able to let in is that one picture—*my* Bug Bradbury moment—that day in the gymnasium during the examination of conscience when we beat Bug until he could hardly breathe. It's funny how the worst things linger on when someone's gone.

•   •   •   •   •

In the TV room after Mass we all tell Blackie that he gave a beautiful tribute. He just cleans his glasses with his sweater, taps his tooth and smiles that lazy smile of his. He says nothing.

"I think they'll forget about the wine stealing now," Oberstein says.

"Jury's still out," Blackie says. "But Saturday's almost here. Everyone ready? No runnin' the next two days. Sleep and eat."

"What's the weather forecast?" I ask.

"Rain," Oberstein says.

"Shit," Blackie says.

"Jesus, Bug," Ryan starts to cry. "You *Brutus*."

"Shhh." Blackie raises his hand. "It's done. Maybe not . . . Maybe he done us the biggest favor of all. Gotta hand it to the Bug. Never said a peep 'bout the marathon. Maybe a good thing you laid that beatin' on him after all."

We all look at each other and shake our heads. Then Blackie laughs the loudest laugh we've ever heard.

•   •   •   •   •

"Mayday! Mayday!" Oberstein whispers as McCann drags out the podium.

Brother McMurtry stands at the front of the cafeteria and claps his hands three times.

Silence. We watch the muscles working in his jaw, his wolf eyes gleaming.

"Mr. Neville, stand up, please."

Blackie stands.

"It seems that Mr. Neville has done something wrong, boys, something terribly wrong. Something sinful, in fact. Something he has admitted, by his own hand . . . and confirmed by Mr. Bradbury. He has performed a little trick on the brothers and Monsignor Flynn. We have another Houdini in our midst. But it was not an impossible trick, mind you. He hasn't turned water into wine or anything like that." McMurtry wrinkles his lip into a half smile and holds up the letter Oberstein and I wrote. "Mr. Neville has admitted that he is a thief. You all know your catechism, boys. You all know the eighth commandment. And what is the eighth commandment, Mr. Neville?"

"Thou shalt not steal."

"And Mr. Neville has not simply stolen, boys. He is not guilty of simply stealing. No, boys. Mr. Neville has stolen from our chapel, thereby committing a more serious sin."

"*A sacrilege,*" McCann interjects, looking on, one hand on his hip.

"No. No, not a sacrilege, Brother McCann. But quite a serious sin, nonetheless. More serious than stealing."

Silence. Murphy bites his parched lip. Ryan is so tense he's shaking. He rubs his sweaty hands along his pants. Oberstein stares at Blackie. We're all thinking about the same thing: the day Ryan was led in on a rope and strapped.

"Come forward, Mr. Neville."

Blackie walks to the front of the cafeteria. McMurtry uncoils his strap. Sunlight streams in through the window beside him.

"I've been told, boys, that there is an unwritten rule among you regarding strapping. A code of sorts, regarding crying or, rather, *not* crying. And I've been told that your ring leader, Mr. Neville, has a reputation of not even blinking when he is strapped. Is that correct, Mr. Neville?"

Blackie is silent.

"Well, we shall soon see if our young thief is capable of repentance. Hands up, sir." *Whack.* The strap hits Blackie's splayed fingers. *Whack.* McMurtry's wolf eyes show no mercy.

"So you don't want to talk about . . ." *Whack. Whack.* ". . . Jesus or the Judgment Day." He pauses and grins. *Whack.* With each swing of the strap there's an angry murmur, a cop movie murmur. *Whack.* "Or about Lazarus." *Whack. Whack.* There is a sheen of sweat on McMurtry's face.

Oberstein keeps count. Tears are rolling down his cheeks as he raises ten fingers.

As McMurtry delivers another blow, I feel the pain. I know what it's like. A bubble surrounds you, and you can only pray that it will soon burst. And that you won't break the secret code: Be a member of a private Klub, the Dare Strapping Klub. Membership is free. There is only one rule. Don't cry. Don't even blink.

"*Blink*, Blackie," Murphy whispers.

"*Blink*, Blackie," Ryan echoes.

"Think of Floyd Patterson!" I want to scream. "There's only a few seconds left in the round. Hang on."

Blackie doesn't make a sound. I close my eyes and see the blinking Celtic cross.

"Jesus, Bug . . ." Oberstein sighs.

Kavanagh says, "*Blink*, Blackie, *please* blink."

Soon our entire table is saying it: "Blink, Blackie, blink."

"Quiet!" McCann yells.

The strapping reminds me of the gunshots at the beginning of *The Rifleman.* I close my eyes and wish Chuck Connors would race in and save Blackie.

King Kelly's table joins in: "Blink, Blackie, blink." The chant drowns out the strapping.

"Quiet! Everyone. Quiet!"

The cafeteria becomes a perfect chorus. Even the little ones are chanting "Blink, Blackie, blink." They think they're part of a spontaneous game. There's a smirk on McMurtry's face that seems to say, See, even your friends are with me. But we're not. We want Blackie to blink so the strapping will stop.

McCann races to a table and cuffs a few boys. He punches Kelly in the head. The chorus grows louder: "Blink, Blackie, blink!"

"Quiet!" McCann screams. "Quiet!"

McMurtry stops the strapping. Blackie's hands are still held high. The chorus falls silent.

"You may go to your dorm, Mr. Neville."

There is a deep silence throughout the rest of the meal and during the washup. Nobody says a word until chores are done.

"How many?" Murphy asks on the way to the dorm.

"Lost count," Oberstein sighs.

"At least twenty," Ryan says.

"But he didn't blink," Murphy says. "Bastard didn't make him blink."

"*God-damn*, Bug," Ryan says.

•   •   •   •   •

Blackie's in the dorm washroom doing what we all do after a good strapping: scrubbing down—running cold water on his burning hands. We do it after a really cold run too. It helps a lot. Ryan is really upset. He cries and mumbles all the way up to the dorm that Blackie didn't blink. He's remembering what it's like to be strapped that way.

"He didn't make you blink, Blackie. The bastard didn't . . ."

Blackie lifts his head, looks in the mirror and stares at the four of us hunched behind him. There's a terrible strain on his face. It looks swelled and cold with shock, and his eyes are red and shrunken.

"I blinked," he says, lowering his head to hide the tears.

19

O'Grady's found his marbles. O'Grady's found his marbles.

IT'S A DECOY CRIER. O'Grady will never find his marbles. He'll never have any to find. The crier is Kavanagh. It means there's an emergency meeting for anyone who can make it.

Besides the checker system, we have a secret writing system for emergencies. If a Klub member wants to send a message to someone about an emergency meeting, but doesn't want anyone else to know, we have a really good method. We write using pee on the back of an innocent-looking piece of paper—a drawing or a comic book cover. The dried urine always remains invisible until you hold it next to a hot radiator or some other heat source. It's a great way to get a message around without others knowing about it. The day before the marathon, Oberstein passes me an odd-looking postcard, and I know right away that there is an important message and I need to get to a heat source fast. I hold the postcard near the flame of Rowsell's Zippo and watch the words materialize: *emerg mtn incnratr 5:00.*

At the incinerator, we learn that Shorty Richardson has the flu. He isn't in bad shape. It looks like he'll be okay for the marathon, but Oberstein is worried that he might get sicker.

"'To everything there is a season,'" Oberstein says. Father Cross has taken his temperature a dozen times. And it's always only slightly above normal.

Blackie's beside himself. He's *resolved*, as Bug would say. He's downcast at the meeting. Like he could get the spells. He hasn't been the same since Bug left the community, as the Kaddish says.

"Never thought there'd be cause for another meeting," Kavanagh says, and looks helplessly at Oberstein, who organizes a team to make sure Shorty gets a good night's sleep and liquids throughout the night.

"Father Cross, you're now Doctor Cross," Blackie says.

The peashooters, who are responsible for stealing their own beans from the kitchen storeroom, are given the job of stealing packages of Tang and cans of apple juice. O'Connor volunteers to steal aspirin from the infirmary. Blackie tells the peashooters to have extra ammunition for the marathon, just in case Shorty's still sick and needs a little help to win the race. He puts Murphy in charge of the shooters.

"Tomorrow's the big day. Practice all day and all night," Oberstein says. "We want deadly accuracy, a bull's-eye every shot."

We think the meeting's over, but we're in for a surprise. Blackie gets that faraway look in his eyes and stares off into space. "I wish I was a ladybug," he says. "I'd just fly away home." He nods to Kelly and O'Connor to stand guard at each end of the swimming pool. Father Cross gives Blackie a new pair of Congress sneakers. "Thank you, Jesus," Blackie says, and takes off his old ones and throws them into the incinerator. He laces up his new sneakers. "Goin' all the way to New York City in these," he says. "Gonna do the impossible trick."

Sighs and murmurs all around. The two guards turn and look at Blackie.

"Last meeting of the Dare Klub . . . for Blackie," he says, and lowers his head. "Soon I'm no longer gonna be with you."

The runners sense what's up. The others stare in astonishment.

"My last day at the Mount."

More murmuring. There's a long silence as he fixes his dark eyes on us, a steady beam.

"You know me. How I love the backup. In baseball. In life. Had a backup all along."

I look at Oberstein. He knows what's coming and he's crying as if his heart is broken.

"Tomorrow I'm gonna slip away, run my own marathon, a Comrades. Got some runnin' and some hitchin' to do. To Argentia. The ferry to the mainland. Then to Harlem. Gotta make it to the ferry in less than six hours. Be slippin' away in the mornin' when we head out for the regatta. Marathon starts 'round noon. Ferry's leavin' at eight. The brothers won't be back for the little ones till six. I'll be long gone. On my way to Nova Scotia. To freedom."

"I wanna go with you," Kavanagh cries out.

"Me too," Ryan says.

"And me," Murphy cries.

Everyone volunteers to go.

"He'll be killed if he's caught," I tell Oberstein. "We gotta stop him."

"'He's as constant as the northern star,'" Oberstein says. "Since the strapping, nothing will change his mind. The rabbis say, 'When one must, one can.' Blackie *must*."

Blackie raises his hand. There's a long silence.

"Goin' it alone. Ain't no other way. 'There is a tide in the affairs of men . . .'"

There's another long silence, and Blackie indicates he wants to say goodbye to each of us, one at a time. He fixes his eyes on Murphy and Kavanagh, pats them both on the shoulders and passes them a piece of paper. "Name of the street I lived on in Harlem," he says, "in case you wanna visit sometime." It's the saddest moment, because we're thinking about what will happen to him if he gets caught. Or worse, if he makes it to Nova Scotia. How will he make out? What will he eat? Where will he sleep? We're worried for him, and sad because we're losing our leader and we know nobody can replace Blackie, *ever*.

When he gets to Oberstein, he hugs him and smiles a long smile and says he's the smartest man in Newfoundland. "Rabbi, you're the noblest norphan of all. Everything kosher?" he asks, and Oberstein says everything's kosher, and Blackie laughs again. He tells him he will send him a postcard from New York. "Gonna sign it Yogi Berra," he says. Oberstein turns away to hide his tears.

He shakes everyone's hand, Roman style. "When you're runnin'," he says to Richardson and Ryan, "be thinkin' of me. When I'm runnin', I'll be thinkin' of you."

When he gets to me, he locks my eyes in a terrible gaze, and my heart jumps. Then he smiles a wide smile, flashes his gold tooth and puts a hand on each shoulder. I can feel the heat of his hands through my sweater. As he speaks, his thumbs press hard against my neck like he is sending a signal for me to listen carefully.

"The last of the Romans . . . There's a writer hidden in you somewhere," he tousles my hair. "All you gotta do is let him out. You got what it takes. Stuff you wrote 'bout Floyd Patterson . . ." He shakes his head. "A sports writer, maybe. Don't let nothin' get in your way. Remember to listen hard when someone speaks. Like Rags. Most people never listen hard." He removes his hands from my shoulders and just stands there with that far-off look on his face. "'Forever and forever, farewell, Cassius.'" I try to speak. The words barely come. "I'll miss you, Blackie," I say, and turn away.

"Gonna miss you too," Blackie says, "for a day or so."

Everyone laughs, and Oberstein starts booming out: "And we'll all glow together . . ."

* * * * *

Ryan wakes me in the middle of the night. "Got a cigarette?" he says.

"You're runnin' tomorrow, Ryan. Jesus."

"I need a cigarette."

I go to Cross's bed and fetch a Viceroy. Ryan sits on my bunk and lights up.

"You okay?" I ask.

"Yeah," he says. "As much as I'll ever be."

He's dragging pretty hard on the cigarette, so I tell him not to inhale so much. He doesn't say anything, so I poke him and tousle his hair, the way Rags does when he wants you to cheer up.

"Don't *touch* me," he says. "You know I hate being touched."

I tell him I'm sorry. We smoke for a while and outta the blue he asks, "Did you ever think you could kill someone?"

I swallow my Adam's apple. "Jesus, Ryan, what are you getting on with?"

"It's been on my mind. Since what he did to Blackie."

"Ryan, we've all been strapped . . ."

"Not like that . . ." he shakes his head. "Not like that."

"But *killing* . . ."

"I know. I know. It's a mortal sin. I'm not saying I'll do it. I'm just saying I *want* to. The thought's entered my mind, that's all. I know I don't have the balls to. But Blackie does. Maybe that's why he's taking off. He told me once that he'd like to kill McCann."

"He didn't mean it. Blackie wouldn't—"

"He *meant* it. One time at the cave he told me he would do it or find someone who could. Someone who could believe strong enough." Ryan passes me the cigarette. "I might not run tomorrow," he says. "I might just see Blackie off and go to the races."

He starts to cry. "Why the fuck did Bug do it? Back-stabbin' Brutus! Blackie was his best friend. Some fucken friend. With friends like that, who needs enemies?" He rocks back and forth, his face grimacing.

"Bug's gone now, Ryan," I say.

"Yeah. Bug's gone. And Blackie's goin'. And I might too. We all should. How far's New York, anyway?"

"Quite a ways! Far as ever a puffin flew."

"Wish we could all fly that far," he sighs. "I'm gonna ask Blackie to let me join him when we head out tomorrow. I know he'll let me go with him. I just know it. He will, won't he?"

"Blackie's goin' alone, Ryan. You know Blackie. Besides, we need you for the marathon."

"Fuck the marathon," he says. "I hope I die of exhaustion. Like the first guy who ran one."

He's so upset I start to worry. "We better get some sleep. Got a big day tomorrow."

"Yeah, the big day," he says, and walks away.

* * * * *

Oberstein rouses me at five o'clock. "The heavens opened an hour ago," he says. "Worse than Noah's flood. It's coming down in buckets."

Murphy appears. "Jesus, it's pissin' out," he says. The rain is so heavy you can hear it pattering on the windowpanes.

Soon all the runners are up. We stare out the open window at the gray rain. The pigeons are cooing mournfully from the shelter of the eaves, as if they know our plight. I lean my head out, straining to see if Nicky's around.

"Never rains but it pours," Oberstein chuckles.

"Shuddup! What's the forecast?" Blackie says.

"Spoze to clear by noon," Oberstein says.

"Shit. I gotta go," Blackie says. "I'm New York–bound. Gotta leave by nine. Got a heavy date."

"It's gonna clear. Relax. It'll clear," Oberstein says.

"Better. Can't run in this shit." Blackie slaps the wet stone of the window frame.

"Don't worry, Blackie, it'll clear."

"Gonna talk to one of your prophets. Noah, maybe?" Blackie's angry and nervous that something might go wrong.

"Noah's not a prophet," Oberstein scoffs.

"Where's your God when we really need him?" Blackie whines. "Always on holiday when he's needed."

The rain beats harder. "Jesus! You can't all run in this shit. Best to let Shorty and Ryan run it alone. Others join the peashooters. Work the sidelines. Gonna be our best chance."

"We've prepared for all conditions," I say. "You're the one who says to believe."

"Shit," Blackie says, staring out the window. "Can't even see Torbay Road. He turns and stares at everyone. "*Shit. Shit. Shit.*"

He kicks one of the wooden lockers. And for the first time, I detect a flash of defeat in his beady black eyes.

Father Cross appears. "Richardson's fine. Slight temp, but he's okay. Says he'll win by a country mile." Oberstein is moody, but determined to beat all odds. "We're taking Blackie's advice," he says. "Only Richardson and Ryan will run. The rest will join the trackers and spotters and peashooters and work from the sidelines. I want the whole Klub peashooting. Make sure we get a medal."

The rain slows after breakfast, around nine o'clock, just before Blackie and Ryan head out. Murphy's transistor informs us that the St. John's Royal Regatta Marathon will take place on a gray, drizzly day. Richardson is up and about, stretching and running on the spot. "He's never looked better," Father Cross says.

When Ryan returns, he refuses to do warm-ups. We learn that he ran with Blackie the short distance across Elizabeth Avenue to Kenmount Road. Blackie stopped there, hugged him and told him to go back. Ryan was shocked. He thought he'd run with him all the way to the Nova Scotia ferry. *To freedom*, Ryan whispers. He felt at first like he was being betrayed, and later like a dog leaving his master. He kept looking back at Blackie running toward the horizon. He tells us he yelled out Blackie's name once and started running toward him. Blackie stopped and laughed and picked up a stone and threw it at him and told him next time he wouldn't miss. He told him to hurry on back to the Mount to help with the marathon. Ryan says he stood and stared until the green boxers disappeared. Then he turned and ran toward the city, crying his eyes out. He was crying so much he said he couldn't see the road. He had to start walking. He couldn't run for the longest time.

He is pouting and downcast. His departure from Blackie has given him a severe bout of the spells. Oberstein is worried. "He's in no mood to run a race," he says. "Go get Kavanagh and try to perk him up."

"Do you want something to eat, Ryan? Some juice?" I ask.

"No," he says.

I try to understand his bitter mood. So much happens at the Mount, your mood can change in a flash. I think of the day he got strapped for running away. Maybe something happened to him that day and it took all this time. Maybe it took seeing it happen to someone else to make him as angry as he is now. I look at him and know that he's thinking of Blackie and wishing he was by his side, running to freedom. I half understand, and I want to go to him and whisper that I wish I had the guts to run away.

Oberstein returns, smoking a cigarette. His fingers are yellow with nicotine.

"Hence, home, you idle creatures," he laughs. "The brothers are all gone. They just left for Hogan's Pond. Only poor little norphs at a norphan home." He looks at Ryan. "Are you gonna warm up? Richardson's been asking where you are. He's down in the yard."

"I'll warm up," he says.

"And you gotta eat, drink some juice."

"I'll drink some juice."

•   •   •   •   •

Quidi Vidi Lake is barely a mile from the Mount, near the bottom of Kenna's Hill, behind Memorial Stadium. We run very slowly, warming up by sprinting and stretching as we go. The air feels wet and salty. Every now and then we backtrack to be with Oberstein, who's chugging along with us. Thousands of people are at the lake. The shores have been turned into a carnival. People with dreamy looks sit on the banks and watch the races or walk around lakeside buying treats and playing games of chance. There are hundreds of stands and bell tents with spin tickets and plush toys. The place is like a gigantic raffle. On the far side of the lake, at the boathouse, a man with a megaphone announces all the races.

All the Dare Klub members have been at the lake since nine o'clock. They're hanging out at the oily pole. The favorite stand of every boy at the Mount is Double Your Dole at the Oily Pole. It's just a greasy pole that you pay a quarter to climb to the top of. If you make it, you get fifty cents back. If you don't make it, you slide back down into a big pool of water. O'Grady's so good, they only let him do it twice.

It's not hard to spot a Mount Kildare boy. We always look like we belong in a Charlie Chaplin movie. We all dress the same, patchy ragamuffin clothes that are either too big or too small. And always the norph glasses and those black-and-white canvas sneakers. You could walk around Quidi Vidi Lake all day just looking at feet and you'd spot every Mount Kildare boy at the regatta.

The racing shells are in the water. They're six-oared boats with fixed seats. There are races all day long and into the night. The biggest trophy of the day is the Silver Cup. The course record is nine minutes and thirteen seconds, and it was set in 1901 by a crew from Outer Cove. Seventy-five years later, the record still stands. The marathon record is three hours and thirty-six minutes. It's broken almost every year. Richardson says he'll break it again today.

We sit on the yellowing grassy bank and watch the first women's race of the day. The women are wearing fiery red shorts and singlets. They all have their hair tied back. A man wearing a baseball cap sits in the coxswain's seat. A little girl is running along the shore screaming to her sister, "Row, Jackie, row. Row, row, row, Jackie, row." And I want to stand and scream, until my head hurts: "Glow, Blackie, glow . . ."

The race is beautiful to watch, the boats lifting out of the water as if they're floating. I look at the way the rowers' bodies move. They move like dancers. And they're like us too, when we run. Together. And I think of all the hard work they must've done to get ready for today—the sores on their hands and bums and the buckets of sweat. And I think of how rowing must be harder than running in a way. All six rowers having to do exactly the same thing at exactly the same time for the whole race. I don't know if I could do that. When you're running, it's just you and the wind and the feel of your sneakers on the road. There's no one else in the whole world. No one to bother you, to tell you what to do. I could never trade that for anything.

Still, I envy them as I watch. I want to be out on the water. I think they must feel and know things only rowers can feel and know. And they remind me of our night running, all of us strung together, running along as one. And I wonder how the runners would do in a boat. I look at the coxswain and see Blackie rocking back and forth, urging us to victory, giving us his strength. And I close my eyes and see us practicing in the early morning, the way we ran, flashlights strapped to each oar, their light cutting into the murky water with every stroke. And for a moment we are all there. Water, boat, and crew are one.

"We could do that," Murphy says. "If we practiced, we'd win a medal."

After the race, we pry our way through the dense crowd and head toward the homemade track.

"Year of the penguin," Oberstein says.

A special lane around the lake has been created for the runners to start and finish. As we approach, dressed in our green boxers, singlets, and new sneakers, the Doyle sisters scream and wave. They are wearing white headbands and colorful halter tops.

"Where's Blackie?" they yell. "Where's Blackie?"

Murphy bolts to tell them to shut up. Ruthie Peckford is with them. She waves to me and wiggles the fingers of her right hand. She is wearing a white blouse and khaki shorts. I wave my hand, the way the queen does on TV. She blows me a kiss. I pretend I'm talking to Oberstein.

Prior to the start of the race, during the registration and warm-up, O'Connor takes out his peashooter and whistles a direct hit at number 28's ear. Luckily, the runner doesn't find the source of the sting. He swats the air like he's been stung by a wasp. Number 29, a skinny guy with glasses, is a bit of a hotshot, showing off his sprinting power and stretching to beat the band. Oberstein orders Murphy to put the peashooters in

line. The plan is to use the shooters during the race at important times, when they are hidden and sure to make a strike.

"I'm worried about number 29, Oberstein," I say. "He looks
really good."

"He's a hot dog," Oberstein says, as he registers Ryan and
Richardson.

An old man with a double chin sits behind a wooden table,
chewing on a cigar.

"Ye all in competition? Two dollars each if ye're in competition." His cigar moves as he speaks.

"Only two in competition," Oberstein says.

"That'll be four bucks," the man says. "Only competitors do
the first lap around the lake," he says.

He hands them their numbers, 116 for Richardson, 117 for
Ryan. We're dressed to run, but we're not in competition. We're
riding shotgun, with a hundred plans and a dozen shortcuts to
make sure that every plan succeeds. Richardson and Ryan are
stretching and running on the spot. Every now and then, Ryan
stops and looks around at the crowd. The man with the megaphone calls the competitive runners to the starting line.

The racing pistol sounds, and the moment is finally here.
The two runners in green boxers and white singlets sprint to a
huge lead. We're all so excited we're jumping and screaming
and shouting. When the cheering dies down, Oberstein
stands, like a statue, and stares at the figures of Shorty
Richardson and Skinny Ryan moving past the still lake. He
beams, and tears roll down his chubby cheeks as he booms in
his loudest voice ever: "Give them wings, Lord . . ."

"That they may fly," we all sing out.

O'Connor and the peashooters are ready. Ned Kelly, the
spotter, is waiting with his stolen bike at the top of Kenna's Hill.

Ryan stays with Shorty and the lead runners for the first
half of the race, but the second time he's heading up Kenna's

Hill in the final miles he stops, hunches over, bites his lower lip and dry-heaves. His knees buckle, and we watch as his body topples to the pavement. Rowsell and Kelly, the two assigned spotters for that leg of the race, run to him and splash him with cold water. They help him up and walk a few yards with him. After he drinks from the water bottle, he tells Rowsell he's fine and starts running again. Kelly bikes ahead at full speed to the next station stop to inform the other spotters that Ryan's in trouble. Before we race back to help Ryan, Murphy tells the peashooters to storm the leads, which means they are to deliberately attempt to pick off anyone ahead of Shorty or Ryan during the last few miles. To knock them out of the race.

When the five of us reach Ryan, we try to lift his spirits. But he falls farther behind. As he slows, we fall back with him.

"C'mon, Ryan, keep up with us, for God's sakes," Brookes says.

"You gotta push Richardson," I tell him. " C'mon, he needs you."

"Yeah, c'mon, Ryan, we're almost there. You can do it," Murphy says. "Remember the day you took Kenna's Hill in a freezing storm. *C'mon!*"

Father Cross offers him a Crown Cola bottle filled with water, but he pushes it aside.

"C'mon, Ryan," Murphy says. "Jesus, we didn't do all that training to finish in the middle of the pack."

"Perk him up, Kavanagh," I say.

"It's useless," Murphy says. "He's out of it."

Brookes starts to cry. "Jesus, all those night runs for nothin', all those laps around the soccer field . . ."

Father Cross offers Ryan a piece of hardtack, but he waves it off. "Leave me alone," he says. "Just leave me alone."

"C'mon, Ryan," Kavanagh says.

"Fuck Bug . . . Fucken Brutus," Ryan says, and starts crying. He looks pitiful, wiping his eyes as he runs. We're sure he'll stop crying soon, but he sobs and breathes heavily for half a mile. Murphy pulls beside him and puts his arm on his shoulder.

"Fuck off, I said. Get away from me. Leave me alone." He stops and walks to a fence and leans against it with both hands, his shoulders rising and falling. We watch as he crouches there, shaking and hugging himself around his knees.

We all fall back and watch him jog along at a pace that is sure to give him a lousy finish.

"What's got into him?" Murphy asks.

"Dunno. Blackie leaving, I guess." I stare at the lopsided 117 on his back.

"Or Bug squealing," Kavanagh says.

"Or dying," Brookes says.

"Dying," Father Cross repeats.

"One thing's for sure," Murphy says. "You can forget about a medal at that pace."

Murphy roars ahead, with Brookes and Kavanagh on his heels, to one of our shortcuts to check with Kelly on how Richardson is doing. Father Cross and I stay with Ryan, jogging behind him.

"Look, Blackie's gonna be fine," I blurt out. "He's gonna make it to the ferry. And he's gonna make it to New York. He'll find his mother too. I know it."

That seems to perk him up a bit, and he picks up speed. But when Cross says he's gotta move faster because Bug is up above, rooting against us, he falls back to his slower pace. After a while, Father Cross and I give up and race on ahead.

The peashooters do their best the last few miles, but it's all for naught. Ryan fades far behind Shorty and the leads. With a mile to go, we know he'll be lucky to finish in the top ten. And we're right. He crosses the finish line in twelfth place, almost fifteen minutes behind Shorty, who runs toward him with his gold medal.

Ryan is dazed and exhausted. He limps past Shorty, ignoring him, and looks around for us. When he spots Oberstein, he starts to cry and lets out an ungodly yell and falls down on all fours, pounding the ground with both fists and cursing, "Jesus, Bug . . . Jesus, Blackie." We run to him and stand him up and tell him it's okay, he did just fine. Shorty Richardson runs in our direction, dodging chanting peashooters jumping toward him: "Shorty won the gold . . ." But their words are hollow. Ryan feels he's let everyone down. He stumbles, bends double and sobs uncontrollably. After he stops crying, he shivers for a long time. Then he gathers strength and pushes us away and wanders off to the side of the road and throws up his guts.

•   •   •   •   •

When they split up at Kenmount Road, Blackie instructed Ryan to be at the pay phone outside Parkdale Pharmacy on Sunday at five o'clock. Everyone knew the spot. It was a ratty old phone booth we robbed quarters from every weekend. Once, on a dare from Blackie, the Klub packed fifteen guys inside it. Ryan was to be there at five o'clock to listen for three rings. Blackie told him not to answer, just to listen for three rings. That would be the signal that he'd made it to Nova Scotia. Three rings would mean that Blackie had performed the impossible trick.

I was with Ryan that Sunday outside Parkdale, waiting by the phone booth. Ryan waited for that phone to ring like a guy losing his mind. When the phone didn't ring at five, he started cursing. At five after five, he was karate-kicking the phone box, punching the walls and yelling and swearing. "Ring, you mother-fucken sonofabitch. Ring, you bastard." People passing by thought he was crazy.

After twenty minutes of kicking and slamming and swearing, he fell to the phone booth floor, exhausted, and wept. His tiny face was as white as a sheet. "Don't come back, Blackie. Please don't come back . . . Please . . ." he cried over and over. "I can see McCann leading him through the cafeteria on a rope." He looked up at me pathetically and cried, "Like they did with me. Only it'll be worse for Blackie. They'll crucify him. They'll shun him for a year." He was beside himself. And the tears wouldn't stop rolling down his baby face. I tried to lift him up, but he just cursed at me and told me to get lost. He didn't move. I was so sad for him and for Blackie that I didn't even care if we made it back to the Mount in time to sign the Doomsday Book.

Then, suddenly, out of the blue, the telephone rang—three times. Ryan jumped to his feet. He listened to the three rings, then grabbed me by the wrist and stared at my Mickey: five-thirty. Then it dawned on us. The time zone. There's half an hour difference between Newfoundland and Nova Scotia time. Newfoundland's always half an hour ahead. Blackie's five o'clock was our five-thirty. Ryan raced out of the phone booth and ran inside Parkdale Pharmacy, screaming his foolish head off that Blackie had made it, that he'd performed the impossible trick. Crotchety old Mr. Noonan, the gray-haired pharmacist, thought he'd gone mad. And he had, in a way. Ryan *had* gone mad, mad with joy. He raced up and down the aisles, screaming and hooting and repeating over and over, "He did it. The impossible trick. He made it. He's New York–bound. The sonofabitch did it. The sonofabitch made it."

Epilogue

FOR AS LONG AS I LIVE, I'll never forget our last contact with Blackie. It was the closest we'd ever been to him, even though he wasn't physically present. And the closest we'd been to each other in all our time together at the Mount. It was so real. As real as Oberstein shouting, "Give them wings, Lord, that they may fly." As real as the homemade bread and bog juice we'd have every day at every meal. As real as the Bat Cave. Our canteen cards. Bug's wheelchair. The Raffle. More real and more powerful than most of my dreams. Blackie wasn't really there, but he really was there.

Rags always said the world of the imagination is a more real world than the one we wake up to every day. Like Oberstein's world of dreams. I didn't know what he was trying to tell us back then. But I do now. It's hard to explain. Like the feeling I get sometimes when I'm out running, and I know with certainty that Blackie and the other night runners are there beside me. Even though they're not. They're not there .. . but they really are. They're just as real as they were when we'd loaf around the Bat Cave, smoking and joshing and humming along to Oberstein's renditions of songs we did in choir.

The gull are squawking madly as the big ferry moves towards the dock in Argentia. The foghorn drowns them out, and the memory of Bug's squeaky voice fades. Standing at the stern, I watch the wide wake the boat cuts in the clear blue water. It's a beautiful day. Surprisingly, I am alone. Well, as Rags used to say, we are never alone. Not as long as we can remember the past. Was it Faulkner who said, "the past is never past"?

I've been crying. A long, tearless cry. The kind that can only come with age. It's my first visit to Newfoundland in many years. I live in Cape Breton now, in an old farmhouse in a small town near a community college, where I teach English literature. I have returned to St. John's to teach a summer-school course at the university.

I drive the long distance that Blackie ran and hiked so many years ago, and I'm amazed at the distance. It's so much farther than he and Oberstein figured. Much farther than a Comrades. Arriving in the oldest city in North America, I stop for a bite to eat at the Golden Eagle Gas Station. The chips and gravy are as good as they always were. I ask the tiny waitress for a spruce beer. She screws up her face and shrugs. "A root beer will be fine," I say.

The new highway to Stavanger Drive takes me to Major's Path. I park the car on the side of the road and walk the few hundred yards to the Bat Cave. It's still there, but the heavy equipment parked nearby means that it's not long for this world. Some developer, I suspect, will destroy it soon to make way for another supermarket.

I walk over the dry earth to the ashes scattered near the opening. The rusty bars are gone, and the heavy steel door is down. I step inside and squint until my eyes adapt to the dimness. The air is musty, and the cave smells of urine. I close my eyes and remember Blackie sitting in his log chair, passing sentence. I hear the roll call and picture the Bank of Newfoundland. I open my eyes and wander about. There is a hole where the bank used to be, and someone has recently built a fire there.

I search the back wall for Father Cross's bat. Only a few faded letters from the Magna Carta remain. The black bat is gone, and in its place someone has scrawled an odd-shaped heart. Inside it is written "Kathy loves Kevin" and "Debbie loves Rob." Beneath the heart is a mattress. I wander toward the entrance, happy that someone besides Father Cross has found love in the cave.

I stand at the opening, close my eyes, lower my head and think of the Dare Klub. Such beautiful memories. I open my eyes and stare at my trouser cuffs and my shoes, my favorite shoes, heavy oxblood brogues. The kind Gene Kelly wore, with wingtips. Wingies, the store clerk called them. And I think of Richardson's run to town the day he was wearing penny loafers.

I walk toward the evergreens. Something catches my eye. A tiny metal disk peeks through the soil. I pick it up and rub it between my fingers, thinking about all the slugs we put in pop machines. After the Golden Eagle, we moved the operation, as Oberstein called it, to Bugden's, a small corner store near Memorial Stadium. How often did Blackie send sprinters from the soccer field to Bugden's Store, to return each time with a bottle of pop and fifteen cents? Blackie knew how to make money more than any of us. He just didn't have the law on his side.

Remembering those runs, I walk toward my car, breathing in the clear Newfoundland air. The fresh air invigorates me. Without realizing it, I am jogging past my car, moving along Major's Path toward Torbay Road and Mount Kildare. A car horn blows, and the bald driver smiles and waves. I must look crazy, running along the highway in my shoes, suit pants, and Arrow shirt. I wave and pick up speed. Feeling light, I think of Nicky. As I pass the Mount, I hear the night runners yelling that they've come to join me. *Believe, believe . . .* I love that about running, the way thoughts jump at you out of nowhere. I don't want to stop. I want to run forever. I fly past the soccer field to Logy Bay Road and Fort Pepperrell and the turnoff to Sugar Loaf Pond before stopping to rest.

I stand in the sunlight and look at the trees and the calm water, listening to memory again. So many great times. Holy, Oberstein might say. But the most sacred of all, the one I'll remember long after the bloodred flickering of the sanctuary lamp, the rosaries and Benedictions, the stations of the cross, the Panis Angelicus, and the Veni Creator Spiritus, the most sacred of all: returning from a long run, the great stone buildings looming in the distance, all of us drenched in sweat, our feet blistered, our throats parched, our thighs chafed, our bodies aching, like tired soldiers finally coming home.

Acknowledgments

MANY PEOPLE HELPED me in the writing of *The Long Run*. I was encouraged and supported by R.J. MacSween, longtime editor of the *Antigonish Review*, and by his successor in that post, George Sanderson, and by Sheldon Currie, one-time fiction editor. *The Antigonish Review* published a number of stories that later became parts of the book. Gert and George Sanderson and Dawn and Sheldon Currie discussed every aspect of the novel with me over a two-year period. Jeanette Lynes, now coeditor of *TAR*, gave the manuscript a detailed and sympathetic reading at a crucial phase in its publication history. Anne Simpson, then fiction editor of *TAR*, read an early version of the book and offered good advice.

Thanks to friends and colleagues who read and/or discussed the manuscript: New Brunswick poet Michael Oliver, novelist Jean Dohaney, Bev and Gavin Matthews, Sarah and Gary Chang, Donna and Robin MacNeil. The memory of Jodean and Brian Tobin's enthusiastic remarks still lingers. Newfoundland poet David Hickey contributed many insightful criticisms, as did novelist Derek Yetman. Special thanks to Dean MacDonald for his encouragement. Also, many thanks to Joyce and Geoff Stirling for their constant support. To

Judith and Al Title, Janet McDonald, and Susan and John Venn, many thanks.

Special thanks to Key Porter, the publisher of the Canadian edition. Thanks also to my good friend, Rick Butler, for his constant encouragement and for the opportunity to work as the writer-in-residence at the Hotel California in Los Angeles and the Savoy Hotel in San Francisco. I am also in debt to my agent, Anne McDermid, who, once she started reading the manuscript, became one of its keenest supporters.

Deepest thanks to my family: my mother, many of whose proverbs and Newfoundland expressions found a home in my book, and my brothers and sisters, always supportive and kind. Jean Chisholm and her Cape Breton family encouraged me in my early literary aspirations. My wonderful children, Rachel, Beth, John-Paul, and Sarah, are constantly supportive and full of praise.

Most of all, thanks to Fluff Cole, whose perfect ear and keen eye guided me through the writing of this book.